WHO'S WHO
IN THE
MARVEL
UNIVERSE

New York • Los Angeles

Written by Steve Behling

Illustrated by:
Steve Kurth, Mike Huddleston, Geanes Holland, Michela Frare, Michela Cacciatore,
Simone Boufantino, Carlos Barberi, Ario Anindito, George Duarte, Eduardo Mello, Dario Brizuela, Gaetano Petrigno,
Cucca Vincenz, Salvatore Di Marco, Roberto DiSalvo, Angela Copolugo, Olga Lapaeva, Vita Efemova, Anna Beliashova,
Tomasso Moscardini, Davide Mastrolonardo, Pierluigi Cosolino, Fabio Pacuilli, Guilla Priori, Ekaterina Myshalova,
Nataliya Torretta, Stefani Renee, and Caravan Studios

For information address Marvel Press, 125 West End Avenue, New York, New York 10023.

First Edition, August 2020

10 9 8 7 6 5 4 3 2 1

FAC-038091-20220

Printed in the United States of America

Library of Congress Cataloging-in-Publication Number: 2019951927

ISBN 978-1-368-06290

Reinforced binding

Visit www.DisneyBooks.com and www.Marvel.com

Table of Contents

SPIDER-MAN & HIS FRIENDS

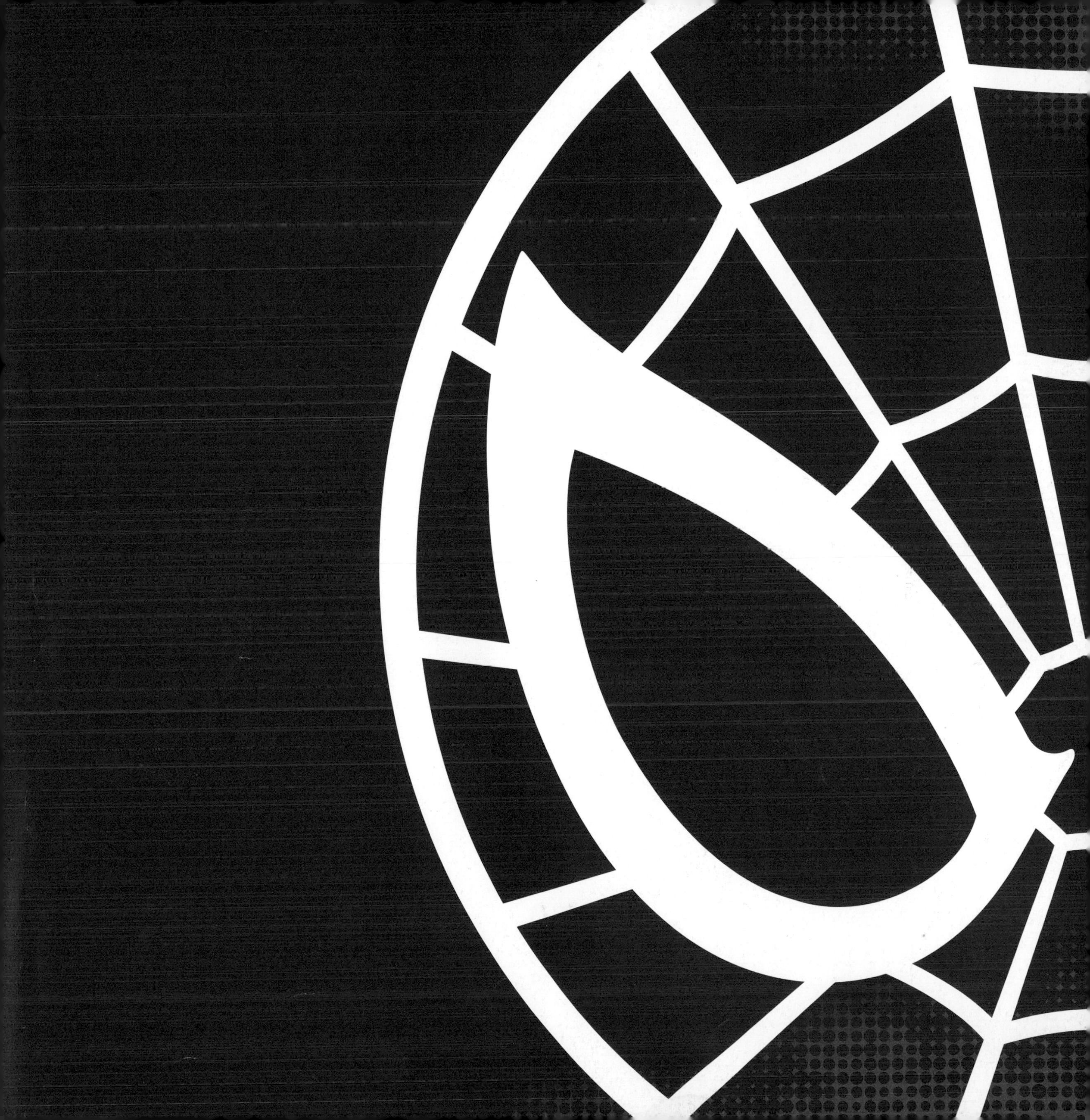

SPIDER-MAN
Peter Parker

Hey! You! Person reading this book! Have you ever been bitten by a radioactive spider? No? Of course you haven't! That's not the sort of thing that happens every day. But it happened to Peter Parker!

HEIGHT: 5' 10"

WEIGHT: 180 LBS

SUPERHUMAN STRENGTH

SUPERHUMAN AGILITY

SUPERHUMAN ENDURANCE

STICKING TO AND CLIMBING WALLS AND OTHER SURFACES

SELF-DESIGNED WEB-SHOOTERS, ALLOWING HIM TO FIRE AND SWING FROM STICKY WEBS

"SPIDER-SENSE" THAT WARNS OF INCOMING DANGER

GENIUS INTELLECT, SPECIALIZING IN CHEMISTRY

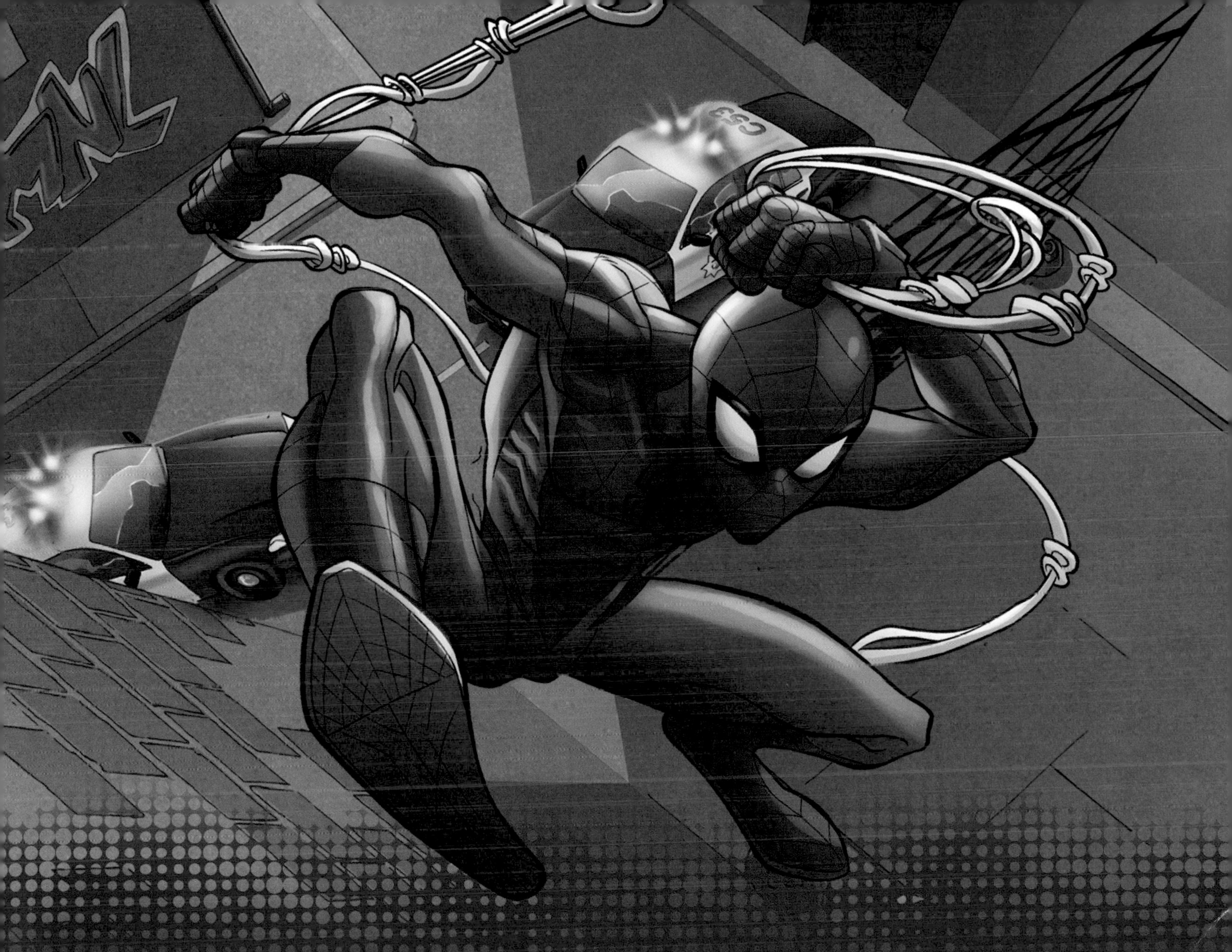

Peter was just a high school student when a strange spider bit him and gave him incredible powers! He became super-strong and could stick to walls. He even had a "spider-sense" that could warn him of danger! After someone close to him got hurt when he failed to stop a bad guy, Peter vowed to use his new powers to make the world a safer place, starting with his own neighborhood. So he made himself a cool costume and a pair of web-shooters. Now he fights crime as Spider-Man!

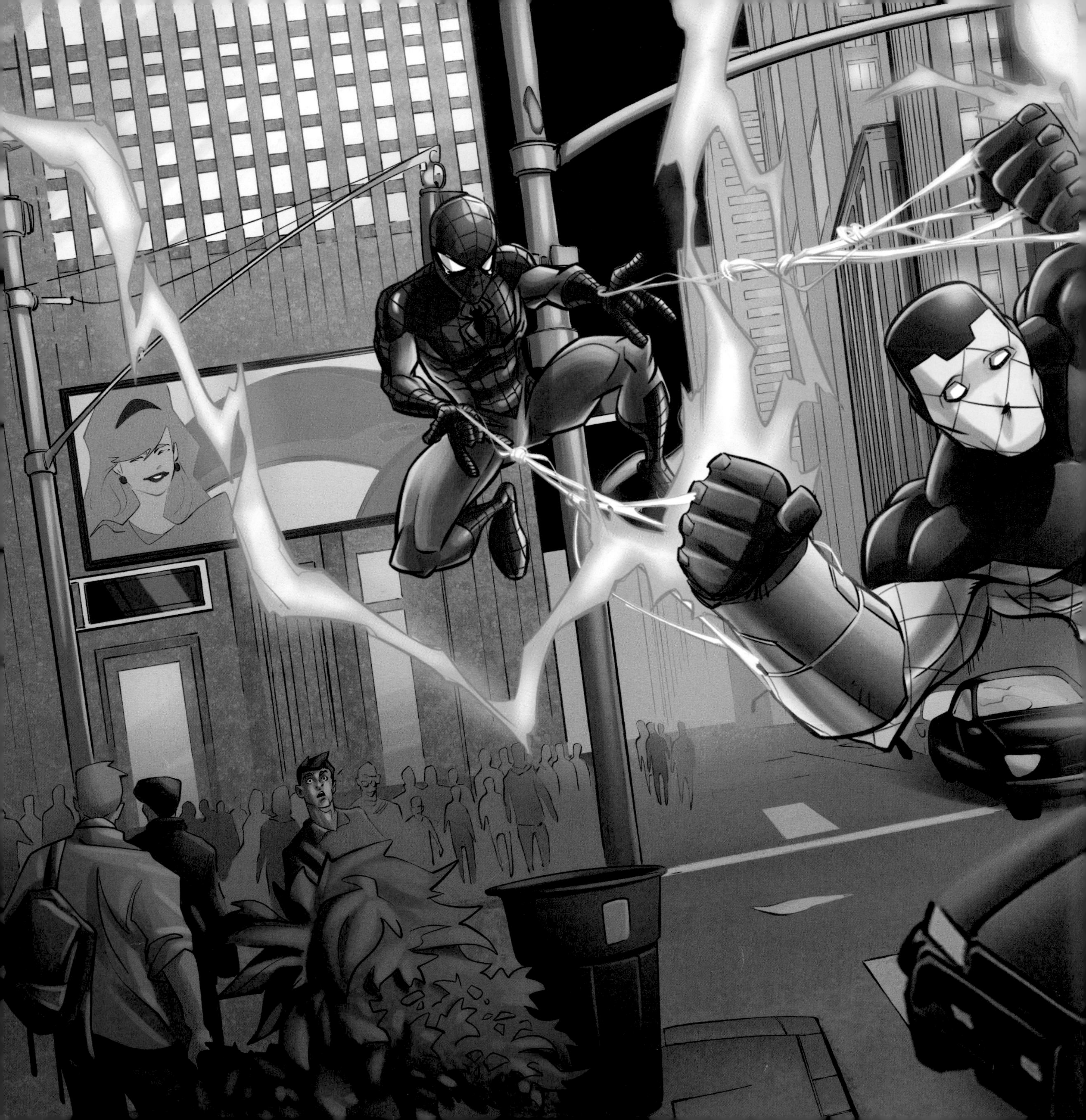

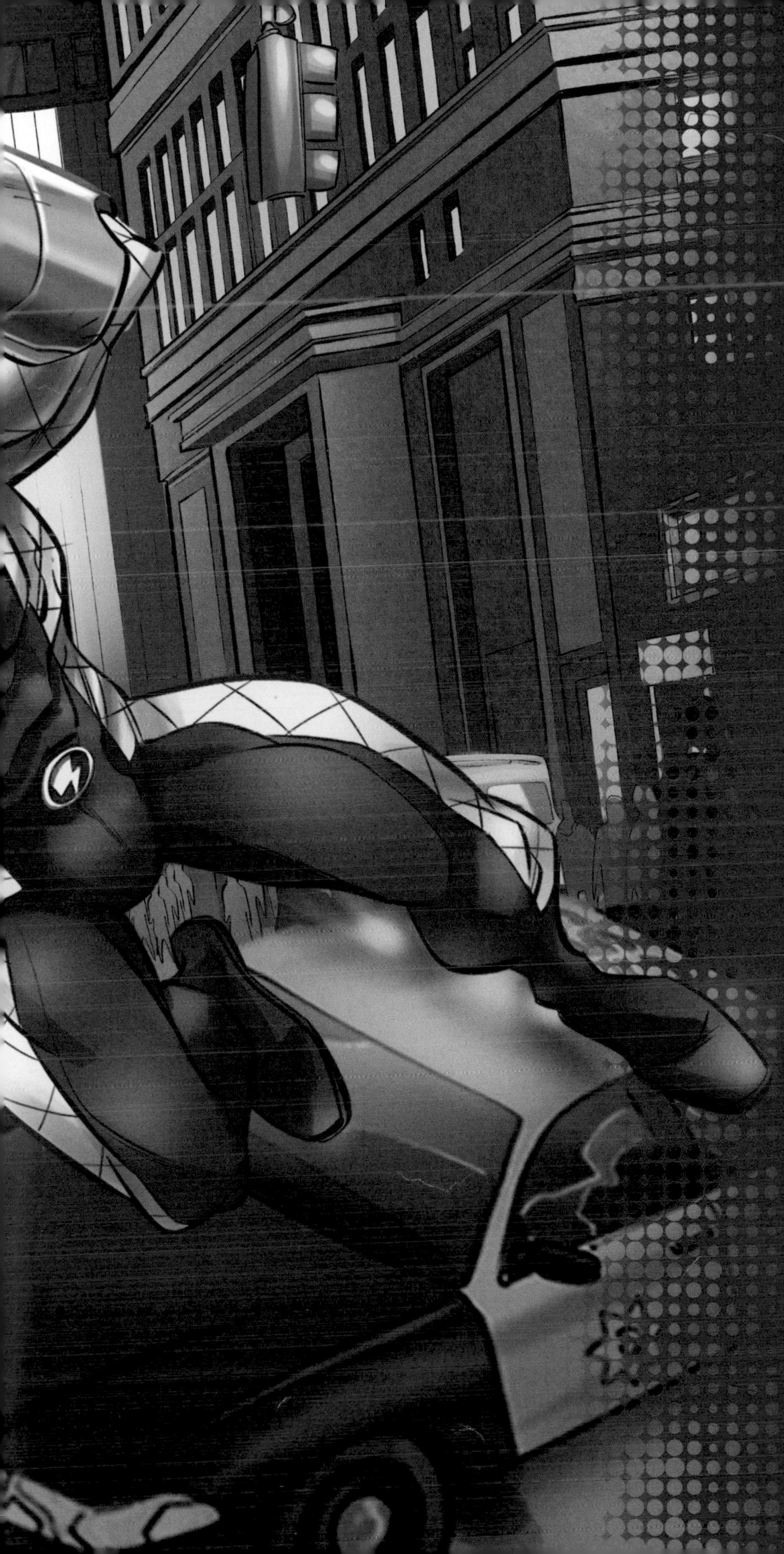

One day, Spidey was swinging through the boroughs of New York City. He was looking out for bad guys, and he was always sure to find one. Suddenly, his spider-sense went wild! Spidey saw one of his old foes—the Shocker! This guy wore bands on each hand that could cause super-strong vibrations. The vibrations were SO strong that he needed a costume with padding to help absorb the shocks. The suit made him look like a bed mattress. At least, that's what Spidey thought.

"Come back, Mattress Man!" Spidey called out. "I wanna introduce you to some friends!"

"You'll have to catch meeeeee!" the Shocker said.

Now, the reason the Shocker said "meeeeee" was because Spidey had just caught the bad guy in his web and yanked him back. Then he turned the Shocker over to the police.

All in a day's work for your friendly neighborhood Spider-Man!

HEIGHT: 5' 5"

WEIGHT: 125 LBS

SUPERHUMAN STRENGTH

SUPERHUMAN AGILITY

SUPERHUMAN ENDURANCE

STICKING TO AND CLIMBING WALLS AND OTHER SURFACES

MECHANICAL WEB-SHOOTERS, ALLOWING HER TO FIRE AND SWING FROM STICKY WEBS

"SPIDER-SENSE" THAT WARNS OF INCOMING DANGER

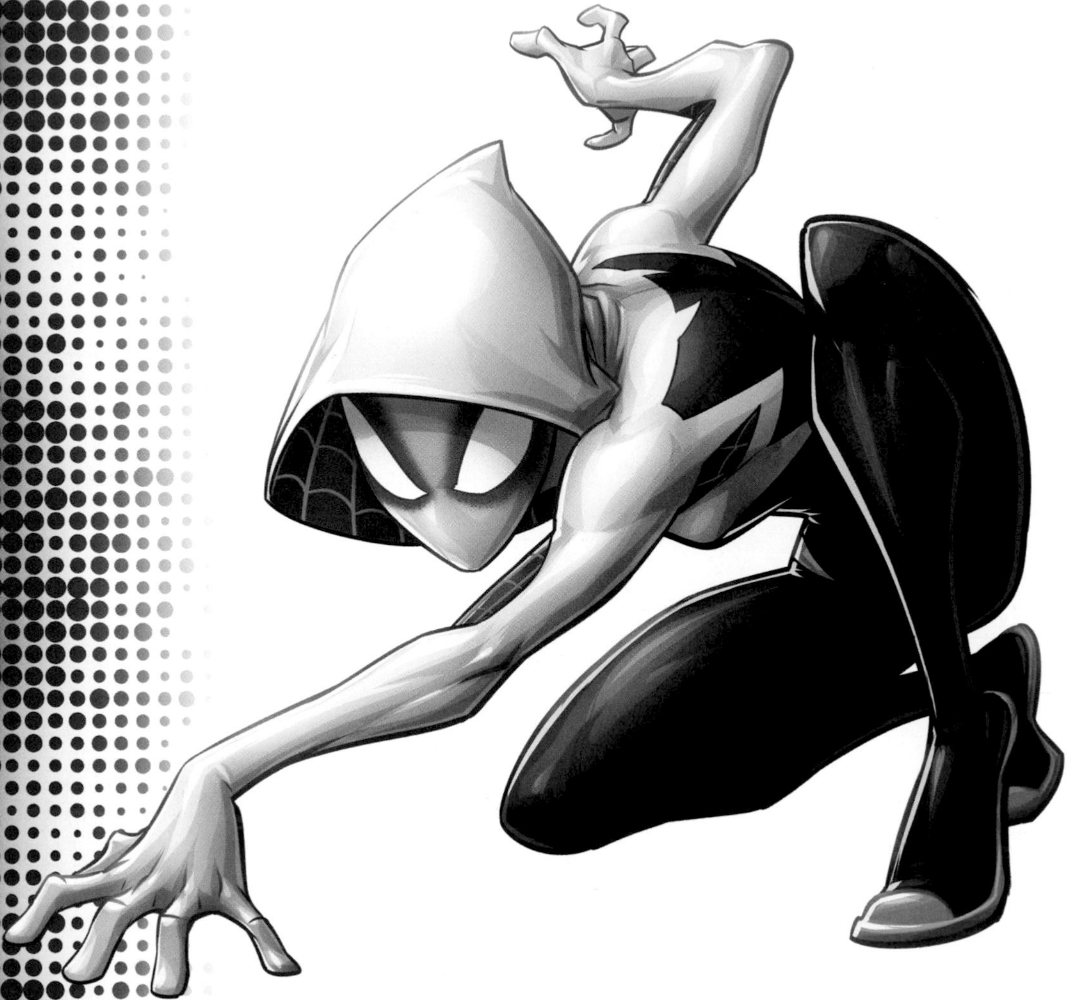

GHOST-SPIDER

Gwen Stacy

What are the odds of a second person being bitten by a radioactive spider? Pretty good, as it turns out—because that's exactly what happened to Gwen Stacy! She was bitten while attending a science demonstration about radioactivity.

Before she became a spidery Super Hero, Gwen was a brilliant science student at Midtown High. She loved to spend time in the laboratory working on all kinds of different experiments. A wizard with electronics, Gwen could build cool gadgets that other kids could only dream of. She was going to need those skills to team up with Spidey!

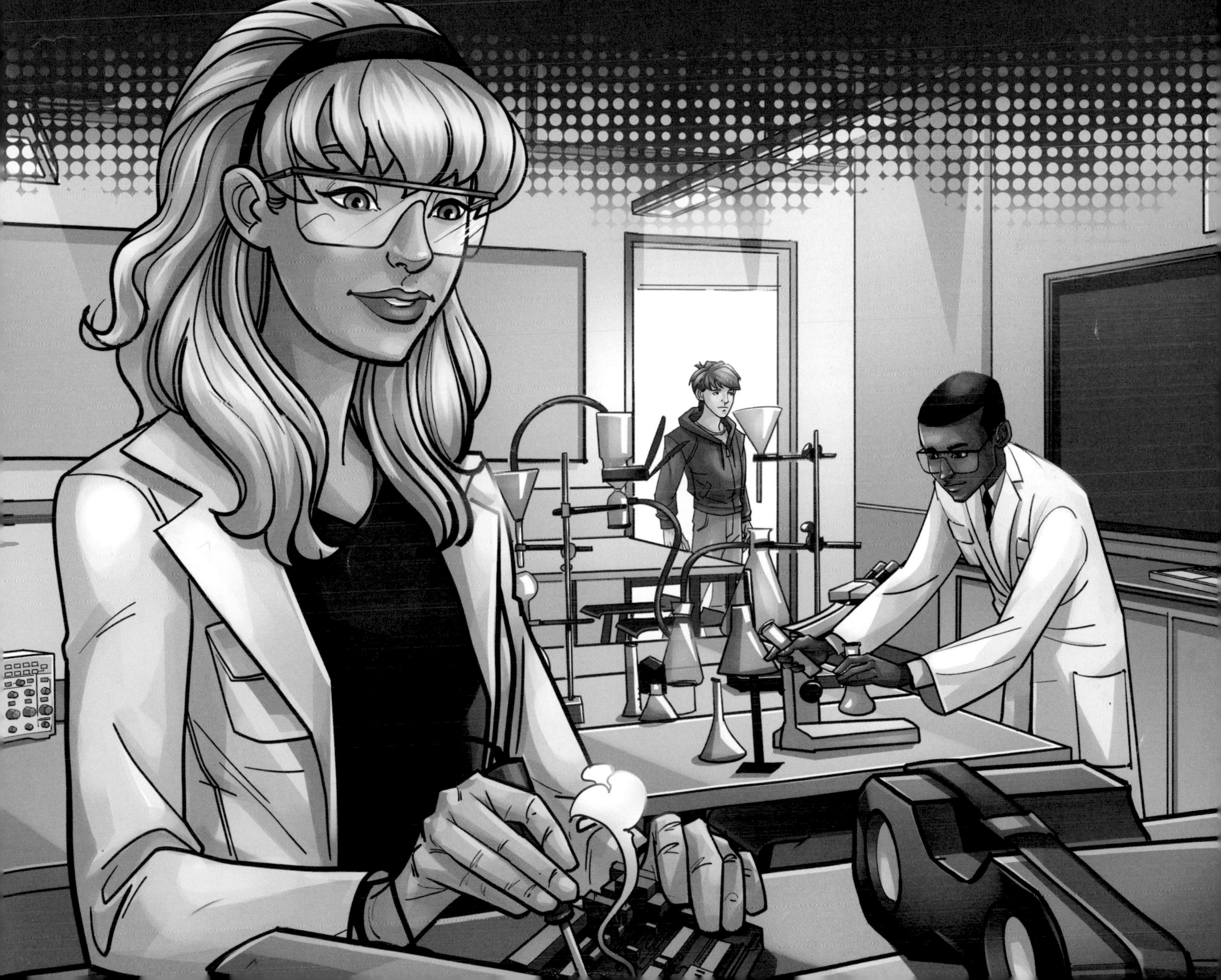

Just like Peter, Gwen can predict danger with her spidey-sense, has the speed and strength of a spider, and can stick to walls. Now Gwen fights crime as Ghost-Spider!

"Come on, guys—keep up!" Ghost-Spider said. She was swinging high above the streets of New York City. Another kid might have been scared out of their wits by the extreme heights. But not Ghost-Spider!

The web-slinging Super Hero was racing against her friends to see who could get to school first. Who were her friends? Glad you asked! Right behind her was Peter Parker, aka Spider-Man, and behind HIM was Miles Morales. Who's Miles Morales? Just turn the page and you'll find out!

"Man, is she fast!" Miles exclaimed.

"There's no way we're going to win this one!" Spider-Man said.

But before Ghost-Spider could respond, her spider-sense went wild. Turn to page 31 to find out why!

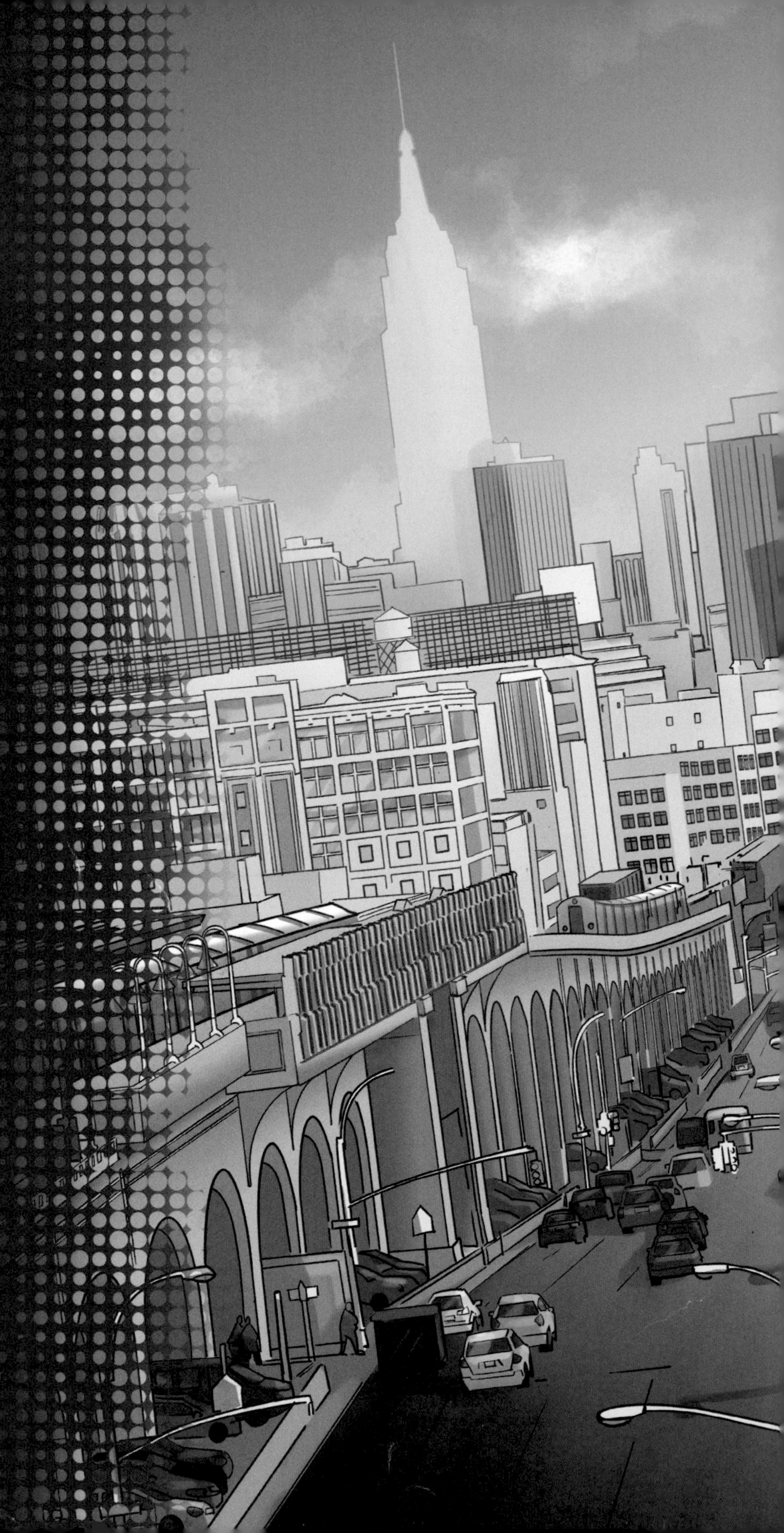

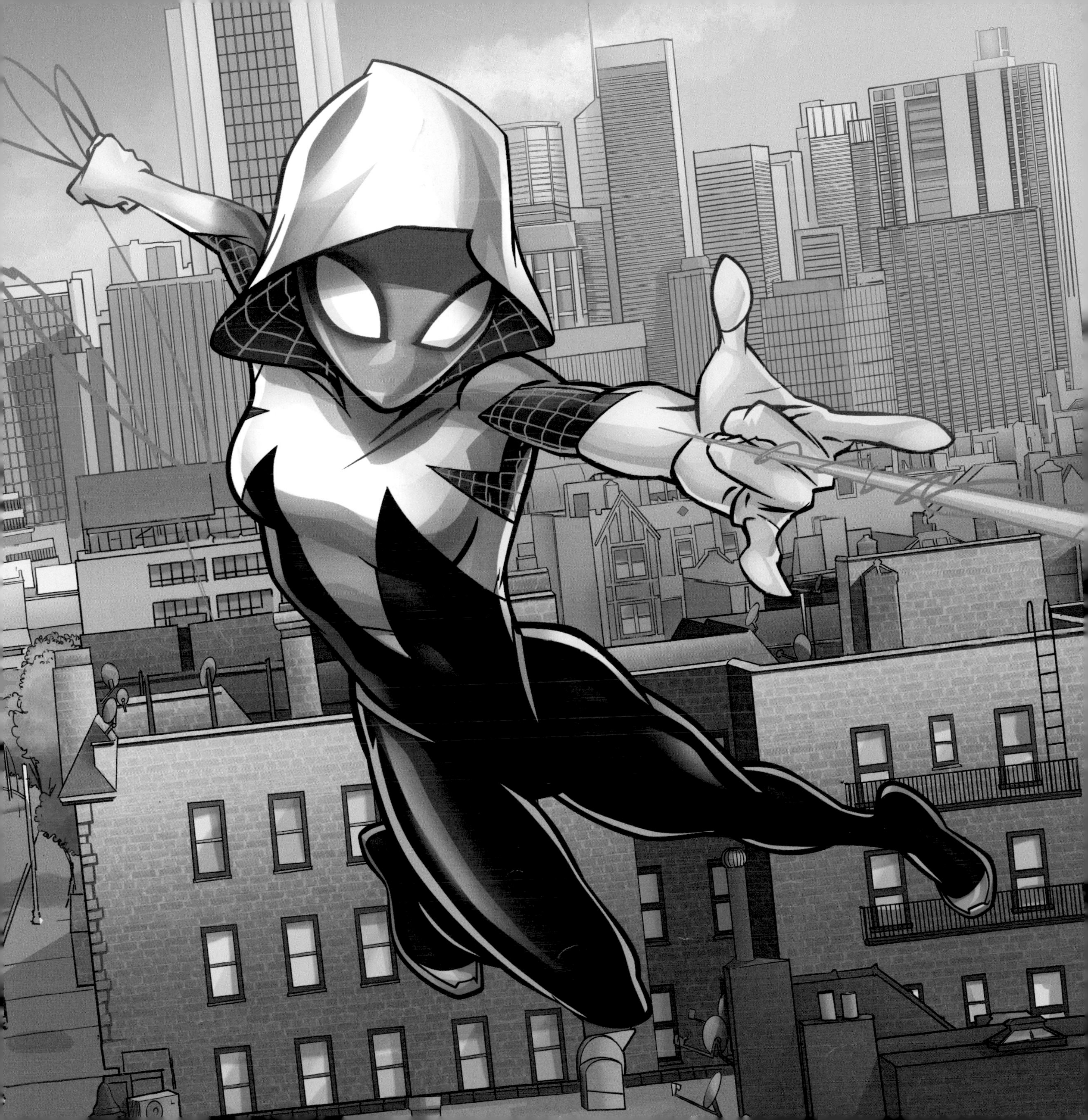

HEIGHT: 5' 7"

WEIGHT: 145 LBS

SUPERHUMAN
STRENGTH

SUPERHUMAN
AGILITY

SUPERHUMAN
ENDURANCE

STICKING TO AND
CLIMBING WALLS
AND OTHER
SURFACES

WEB-SHOOTERS

CAN CAMOUFLAGE
HIMSELF AND
HIS CLOTHING,
BECOMING NEARLY
INVISIBLE

DISCHARGES
POWERFUL
ELECTRICAL VENOM
STRIKES

"SPIDER-SENSE"
THAT WARNS OF
INCOMING DANGER

SPIDER-MAN

Miles Morales

Guess what! Peter Parker and Gwen Stacy aren't the only spiders in town! Meet Miles Morales, a high school student and friend of Peter Parker and Gwen Stacy. Miles was bitten by a—you guessed it—spider! This one was genetically modified instead of radioactive.

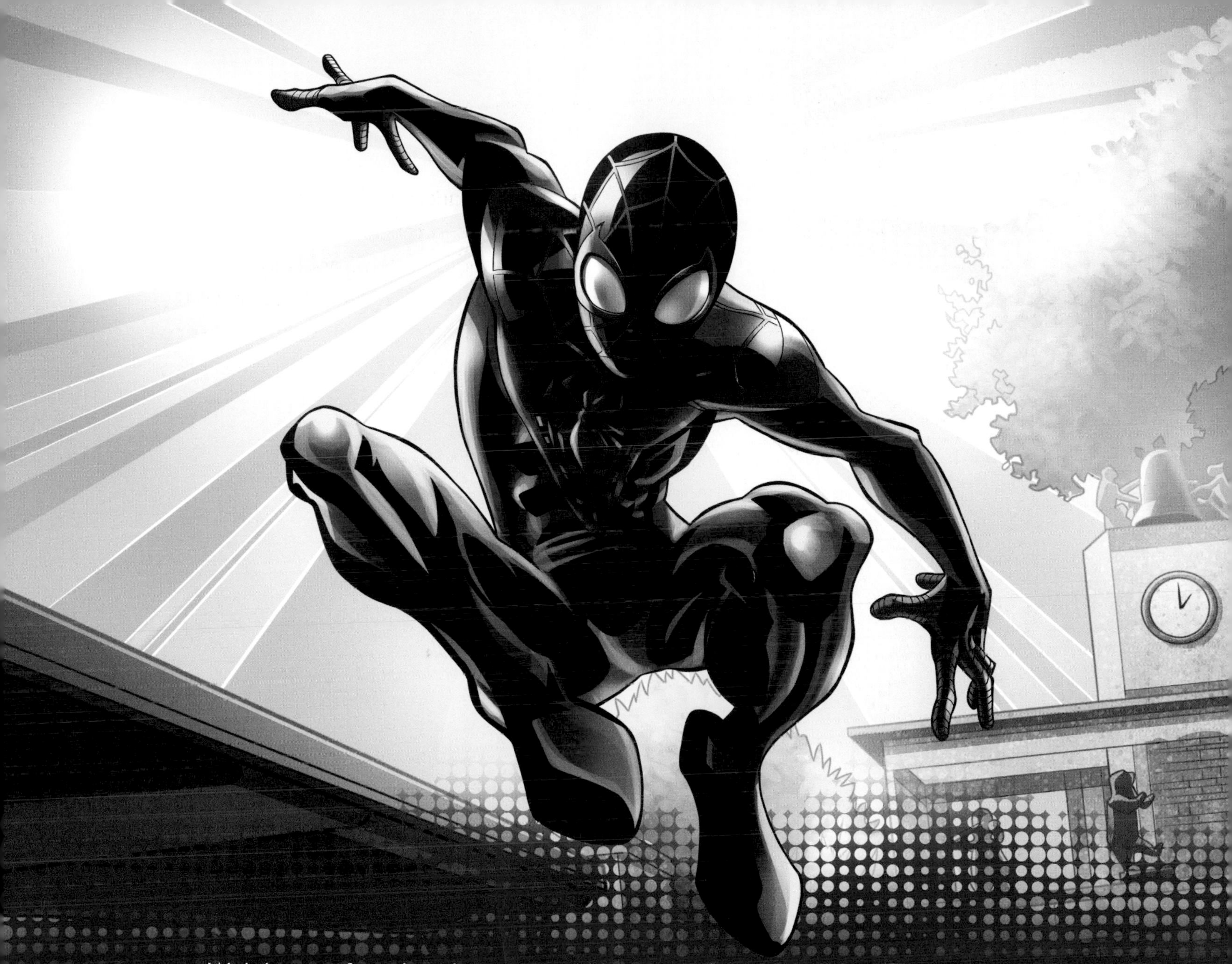

With his newfound spider-powers, Miles joined Spider-Man and Ghost-Spider in their fight against crime. Not only does Miles have the speed and strength of a spider and the same spidey-senses that Peter and Gwen have, but he also has a venom strike, a powerful form of energy that he can use to fight off the biggest bad guys in the city. Bonus: Miles can turn invisible, too! These powers come in handy whenever he fights crime in the city—whether it's by himself or as part of the spider-people team.

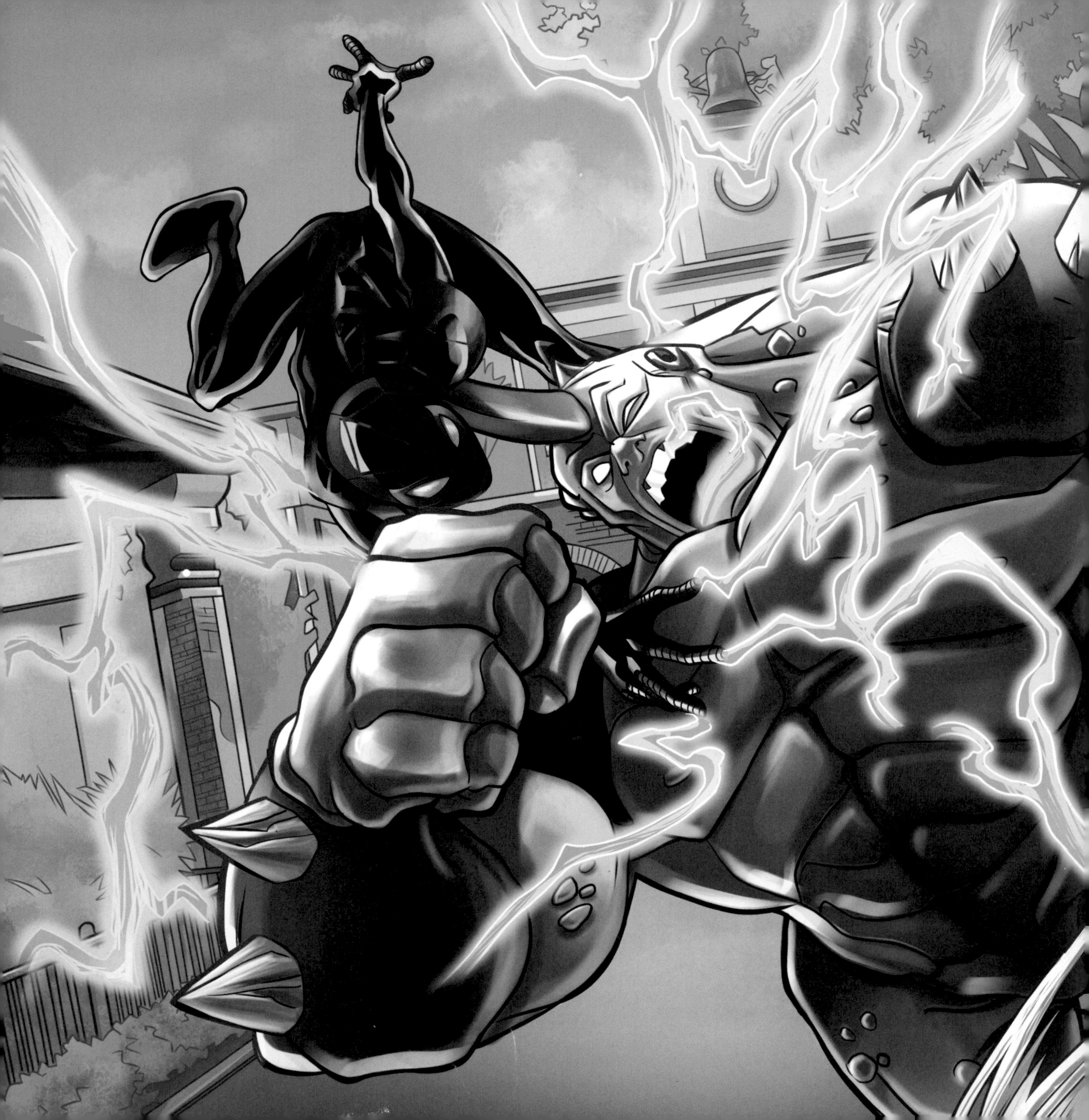

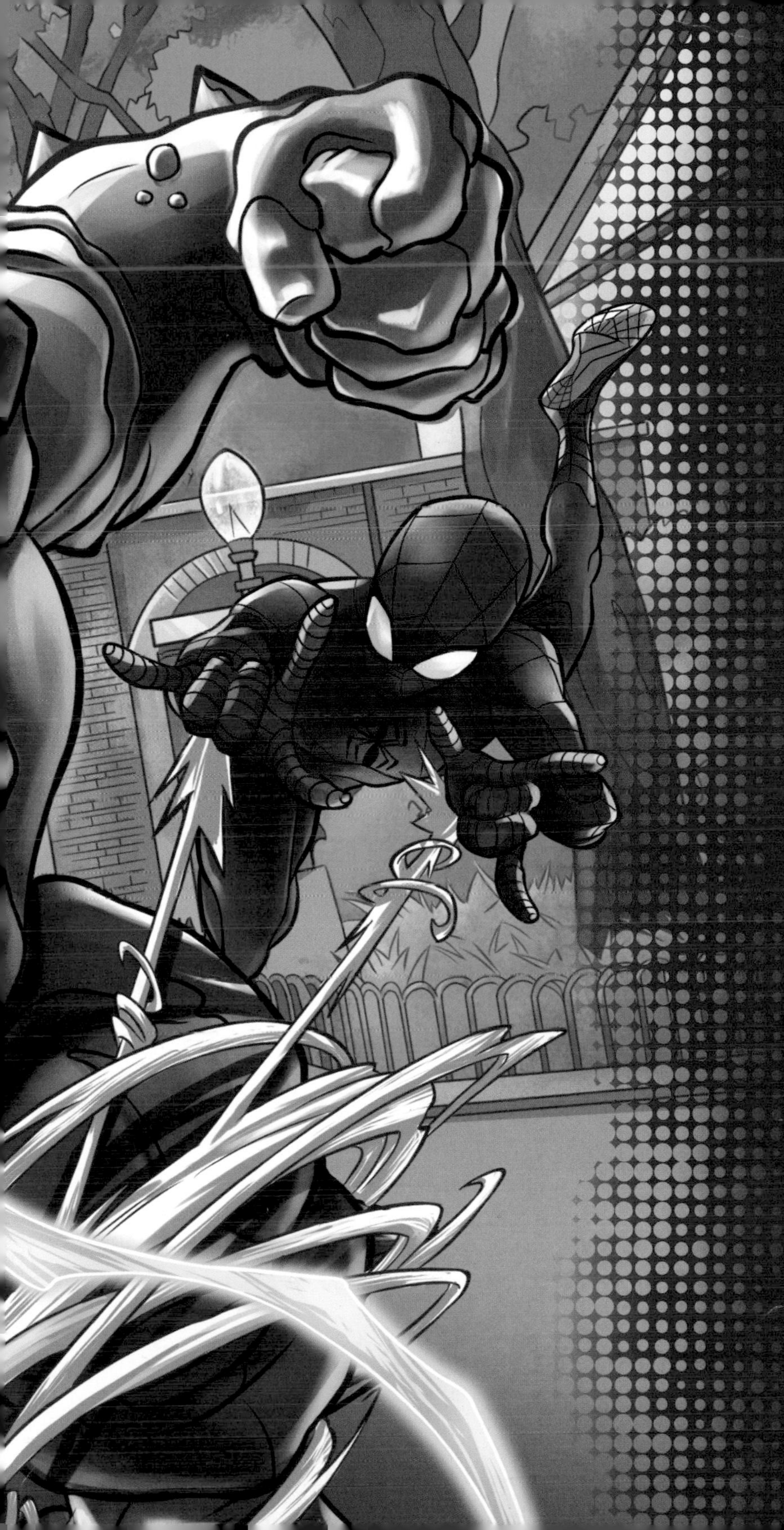

Have you ever faced the rampaging Rhino? No? Of course you haven't. But it's all in a day's work for Miles Morales!

"Hey, hornhead!" Miles said, swinging above New York City's Central Park. "Didn't you see the 'No Rhinos Allowed' sign?"

"I don't think he's much of a reader," Spidey said.

"Enough talk!" Rhino said, and he charged the Super Heroes."I'm gonna run right over you clowns and flatten you like a couple of, uh, clowns!"

"I'll take the high road!" Miles shouted, and unleashed his venom strike at Rhino.

"And I'll take the low road!" Spidey answered, webbing Rhino's feet.

WHAM!

The Super Villain hit the ground hard.

"You spider-people are the worst," Rhino said, right before he passed out.

VILLAINS

MYSTERIO

Quentin Beck

Meet Mysterio, the master of illusion! Except right now, he's the master of getting kicked in the face by the amazing Spider-Man!

HEIGHT: 5' 11"

WEIGHT: 175 LBS

MASTER OF PHYSICAL STUNT WORK AND MECHANICAL AND VISUAL SPECIAL EFFECTS

SUIT INCLUDES GLASS HELMET WITH THIRTY-MINUTE AIR SUPPLY, HOLOGRAPHIC PROJECTORS, AS WELL AS GLOVES AND BOOTS THAT EMIT HALLUCINOGENIC GAS THAT CAN RENDER SPIDER-MAN'S SPIDER-SENSE USELESS

SKILLED ACTOR

TRAINED IN HYPNOTISM AND BASIC PSYCHIATRY

CREATED HIS OWN VERSION OF SPIDER-MAN'S WEBBING

MEMBER OF THE SINISTER SIX

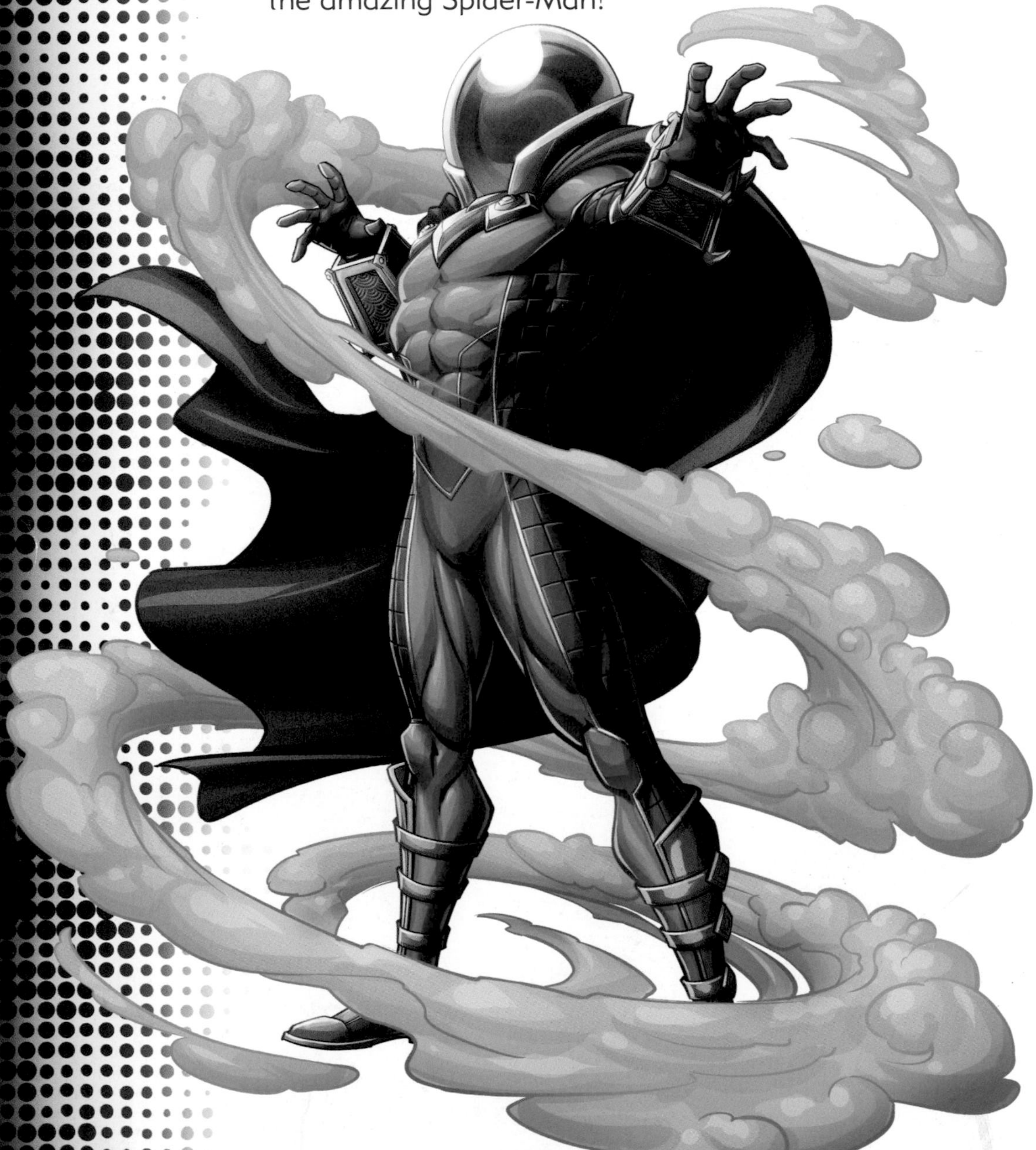

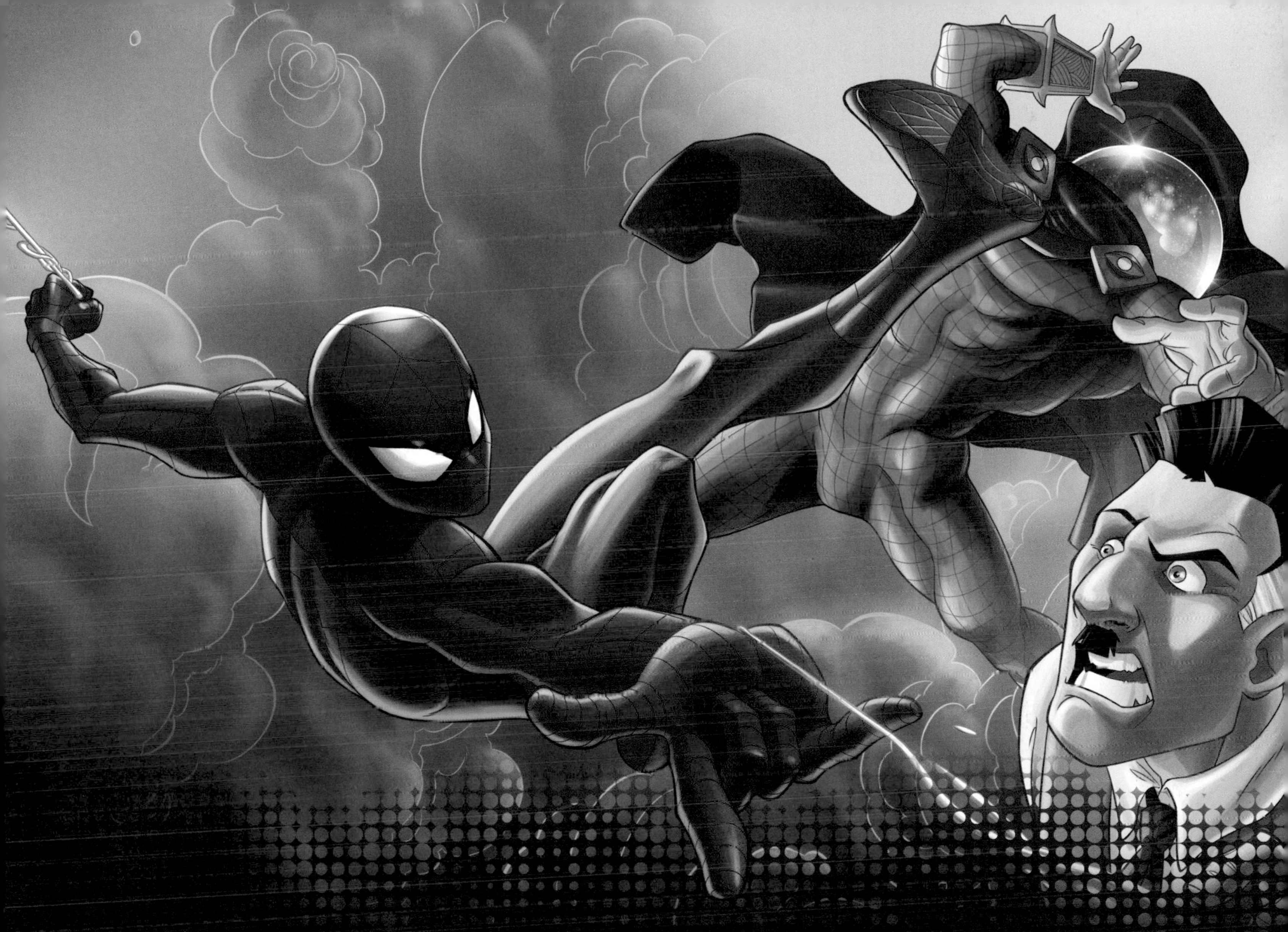

"Get him, Mysterio!" J. Jonah Jameson yelled. He was the publisher of the *Daily Bugle* newspaper. He really, really didn't like Spider-Man, and had hired Mysterio to defeat the wall-crawler.

"I think the only thing Mysterio's going to get is jail time!" Spidey said.

"Curse you, Spider-Man!" Mysterio said as Spider-Man webbed him up. "How did you see through my illusions?"

"It was easy," Spidey said. "I just closed my eyes!"

HEIGHT: 6' 8"

WEIGHT: 550 LBS

SUPERHUMAN STRENGTH

SUPERHUMAN STAMINA

SUPERHUMAN AGILITY

SUPERHUMAN DURABILITY

RESISTANT TO CONVENTIONAL INJURIES

INFLICTS GRAVE INJURIES USING HIS SAVAGE TEETH, CLAWS AND WHIP-LIKE TAIL

CAN TELEPATHICALLY COMMUNICATE WITH AND CONTROL NEARBY REPTILES

MEMBER OF THE SINISTER SIX

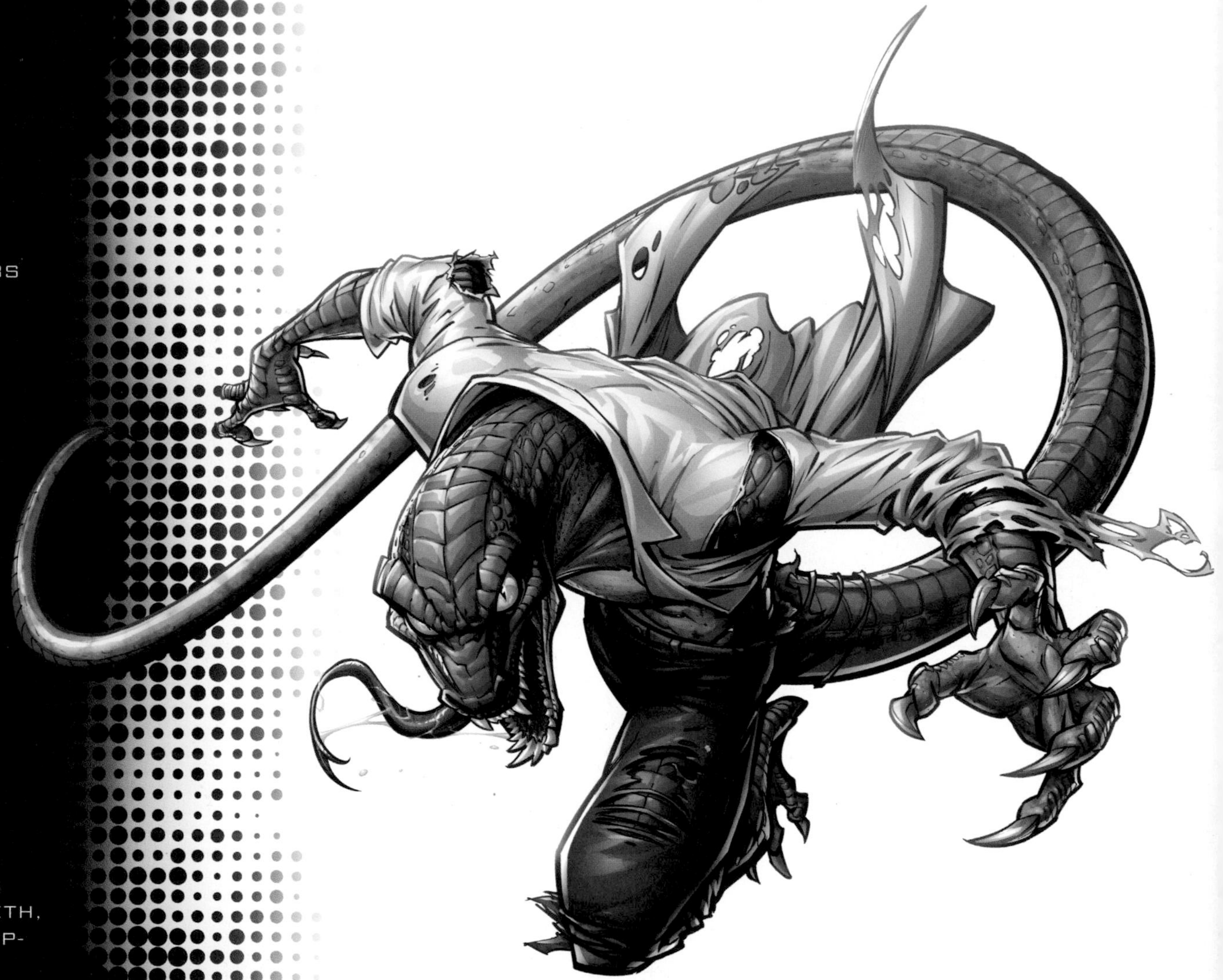

LIZARD

Dr. Curt Connors

The Lizard is really Dr. Curt Connors, a friend of Spidey's. In an attempt to regrow his missing right arm, the scientist turned himself into a giant lizard! (Which, you know, is kind of a problem.)

"Sssstay sssssstill, Ssssssspider-Man!" the Lizard hissed.

"Why, sssssssso your sssssssnakes can bite me?" Spider-Man teased.

The Lizard was so angry, he lashed out at Spidey with his tail. The web-slinger jumped up, and the tail missed. Then Spidey leaped right at the Lizard, and poured a vial down the creature's throat! The vial contained an antidote that turned the Lizard back into Dr. Connors.

"How can I ever thank you, Spider-Man?" the doctor asked.

"You could get these snakes away from me," Spidey joked.

THE SPOT

Jonathan Ohnn

The Spot is a scientist named Jonathan Ohnn who can summon big black spots. He can walk into one spot and exit from another! He can also stick his hand through a spot to attack Spider-Man!

HEIGHT: 5' 10"

WEIGHT: 170 LBS

RECEIVED SPOTS AND POWERS BY INADVERTENTLY VISITING THE SPOTTED DIMENSION WHEN ATTEMPTING TO MIMIC PORTALS UTILIZED BY THE HERO CLOAK

CAN TELEPORT USING HIS SPOTS, WHICH CAN BE SUSPENDED IN MIDAIR

SCIENTIST SPECIALIZING IN PHYSICS

CANNOT THROW AN UNLIMITED NUMBER OF SPACE WARPS AS THEY ARE DRAWN FROM HIS OWN BODY

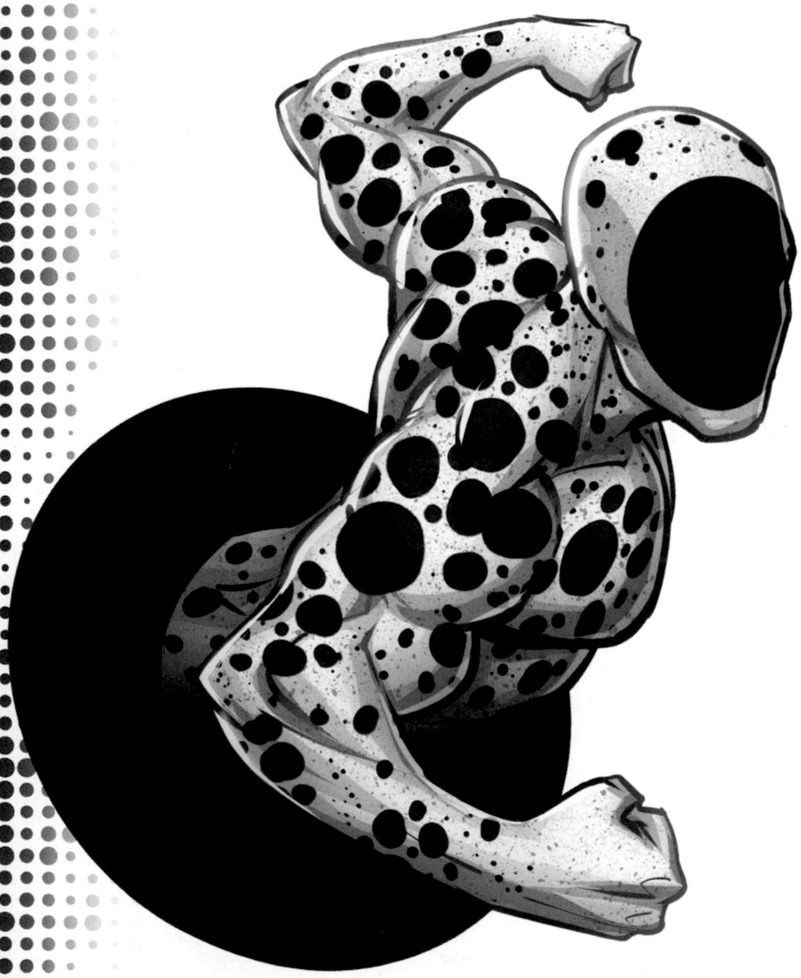

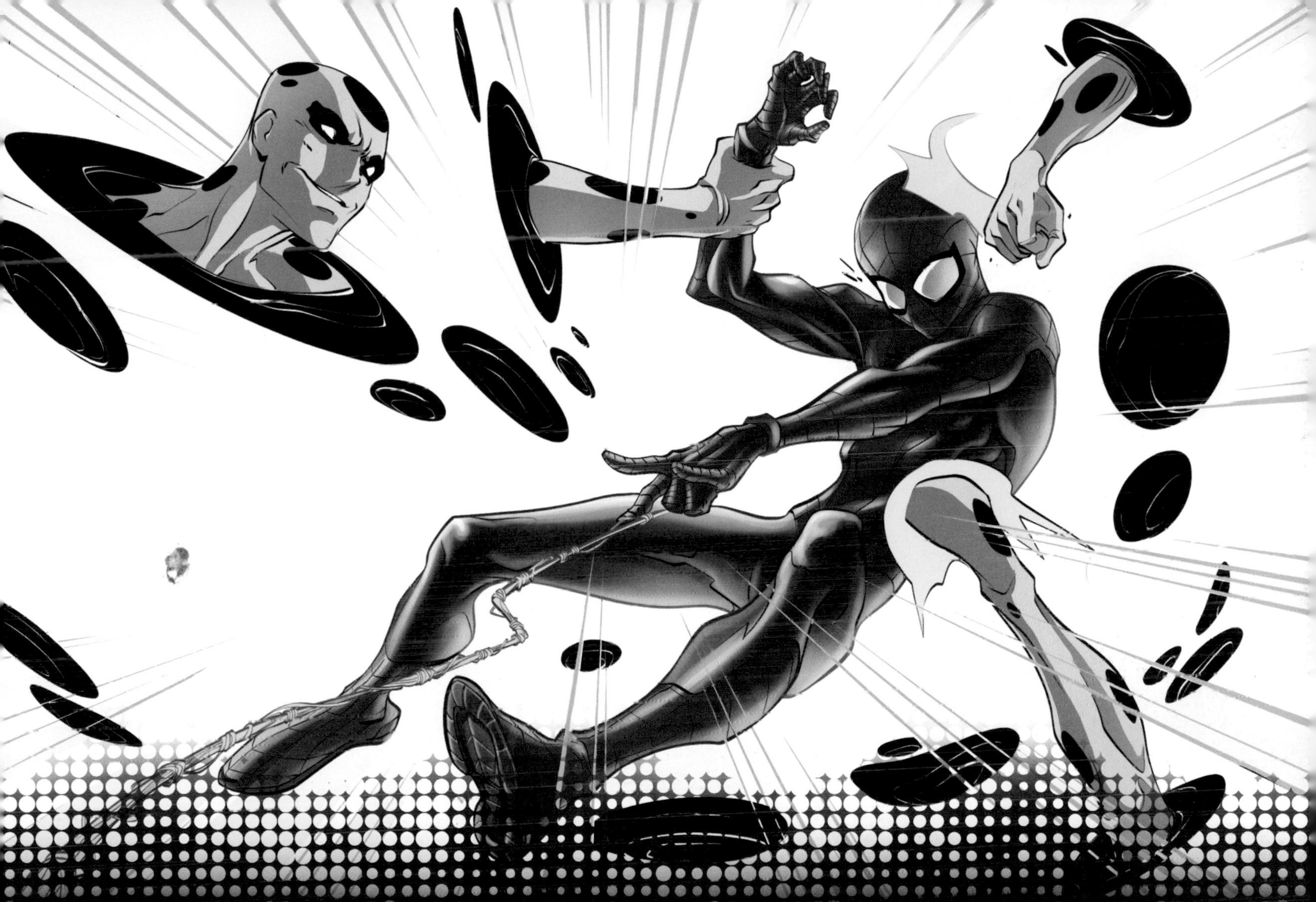

"How about some PUNCH, Spider-Man?" The Spot laughed.

"No thanks," Spidey said. "I had some before I left the house!"

In case you didn't know, Spidey REALLY didn't like The Spot.

Before The Spot could strike again, Spidey spun a web, sticking the villain's arms to his body.

"I can't summon my spots!" The Spot said.

"Too bad I can summon the cops!" Spidey replied.

HEIGHT: 6' 0"

WEIGHT: 235 LBS

SEEKS TO DEFEAT SPIDER-MAN TO PROVE HE'S THE GREATEST HUNTER IN THE WORLD

UTILIZES HAND-TO-HAND COMBAT AND EXPERT KNIFE-FIGHTING

AFTER INGESTING A MYTHICAL POTION, HE WAS GIVEN SUPERHUMAN STRENGTH, SPEED, STAMINA, AND DURABILITY

MASTER HUNTER AND TRACKER

MEMBER OF THE SINISTER SIX

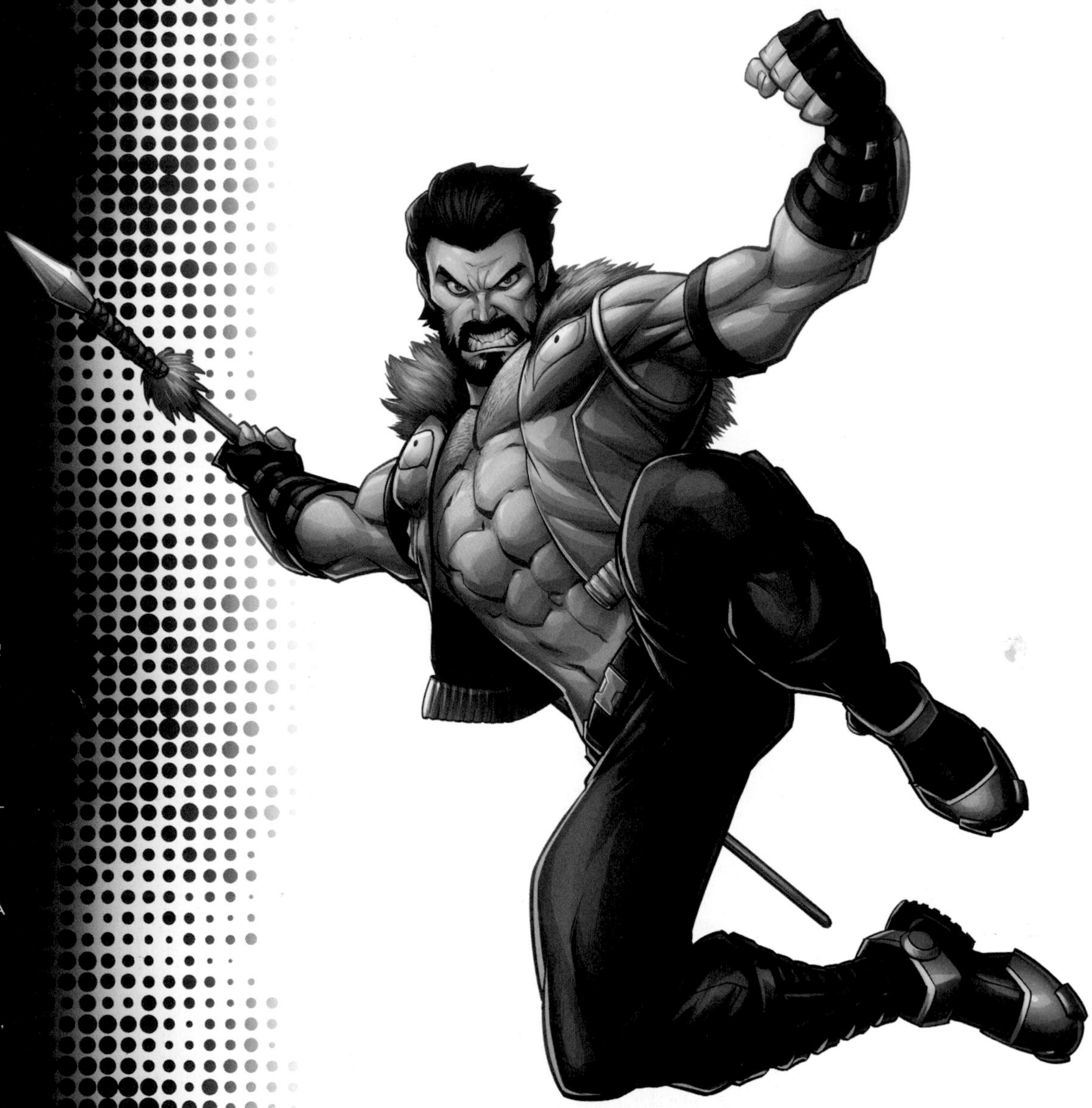

KRAVEN the HUNTER

Sergei Kravinoff

Kraven is the world's most famous hunter, and he came to New York City to capture the most dangerous prey of all—the wondrous wall-crawler! But Spider-Man had other plans. Plans that didn't involve him getting captured by Kraven!

WHOOSH!

Kraven's knives sliced through the air, just missing Spider-Man.

"What's the matter? Can't catch a little Spider?" Spider-Man asked. "Guess I'll have to catch YOU instead!" Spidey said, spinning his webs, ensnaring the hunter.

The web-slinger had turned the tables!

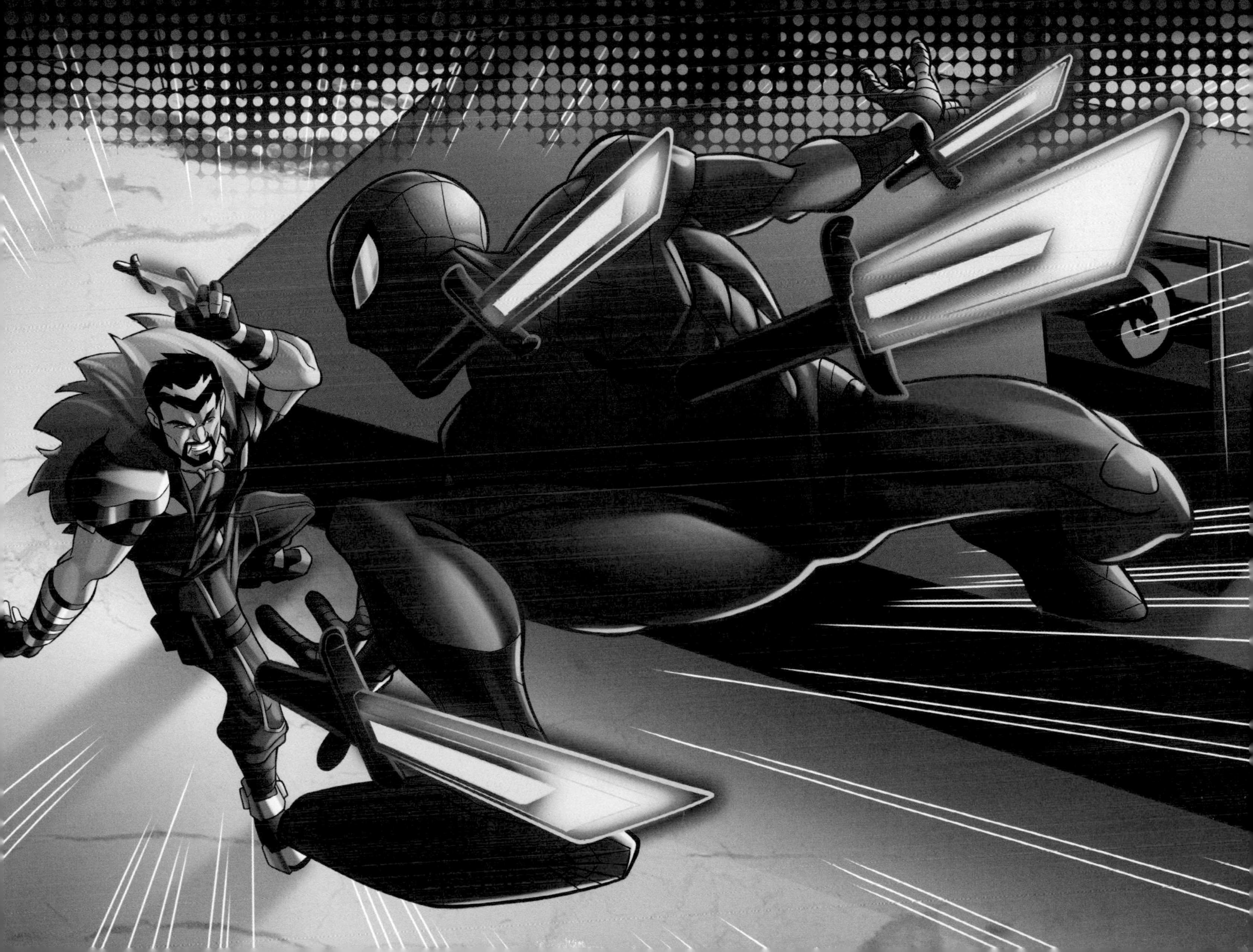

VULTURE

Adrian Toomes

The Vulture is really a guy named Adrian Toomes. Toomes created an incredible flying harness that allowed him to take to the skies. Instead of using this newfound power for good, Toomes decided to use it for his own twisted purposes. He's a bad guy, is what we're saying.

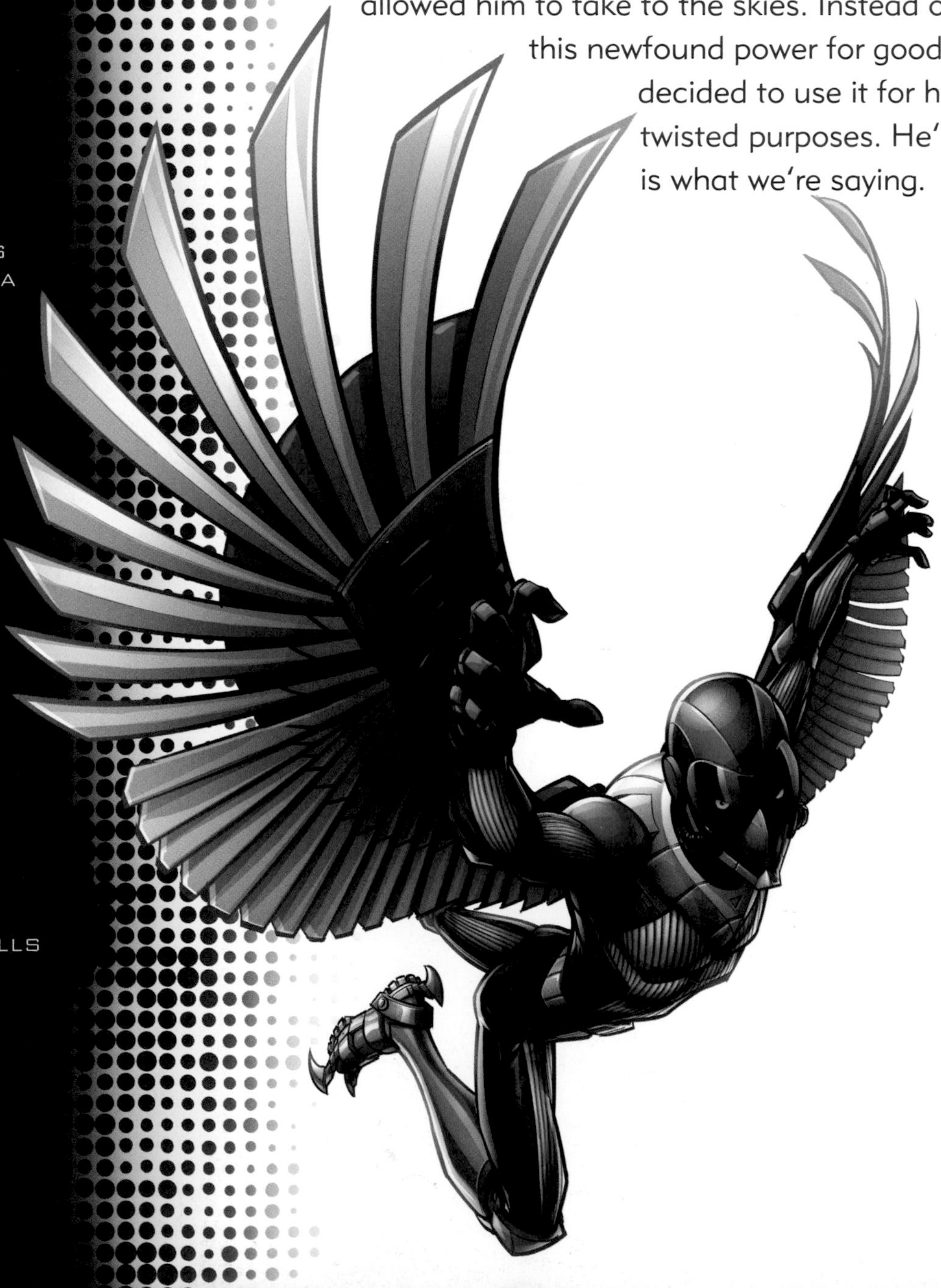

HEIGHT: 5'11"

WEIGHT: 160 LBS

INVENTOR WHO CREATED HIS WINGED HARNESS AND USES IT FOR A LIFE OF CRIME

SUPERHUMAN STRENGTH WHEN USING HIS MECHANICAL HARNESS

FLIGHT AT HIGH SPEEDS WITH HARNESS

RAZOR-SHARP TALONS WITH HARNESS, CAPABLE OF TEARING THROUGH STEEL

ADVANCED ENGINEERING SKILLS

MEMBER OF THE SINISTER SIX

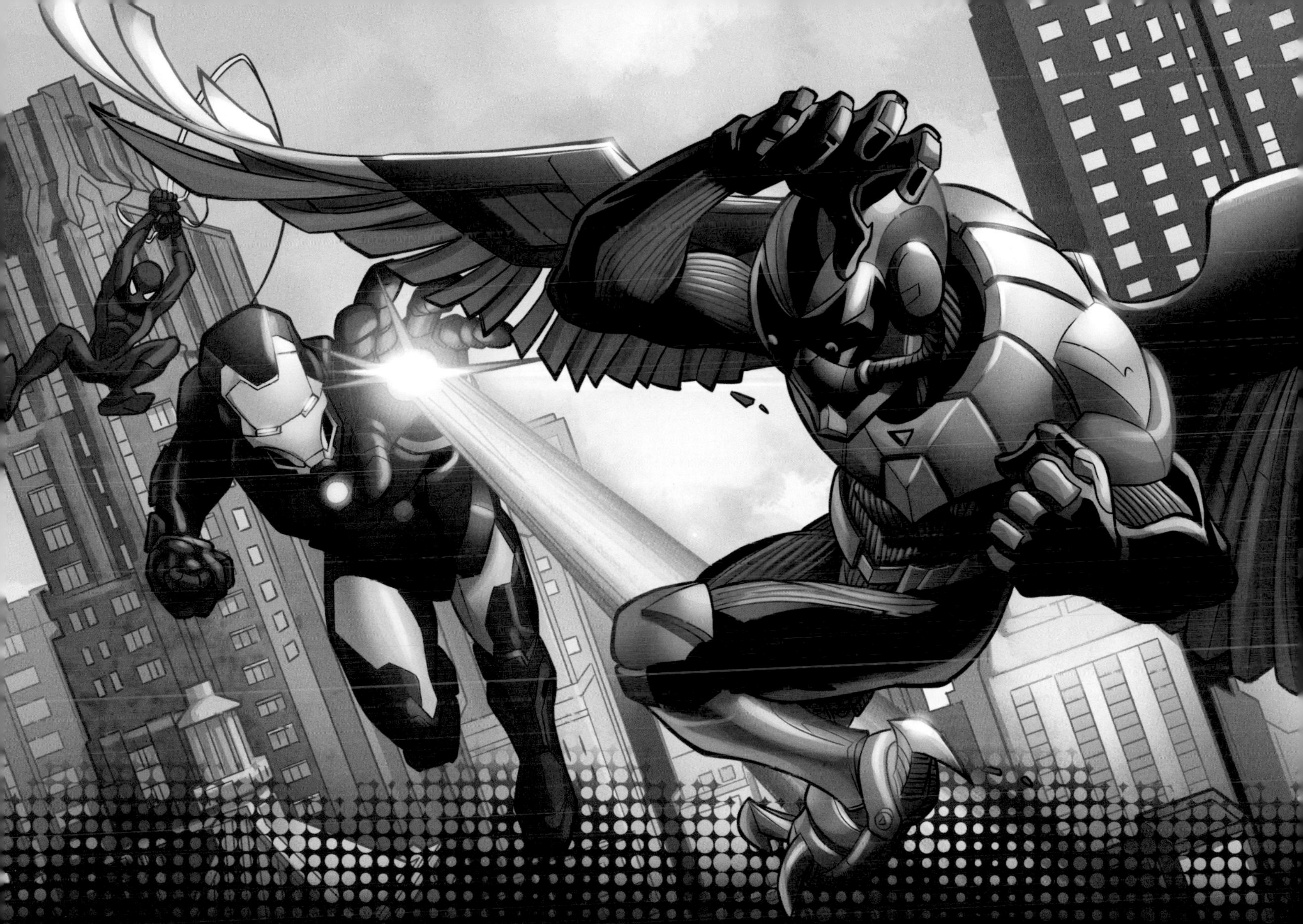

The Vulture had stolen a fortune in rare diamonds, but Spider-Man wasn't going to let him get away with it!

Man, I sure wish I could fly, Spidey thought. Suddenly the web-slinger heard the sound of rocket engines, and Iron Man soared into view.

"Need a hand, web-head?" Iron Man asked.

"Two against one!" the Vulture sneered. "That's not fair!"

"Neither is stealing!" Spidey shouted as the heroes grounded the Vulture for good.

HEIGHT: VARIABLE

WEIGHT: VARIABLE

SYMBIOTIC BEING WHO HAS BONDED ITSELF TO A HUMAN HOST

AMORPHOUS COSTUME-LIKE ENTITY WHO CAN TAKE A VARIETY OF SHAPES AND CAMOUFLAGE ITSELF

GRANTS ITS HOST SUPERHUMAN STRENGTH, AGILITY, AND DURABILITY

EXTRUDES TENDRILS AND A LONG TONGUE

CAN CREATE AND PROJECT A WEB-LIKE FLUID FROM ITS OWN SUBSTANCE

CAN MIMIC SPIDER-MAN'S POWERS

MEMBER OF THE SINISTER SIX

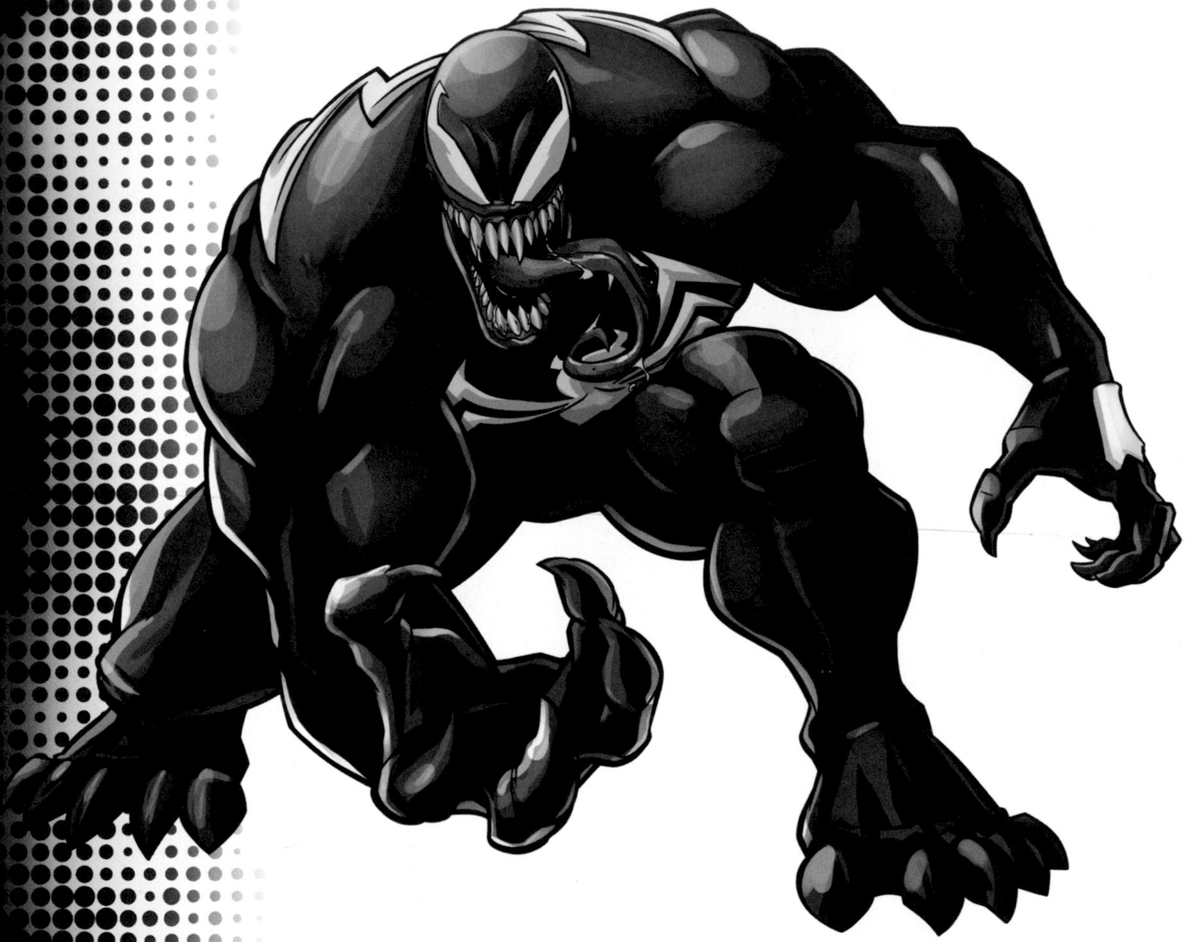

VENOM

Eddie Brock

Venom is one weird dude! Part man and part alien creature, Venom really doesn't like Spider-Man and his friends. He even has most of the same powers as Spider-Man. Venom can climb up walls, and he is super-strong. Oh, and let's not forget about the scary teeth!

"Three little spiders!" Venom growled. "I can't wait to stomp on you!"

Venom screamed and lashed out with his tendrils. They hit Spider-Man hard!

Then Miles tried to stop him, but the creature just shrugged off the attack.

"Hey, ugly! Over here!" Ghost-Spider yelled, drawing Venom's attention. Then she held out her sound cannon. Ghost-Spider remembered Venom's weakness—really loud sounds. So she cranked up the volume, and blasted Venom right in the ear.

"Aaarrrgh!" Venom shouted as the Spiders caught the creature.

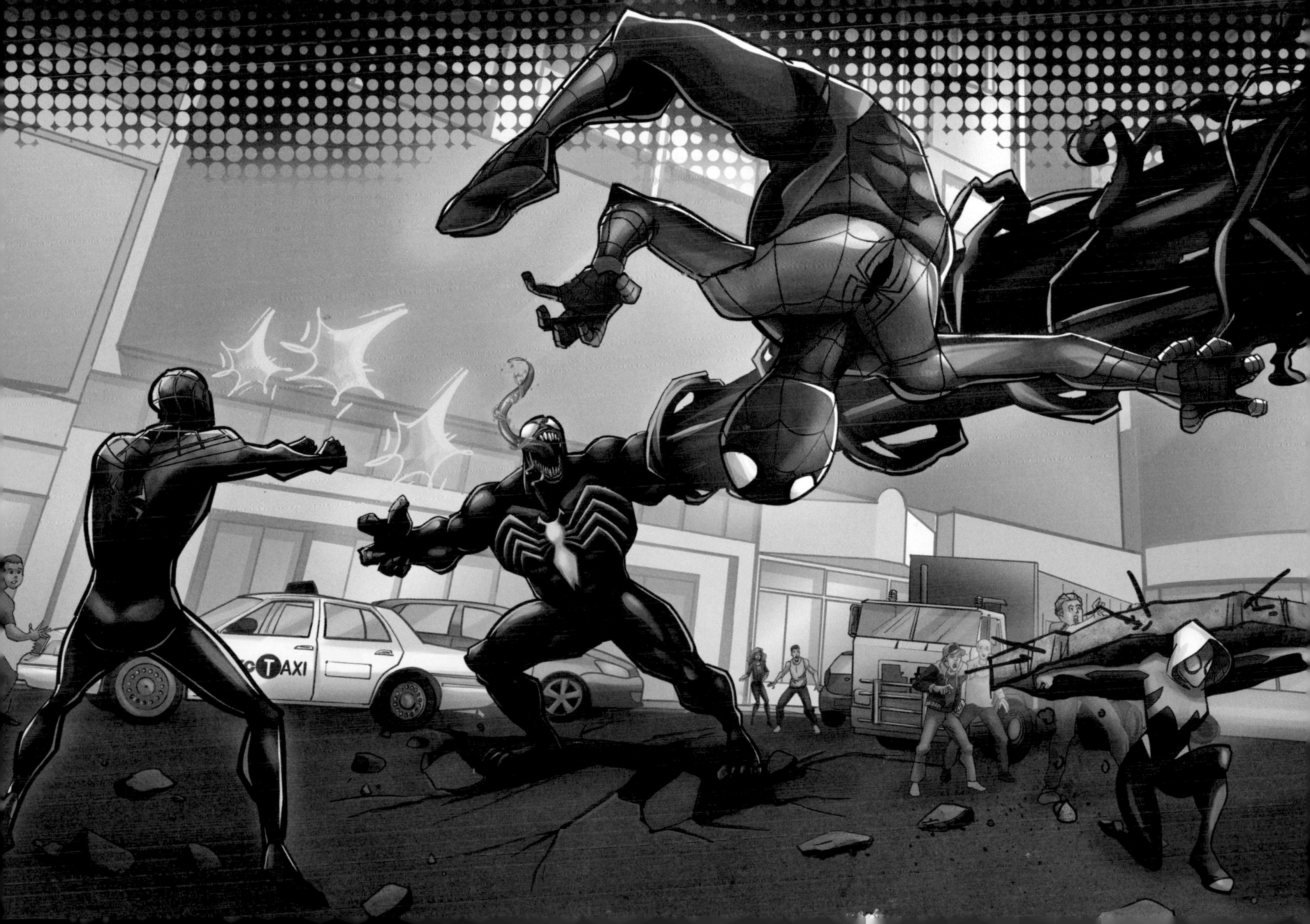
TAXI

CHAMELEON

Dmitri Smerdyakov

Chameleon was originally a spy named Dmitri Smerdyakov (try saying that ten times fast!). Not only was Chameleon a spy, he was also a master of disguise. Chameleon realized he could use this to his advantage! Now he can make himself look like anyone else. He can even trick Super Heroes into thinking he is one of the good guys! Which makes him a pretty bad guy.

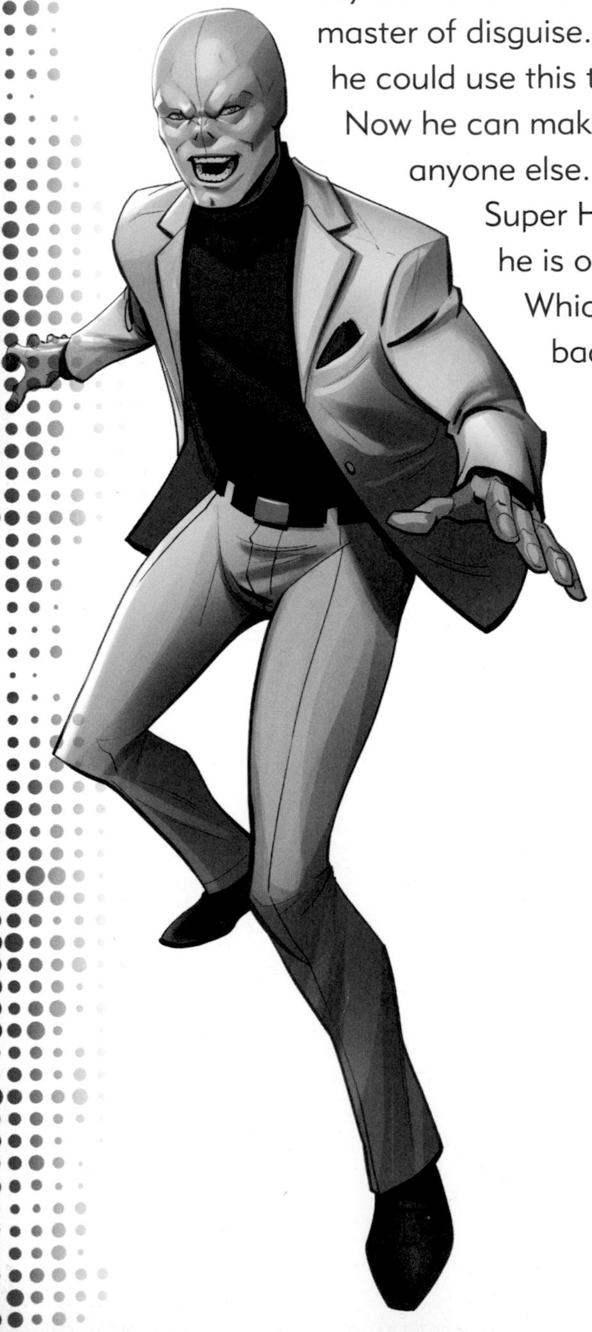

HEIGHT: UNKNOWN

WEIGHT: UNKNOWN

MASTER OF DISGUISE

INITIALLY DESIGNED A COSTUME THAT COULD MIMIC ANY CLOTHING, INCLUDING A HOLOGRAPHIC BELT THAT COULD STORE THE APPEARANCES OF PEOPLE HE CAME INTO CONTACT WITH TO USE WHENEVER HE NEEDED

EVENTUALLY USED A SERUM THAT ALLOWED HIM TO CHANGE HIS APPEARANCE AT WILL

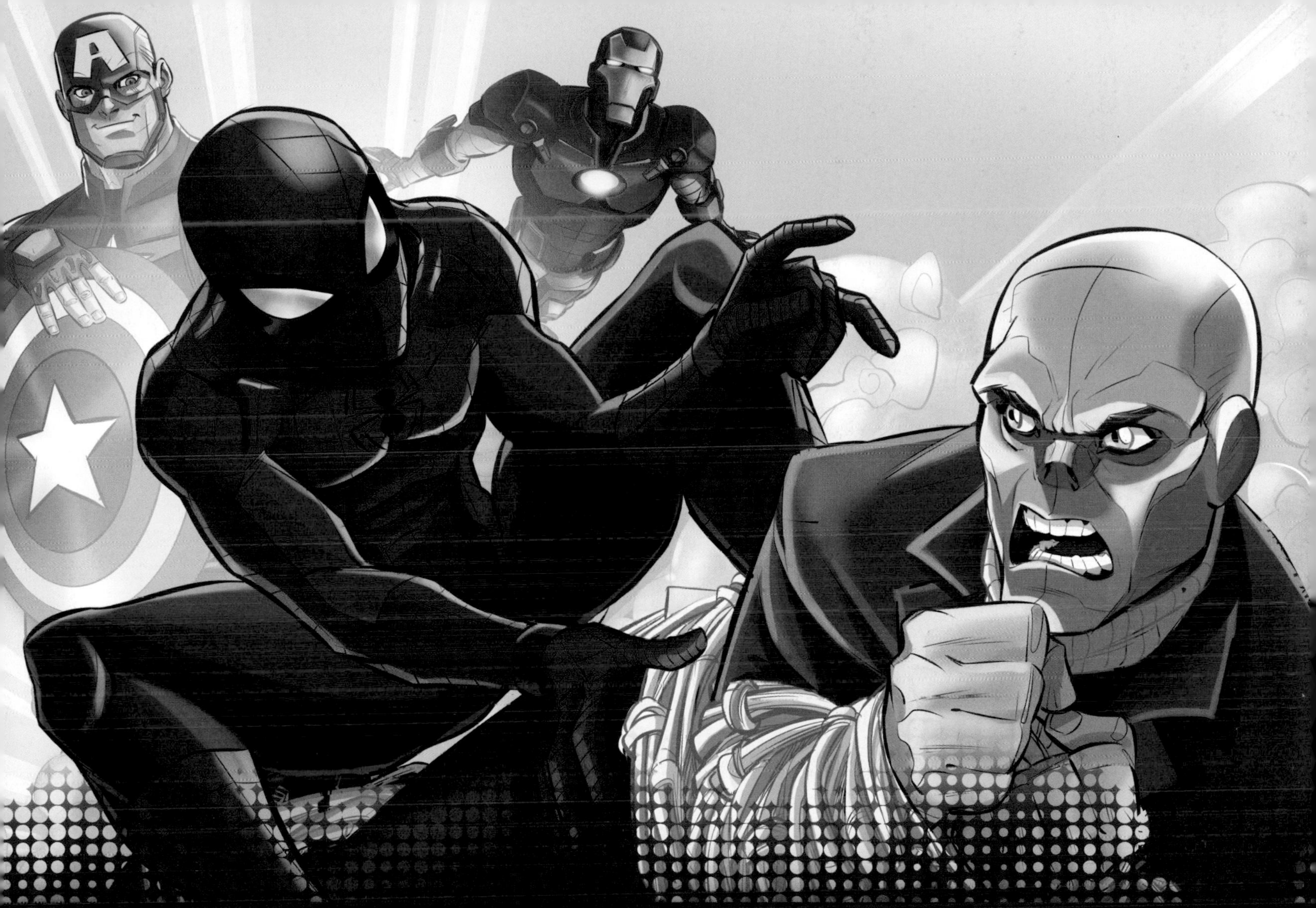

"Ow!" Spidey yelled. "Why are you hitting ME?"

"Put Nick Fury down!" Iron Man ordered. He had just arrived on the deck of the helicarrier, only to see Spidey fighting with the leader of S.H.I.E.L.D.

"That's not Fury!" Spidey said. "That's my old enemy—the Chameleon!"

"He's lying!" Fury replied.

"Oh yeah?" Spidey said, spinning a web at Fury's face. He pulled off a mask, revealing Chameleon underneath! "Now do you believe me?"

"Sorry I ever doubted you, web-head!" Iron Man replied.

As you can see, it's not all fun and games being a Spider-Hero. But it's STILL pretty awesome.

"Hey, guys," Miles said. "I think Venom just woke up from his nap. . . ."

Looks like it's time for our heroes to get back to work!

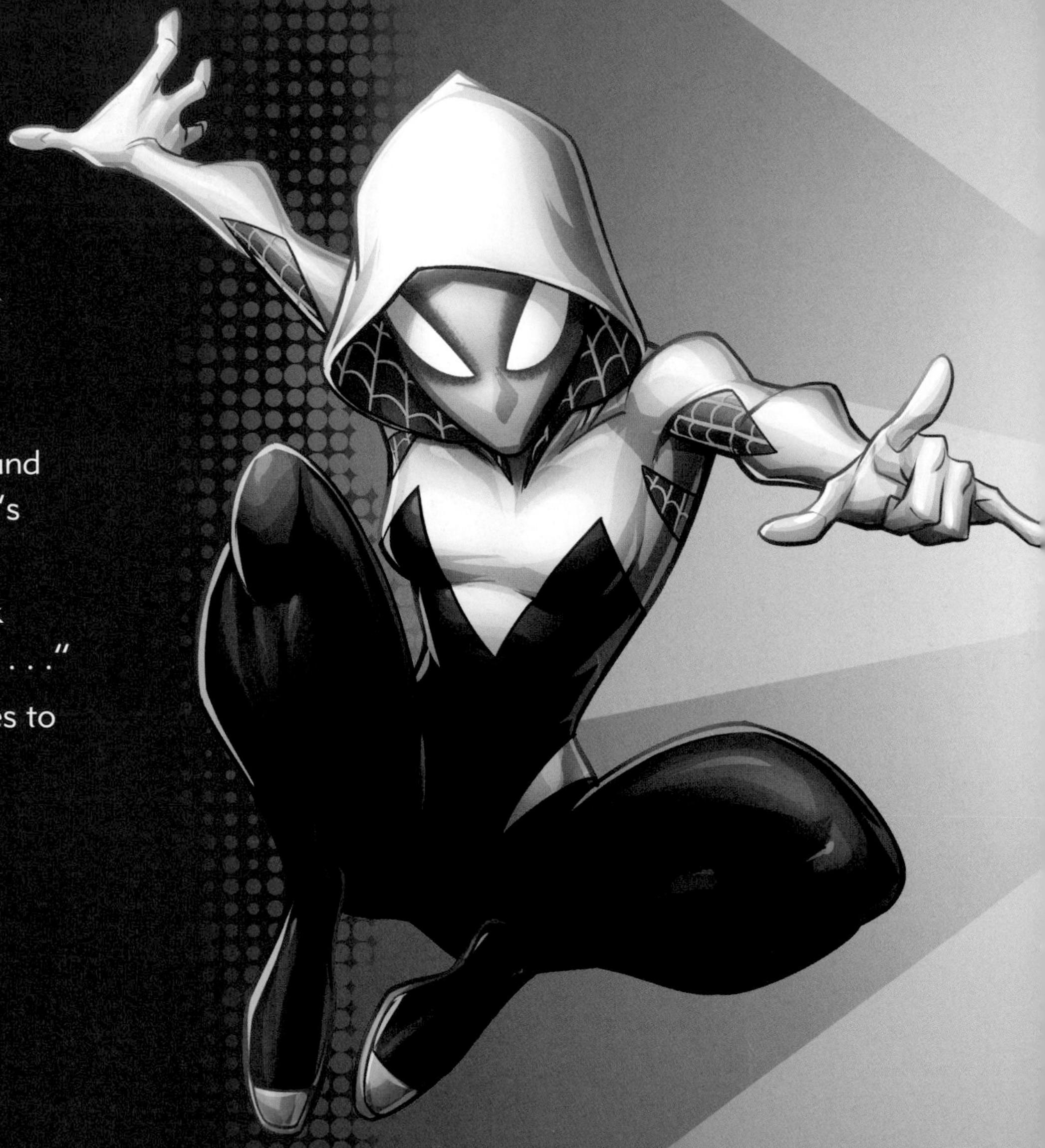

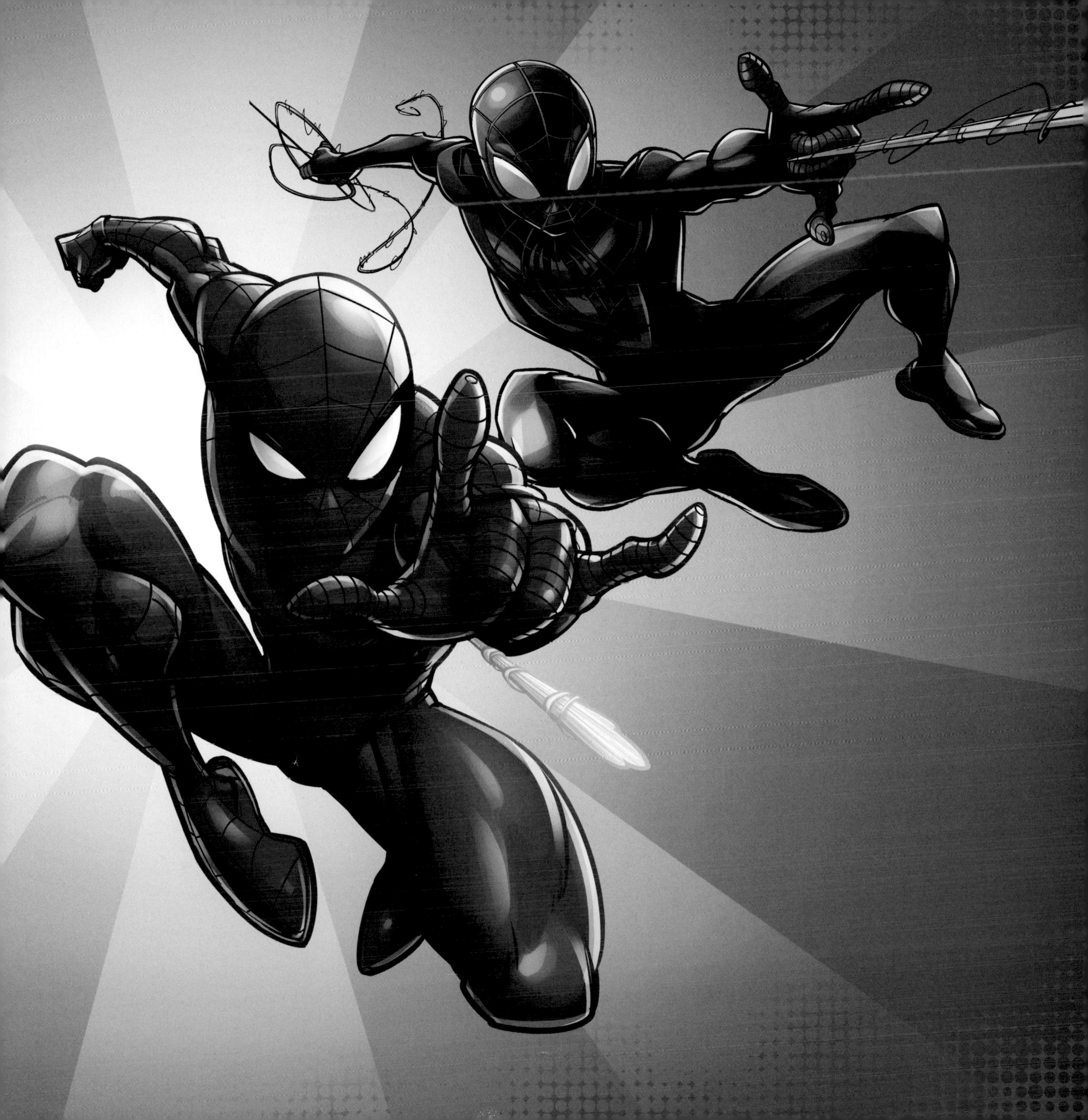

GUARDIANS OF THE GALAXY

HEIGHT: 6'1"

WEIGHT: 175 LBS

HALF HUMAN,
HALF ALIEN

ADEPT HAND-TO-HAND COMBATANT AND MARKSMAN

GIFTED STRATEGIST, WITH APTITUDE FOR THINKING OUTSIDE THE BOX

HAS A UNIQUE BLASTER THAT ONLY WORKS IN HIS HANDS

HIGH-TECH MASK GRANTS A VARIETY OF VISION MODES AND SUPPLIES OXYGEN EVEN IN THE VACUUM OF SPACE

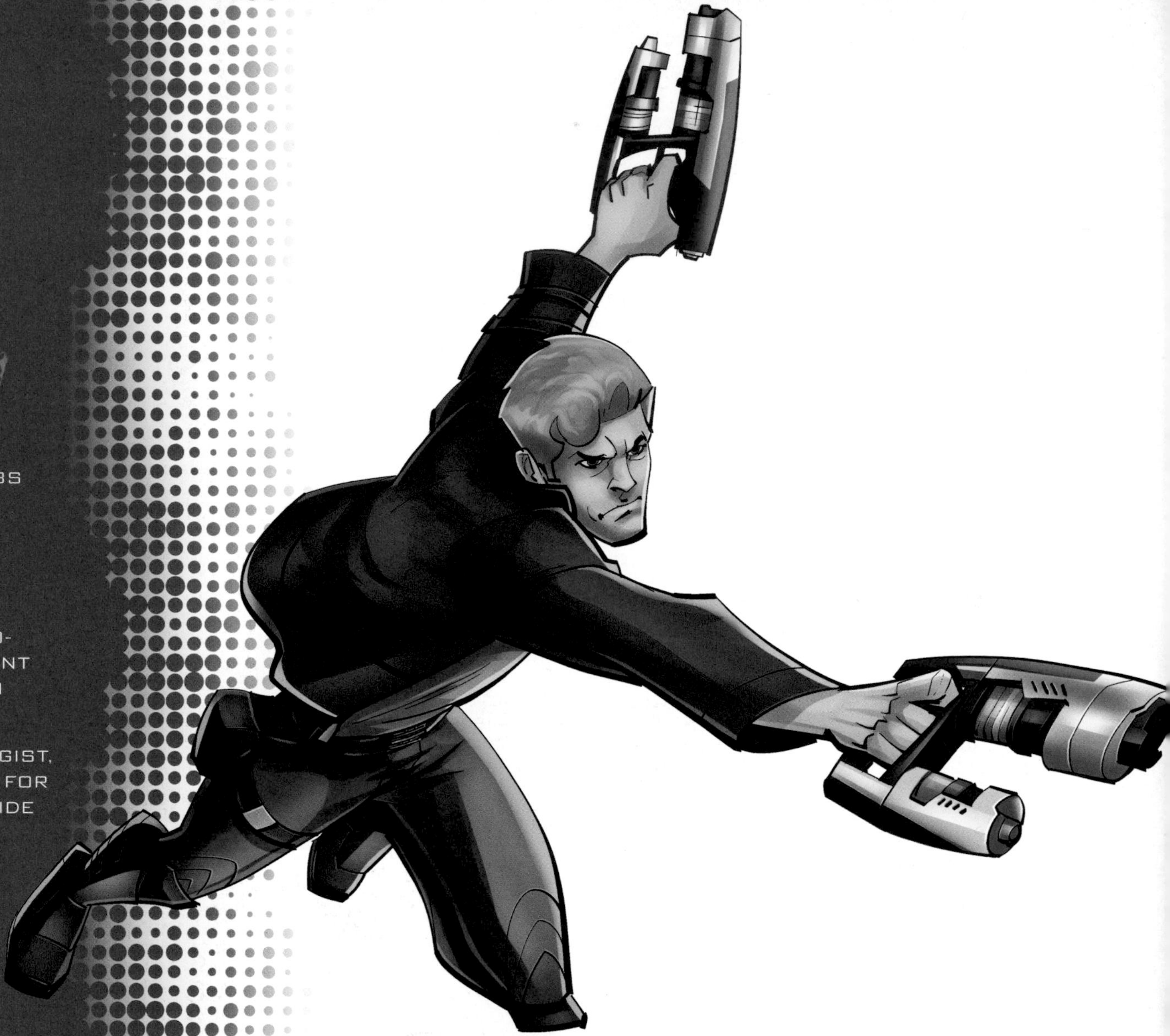

STAR-LORD

Peter Quill

Have you ever been to outer space? Lived in it? Worked in it? Joined forces with four aliens to save the galaxy? No? Same here. But Peter Quill has! As a member of the heroic Guardians of the Galaxy, Peter travels throughout space to right intergalactic wrongs.

It wasn't always that way, though. When he was a kid growing up on Earth, Peter only dreamed of having adventures in outer space. Peter studied and practiced very hard to become an astronaut so he could live out those adventures for real! As Peter grew up, he took the name Star-Lord and teamed up with Gamora, Drax, Rocket, and Groot to form the Guardians of the Galaxy.

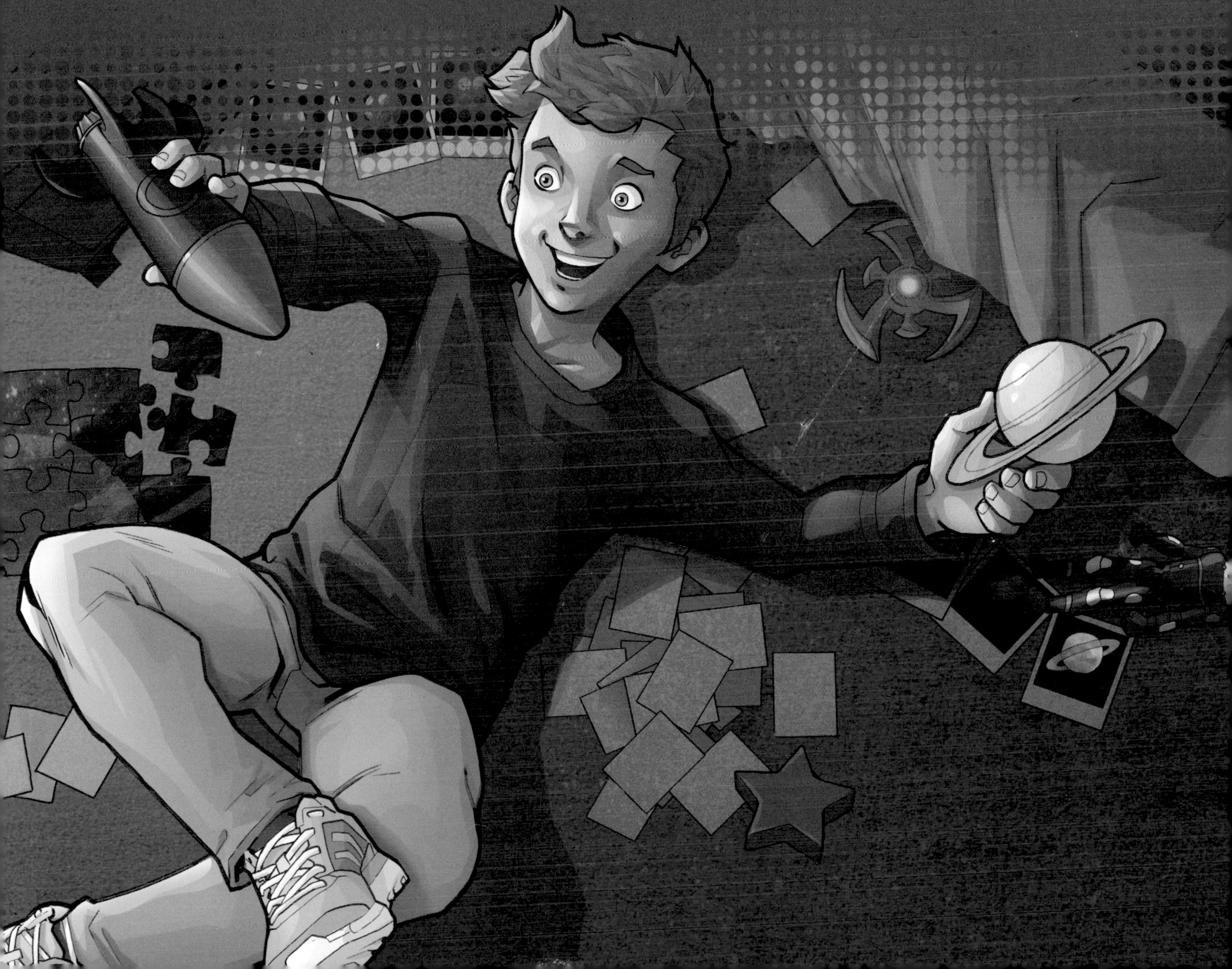

The Guardians had just arrived at their latest mission. Their ship, the *Milano*, hovered in the sky. If anything went wrong on the mission, they would have to make it back to the ship as fast as they could to escape.

"Watch where you're pointin' that thing!" Rocket said as Peter jumped past him. "I don't wanna get hurt BEFORE we go into battle!"

"Then maybe you should stay behind me," Peter said. "I mean, I AM the leader."

"Will you two stop bickering?" Gamora sighed.

"Yes, this argument is ridiculous," Drax added, before letting loose a bloodcurdling battle cry.

"I am Groot," Groot said.

"Fine," Peter said. "But stay out of my way, raccoon."

"I ain't no raccoon!" Rocket said. Peter was pretty sure that he was.

It was just another typical day for the Guardians of the Galaxy.

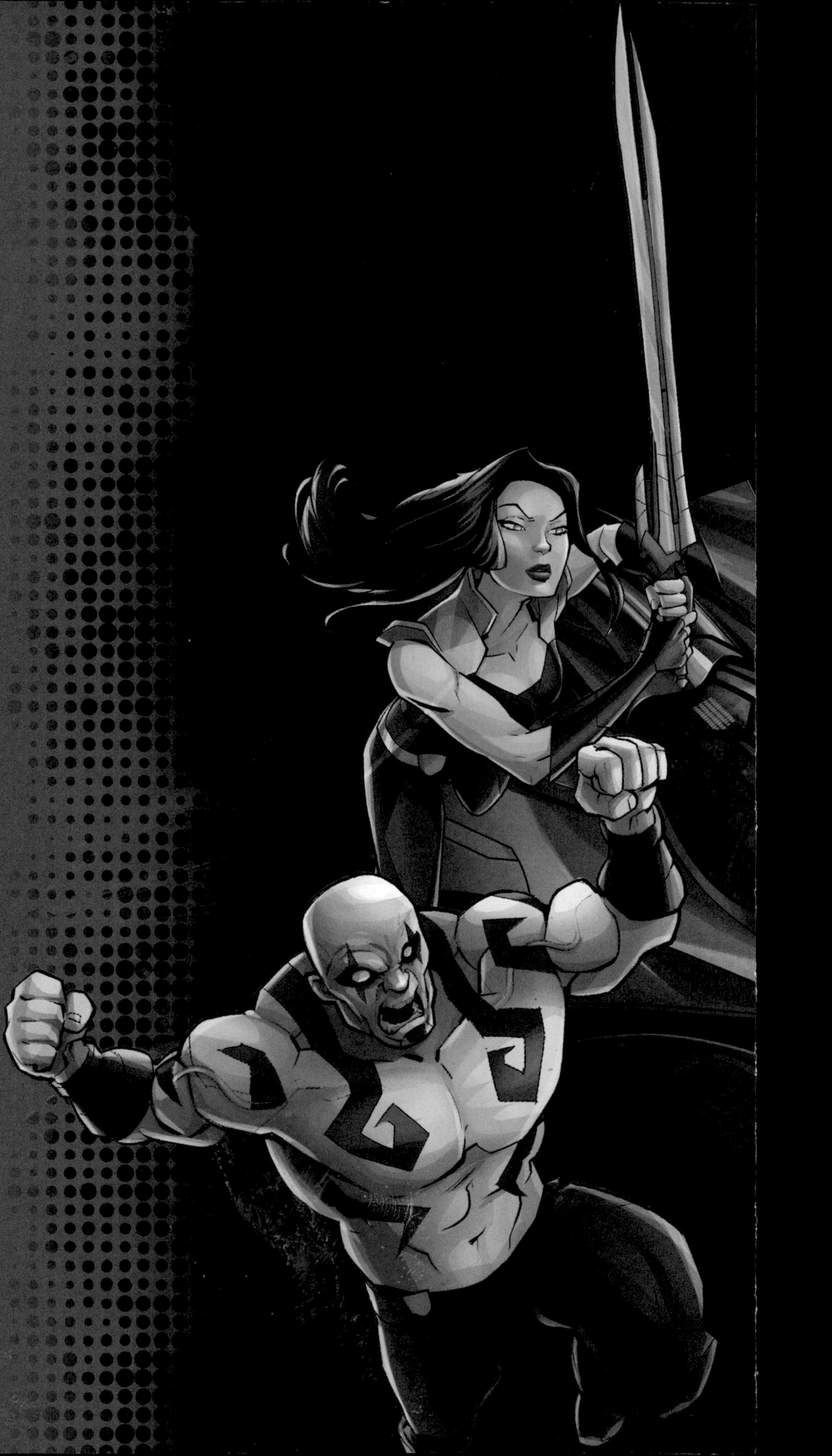

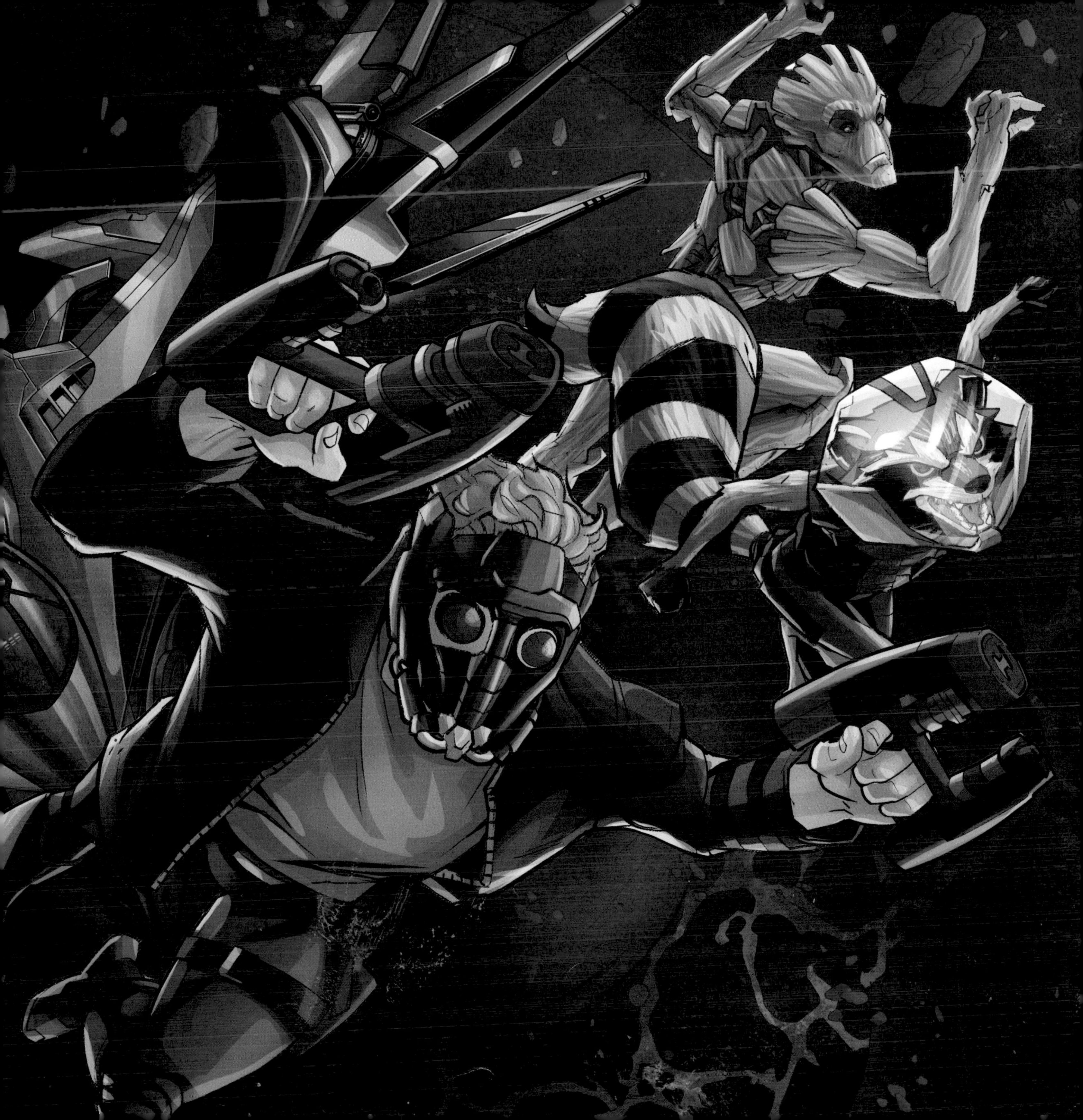

GAMORA

The Deadliest Woman in the Galaxy

HEIGHT: 5'9"

WEIGHT: 170 LBS

ADOPTED DAUGHTER OF THANOS, RAISED WITH HER ADOPTED SISTER, NEBULA

STRENGTH, AGILITY, PHYSICAL CONDITIONING, AND HEALING RATE HEIGHTENED BY CYBERNETIC IMPLANTS AND GENETIC ALTERATION

UNPARALLELED WARRIOR, MASTER OF HAND-TO-HAND COMBAT

EXPERIENCE IN VIRTUALLY ALL KNOWN MARTIAL ARTS

PROFICIENT IN A WIDE VARIETY OF WEAPONRY

HIGHLY SKILLED IN THE ART OF SUBTERFUGE

If there's anyone more dangerous in the galaxy than Gamora, we haven't met them! (We haven't met a lot of people, but that's beside the point.) When Gamora was just a little girl, the Mad Titan, Thanos, came to her planet and wiped out her people, but "saved" Gamora and trained her to fight better than anyone so he could use her to fight his battles.

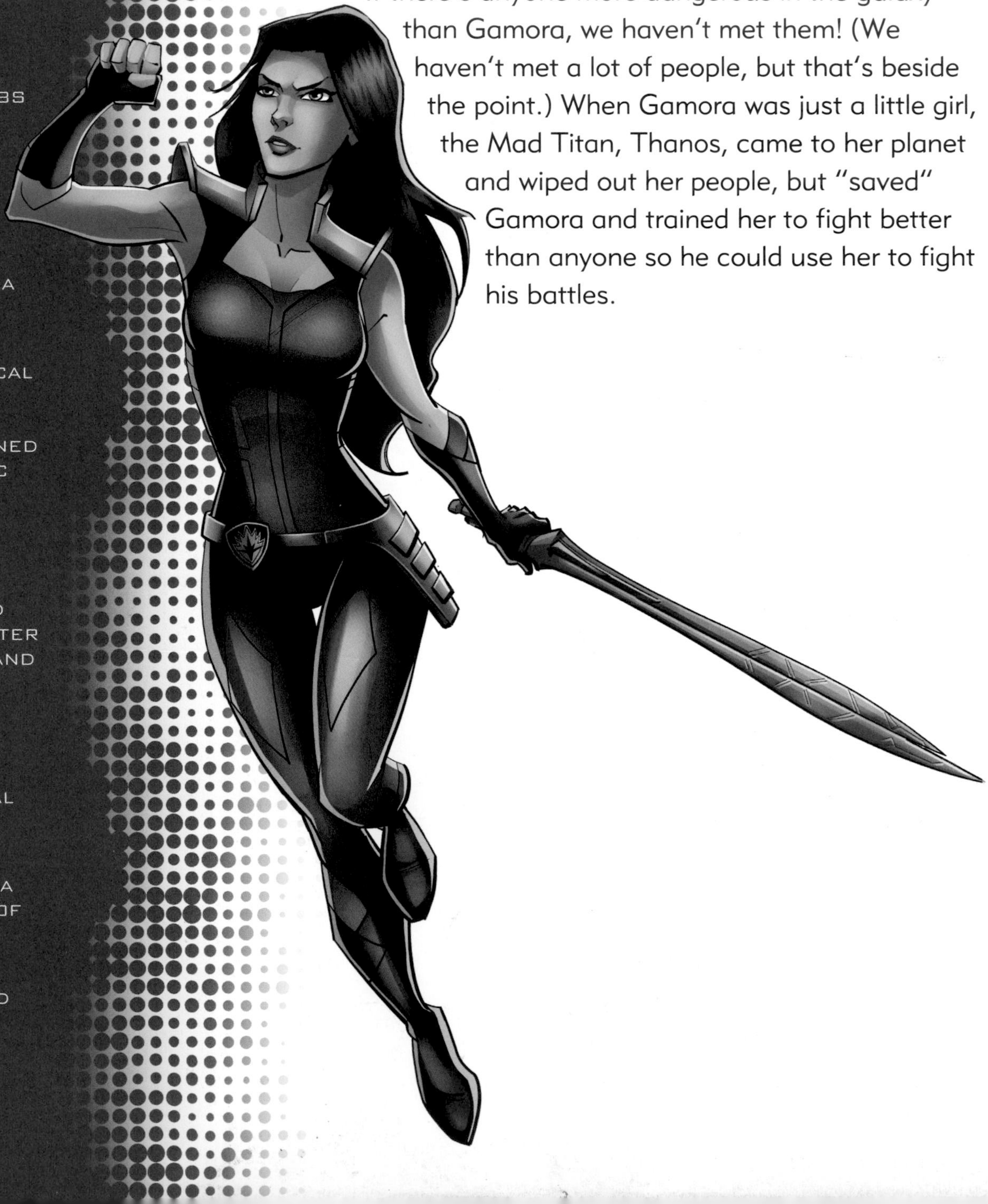

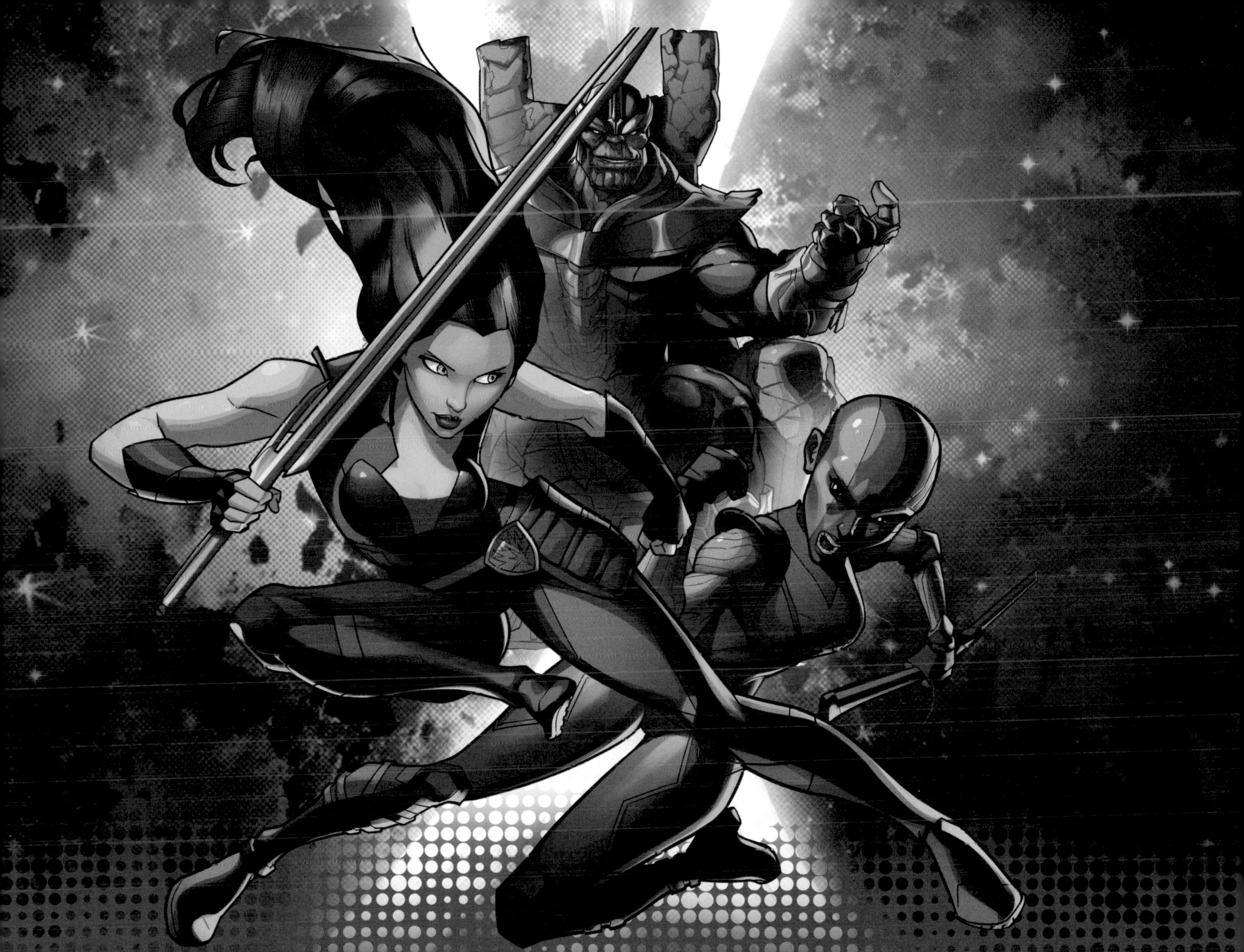

Thanos also adopted another girl, named Nebula (more on her later!), and Nebula became Gamora's sister. But they were forced by Thanos to fight one another constantly. They both became powerful warriors, but because they were always competing, the sisters came to dislike each other. Eventually Gamora went against her father and joined the Guardians of the Galaxy. She was an extremely skilled fighter and became known as the deadliest woman in the galaxy!

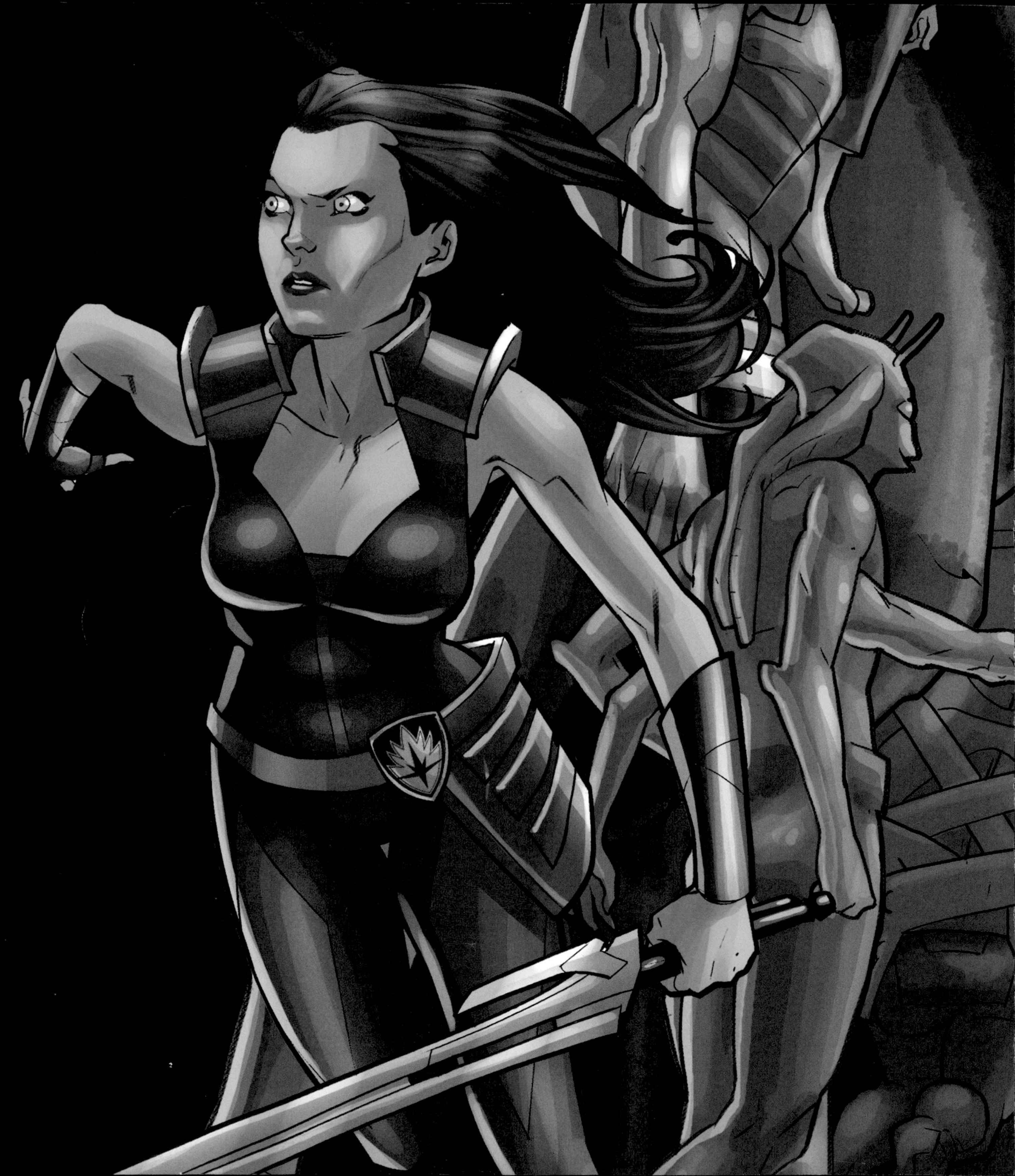

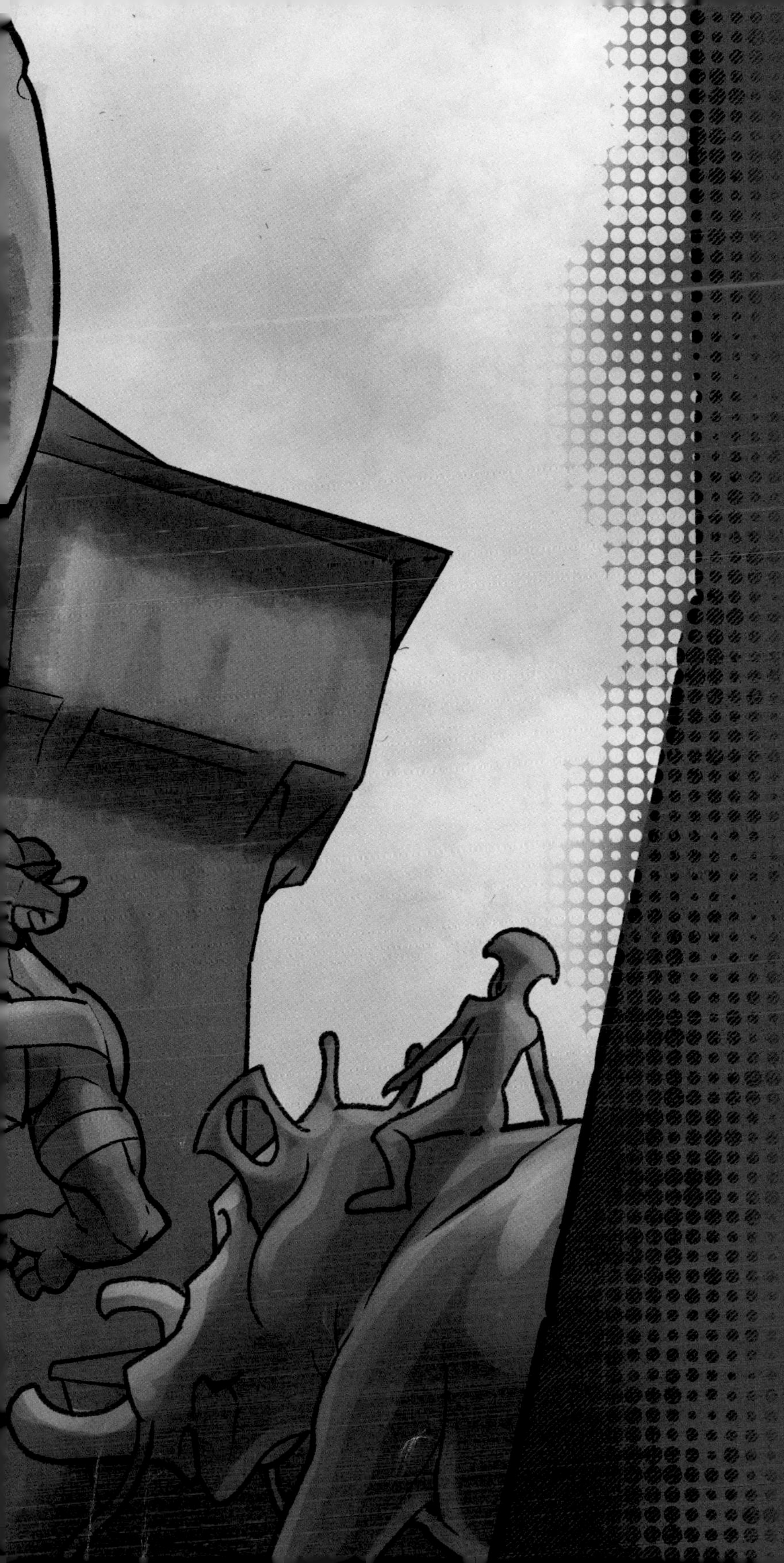

The Guardians had landed on the planet Morag, and it was chaos on the planet's surface. The Guardians had been forced to split up, and Star-Lord was trying to keep track of his team.

"Where are you, Gamora?" Peter said over his comms link. "I've been trying to reach you for an hour, and all I'm getting is static!"

"I'm running through the streets of an alien city, chasing after my sister!" Gamora said angrily. "Now stop bothering me!"

"Sheesh," Peter replied. "I was just asking a question."

Gamora had been searching for Nebula, trying to persuade her to join the Guardians.

Suddenly a bright flash of light appeared, and Gamora couldn't see. When her vision cleared, she saw Thanos sitting on his throne. Nebula was there, too.

"Hello, daughter," Thanos said. "Let the combat begin!"

HEIGHT: 6'5"

WEIGHT: 680 LBS; UP TO 1050 LBS IN MOST POWERFUL BODY

FUELED BY REVENGE FOR HIS FAMILY

SUPERHUMAN STRENGTH AND DURABILITY

FEROCIOUS HAND-TO-HAND COMBATANT

HIGHLY SKILLED WITH BLADES AND OTHER CLOSE-COMBAT GEAR

DIRECT BUT ROUGH-EDGED IN COMMUNICATION

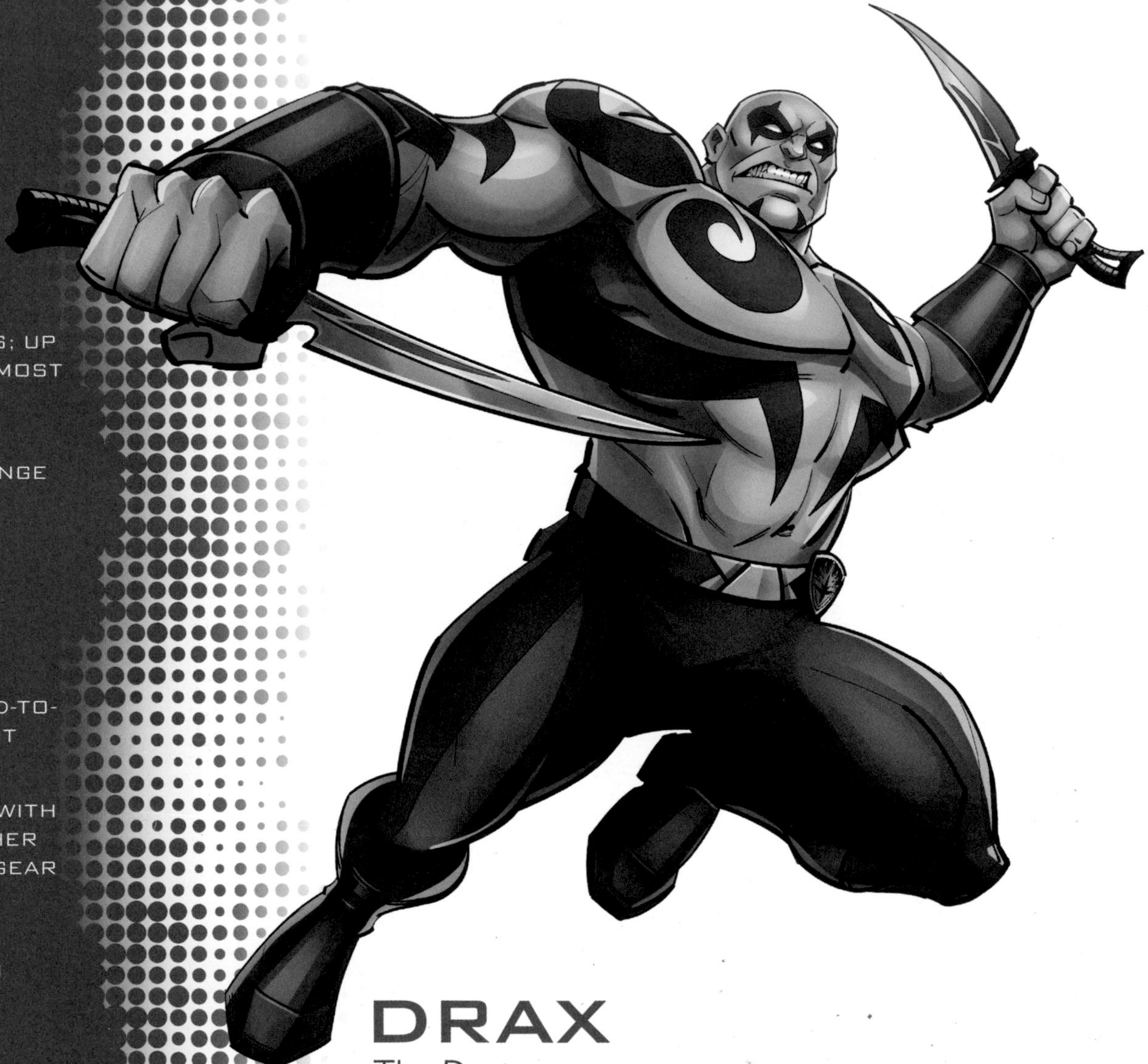

DRAX

The Destroyer

Gamora wasn't the only incredible warrior who joined the Guardians. A large alien named Drax the Destroyer, who has super-strength, also joined Peter Quill's space-faring team. Fierce and powerful, Drax is great to have in any battle.

Years ago, Drax lost his family. Since then, he has roamed the galaxy looking for Thanos, who took his family from him. He joined Gamora and Peter, glad to be part of a family once more. Drax is an incredible warrior, braver than anyone the Guardians have ever met. But Drax has one teeny, tiny flaw. He takes everything literally. For example, if you said something was so funny you forgot to laugh, from then on Drax would remind you to laugh. You know, so you wouldn't forget!

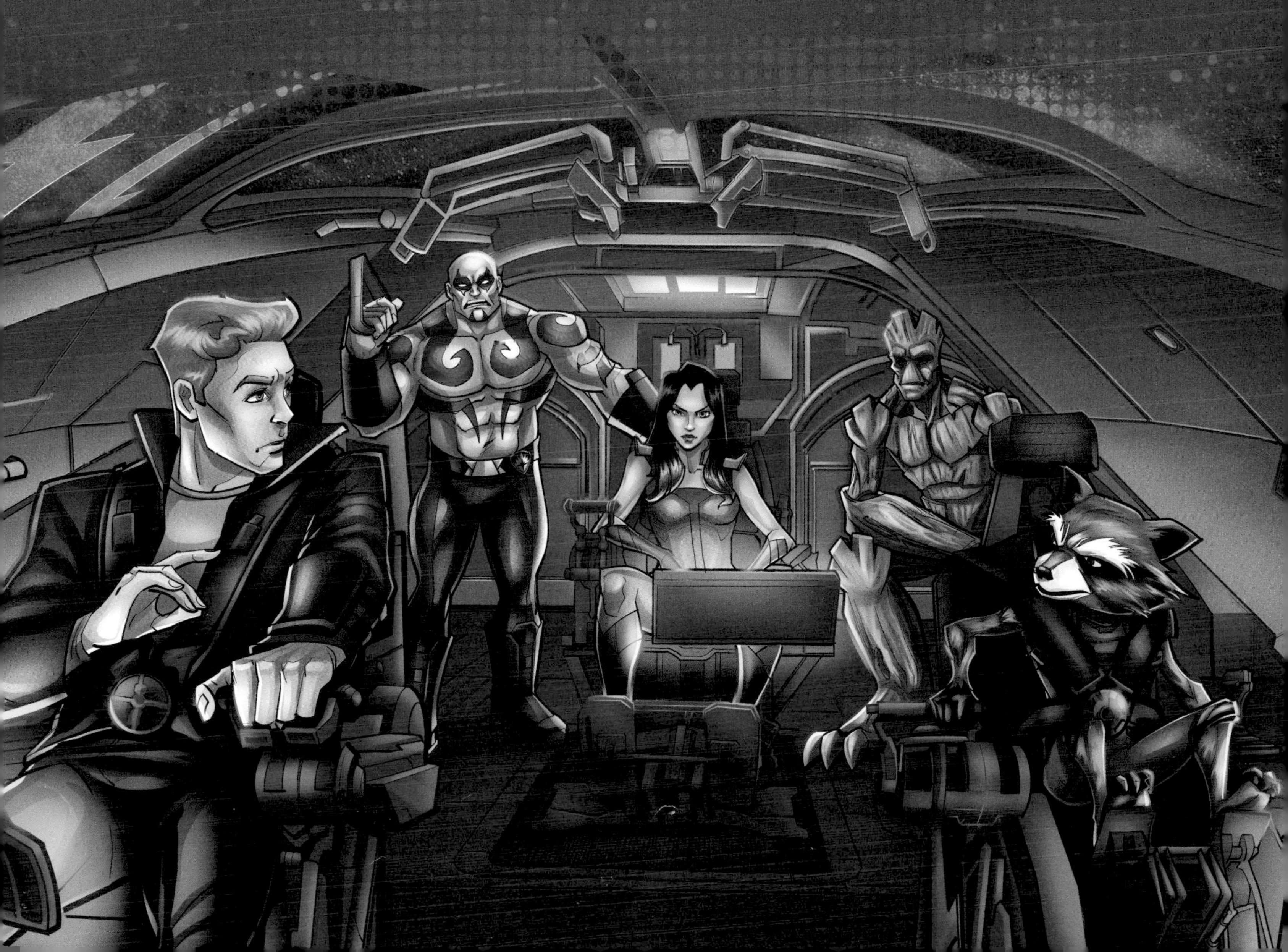

"Something's wrong with Iron Man!" Star-Lord said.

"That is obvious," Drax replied. Remember when we said that he took everything very literally? Well, he was doing it again. "He is acting like a jerk."

"I don't think he's acting," Rocket added.

"Drax!" Star-Lord shouted. "Get the people out of here before Shellhead does some serious damage!"

As Iron Man blasted the Guardians of the Galaxy, Drax moved quickly. He protected one of his friends. He was always loyal to those who cared about him and those who most needed help.

Thankfully, the team figured out that Iron Man wasn't really Iron Man at all! Thor's evil brother, Loki, had hijacked one of Tony Stark's Iron Man suits, and was using it to try to destroy Thor. But Loki hadn't counted on the Guardians of the Galaxy showing up!

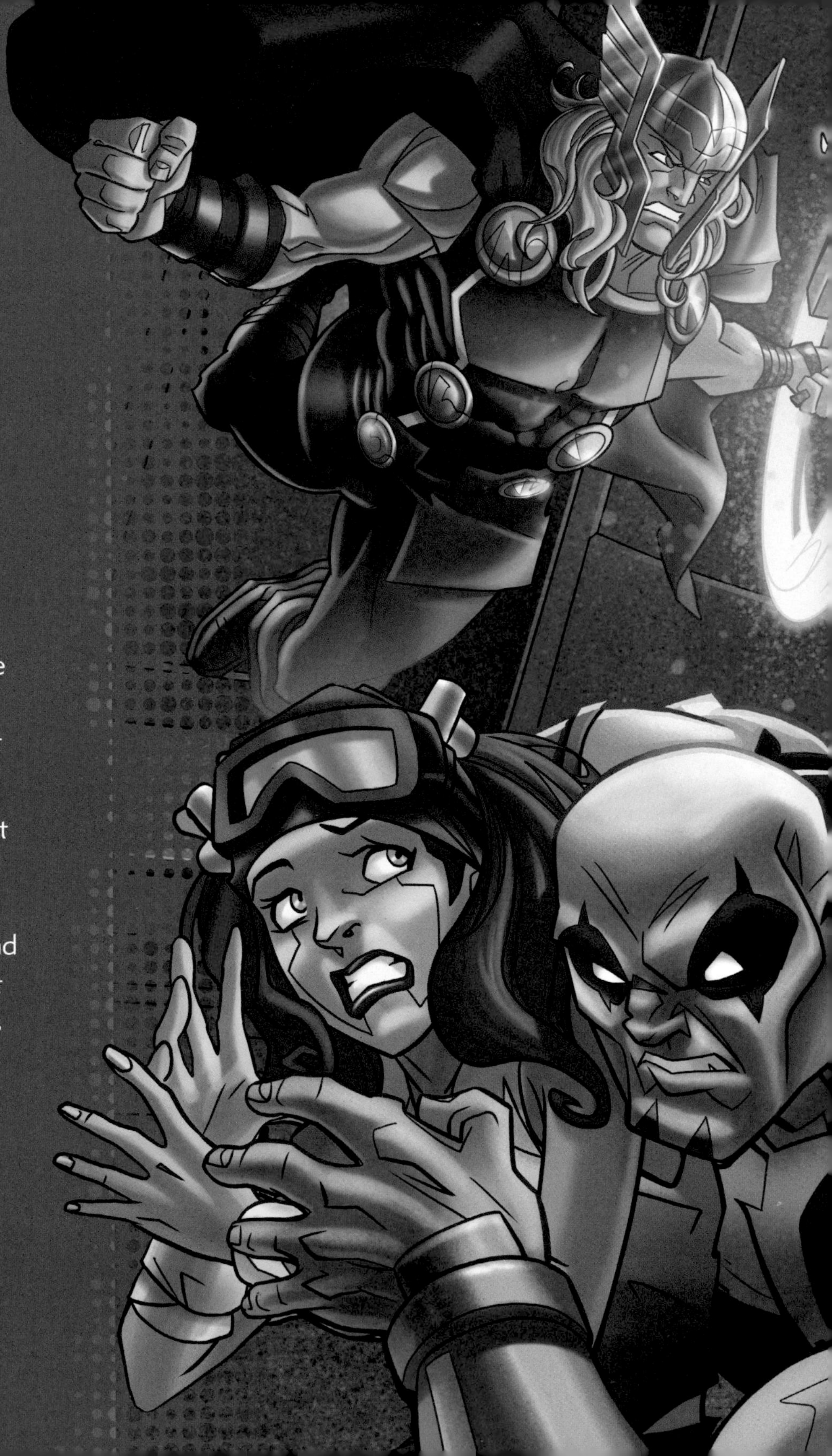

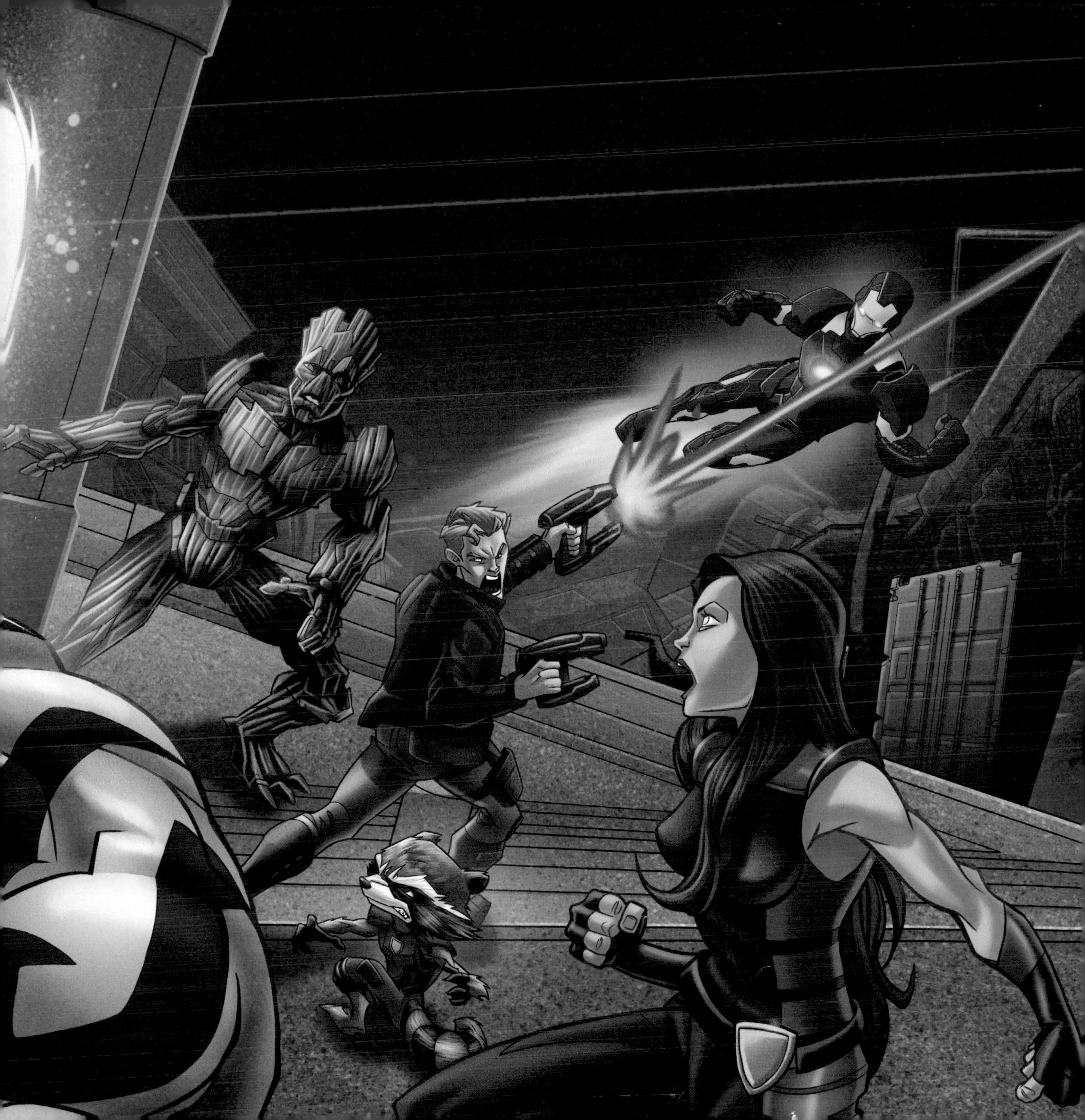

ROCKET

Not a Raccoon

HEIGHT: 3'

WEIGHT: UNKNOWN

NOT A RACCOON

MASTER PILOT, ENGINEER, MARKSMAN, AND WEAPONS SPECIALIST

GENETICALLY AND CYBERNETICALLY ENHANCED

HIGHLY AGILE

MECHANICAL GENIUS (ESPECIALLY IN ENGINEERING, VEHICLES, AND HEAVY MUNITIONS)

TOUGH TALKER

If you travel the galaxy far and wide, you'll never meet anyone like Rocket! That's because only Rocket is like Rocket! That makes sense, right? Anyway, Rocket was kind of like a raccoon, we guess, until a team of scientists experimented upon the little guy. He has all the abilities of a raccoon—a heightened sense of sight, sound, and smell—but he was also given increased intelligence. That Rocket is one smart creature!

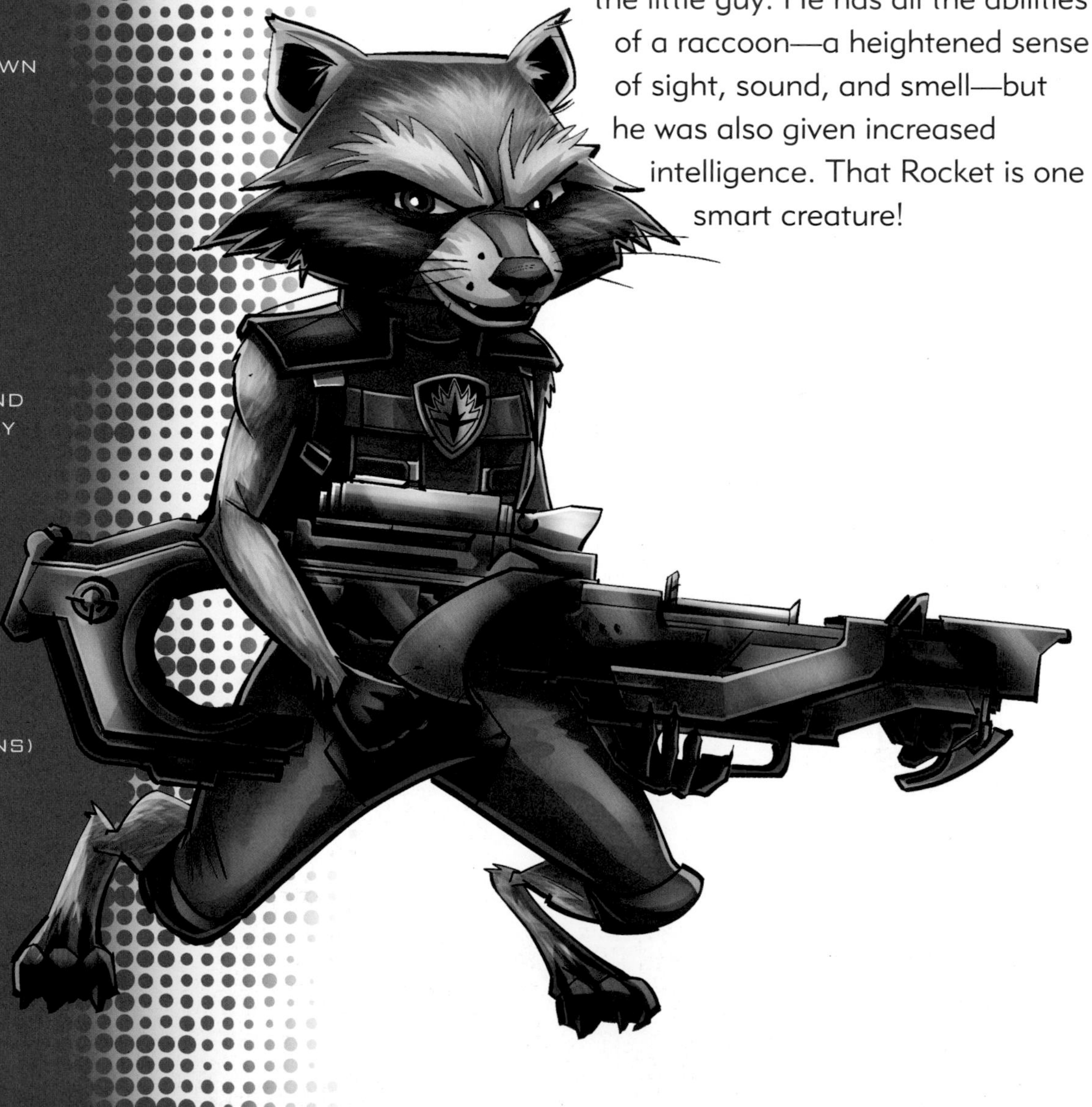

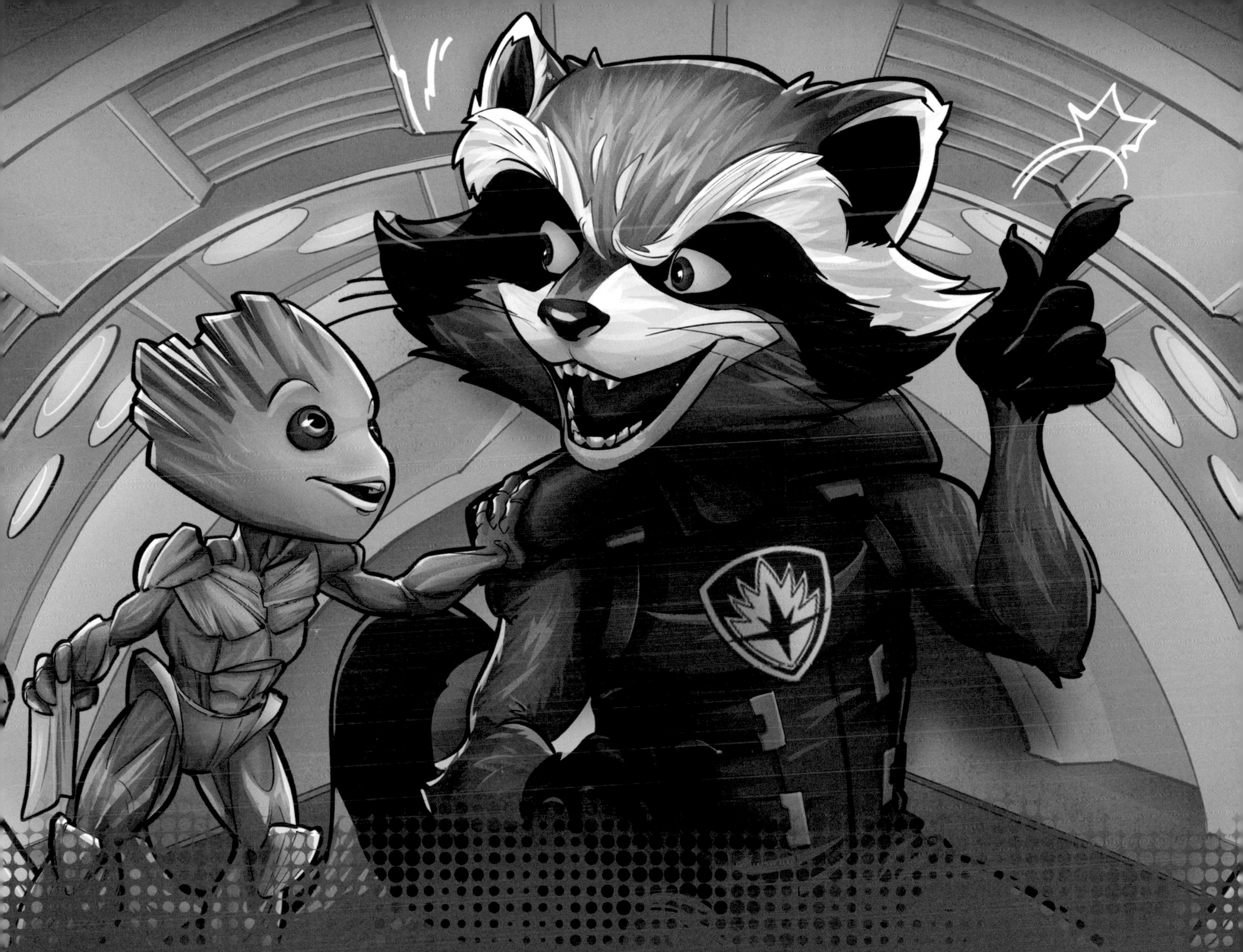

Even though he may look like a furry, fuzzy woodland creature, Rocket is anything but. He's tough, scrappy, and always ready for a fight. And if you call him a "raccoon," you'll find all that out really quick! (Hint: Don't call him a raccoon.) Rocket's also a master of all kinds of weapons, and comes up with great battle plans. Rocket's best friend is a talking tree named Groot. Together, they joined the Guardians of the Galaxy, and when they're not fighting with each other, they're saving the universe. Or parts of it, anyway.

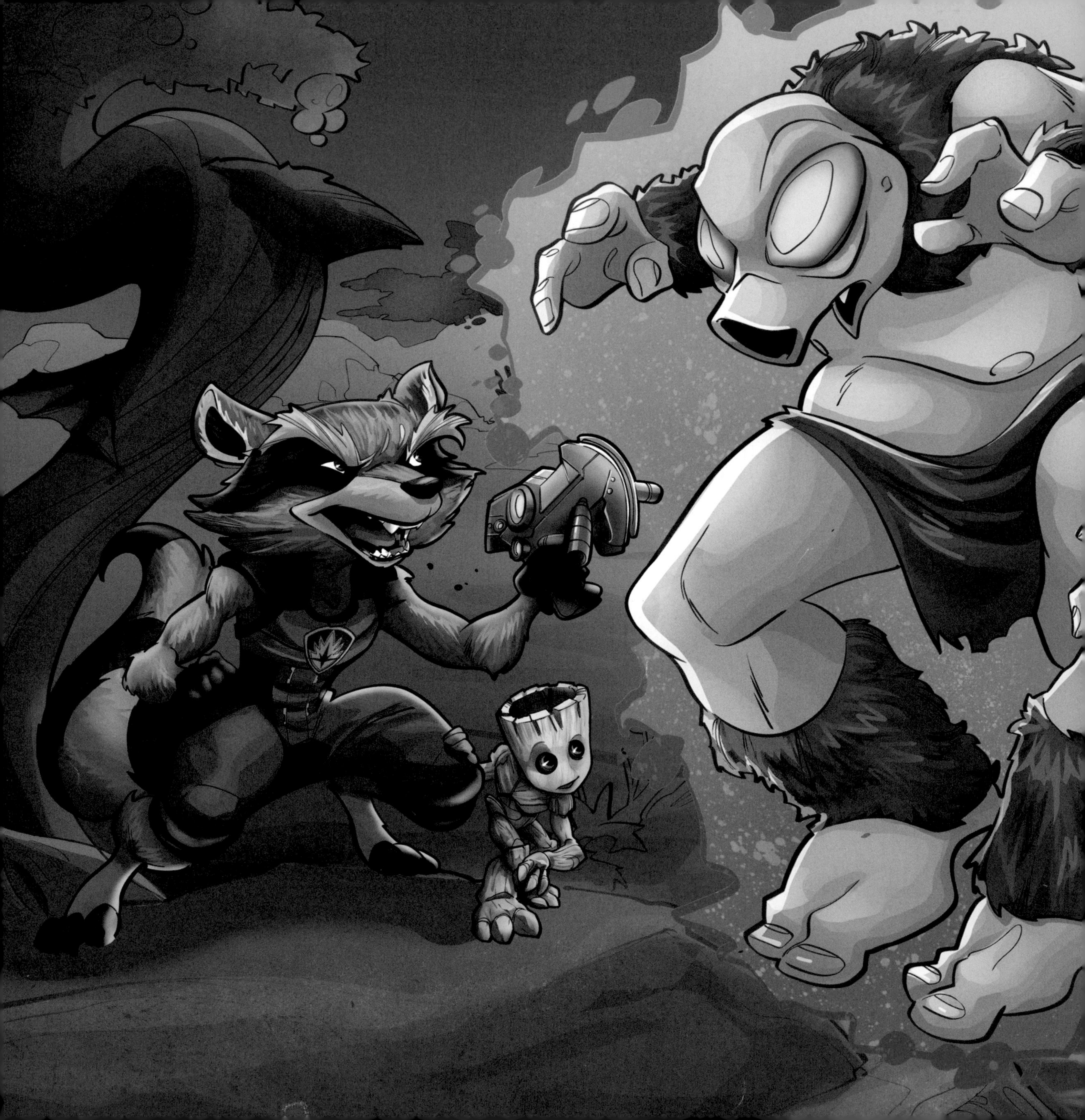

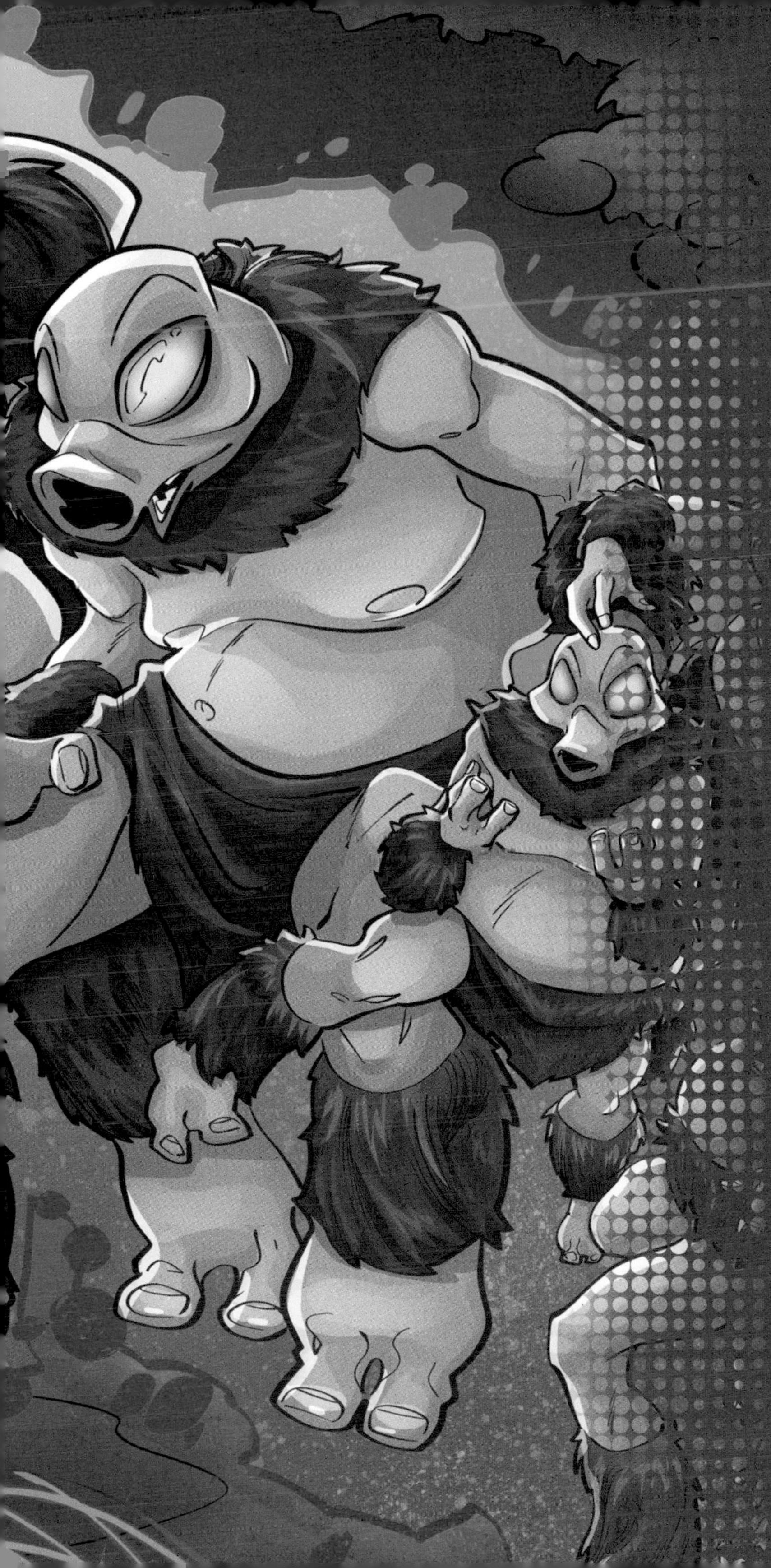

Rocket and Groot landed on a planet called Blorf, looking to refuel their ship. Instead of finding fuel, they met a group of piglike aliens called Kodabaks. Turned out the Kodabaks didn't want to meet THEM. So the Kodabaks attacked.

Usually, Rocket was the one who was spoiling for a fight. But not this time. "Look, guys—I don't wanna fight!" Rocket said. "I just wanna get our fuel and go! Y'know, fuel? What goes in a ship? Aside from us?"

Groot looked at Rocket and thought for a second. Then he shouted, "I. AM. GROOT!"

Suddenly the Kodabaks stopped running. One of them smiled and said, "I am Groot!"

"Whaddaya know?" Rocket said. "I guess they speak Groot!"

The Kodabaks took Rocket and Groot to their refueling station, and everything was great, until Rocket and Groot got into trouble again.

HEIGHT: VARIABLE

WEIGHT: VARIABLE

MEMBER OF A TREELIKE ALIEN RACE

SUPERHUMAN STRENGTH

ABILITY TO QUICKLY REGENERATE AFTER ENDURING PHYSICAL DAMAGE

PLANTLIKE FORM ENABLES HIM TO GROW OR RESHAPE HIS LIMBS AND ROOT HIMSELF IN PLACE FOR ENHANCED STABILITY

CAN EMIT GLOWING SPORES

ONLY SAYS THE PHRASE "I AM GROOT"

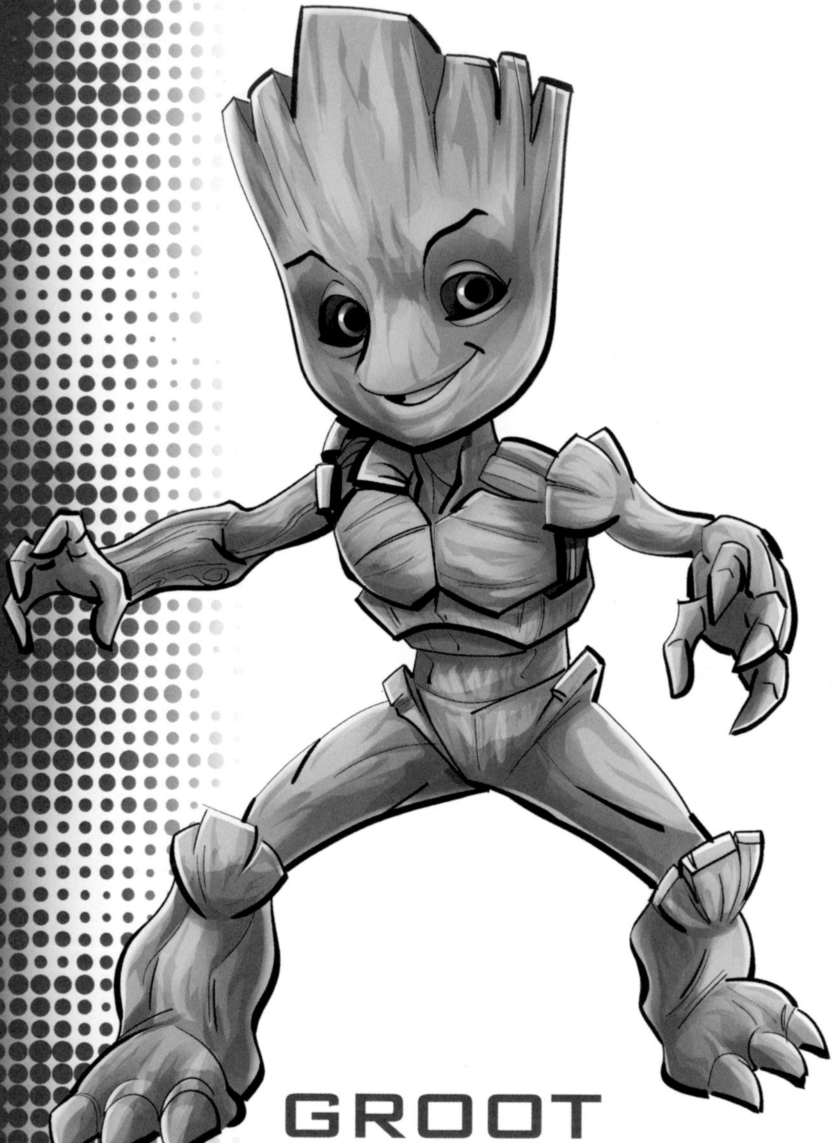

GROOT

He is Groot

This is Groot! He's a tree. Well, sort of. He comes from Planet X, where a race of treelike beings dwells. The only thing Groot can say is "I am Groot." At least, that's what it sounds like to us. But to somebody who speaks Groot's language, it can mean practically anything!

Groot is always looking out for his friends—he is very loyal and thinks it is important to protect those who need help. He is usually pretty chill, and when he joined the Guardians of the Galaxy, he became the most chill member of the team! But one thing can really set Groot off—tiny alien pests called Orloni. They can live on land or in water, so you never know when you might stumble upon one! Groot can't stand them. They make him so mad, he will shout, "I AM GROOT!"

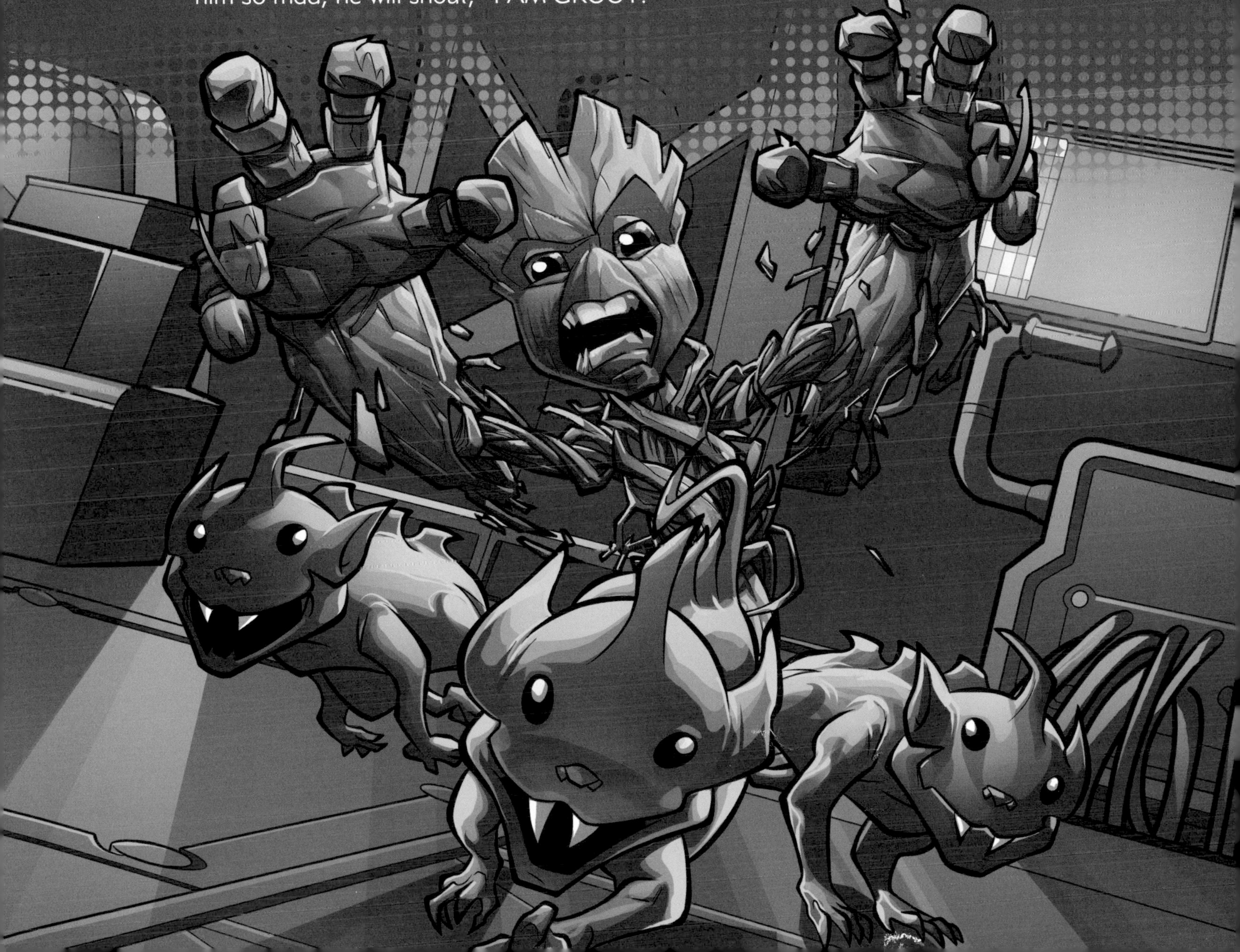

Which is precisely what Groot was doing at that exact moment.

"I am Groot!"

Something was wrong with the Guardians' ship, the *Milano*. The engines wouldn't work! Groot suspected it might have something to do with a particularly pesky Orloni. So he did EXACTLY what he shouldn't have done, and dove into the engine pipes to see what was wrong!

"Get outta there, Groot!" Rocket yelled. He was worried for his friend!

"I am Groot!" Groot replied as he kept after the Orloni. He was determined to catch the alien wreaking havoc on his ship!

Soon, the Orloni raced right into a big blob of engine goo (yes, that's a thing). The Orloni was using it to build a nest! The Orloni was afraid of Groot, and burst right through the blob. Now the engines would work!

"Great job, pal!" Rocket said. "But next time, try not to jump in the engine, okay?"

"I am Groot!"

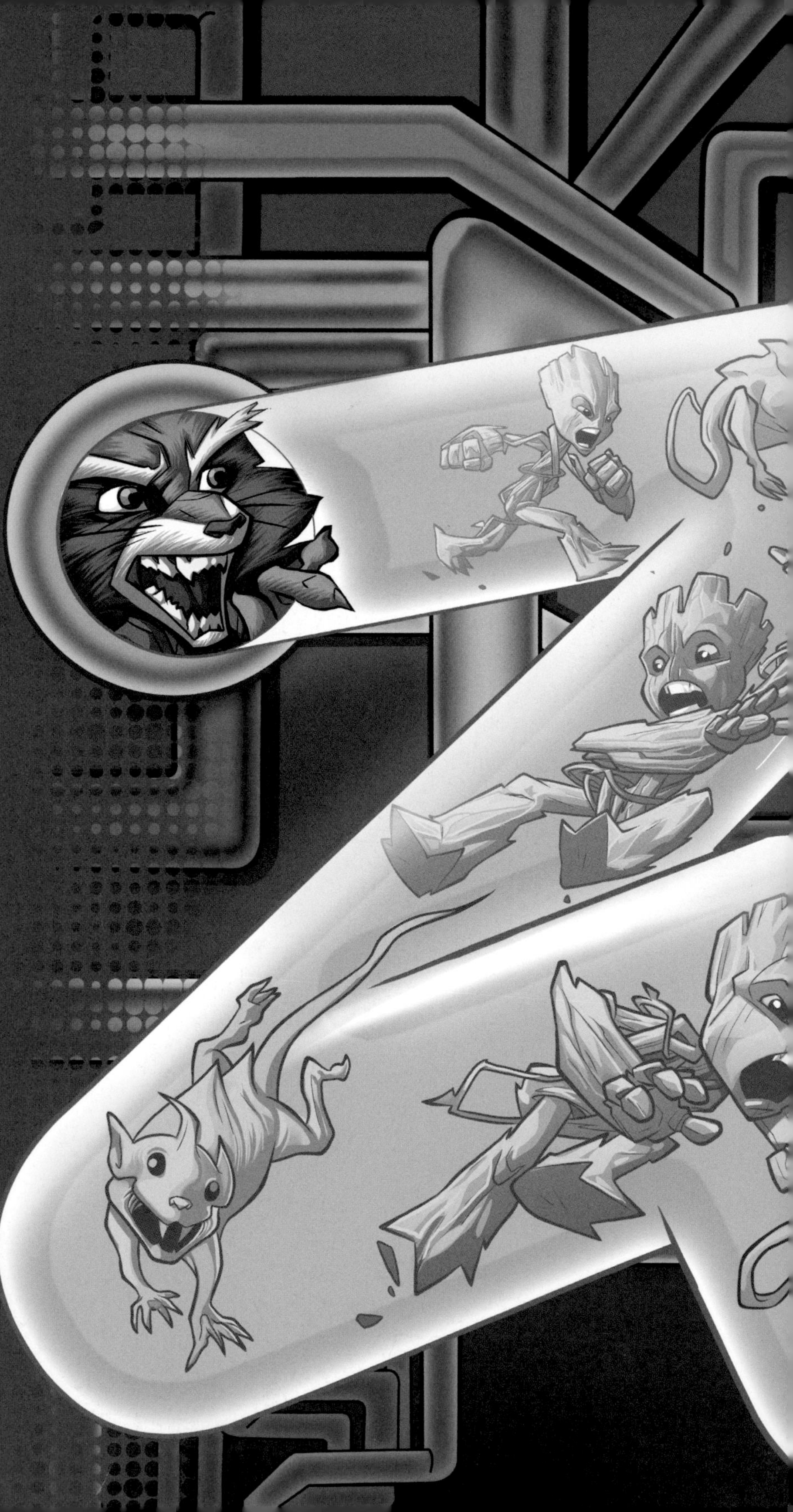

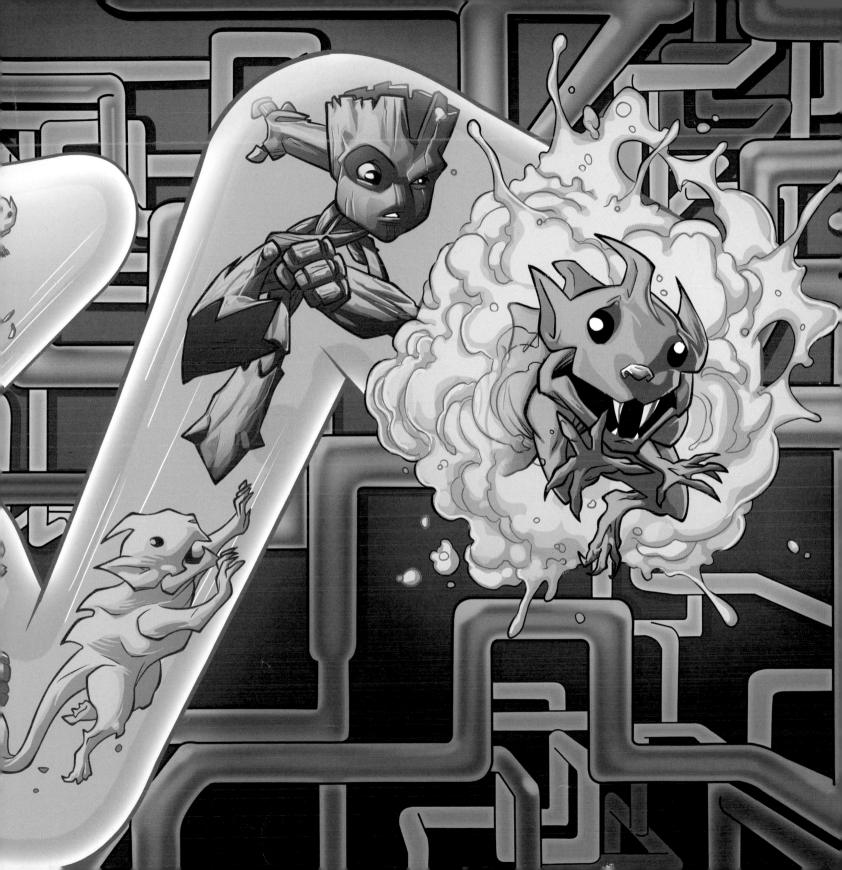

VILLAINS

HEIGHT: 6'5"

WEIGHT: UNKNOWN

SUPREME ACCUSER OF THE KREE EMPIRE, DEDICATED TO JUSTICE AND ANCIENT TRADITION

SUPERHUMAN STRENGTH, ENDURANCE, AGILITY, AND DURABILITY

EXPERT HAND-TO-HAND COMBATANT, WITH MASTERY OVER A VARIETY OF KREE FIGHTING STYLES

WIELDS THE UNIVERSAL WEAPON, A HAMMER-LIKE STAFF CAPABLE OF ABSORBING AND PROJECTING ENERGY, MANIPULATING GRAVITATIONAL FORCES, AND INFLICTING MASSIVE PHYSICAL DEVASTATION

EXPERIENCED SOLDIER WITH A HONED MILITARY MIND

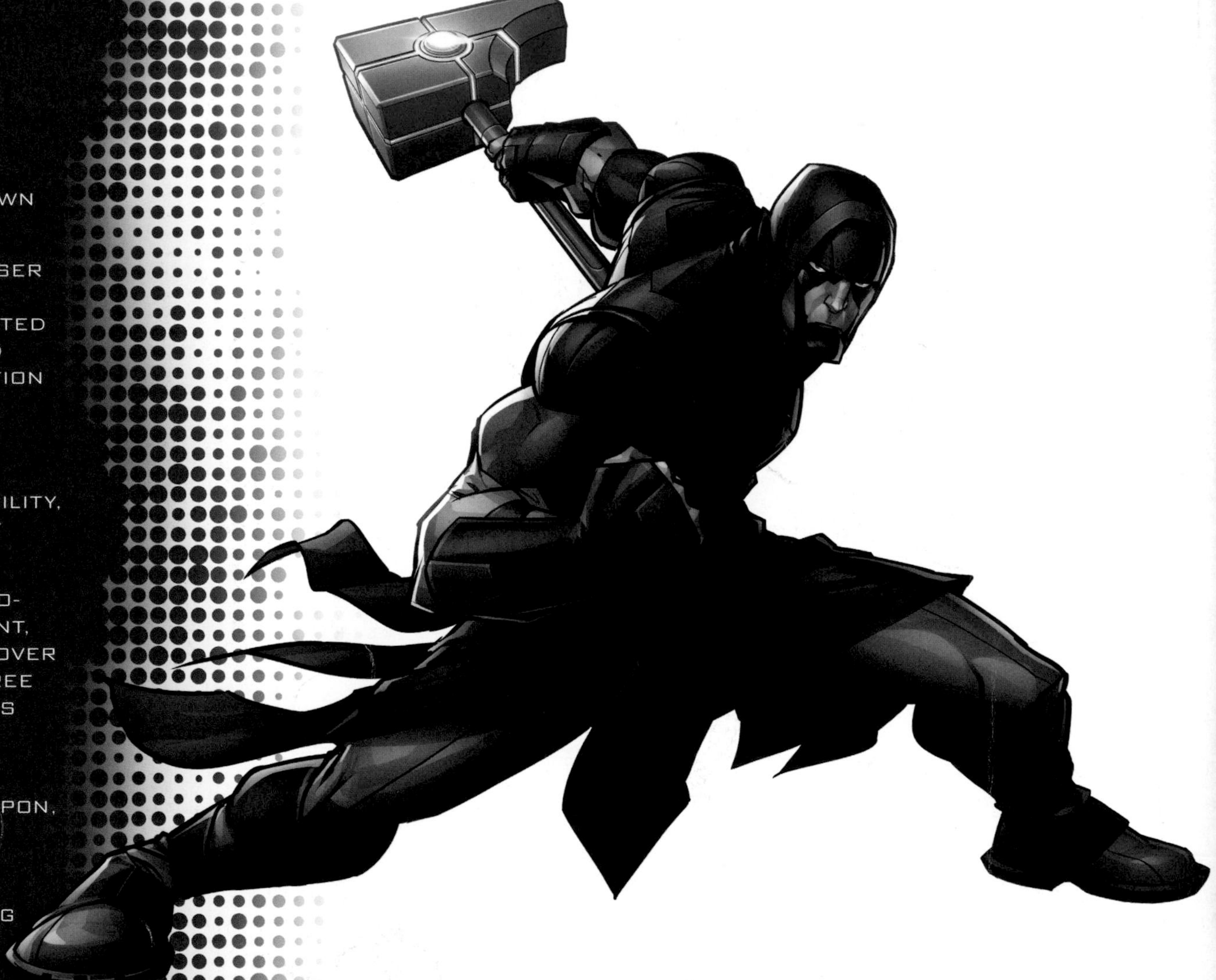

RONAN

The Accuser

As you might have guessed, the galaxy is full of bad guys—bad guys like Ronan the Accuser. Ronan is a Kree warrior who wants to punish anyone who stands in his way. And unfortunately for the Guardians, they're usually standing in his way!

Ronan had found Drax, who was trying to protect a group of aliens from the Kree's wrath. Ronan was wielding the cosmi-rod, a weapon that gave Ronan great power.

"You are a monster," Drax said. "And you'll harm no one. I won't allow it!"

"You are in a position to allow nothing," Ronan said, unleashing a blast at Drax.

But Ronan had not counted on Drax's incredible strength, or his ability to withstand pain. "If that's the best you can do," Drax said, "you might want to run."

Ronan was starting to think that Drax was right!

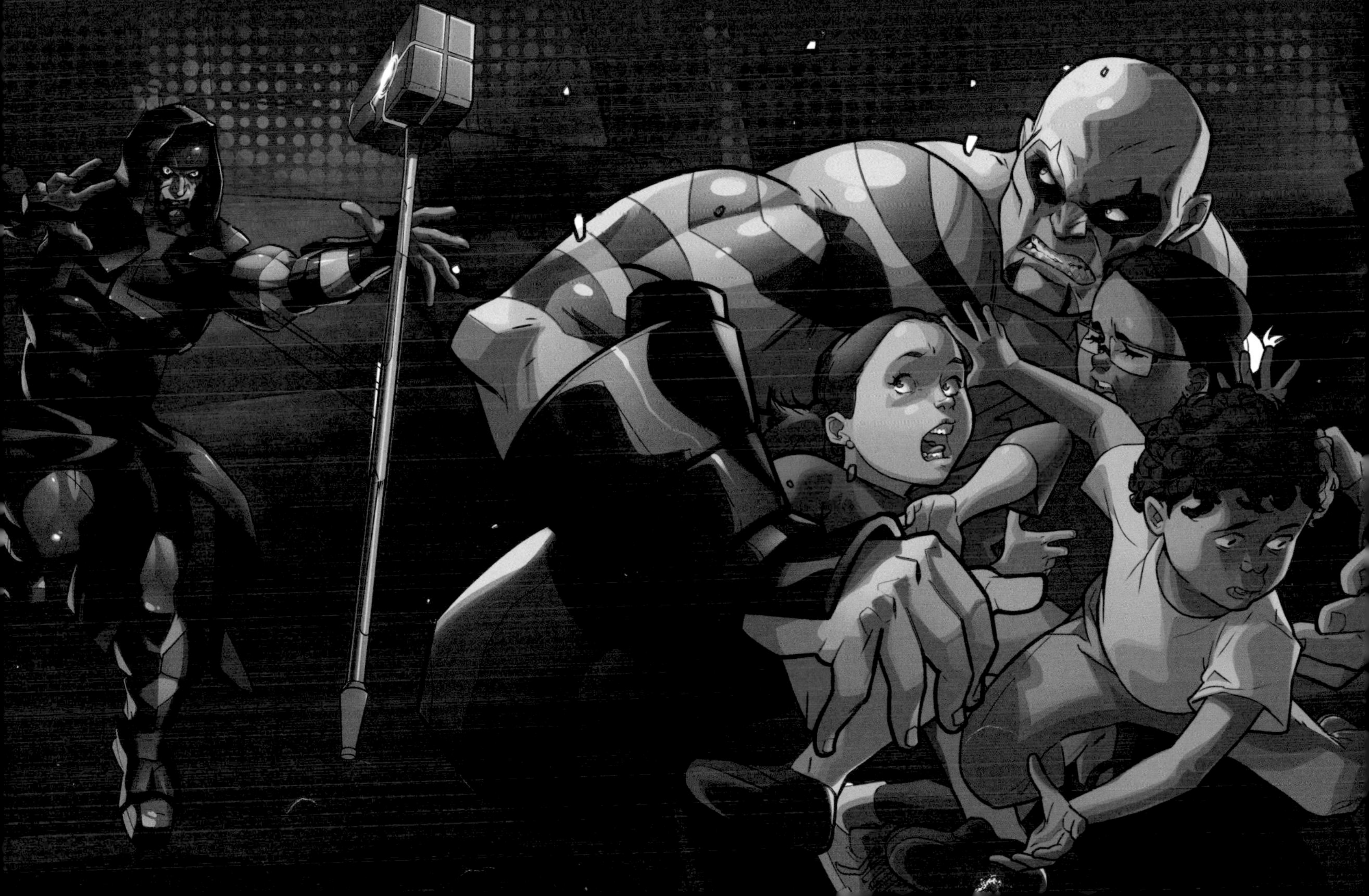

THE COLLECTOR

Taneleer Tivan

While some might not call The Collector a villain, he certainly has a wicked side. One of the Elders of the Universe, The Collector spends his days acquiring anything and everything that catches his interest. Usually it's rare, one-of-a-kind objects that attract his attention—and in some cases it isn't objects, but rare, one-of-a-kind beings!

HEIGHT: 6'2"

WEIGHT: 450 LBS

INTERGALACTIC DEALER AND COLLECTOR OF RARE AND UNUSUAL ITEMS

INFAMOUS FOR HIS ECCENTRIC TASTES

CONTROLS AN EXPANSIVE ESTATE

HAS NUMEROUS POLITICAL AND CRIMINAL CONNECTIONS ACROSS THE GALAXY

POSSESSES GREAT WEALTH AND RESOURCES

SEEKS TO PURCHASE OR ACQUIRE TECHNOLOGY, WEAPONS, SERVICES, AND MORE AS PART OF HIS VAST COLLECTION

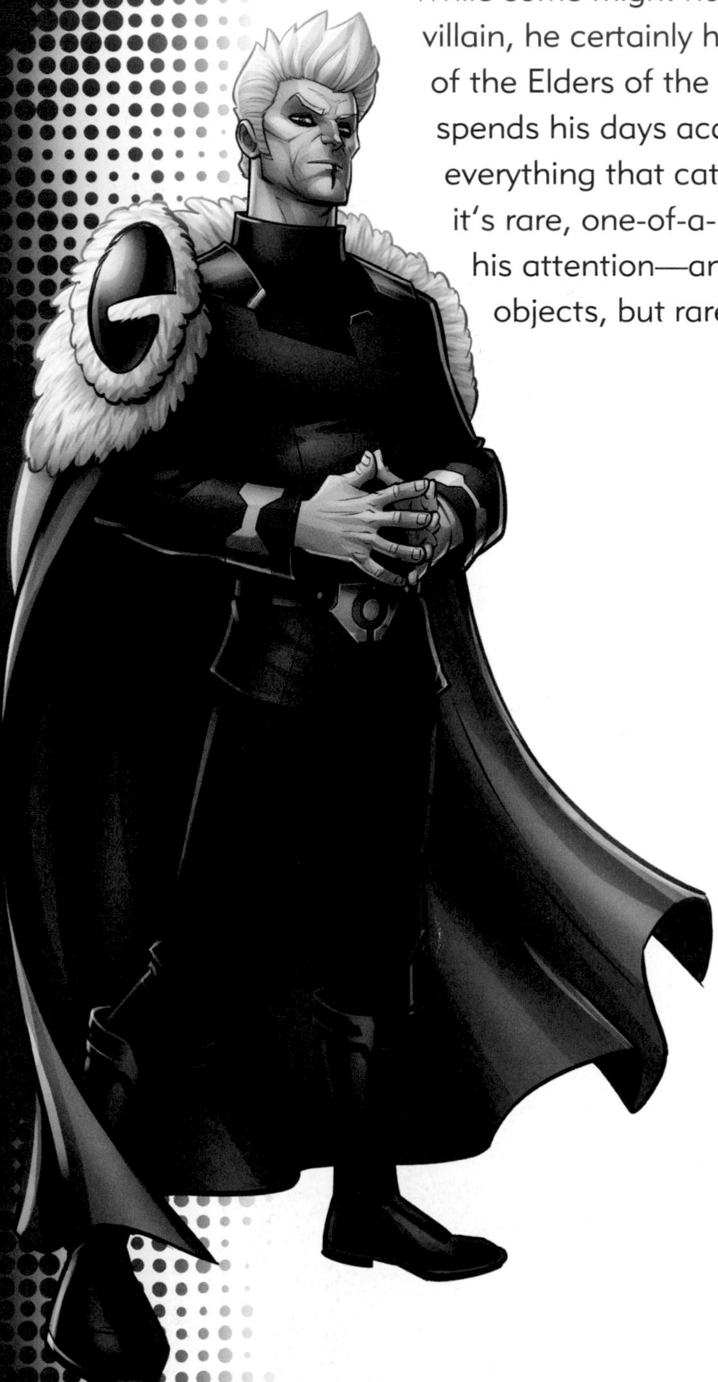

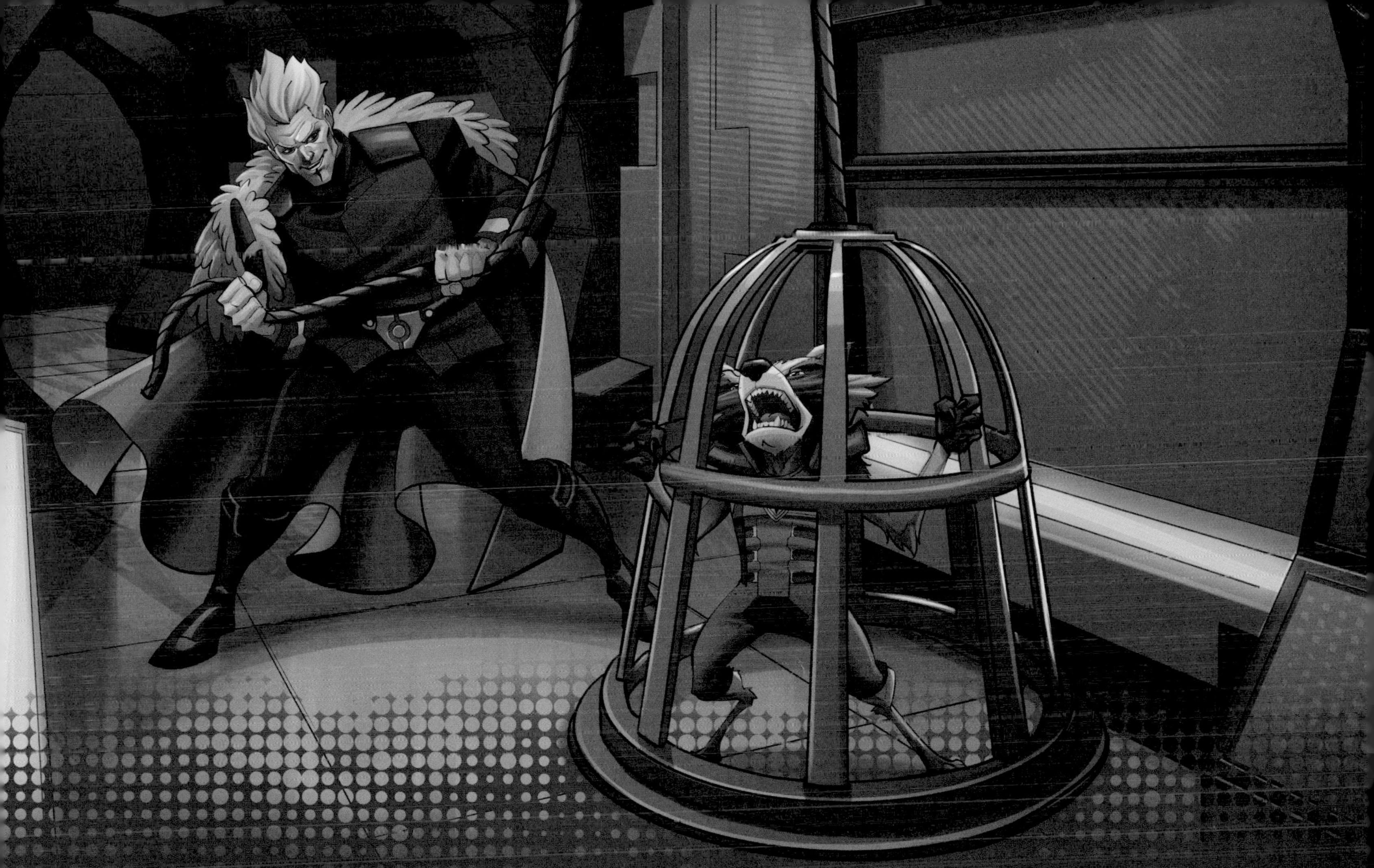

Perhaps that's why The Collector had his sights set on Rocket!

"What manner of creature are you?" The Collector said.

"I ain't no creature," the tiny Guardian snarled. "I'm Rocket!"

"Regardless," The Collector said, "I will add you to my collection." He pressed a button on a control pad, springing an elaborate trap. But Rocket pried the bars open. He jumped atop the villain's head and pulled his hair.

"Ahhh!" The Collector shouted. "What are you doing?!"

"Say you'll leave me alone, and I'll stop," Rocket replied.

"Fine!" The Collector said. "You seem more annoying than you're worth anyway. Begone."

HEIGHT: 5'11"

WEIGHT: 185 LBS

MERCILESS SPACE PIRATE

ADOPTED DAUGHTER OF THANOS AND ADOPTED SISTER OF GAMORA

HEIGHTENED STRENGTH, AGILITY, DURABILITY, AND REFLEXES DUE TO EXTENSIVE CYBERNETIC AUGMENTATION

SKILLED PHYSICAL COMBATANT, WITH EXPERTISE IN A VARIETY OF ADVANCED WEAPONRY

CUNNING TACTICIAN, MANIPULATOR, AND STRATEGIST

SEEKS TO ACHIEVE VICTORY AND POWER BY ANY MEANS

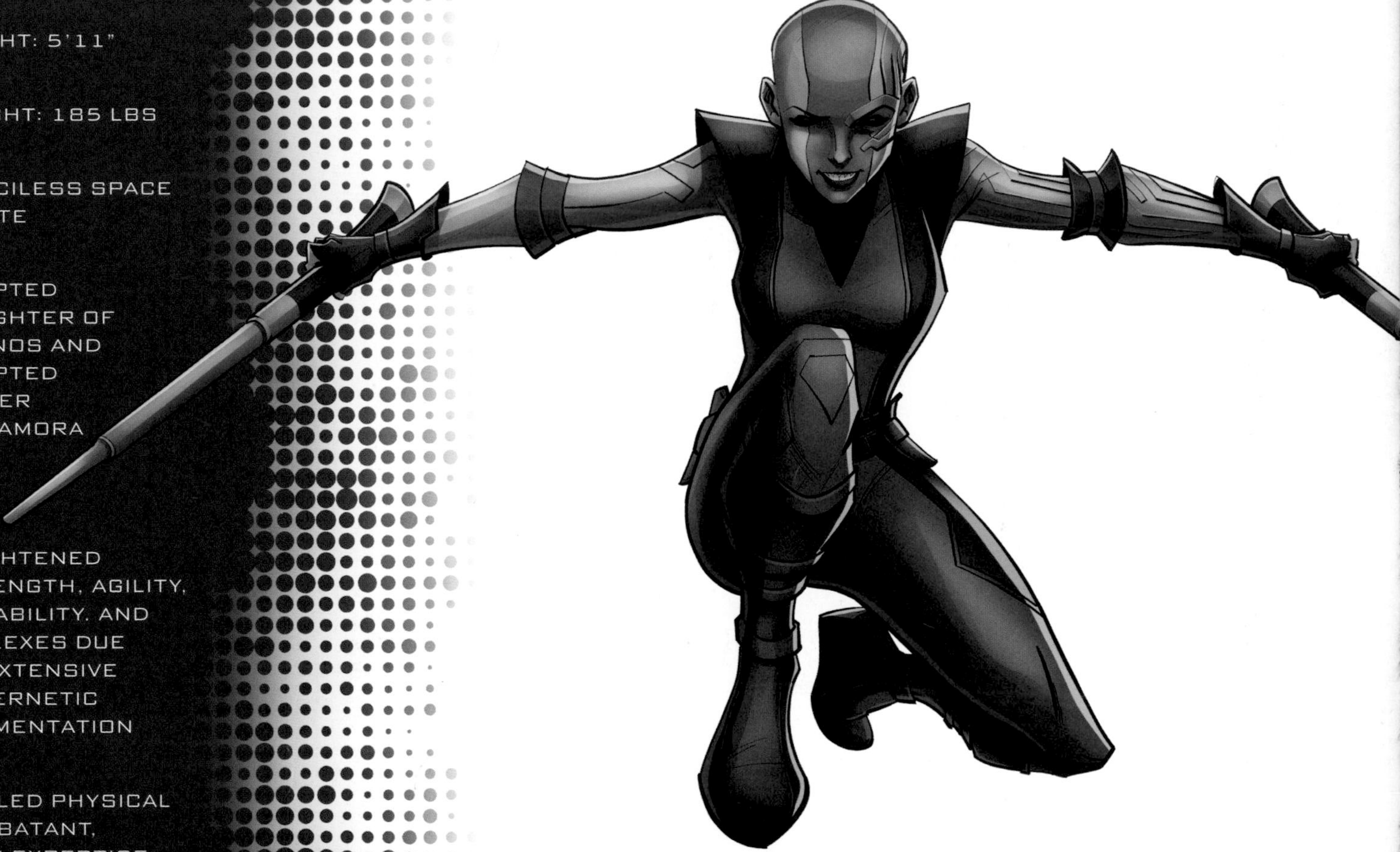

NEBULA

Daughter of Thanos

Do you remember back on page 43 when we said we'd tell you more about Nebula later? Well, now it's later! Nebula is a cunning warrior, and every bit as deadly as her sister, Gamora. Part machine, Nebula's strength and speed have been increased, making her a real threat to the Guardians of the Galaxy. She would destroy them just to get at her sister.

Sometimes, when fighting with Gamora, Nebula would be winning, and she would think victory was within her grasp. But then the Guardians would somehow pull off a miracle and capture Nebula.

Over time, Gamora realized that she loved her sister, even if Nebula WAS trying to destroy her most of the time.

Gamora hoped that maybe one day, instead of fighting against each other, she and Nebula could fight together. Then, with their combined might, they could beat Thanos once and for all!

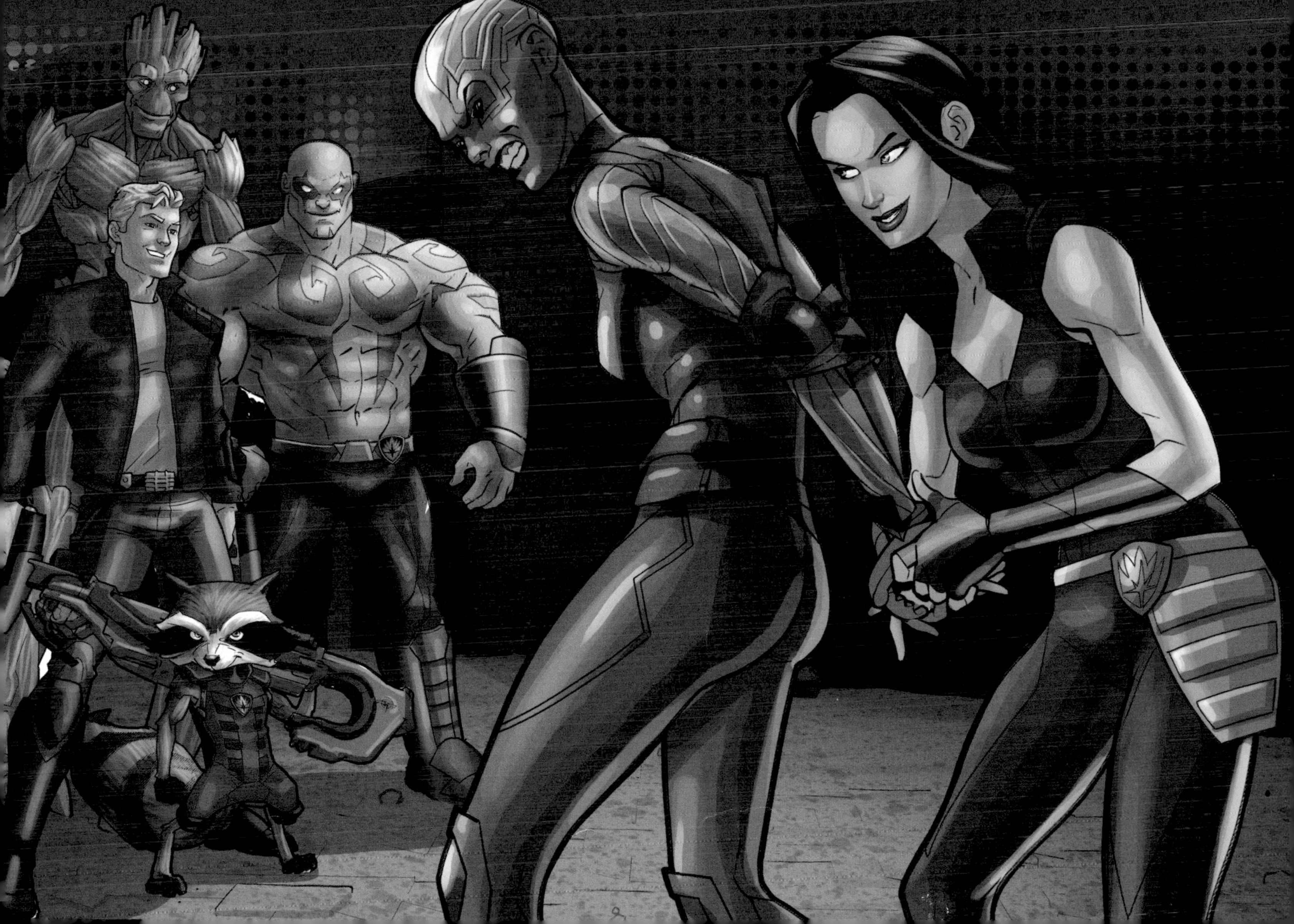

As you can see, the Guardians certainly have their hands full keeping the galaxy safe. While they may have started out as a group of misfits, they banded together for the greater good. Lucky for us, they're more than prepared for the job. Doesn't it feel reassuring, knowing that a talking tree and a not-a-raccoon are somewhere in space right now, beating the bad guys?

(Look, just do us a favor—if you see Rocket, don't tell him about the whole "not-a-raccoon" thing, okay? No need to distract him from that "greater good" we were talking about earlier.)

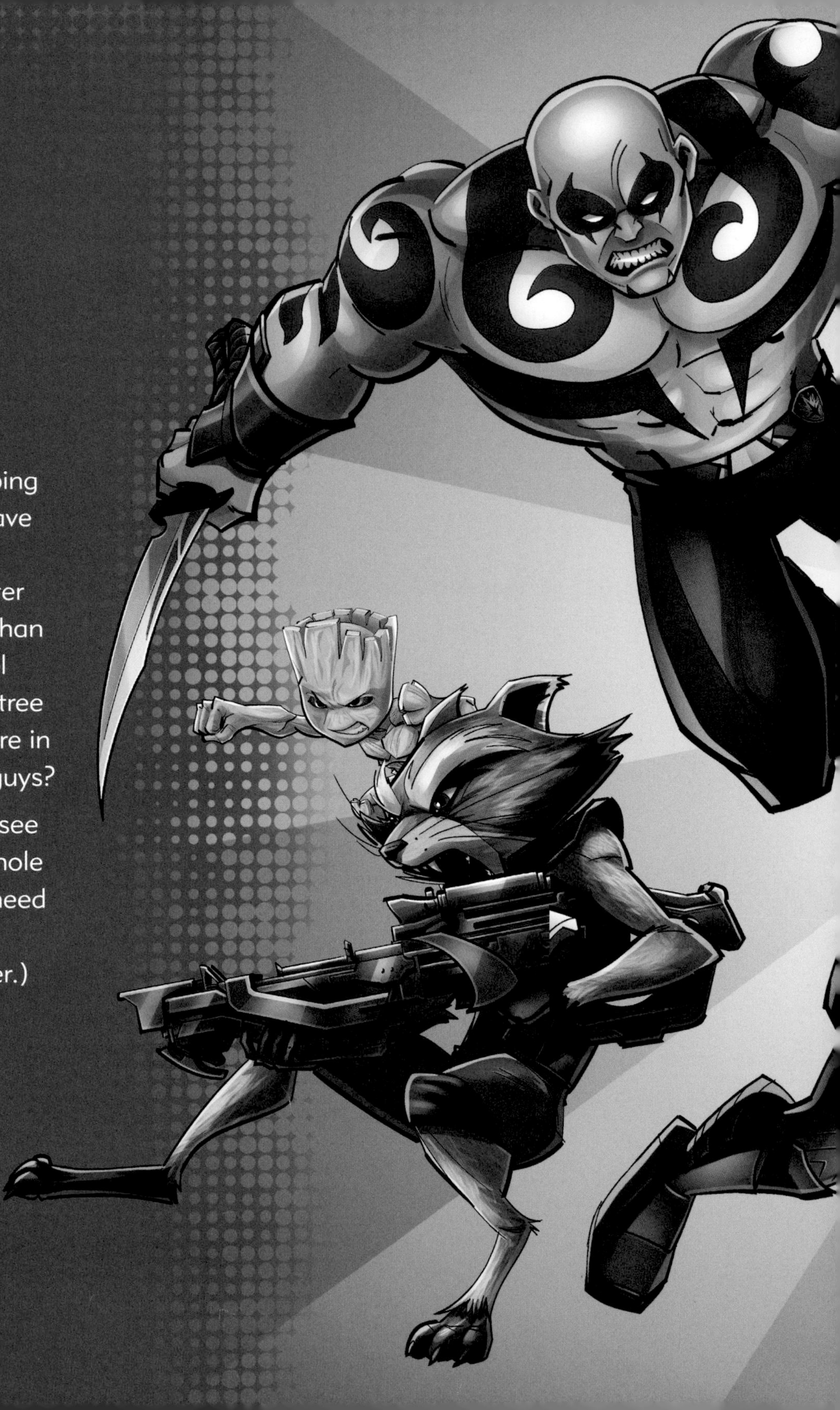

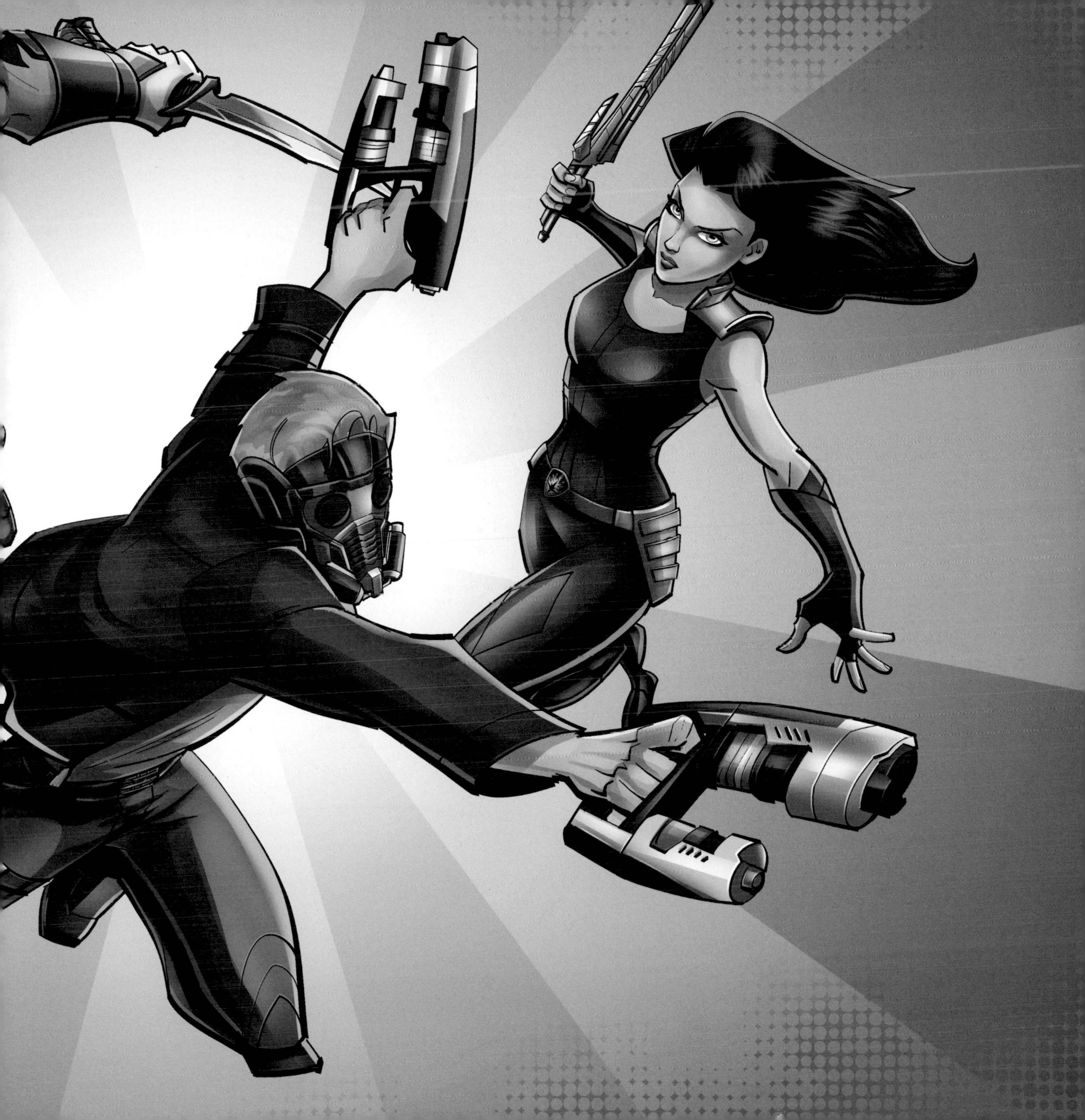

THE AVENGERS

IRON MAN

Tony Stark

Tony Stark was very rich and incredibly smart. He graduated from college at a very young age and inherited his dad's company, Stark Industries. They made all kinds of weapons and sold them to the army. Tony didn't like to think about how those weapons were used.

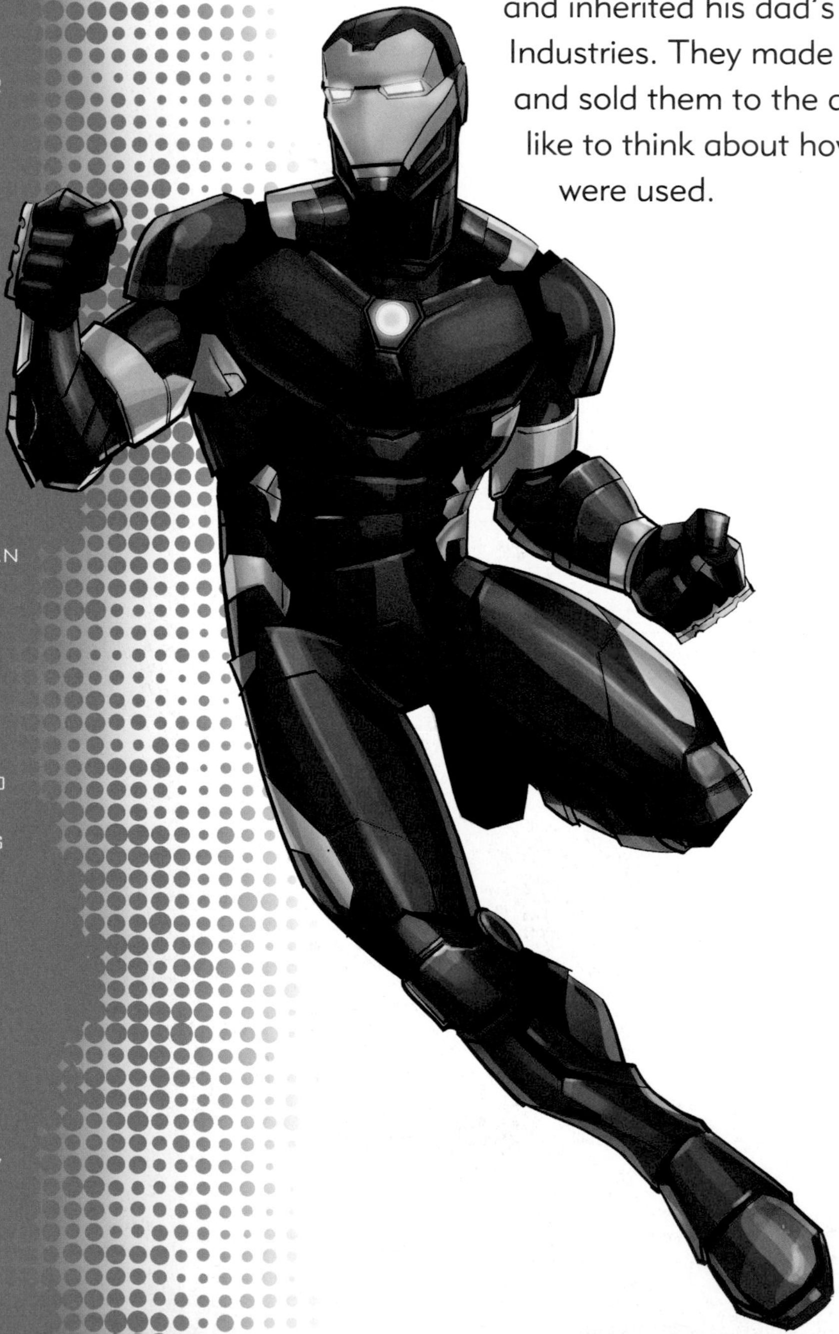

HEIGHT: 6'1" / 6'5" IN ARMOR

WEIGHT: 190 LBS / 425 LBS IN ARMOR

GENIUS-LEVEL INTELLECT WITH PARTICULAR APTITUDE IN INVENTION AND ENGINEERING

BILLIONAIRE INDUSTRIALIST

WEARS MODULAR ARC-REACTOR-POWERED IRON MAN ARMOR GRANTING SUPERHUMAN STRENGTH AND DURABILITY

ARMORED SUIT GRANTS ABILITY TO FLY AND PROJECT REPULSOR BLASTS

ARMOR IS OUTFITTED WITH COMPLEX TECH, INCLUDING A CUTTING-EDGE ARTIFICIAL INTELLIGENCE, SOPHISTICATED SENSOR SYSTEMS, AND OTHER GADGETRY

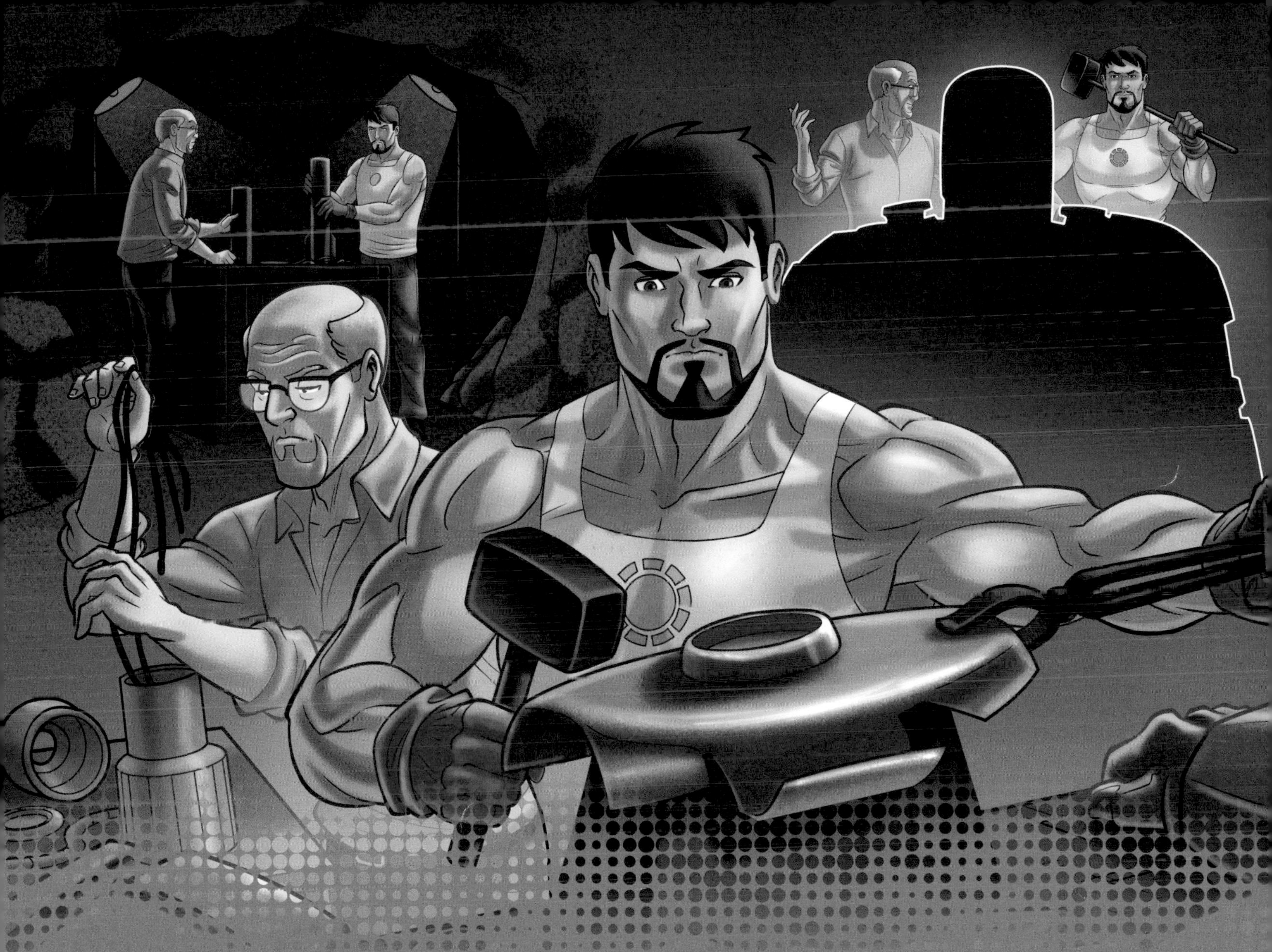

But one day, he had no choice. While he was showing some soldiers how to use his weapons, Tony was attacked and held captive by enemies of the United States who wanted Tony to make a weapon for them!

With the help of another prisoner, Dr. Ho Yinsen, Tony DID build a weapon. But not the weapon that the bad guys wanted! Instead, Tony built an incredible suit of armor that he used to escape. Tony decided to stop selling weapons. Now he fights to make the world a safer place as the invincible Iron Man!

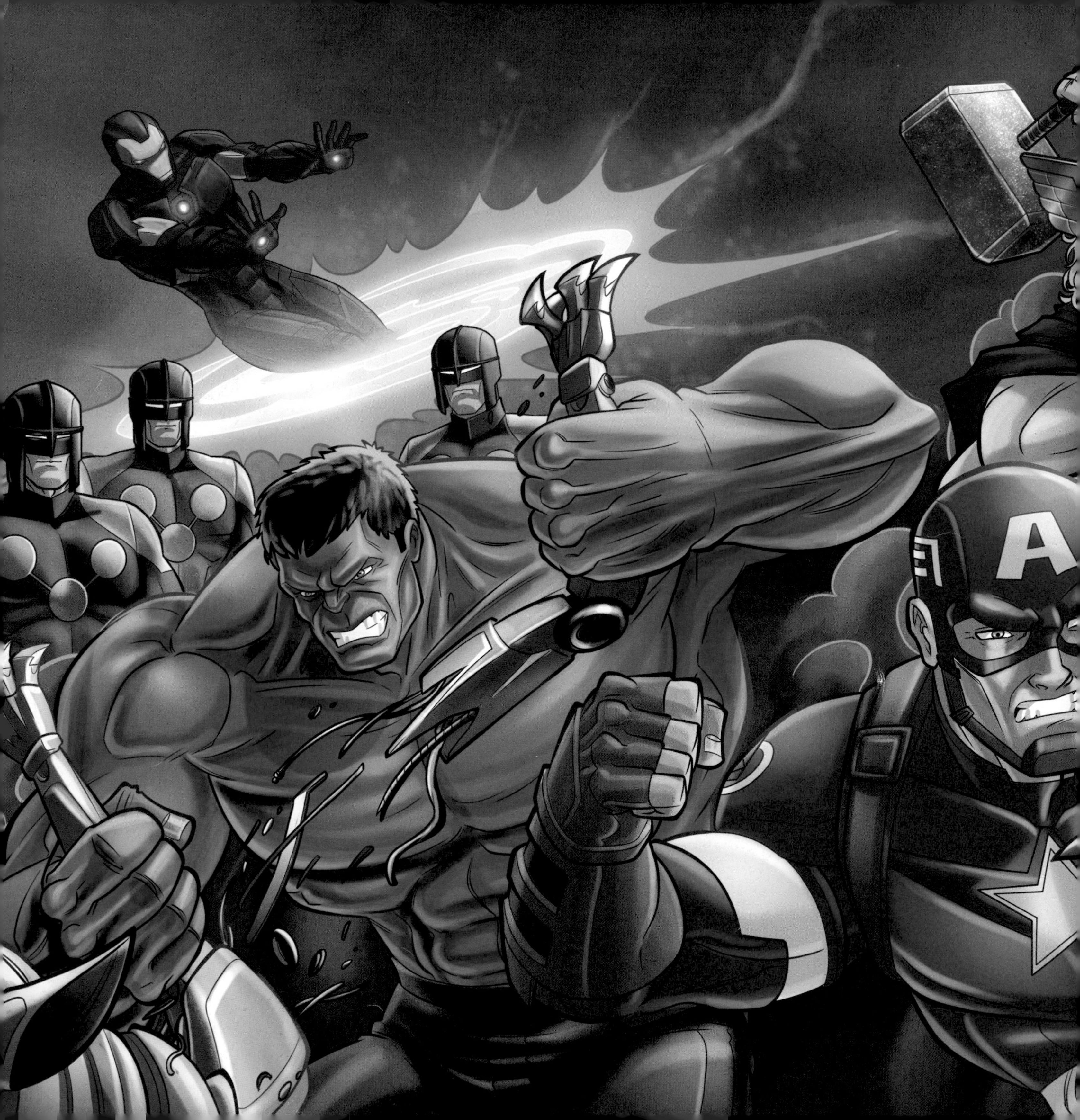

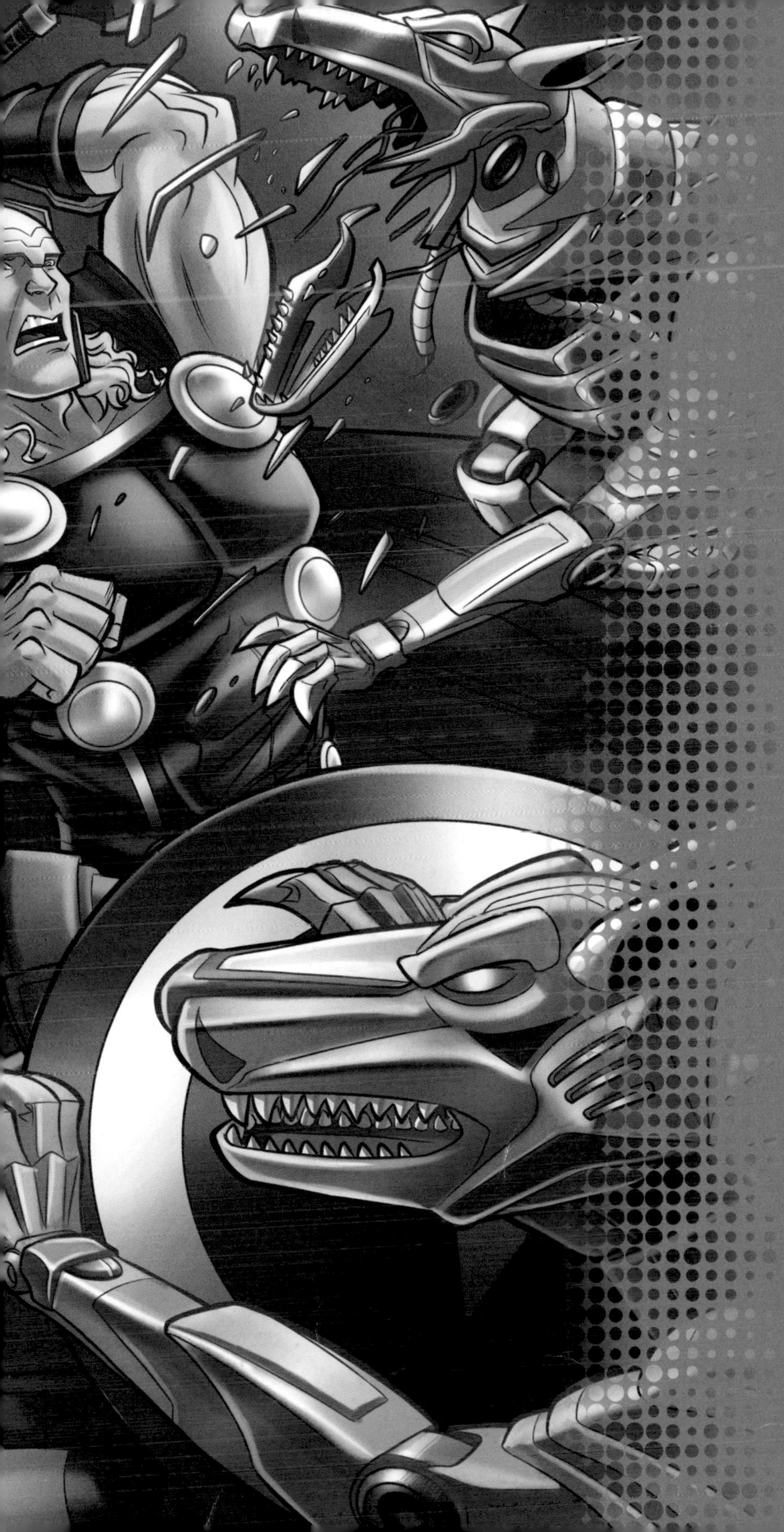

One of the great things about being Iron Man was having a high-tech headquarters in New York City.

One of the not-so-great things about being Iron Man? Evil aliens called Chitauri that wanted to attack his high-tech headquarters in New York City!

"I'm sorry," Iron Man said as he blasted a Chitauri warrior. "What part of 'Stay down' don't you understand?"

As Iron Man kept the enemy busy, the Avengers arrived at the scene, along with the Nova Corps. The Chitauri warriors thought they would conquer Earth easily, but they hadn't counted on Iron Man!

With the help of the other Avengers, Iron Man made short work of the Chitauri and their cybernetic creatures.

"Hulk smash!" Hulk said as he slammed his fists into a metal beast.

"You do good work, Hulk!" Iron Man said.

Captain America smiled as the Avengers saved the day.

HEIGHT: 6'2"

WEIGHT: 230 LBS

RECIPIENT OF THE SUPER-SOLDIER SERUM

THE PINNACLE OF HUMAN PHYSICAL POTENTIAL

HEIGHTENED STRENGTH, ENDURANCE, AND AGILITY

MASTER HAND-TO-HAND FIGHTER

SKILLED MILITARY LEADER AND STRATEGIST WITH A STRONG SENSE OF HONOR AND JUSTICE

EQUIPPED WITH A VIRTUALLY INDESTRUCTIBLE VIBRANIUM SHIELD

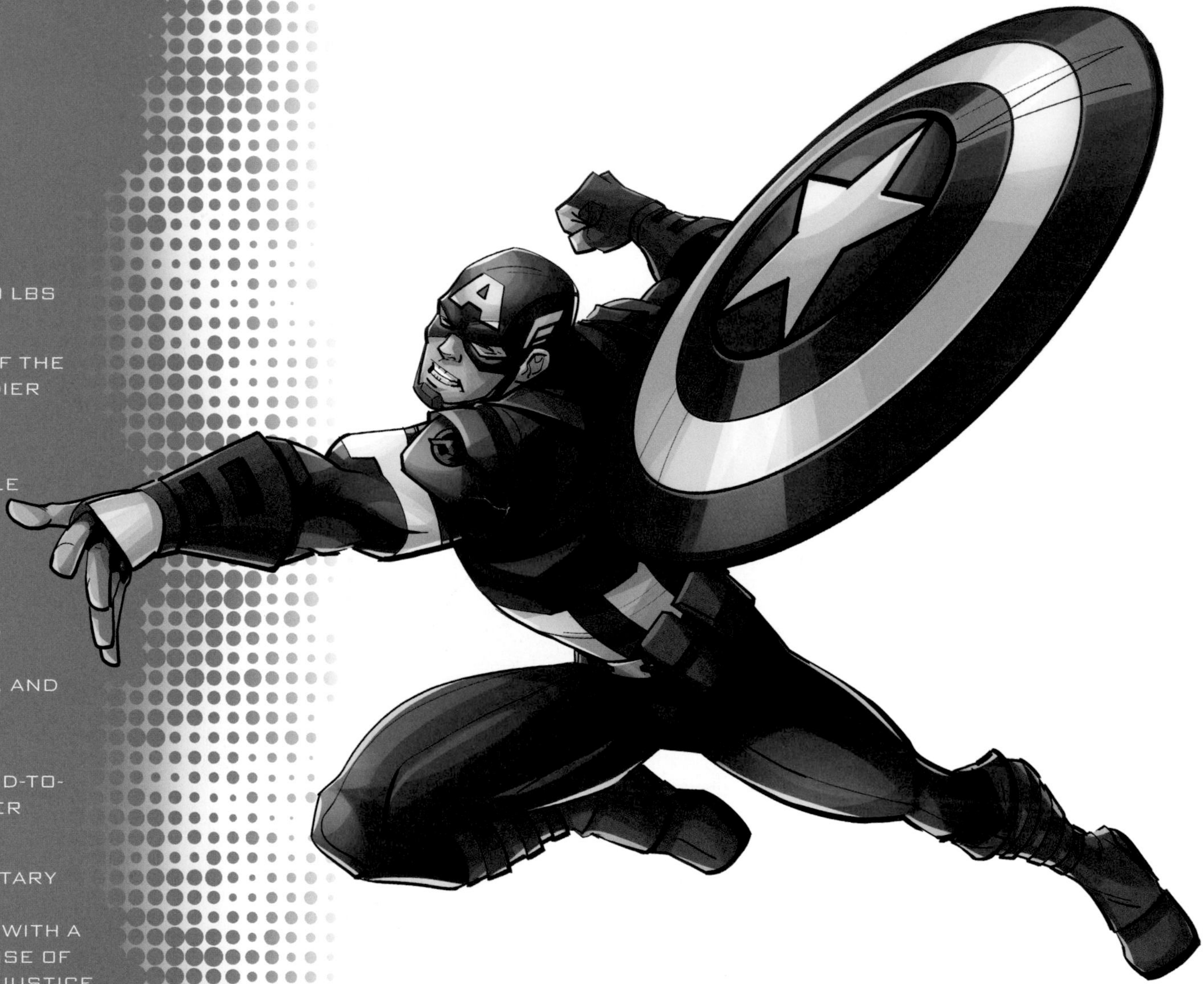

CAPTAIN AMERICA

Steve Rogers

Are you ready to travel back in time? Good! Because we're headed back to the 1940s, when the world was at war! This is where we meet Captain America, but before he was Captain America, he was Steve Rogers!

Frail Steve Rogers wanted to serve his country, but the U.S. Army told him that he was too small and not healthy enough. But a man named Dr. Erskine thought Steve had heart. So he picked him for his top-secret Super-Soldier experiment! Steve was given a special formula and bombarded with Vita-Rays. In seconds, Steve became strong—stronger than he could ever have hoped to be!

Steve was given a costume and an indestructible shield, and became Captain America! Cap stood for everything that was good in the world, and fought back the forces of evil during the war. But he was frozen in a freak accident. He spent decades on ice, until he was revived in the present day!

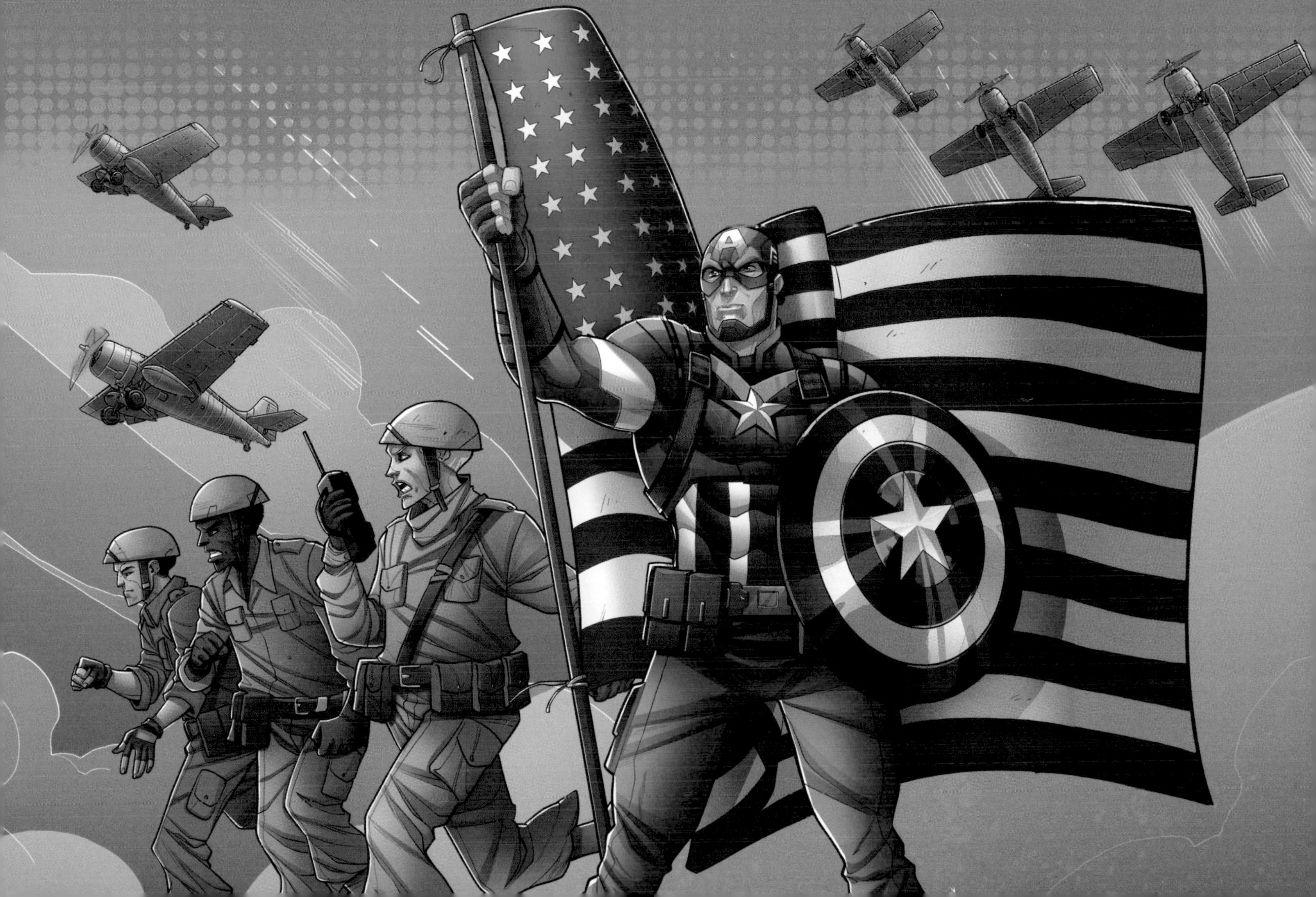

It was going to take some time for Captain America to adjust to life in a new era. Lots of things had changed for good. Computers and medicines made life better for people. But sadly, some things remained the same.

By *some things*, we mean "Bad guys were still bad guys."

"Destroy Captain America!" Baron Strucker screamed at an evil Hydra soldier.

Before the Hydra soldier could fire, Captain America hurled his mighty shield. He knocked the weapon out of the soldier's hand.

"If you were thinking of surrendering, now's the time," Cap said.

"Never!" Strucker sneered. "We are Hydra! Cut off a limb, two more shall take its place!"

"Are you sure about that?" Cap asked. "Maybe Hulk can change your mind!"

The Avengers had arrived. And in case you were wondering, Hulk DID change Strucker's mind, and Hydra DID surrender. It helps to have a Hulk!

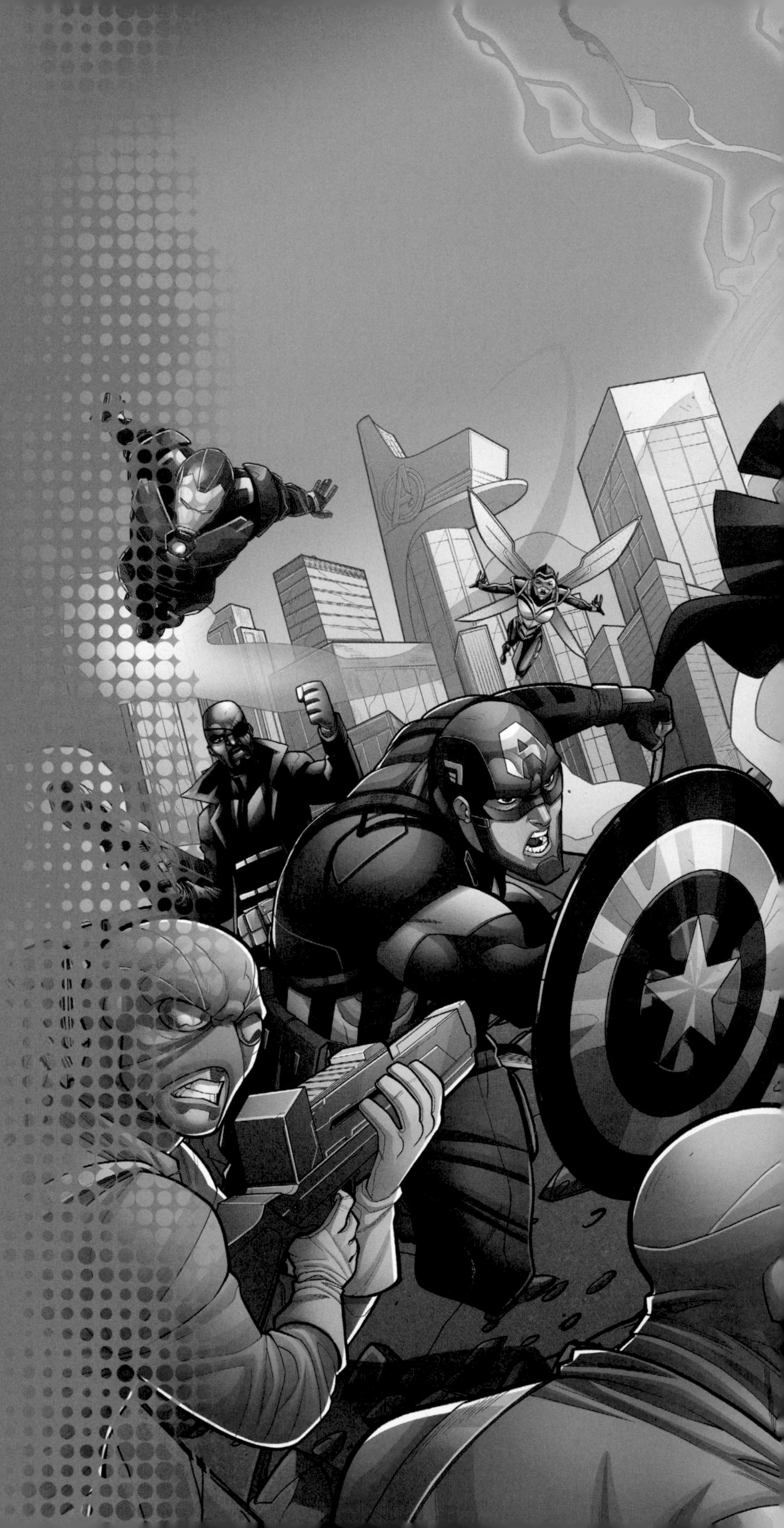

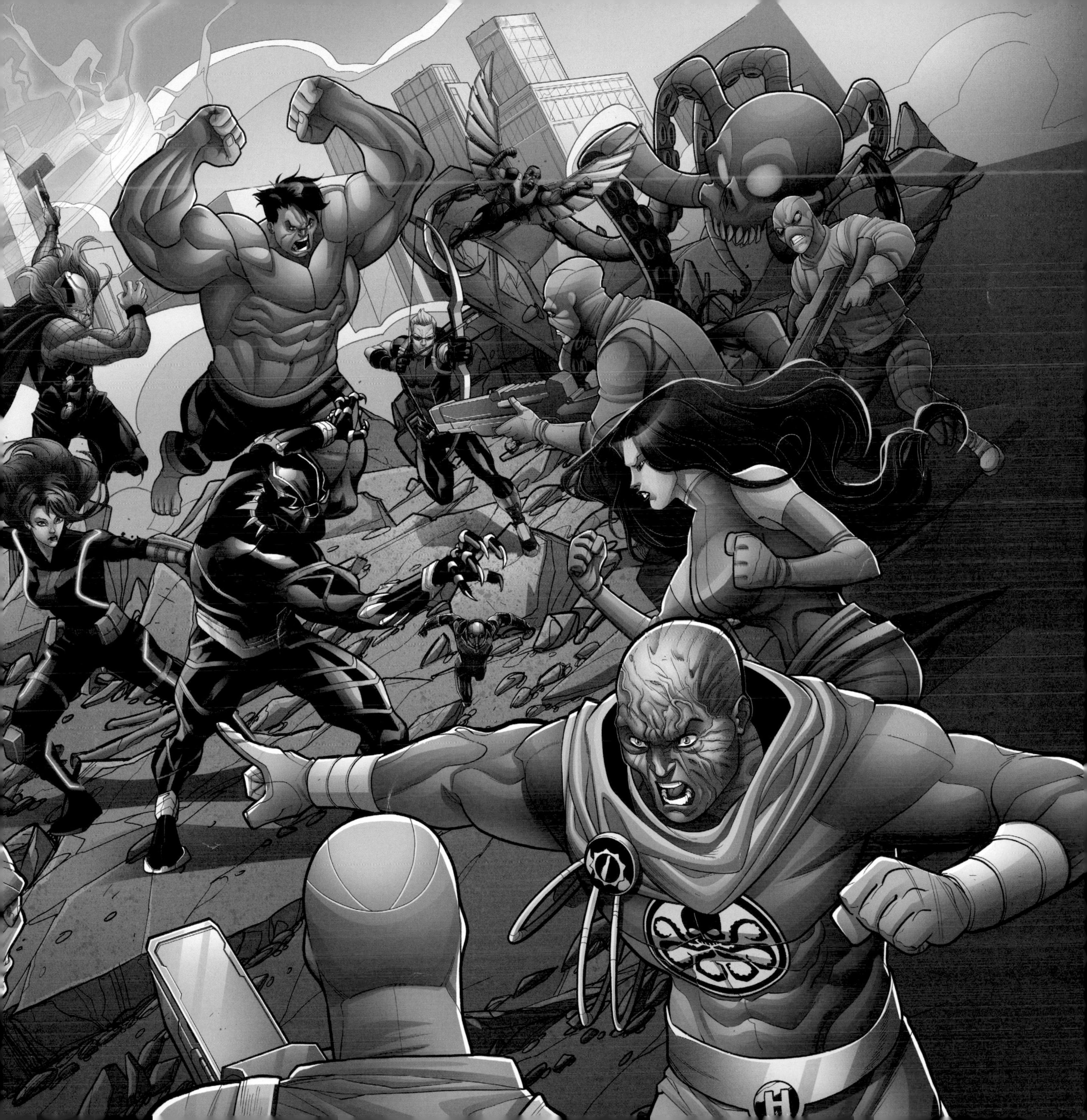

THOR

Prince of Asgard

Did you know that Thor is from a realm called Asgard? That his father is a guy named Odin? And that he wields a mystic hammer named Mjolnir?

And did you know that Thor wasn't always Thor?

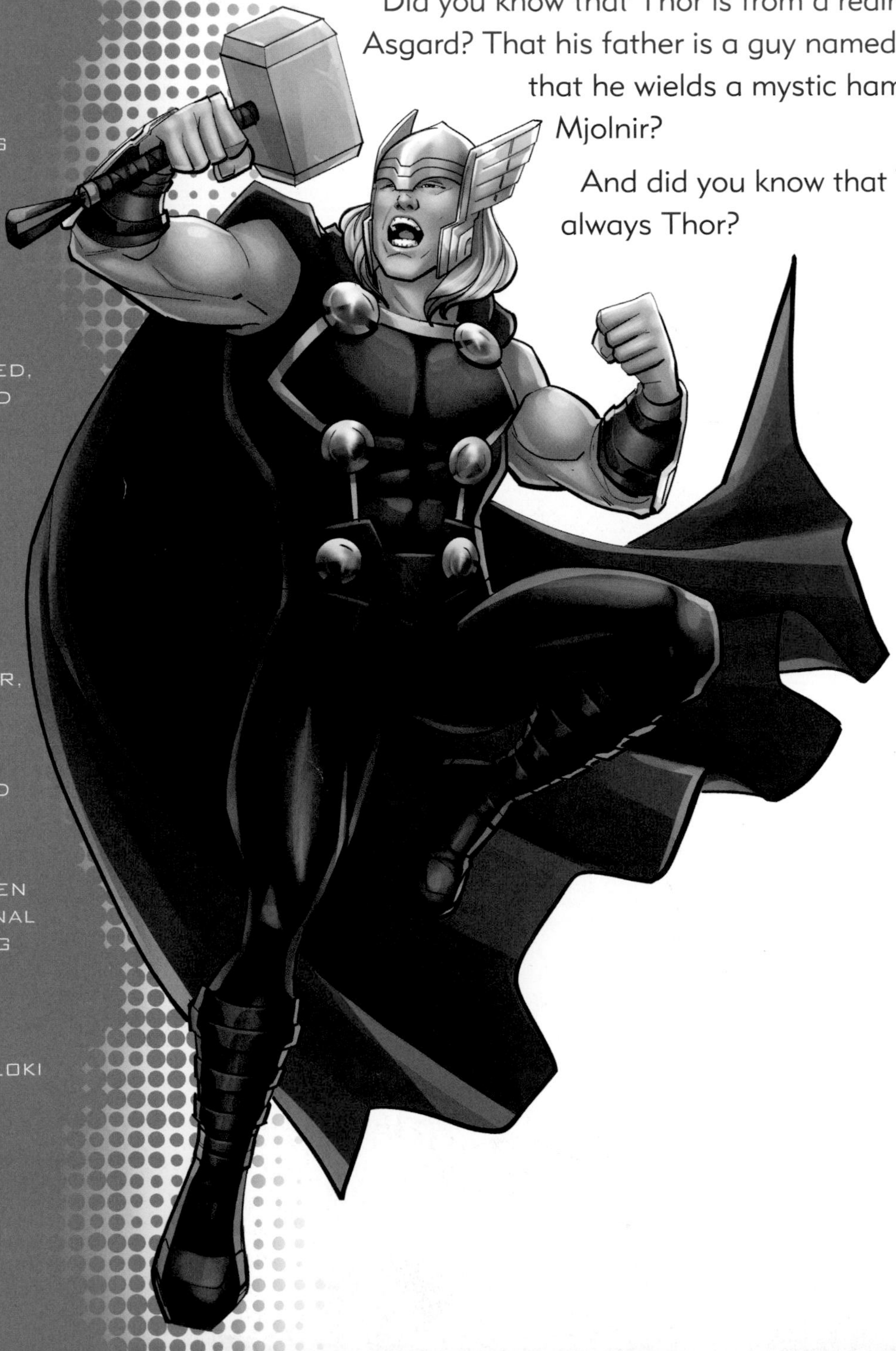

HEIGHT: 6'6"

WEIGHT: 640 LBS

SON OF ODIN AND PRINCE OF ASGARD

SUPERHUMAN STRENGTH, SPEED, ENDURANCE, AND RESISTANCE TO INJURY

VIRTUALLY IMMORTAL

WIELDS THE ENCHANTED HAMMER MJOLNIR, WHICH GRANTS MASTERY OVER THE ELEMENTS OF THUNDER AND LIGHTNING

CAN FLY AND OPEN INTERDIMENSIONAL GATEWAYS USING MJOLNIR

RAISED AS A BROTHER WITH LOKI THE TRICKSTER

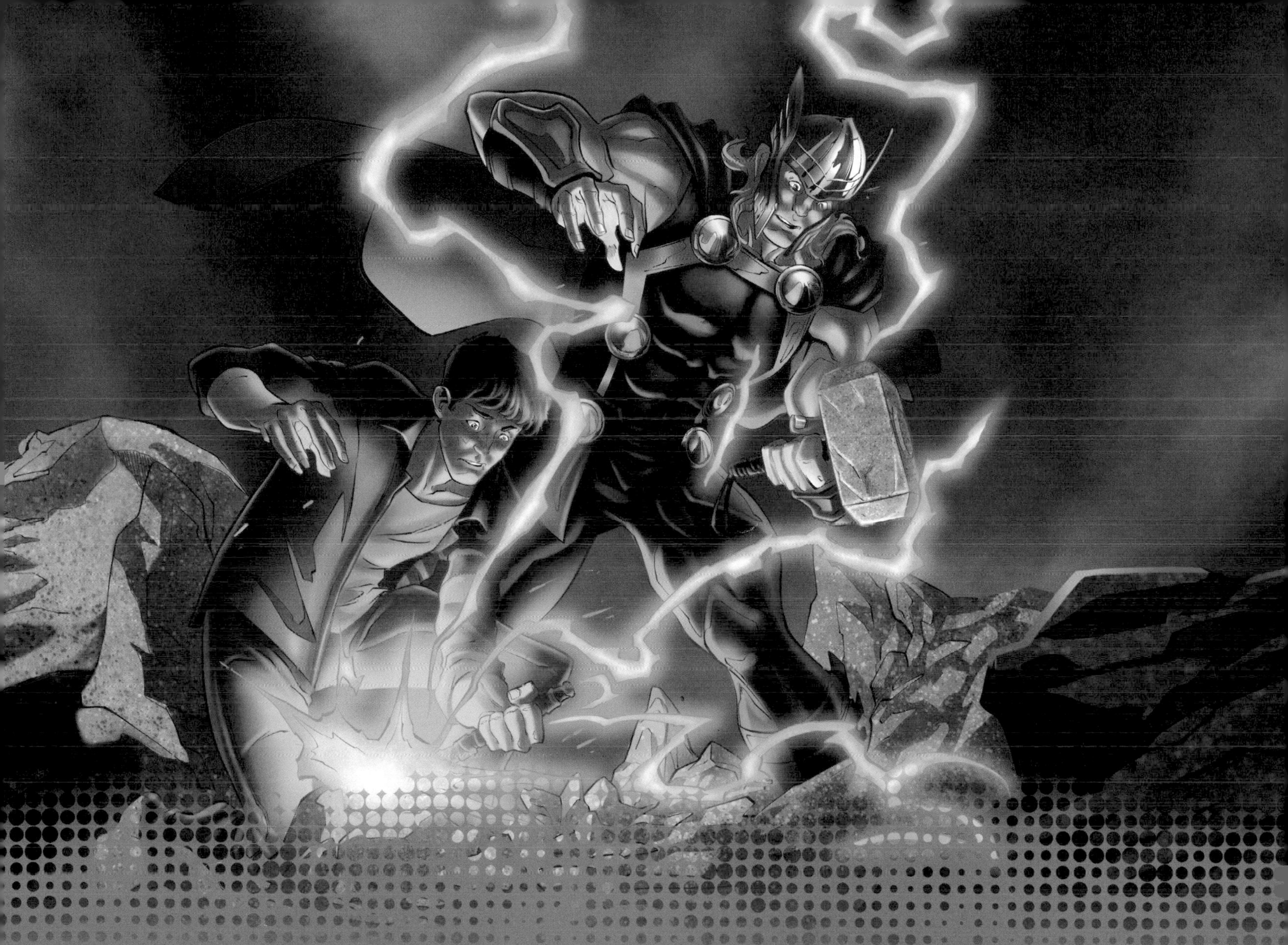

In his youth, Thor was very full of himself. He thought he was the best, and had no problem letting everyone know it. But his father, Odin, thought Thor needed to be taught a lesson. So he took away his powers, erased his memory, and sent him to live on Earth as Doctor Don Blake. Ouch.

There, the Asgardian learned how to be kind and to care about people. Since Don had proved his worth, Odin allowed his son to find an old cane. When Don struck the cane on the ground, lightning appeared and Don Blake became his true self, the mighty Thor, once more!

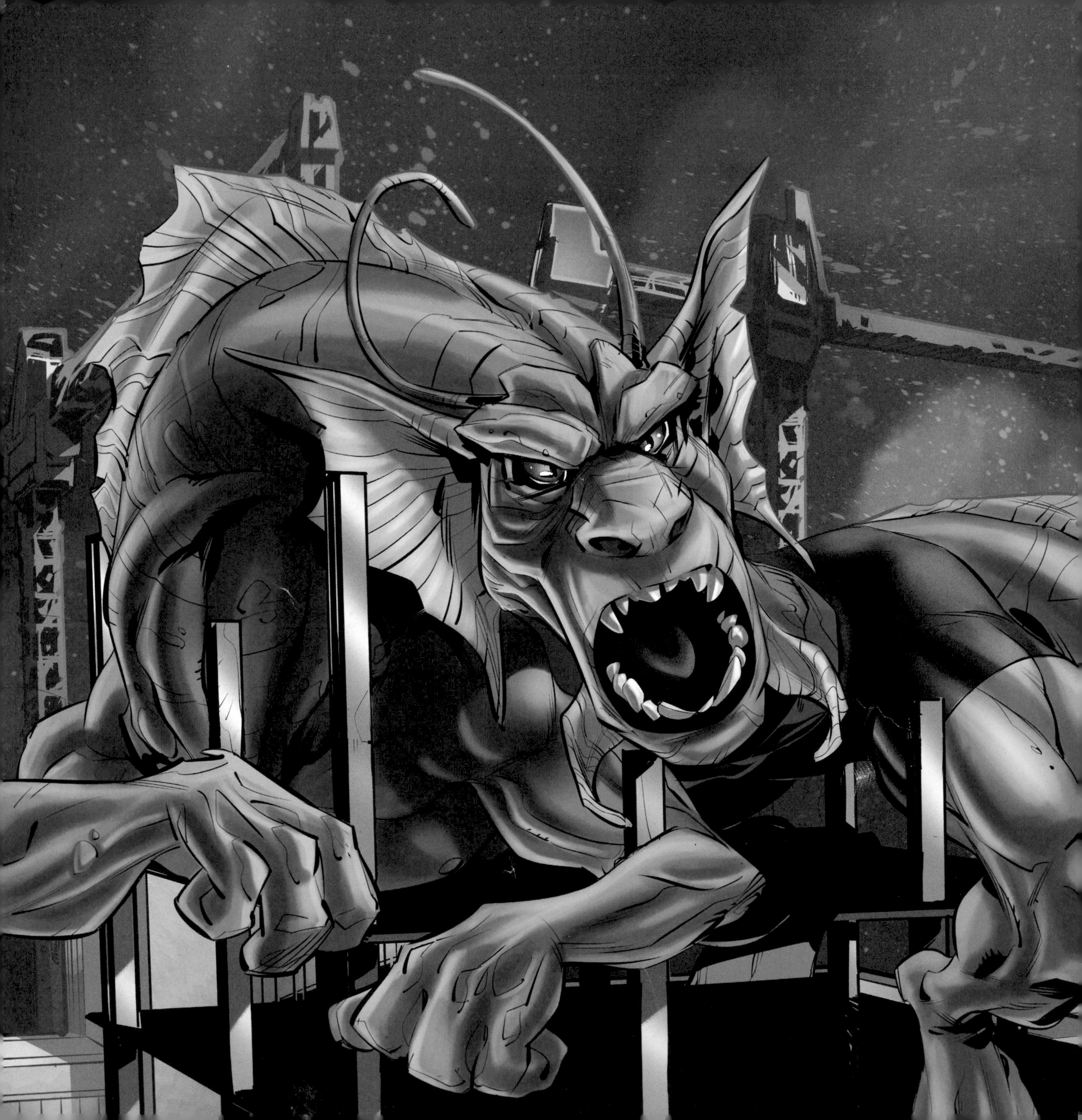

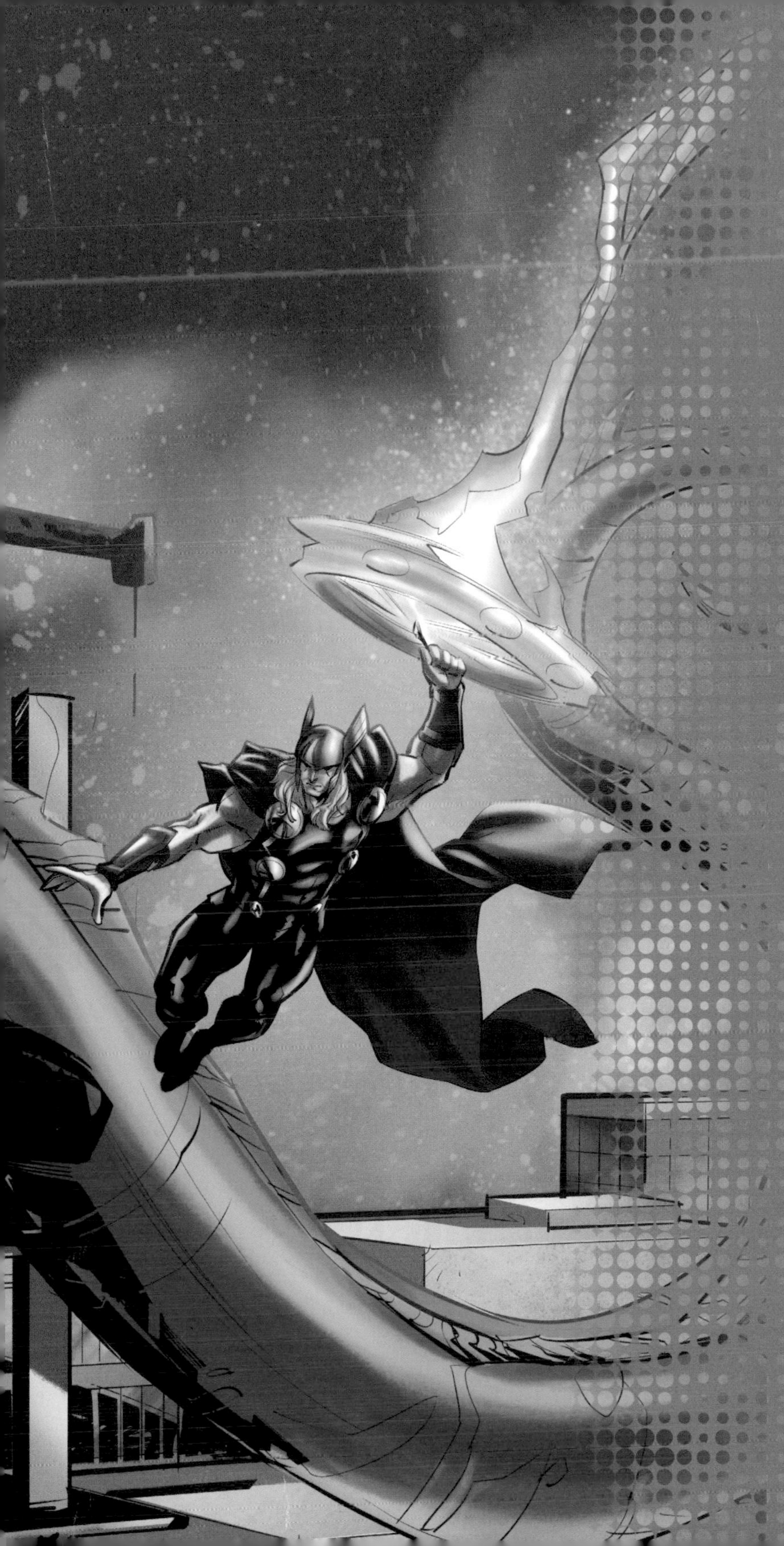

Now that Thor knew what it meant to be a hero, he would join the Avengers and help them save countless realms!

As an Avenger, Thor defends the world from giant monsters like Fin Fang Foom, who want to eat it! Okay, so maybe Fin Fang Foom doesn't want to eat the world. But this enormous alien dragon sure wouldn't mind ruling it! Thankfully Thor will always stand ready to stop him.

"Hold, dragon!" Thor ordered, hurling his hammer at Fin Fang Foom.

"Bah!" the beast grunted as it landed atop a skyscraper under construction. "Your powers are puny compared to mine!"

"Perhaps," Thor said, holding his hammer up to the sky. "But how do you think you'll fare against the power of nature itself?"

With those words, lightning struck Thor's hammer. Then Thor pointed the hammer at Fin Fang Foom. The creature was blasted by lightning bolts until it collapsed on the building.

"Good news, Avengers," Thor said over his comms link. "I've caught Fin Fang Foom. Bad news—I have no idea how to get him down from here!"

HEIGHT: 5'7"

WEIGHT: 130 LBS

SUPER-SPY

MASTER IN THE COVERT ARTS OF ESPIONAGE, INFILTRATION, AND SUBTERFUGE

EXPERT MARTIAL ARTIST

EXCEPTIONAL AGILITY AND ATHLETIC ABILITY

UTILIZES ADVANCED WEAPONRY

TRAINED FROM AN EARLY AGE IN THE TOP-SECRET RED ROOM PROGRAM

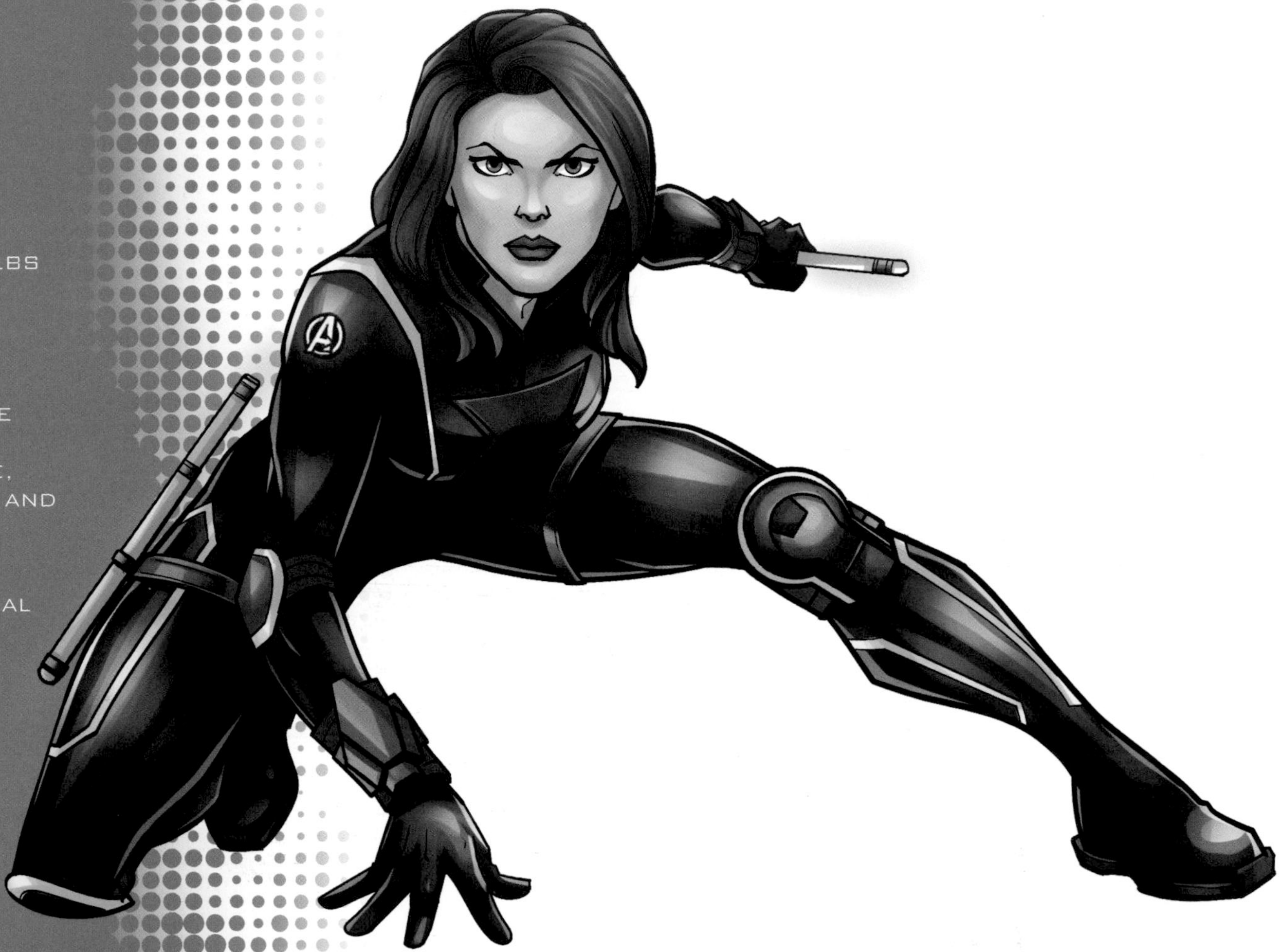

BLACK WIDOW

Natasha Romanoff

Everyone knows that a black widow spider is dangerous. And if you DIDN'T know it, you do now, because we just told you. Anyway. Meet Natasha Romanoff, aka Black Widow. She's every bit as dangerous as her namesake!

From the time she was a child, Natasha trained to be a spy. She used to be an enemy agent before she met a Super Hero named Hawkeye.

Then she switched sides to work for Nick Fury (this guy in the picture) and S.H.I.E.L.D. Then she became an Avenger!

Oh yeah, we keep forgetting to mention what S.H.I.E.L.D. stands for! It means Strategic Homeland Intervention, Enforcement, and Logistics Division! Try saying THAT ten times fast!

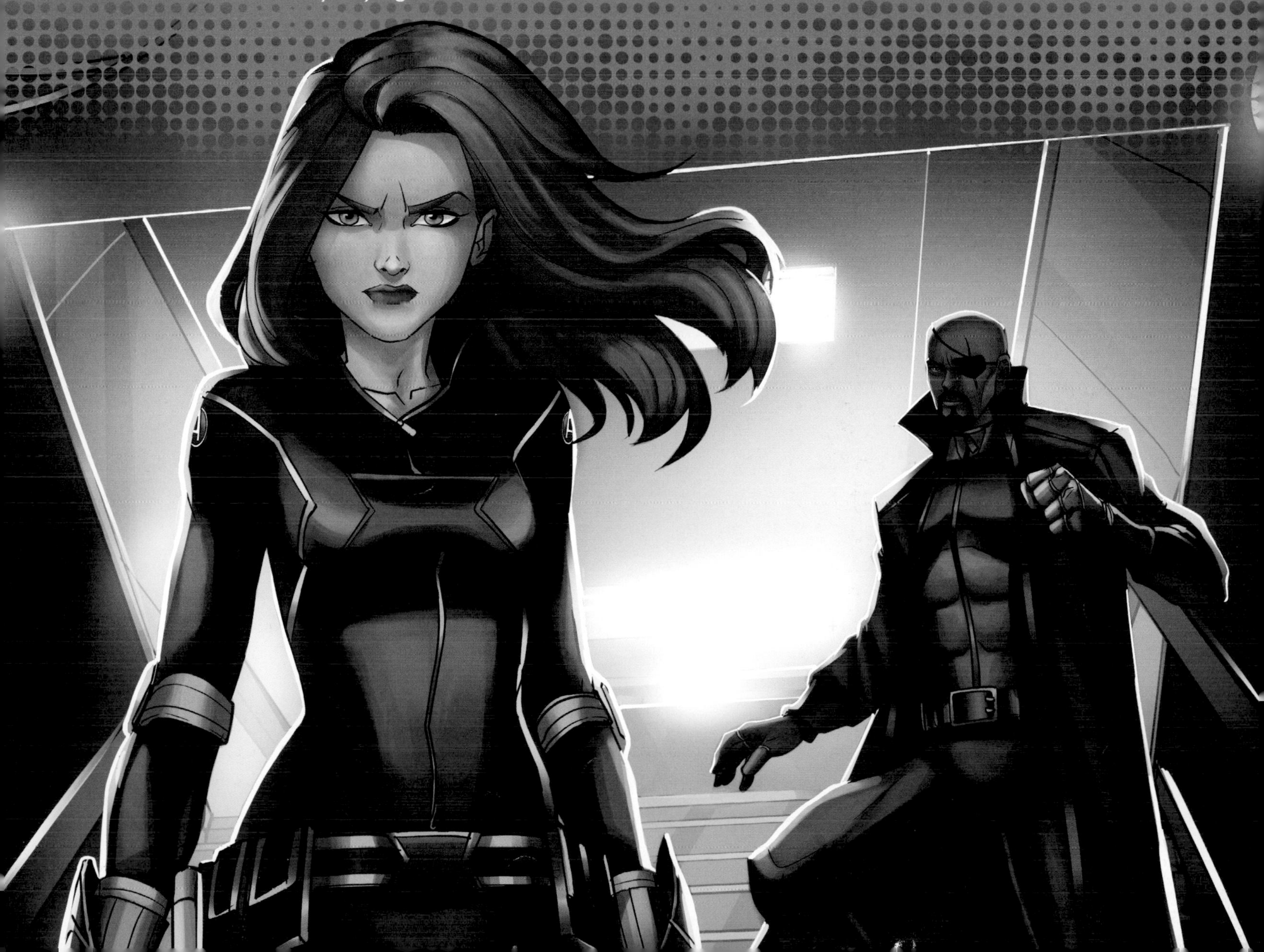

Yikes! A strange group of aliens appeared in New York City's Times Square and started to wreak havoc, which is not something you want to have wreaked.

Black Widow jumped right into the battle and took down a towering creature with one of her batons. Another tried to punch her, but she fired her Widow's Bite at the alien. The electric shock dropped the creature to the ground. Black Widow landed on her feet, and she turned to face her next attacker.

"Any idea who these guys are, Hawkeye?" Black Widow said as the creatures continued to attack.

"They're not from around here!" Hawkeye said, firing his arrows.

Black Widow laughed, but the situation was very serious. The Avengers had to stop the aliens before they destroyed Times Square, or worse!

But she wasn't worried. She knew her teammates could handle anything. And together, that's exactly what they did!

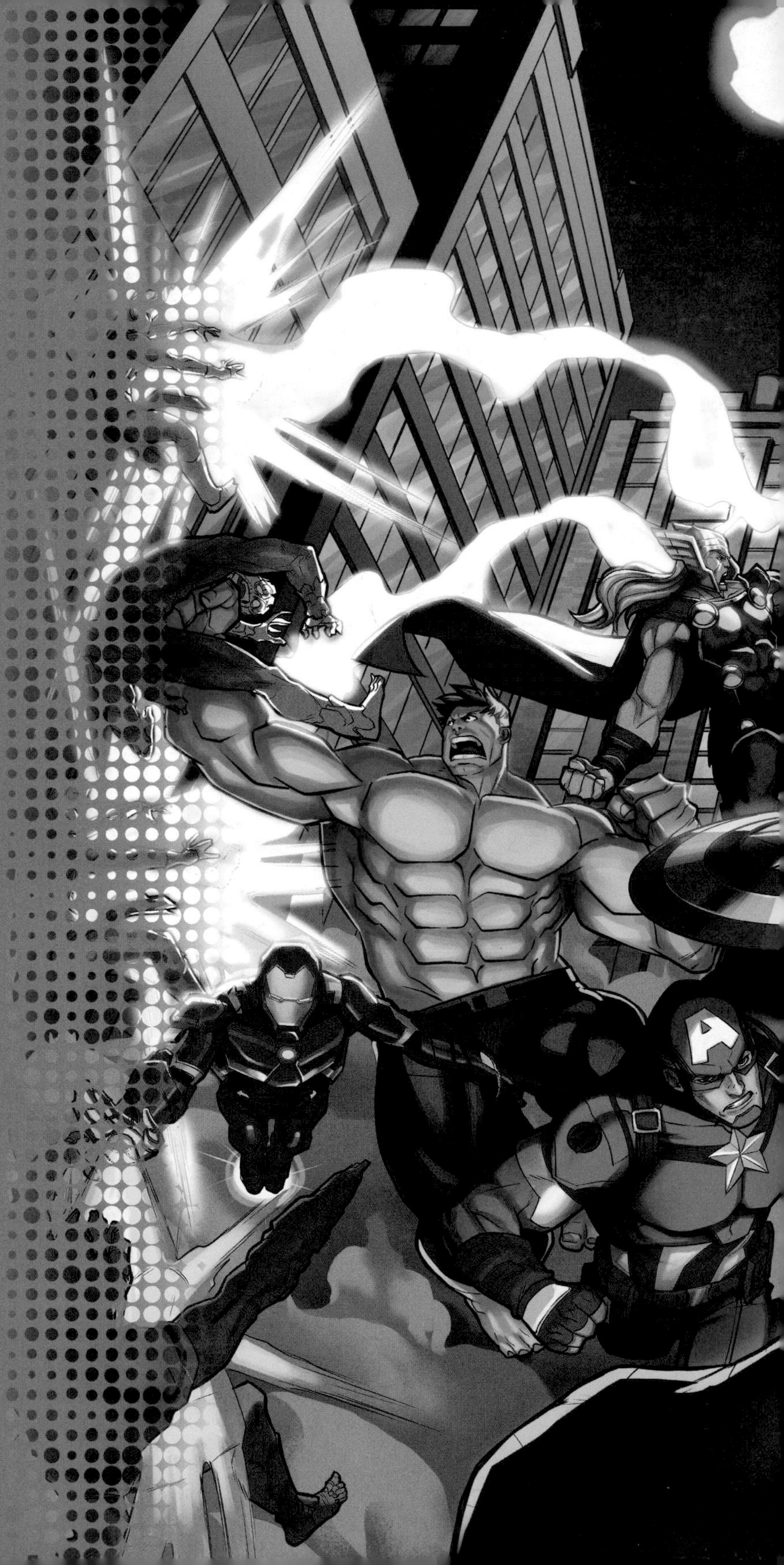

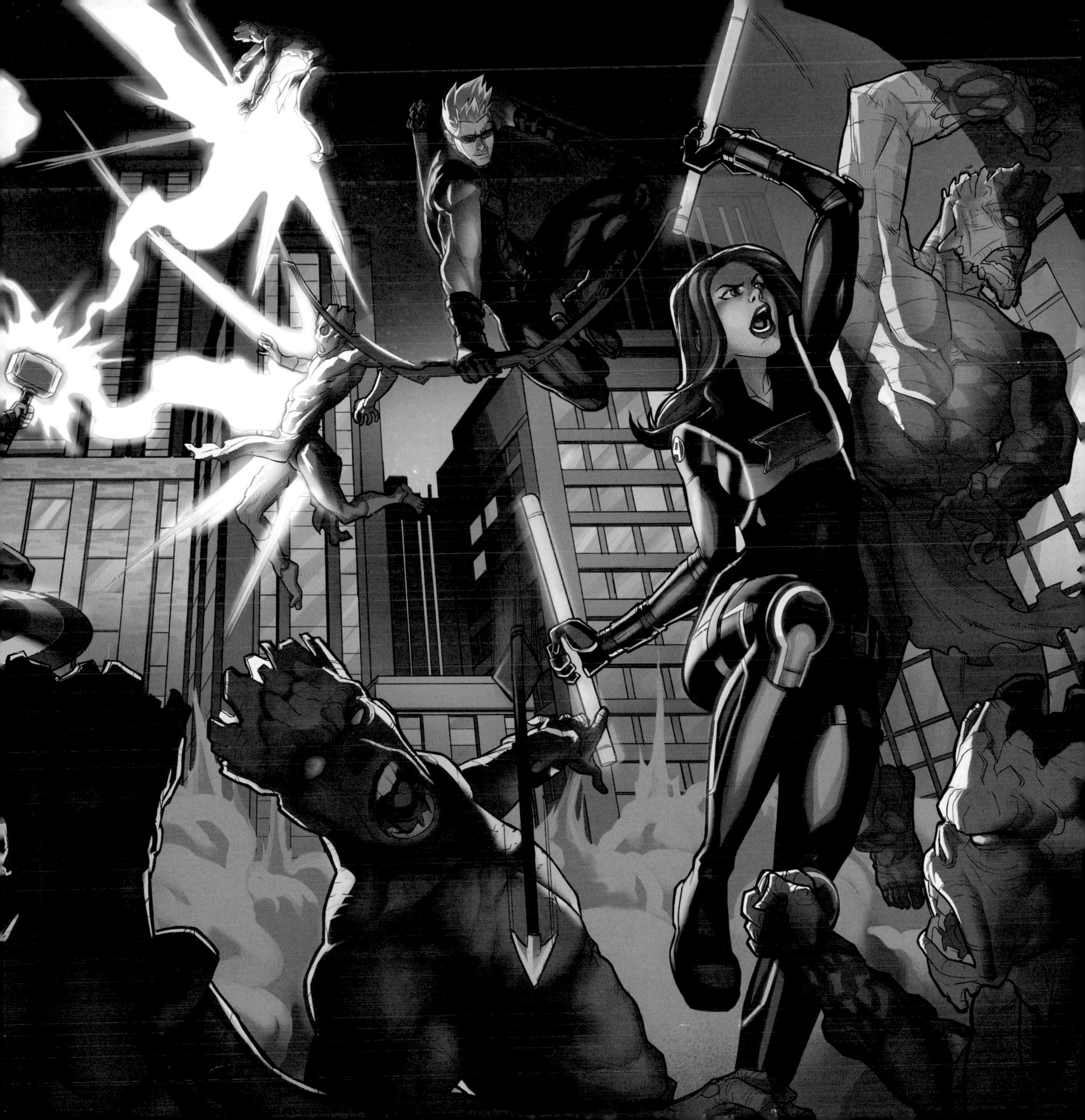

HEIGHT:
5'9" AS BRUCE /
8'5" AS HULK

WEIGHT:
145 LBS AS BRUCE /
1040 LBS AS HULK

EXPOSED TO A
MASSIVE DOSE OF
GAMMA RADIATION

TRANSFORMS FROM
BRUCE BANNER TO
HULK WHEN MADE
ANGRY OR ANXIOUS

INCREDIBLE
SUPERHUMAN
STRENGTH,
DURABILITY, AND
HEALING FACTOR

BECOMES MORE
POWERFUL AS HIS
ANGER INCREASES

AS BANNER,
POSSESSES A
GENIUS-LEVEL
INTELLECT

MISUNDERSTOOD BY
THOSE AROUND HIM
DUE TO THE DAMAGE
HE CAN CAUSE

HULK

Bruce Banner

Scientists don't come much smarter than Bruce Banner! He was an expert on gamma rays. In fact, his work with gamma rays eventually led him to become the Hulk! But that wasn't really what Bruce wanted. . . .

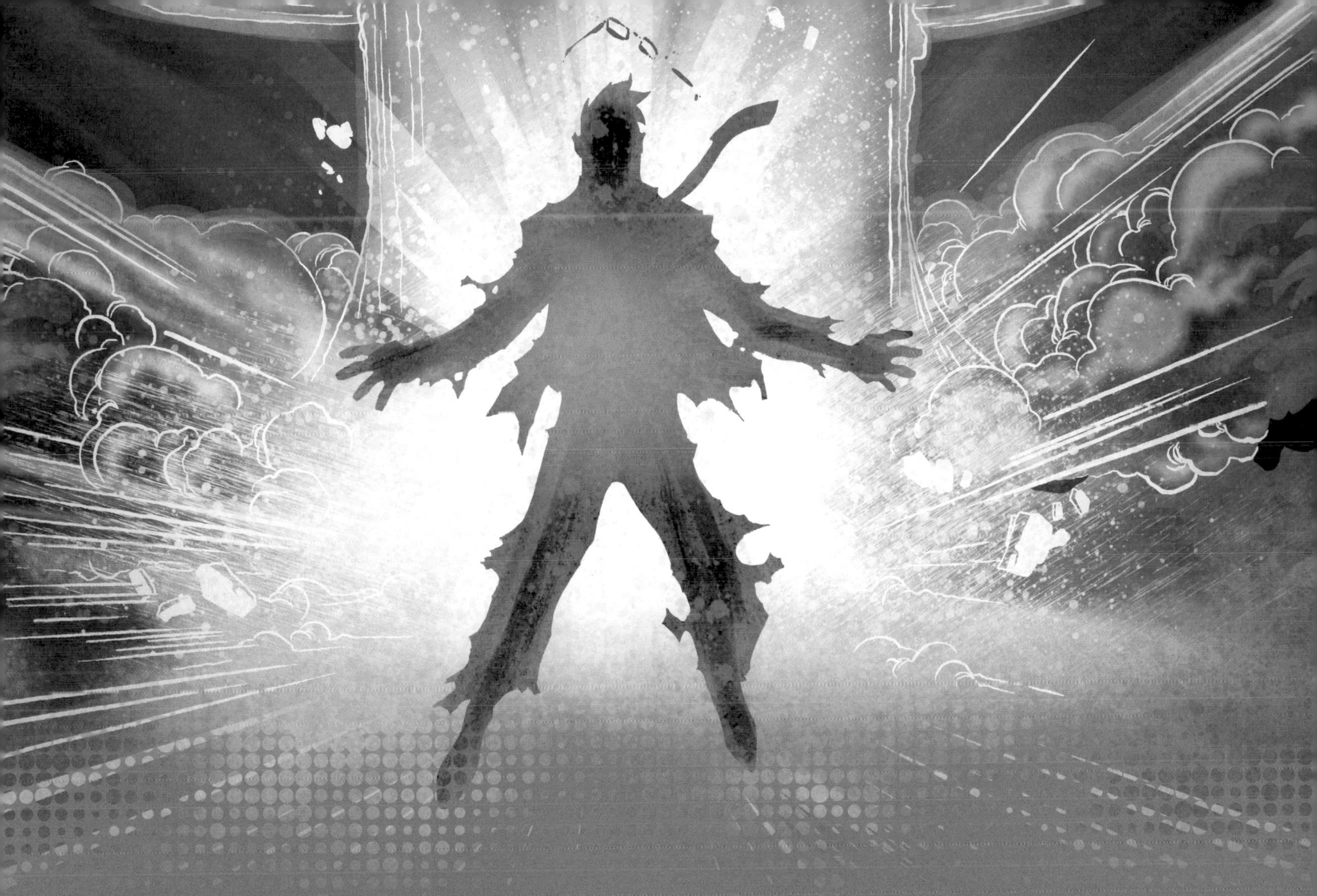

The army wanted Bruce to build a gamma bomb for them. He felt that it was wrong, but was bullied into it by General Thunderbolt Ross. When the army was about to detonate the bomb, Bruce saw a teenager drive onto the test site! He told some soldiers to save the boy, but no one listened. So Bruce ran out to save the kid himself!

Bruce did save the teenager. But just as he pushed the kid into a protective trench, the bomb exploded! Bruce was caught in the blast. His body absorbed more gamma radiation than anyone ever had before! Those gamma rays caused a startling change in Bruce. When he became angry, he turned into a huge, super-strong, green-skinned giant called Hulk!

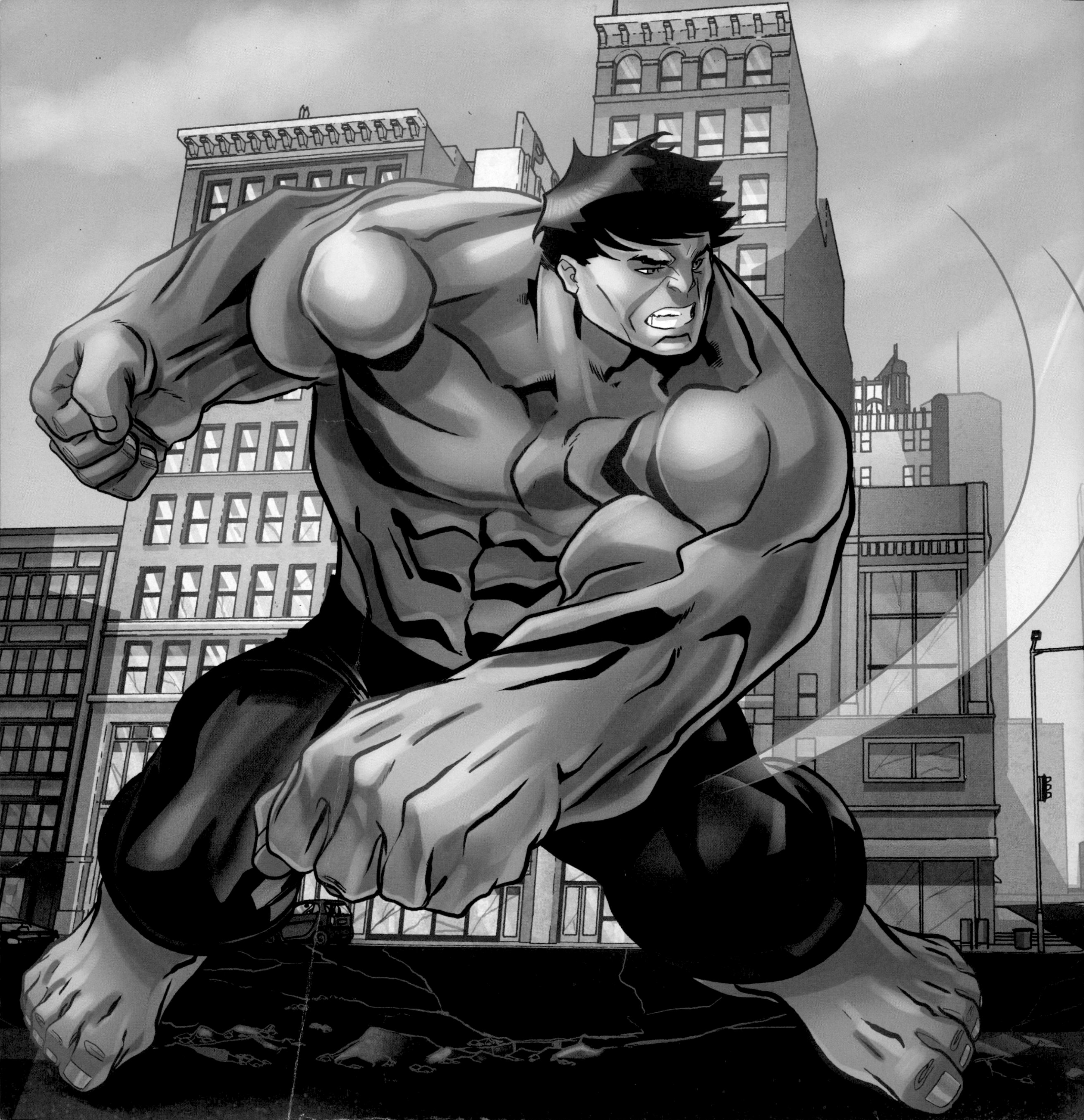

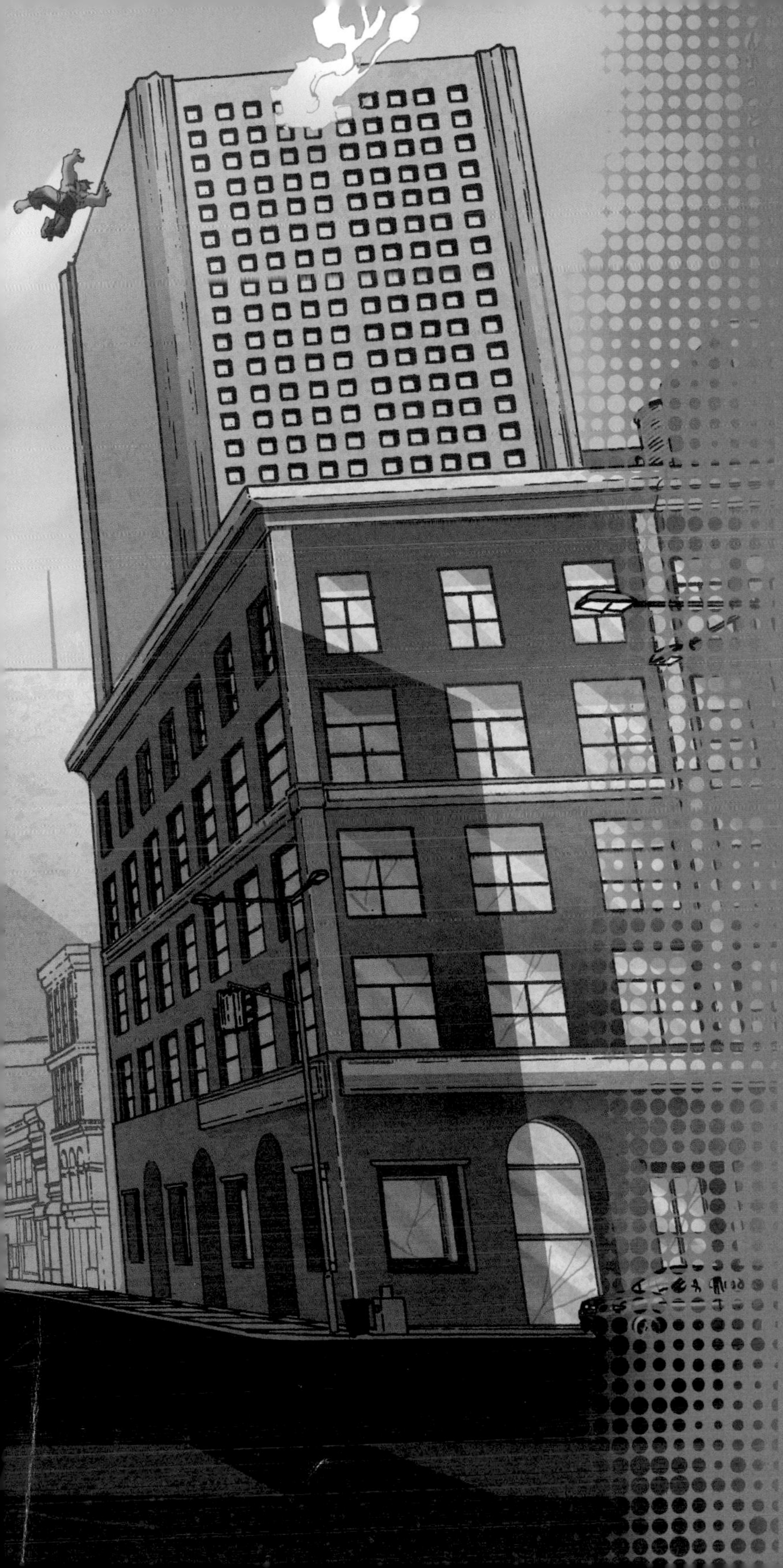

As the Hulk, Banner is one of the strongest beings on Earth! He decided to use his newfound power for good (and a little destruction).

"Hulk tired of fighting puny Ravage!" Hulk said. He clapped his massive green hands together, making a shock wave that knocked Ravage off his feet.

Ravage was really Professor Crawford, an old friend of Bruce Banner's. Crawford had turned himself into a Hulk-like creature, too, and now he was fighting the real Hulk!

"You're no match for me!" Ravage growled. He got up from the ground. Then he took a swing at Hulk.

And missed.

"Hulk want to get back to Stark Tower, watch TV!" Hulk said. Then HE took a swing at Ravage.

And DIDN'T miss.

Ravage soared through the sky and into a building.

"All done," Hulk said, and he jumped into the air, because TV.

HEIGHT: 6'

WEIGHT: 185 LBS

MASTER MARKSMAN WITH NEAR-PERFECT AIM

UTILIZES A UNIQUE BOW AND A QUIVER OF TRICK ARROWS WITH A VARIETY OF EFFECTS

EXPERT HAND-TO-HAND COMBATANT, ATHLETE, AND ACROBAT

TRAINED FROM AN EARLY AGE IN THE ART OF ARCHERY, HIS SKILLS EARNED HIM THE NICKNAME HAWKEYE

INSPIRED BY THE DEEDS OF IRON MAN AND CAPTAIN AMERICA, HE PUTS HIS SHARPSHOOTING SKILLS TO WORK AS A MEMBER OF THE AVENGERS

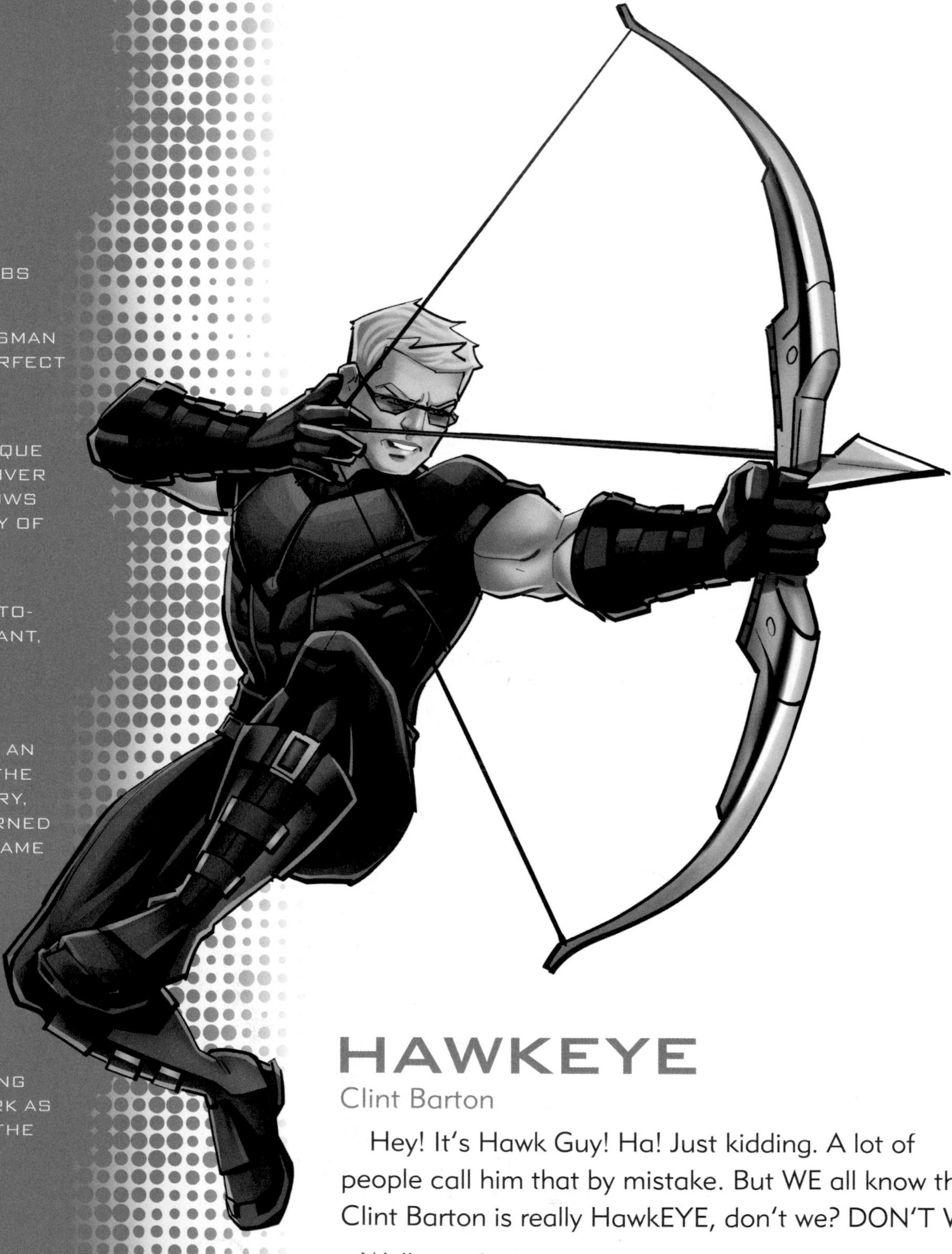

HAWKEYE

Clint Barton

Hey! It's Hawk Guy! Ha! Just kidding. A lot of people call him that by mistake. But WE all know that Clint Barton is really HawkEYE, don't we? DON'T WE?

Well, we do now.

Clint Barton is an expert archer, maybe the best who ever lived. With his incredible aim, he can hit nearly any target! Taking the name Hawkeye, Clint wanted to become a Super Hero like Iron Man. But he was mistaken for a Super Villain instead!

Eventually everyone came to realize that Clint really was a hero, and he went to work for Nick Fury and S.H.I.E.L.D. He became one of their top agents!

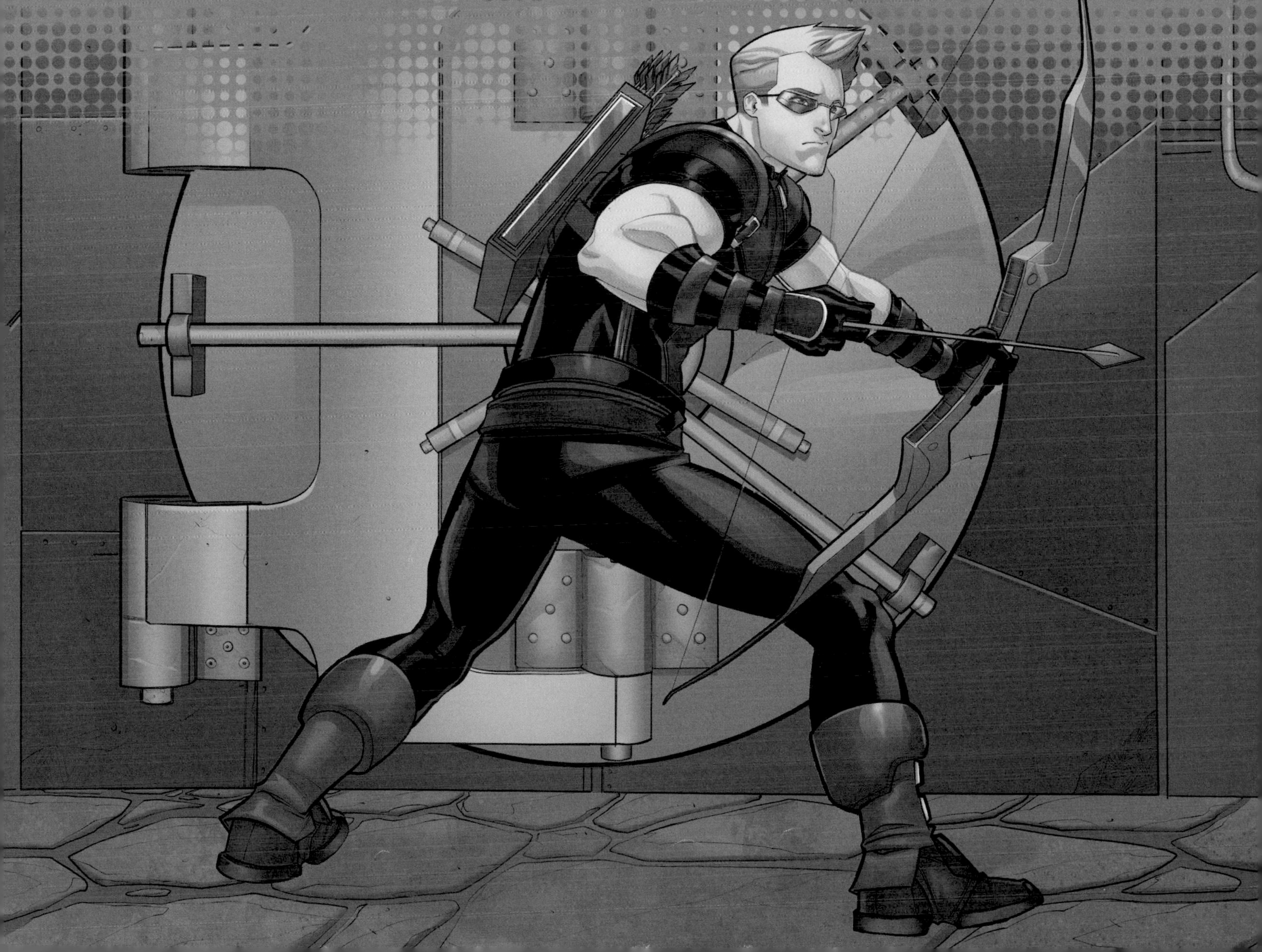

On one of his missions for S.H.I.E.L.D., Hawkeye encountered an enemy like no other he had faced before. She was called Black Widow, and she could outmatch Hawkeye every time! Even with his incredible archery ability and hand-to-hand combat skills, Hawkeye couldn't seem to beat her.

They clashed again and again. Over time, Hawkeye came to realize that Black Widow wasn't really his enemy. He knew what it was like to have everyone think you were a bad guy. Maybe all Black Widow needed was a chance to prove that she could do something good with her life.

Hawkeye thought that Black Widow would be able to do exactly that by joining S.H.I.E.L.D. From that point on, the two heroes worked together to make the world safe from all kinds of terrible threats. Then they joined the Avengers, and the rest is history!

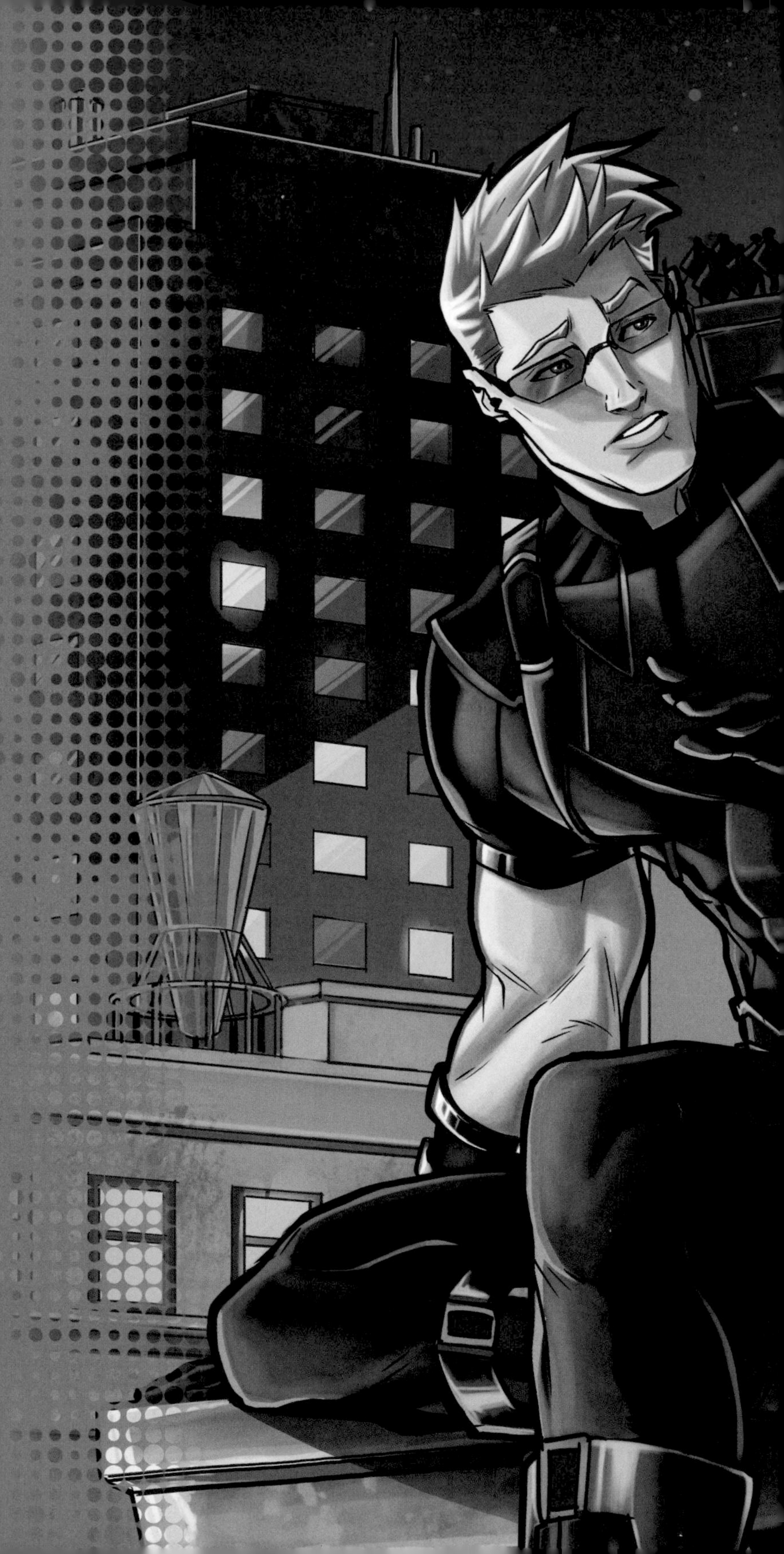

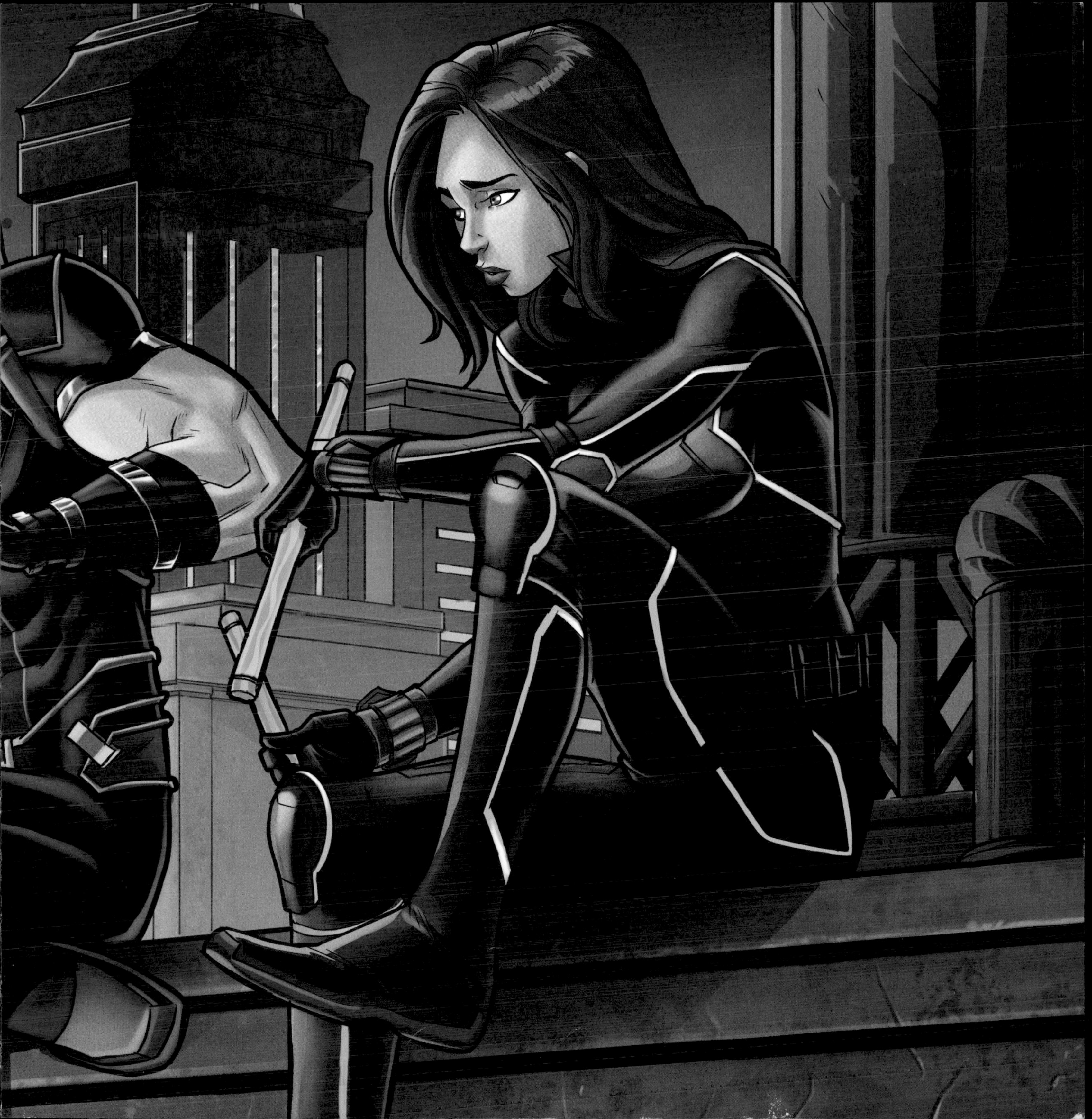

CAPTAIN MARVEL

Carol Danvers

Carol Danvers was one of the best pilots the U.S. Air Force had ever had! But she didn't want to just fly airplanes—she wanted to soar into the stars! • Carol would one day get her wish—just not quite the way she expected.

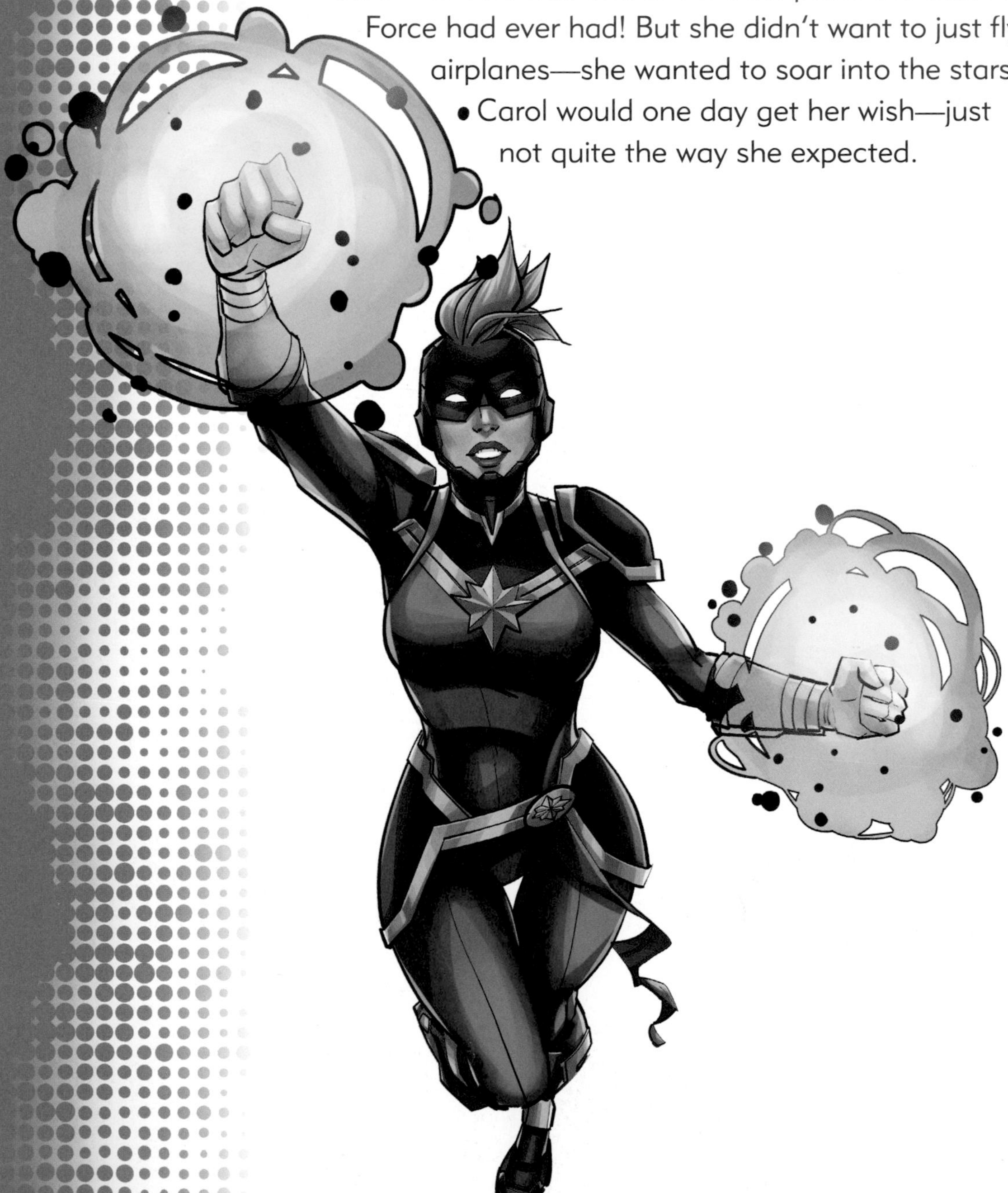

HEIGHT: 5'11"

WEIGHT: 155 LBS

SUPERHUMAN STRENGTH, STAMINA, AND DURABILITY

CAN FLY AT HIGH SPEEDS AND PROJECT INTENSE ENERGY BLASTS

CAN TAP INTO AND ABSORB DIFFERENT FORMS OF ENERGY, TRANSFORMING INTO A POWERFUL ALTERNATE FORM KNOWN AS BINARY

EXPERIENCED ESPIONAGE AGENT AND HAND-TO-HAND COMBATANT

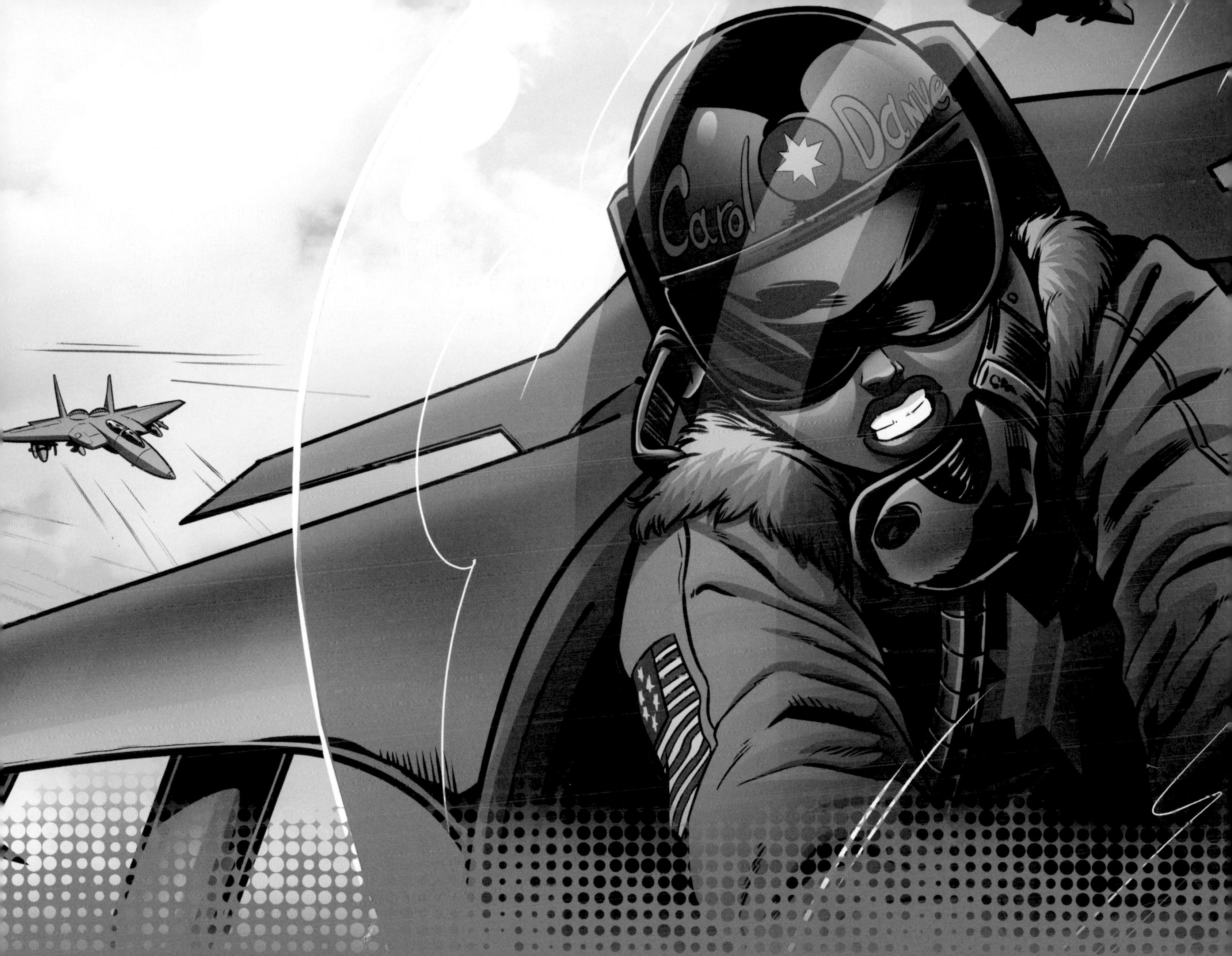
Carol

While working for NASA, Carol encountered a race of aliens known as the Kree. One of them, an evil warrior named Yon-Rogg, captured Carol along with a strange alien device. The device exploded, and Carol was caught in the blast. But she wasn't hurt! Instead, she gained the power to harness photon energy. It seemed like nothing could hurt her—she could even fly into space! Thus she became the Super Hero called Captain Marvel.

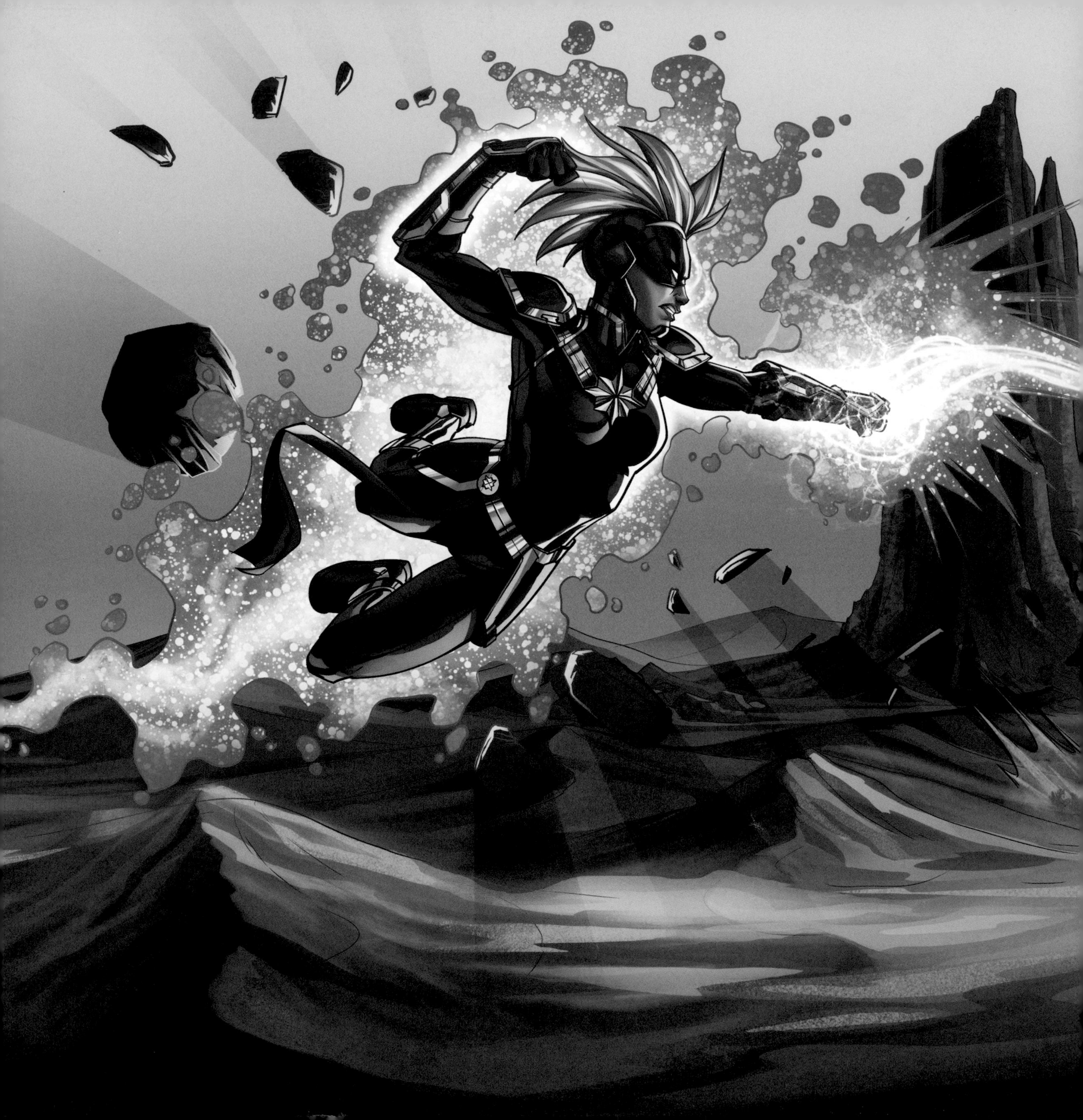

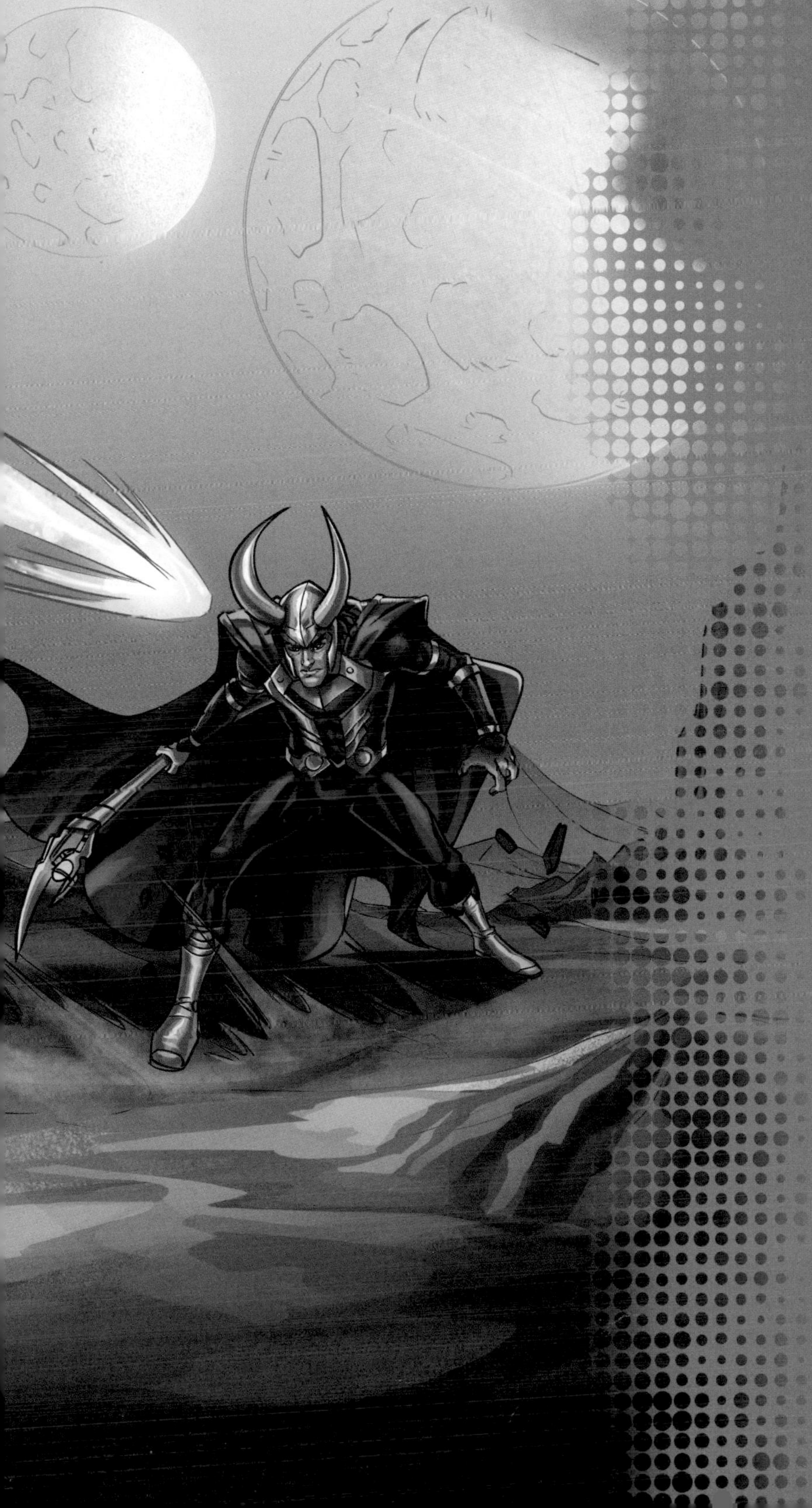

As Captain Marvel, Carol faced all kinds of interstellar threats. That's exactly what happened when she encountered Thor's evil brother, Loki.

"What brings you to this corner of the galaxy?" Captain Marvel asked.

"Others may enjoy your sense of humor," Loki said. "I do not." With a wave of the magical gem in his hand, Loki hurled asteroids at the hero.

"Y'know, others may enjoy it when you throw asteroids at them," Captain Marvel joked as she blasted the boulders into atoms. "I do not."

"Touché, Captain," Loki said. The Asgardian was about to launch another attack, when Captain Marvel soared into the air, swooping in behind him. "What—what are you doing?" Loki stuttered.

"Nothing important," Captain Marvel said as she snatched the gem from Loki's hands. "Just taking this back to its rightful owners."

As Captain Marvel flew away, she saw Loki shaking his fist angrily. She made sure to laugh extra loud, so he could hear it!

HEIGHT: 6'

WEIGHT: 170 LBS

INSPIRED BY AN ENCOUNTER WITH CAPTAIN AMERICA TO BECOME A SUPER HERO

WEARS A SOPHISTICATED HARNESS GRANTING HIGH-SPEED FLIGHT AND PRECISE AERIAL MANEUVERABILITY

HARNESS CAN DETACH AND OPERATE AUTONO-MOUSLY IN "REDWING MODE"

SUPERB ATHLETE AND HAND-TO-HAND COMBATANT

HIGHLY INTELLIGENT WITH PROFICIENCY IN ADVANCED TECHNOLOGY

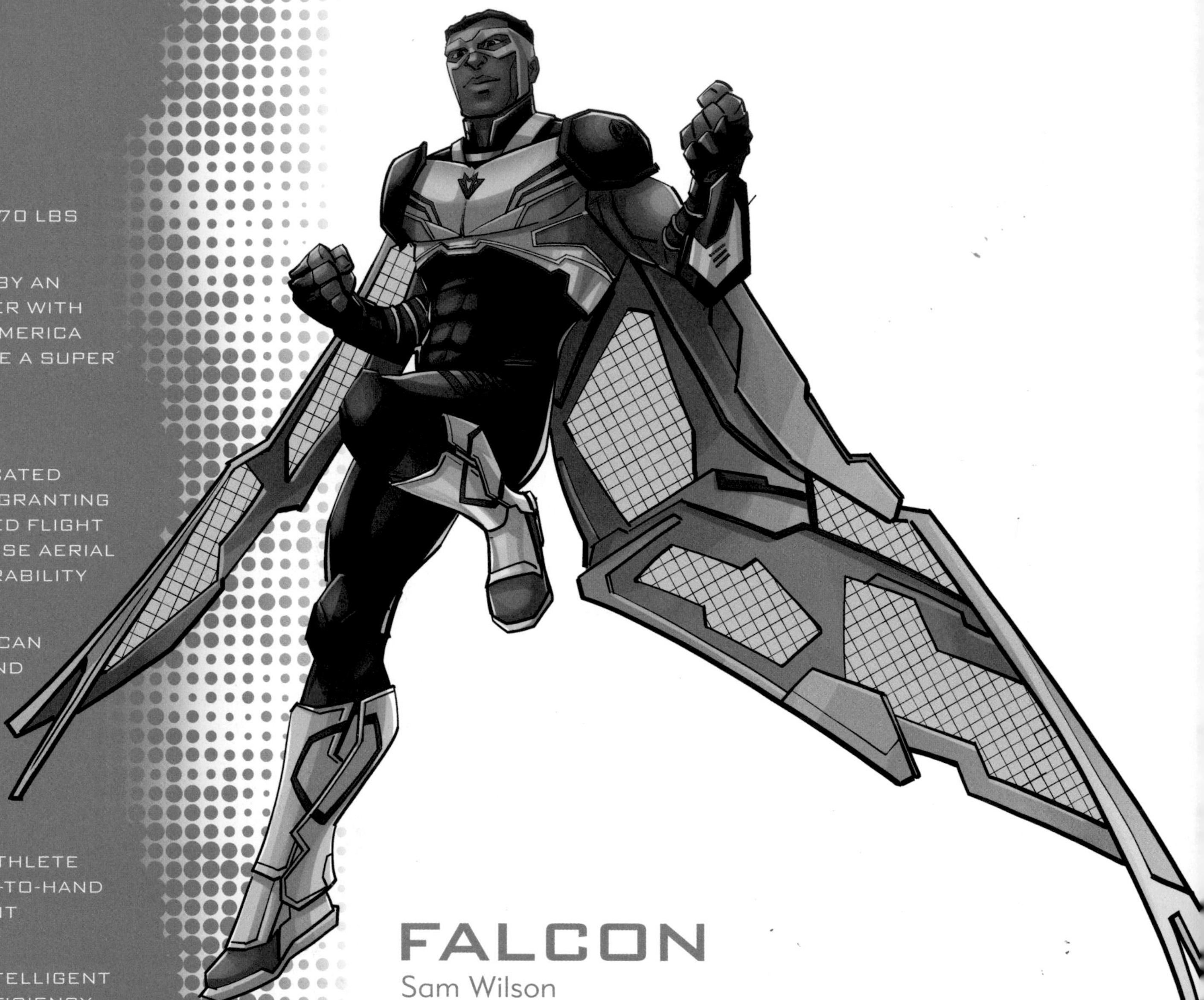

FALCON

Sam Wilson

Not all heroes wear capes, but some of them DO wear wings! Take Sam Wilson, also known as Falcon.

This Avenger patrols the skies to keep everyone safe from all kinds of aliens, Super Villains, and giant, earth-shattering monsters.

Sam was friends with Captain America, and wanted to help him make the world a better place. He was kind and tough, so Cap helped him come up with a costumed identity of his own! Falcon's wings were designed by Black Panther (more on him soon) and are made out of lightweight titanium. They can even convert sunlight into electricity to power the rest of his suit! Not only did Sam better the world fighting alongside his pal Captain America, but he even joined the Avengers!

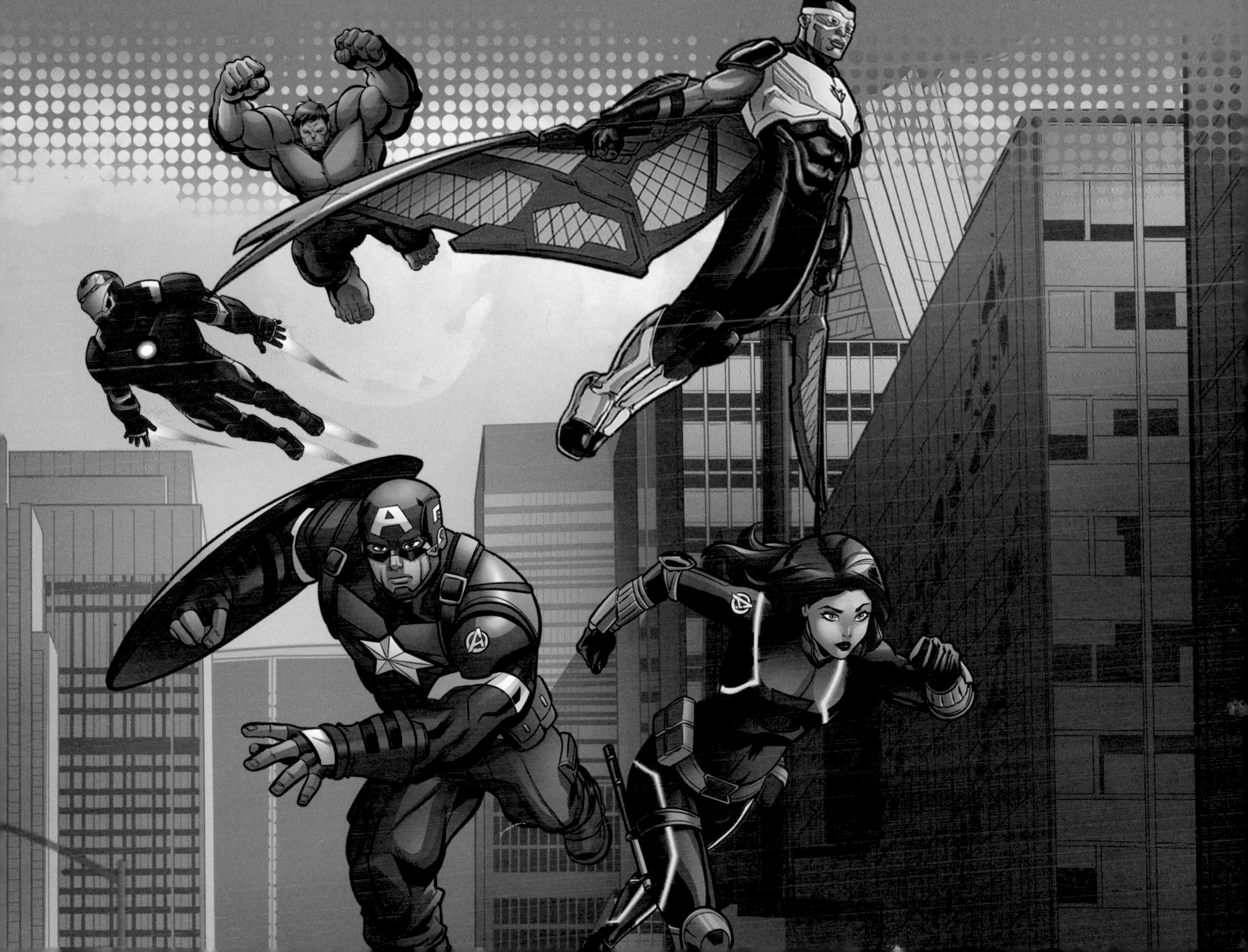

Falcon's ability to fly made him a perfect choice to scout ahead for approaching enemies, and the Avengers were always happy to have him keeping an eye out from above.

"See anything, Falcon?" said Captain America, standing atop Avengers Tower.

"Looks like clear skies!" Falcon replied as he flew above the city. "I've got a clear view all the way past the Hudson River. Nothing so far!"

The Avengers had received a report that Hydra was planning to attack the Avengers in their own headquarters. So the team had gathered to stop them!

Just as he was about to turn around and head back to Avengers Tower, Falcon saw something out of the corner of his eye. "Wait!" Falcon shouted. "I see something now—looks like Hydra's coming in hot! Gather the troops, Cap, we've got company."

As the Super Villains approached, the Avengers stood ready—thanks to an early warning from Falcon!

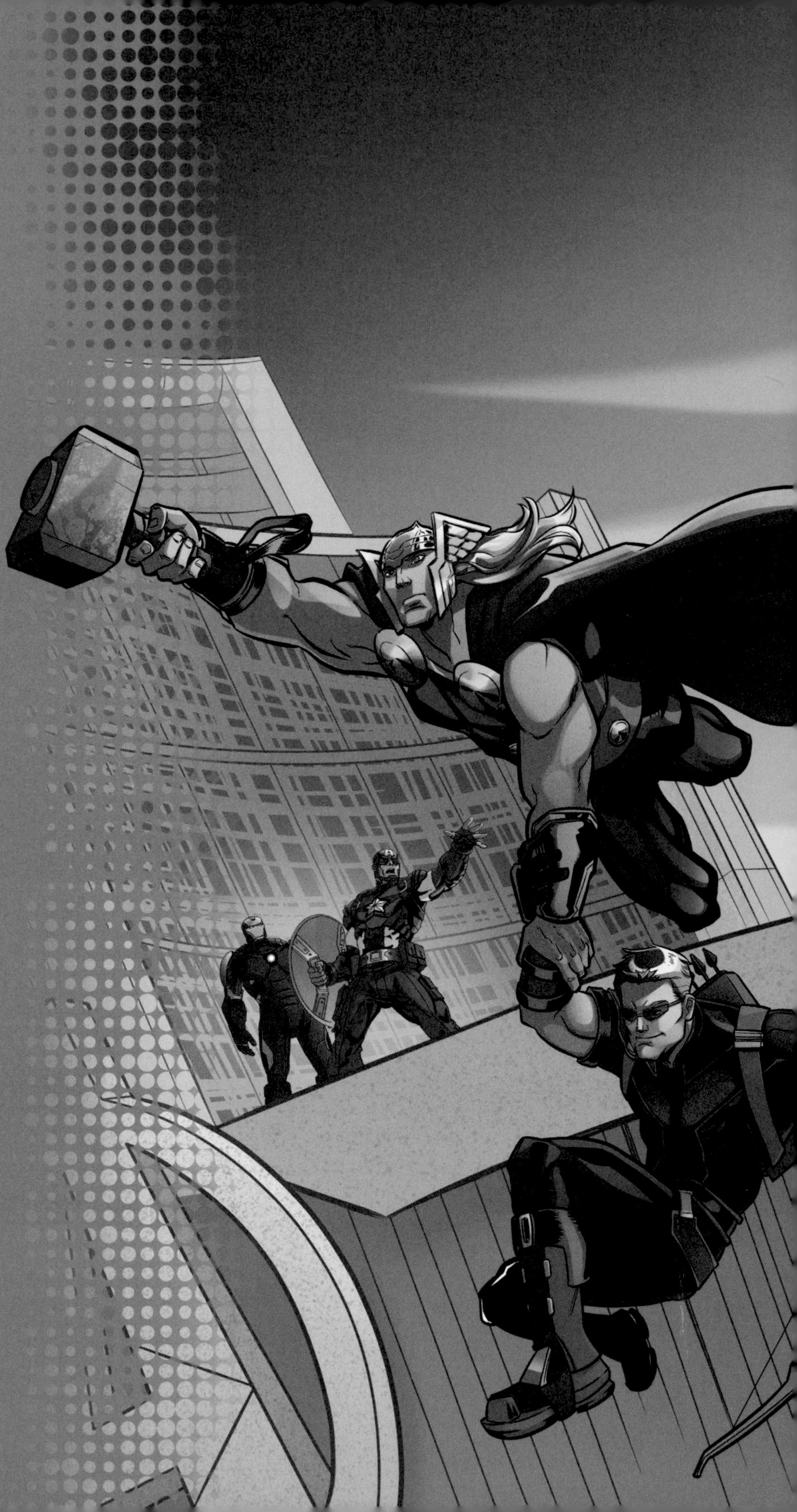

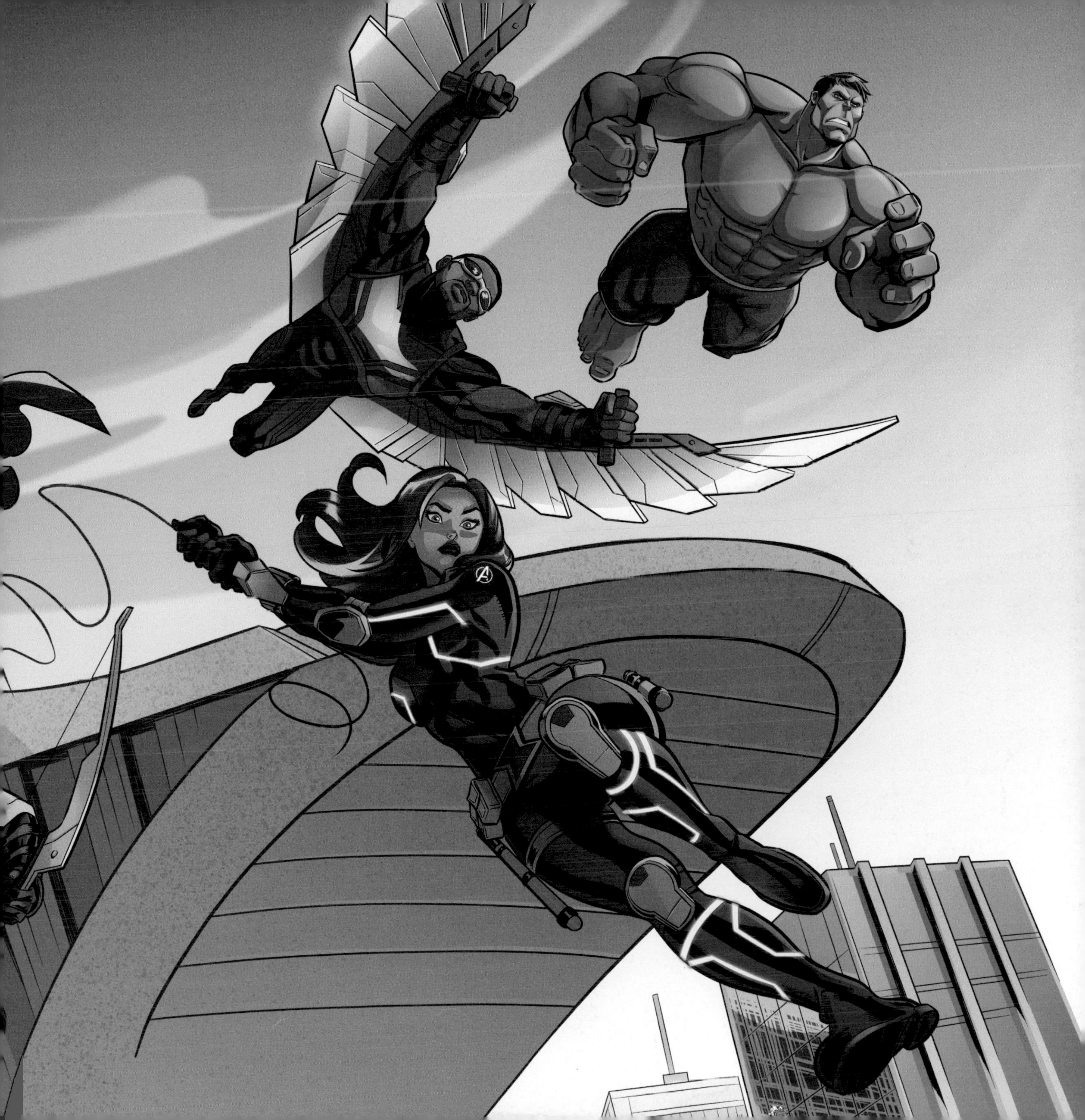

WINTER SOLDIER

James Buchanan "Bucky" Barnes

James Buchanan Barnes, known to his friends as "Bucky," is an amazing fighter and a brilliant strategist. Oh yeah, he also has a super-cool, super-strong cybernetic arm!

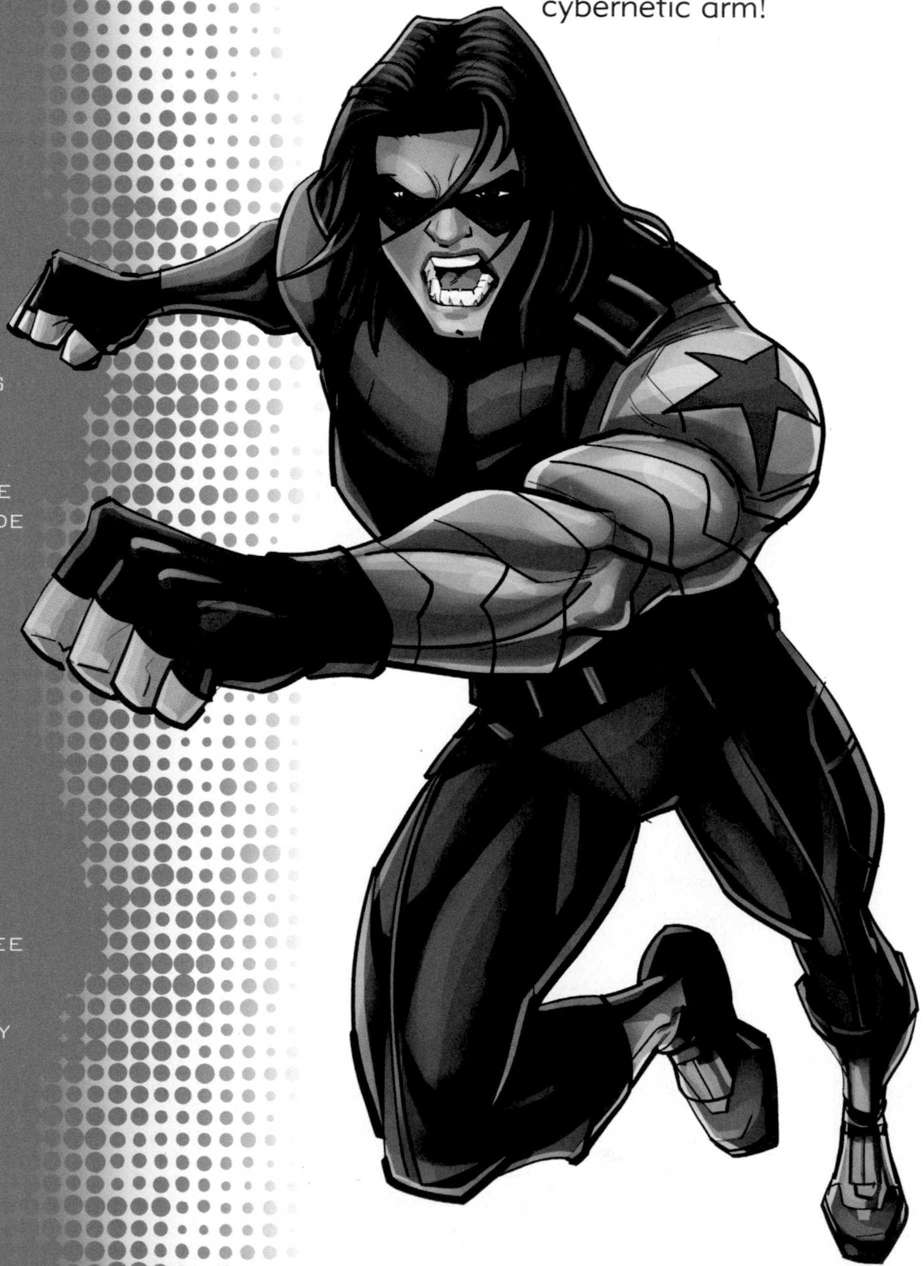

HEIGHT: 5'10"

WEIGHT: 195 LBS

SUBJECTED TO MENTAL AND PHYSICAL EXPERIMENTS

REBORN AS THE WINTER SOLDIER, WHO COULD BE ACTIVATED FROM CRYOSTASIS TO UNDERTAKE SPECIAL MISSIONS

FREED FROM BRAINWASHING, HE NOW FIGHTS BESIDE HIS BEST FRIEND, CAPTAIN AMERICA

MASTER OF HAND-TO-HAND COMBAT, INFILTRATION, ESPIONAGE, AND MARKSMANSHIP

EQUIPPED WITH AN ADVANCED CYBERNETIC ARM GRANTING A DEGREE OF SUPERHUMAN STRENGTH AND HOUSING A VARIETY OF HIDDEN TOOLS INCLUDING AN EMP GENERATOR AND A HOLOGRAPHIC CAMOUFLAGE UNIT

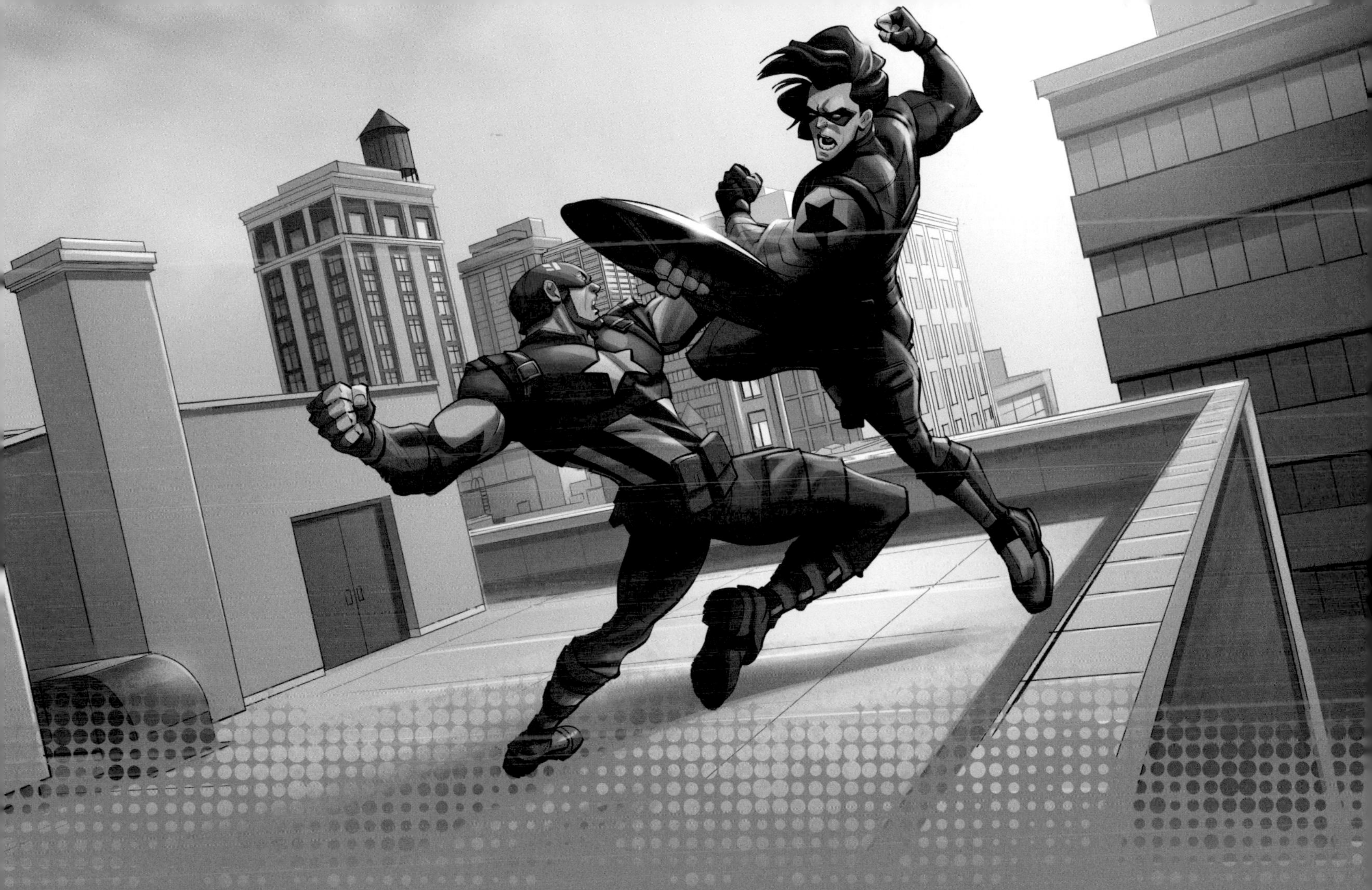

Bucky fought alongside Captain America in World War II. While on a mission with Cap toward the end of the war, Bucky was believed to have been lost in battle. But really, he had been captured by enemy agents and brainwashed so he would obey their orders. His left arm was replaced with a bionic one, and Bucky became Winter Soldier. Like Cap, he was frozen. But unlike the star-spangled Super Hero, Winter Soldier was thawed out by his captors when they needed him to do their dirty work.

In the present day, Captain America fought Winter Soldier, eventually learning that his new enemy was really his old friend! With Cap's help, Bucky recovered his memories and became one of the good guys. Now he teams up with the shield-slinger and his squad, the Avengers.

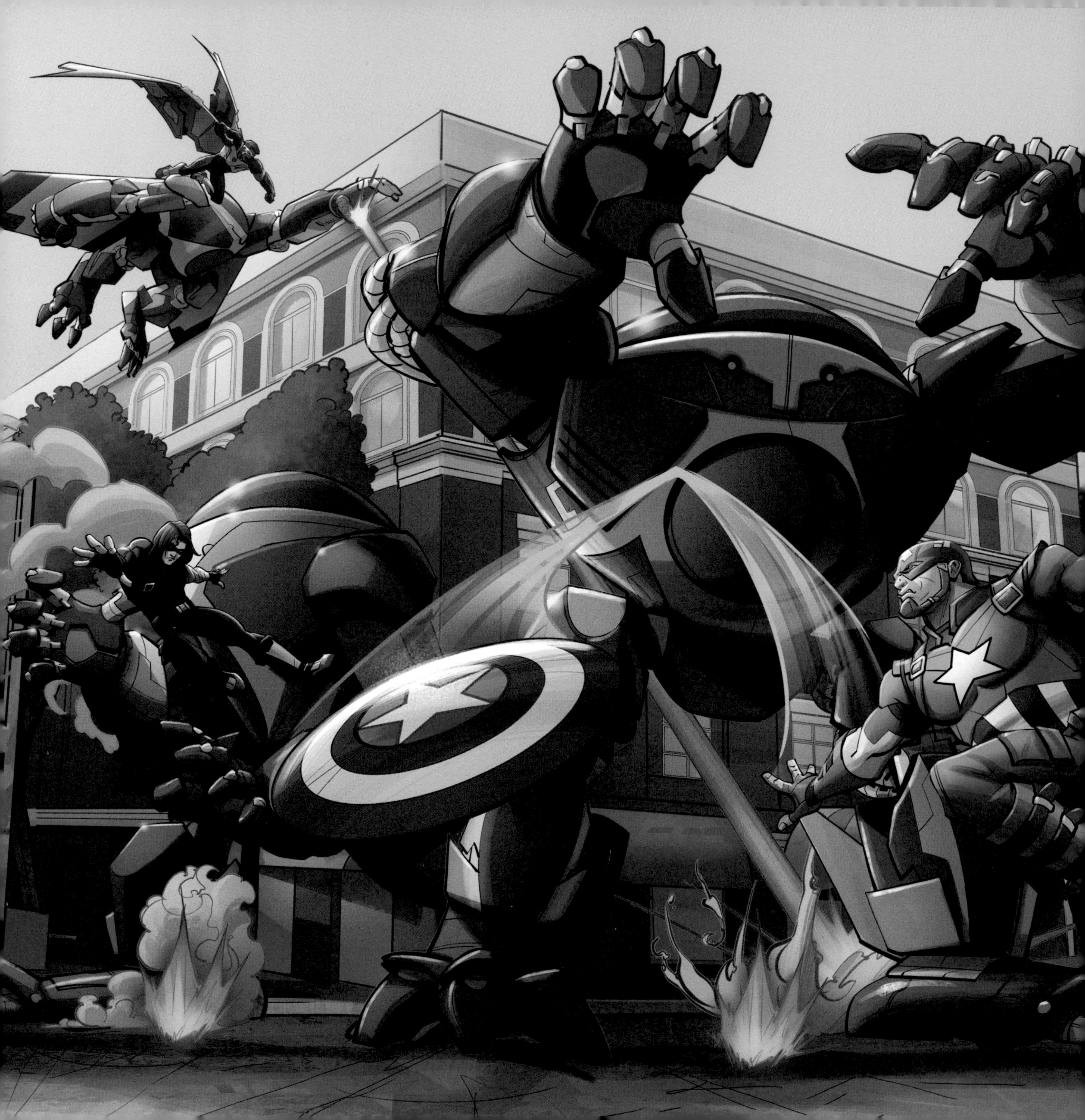

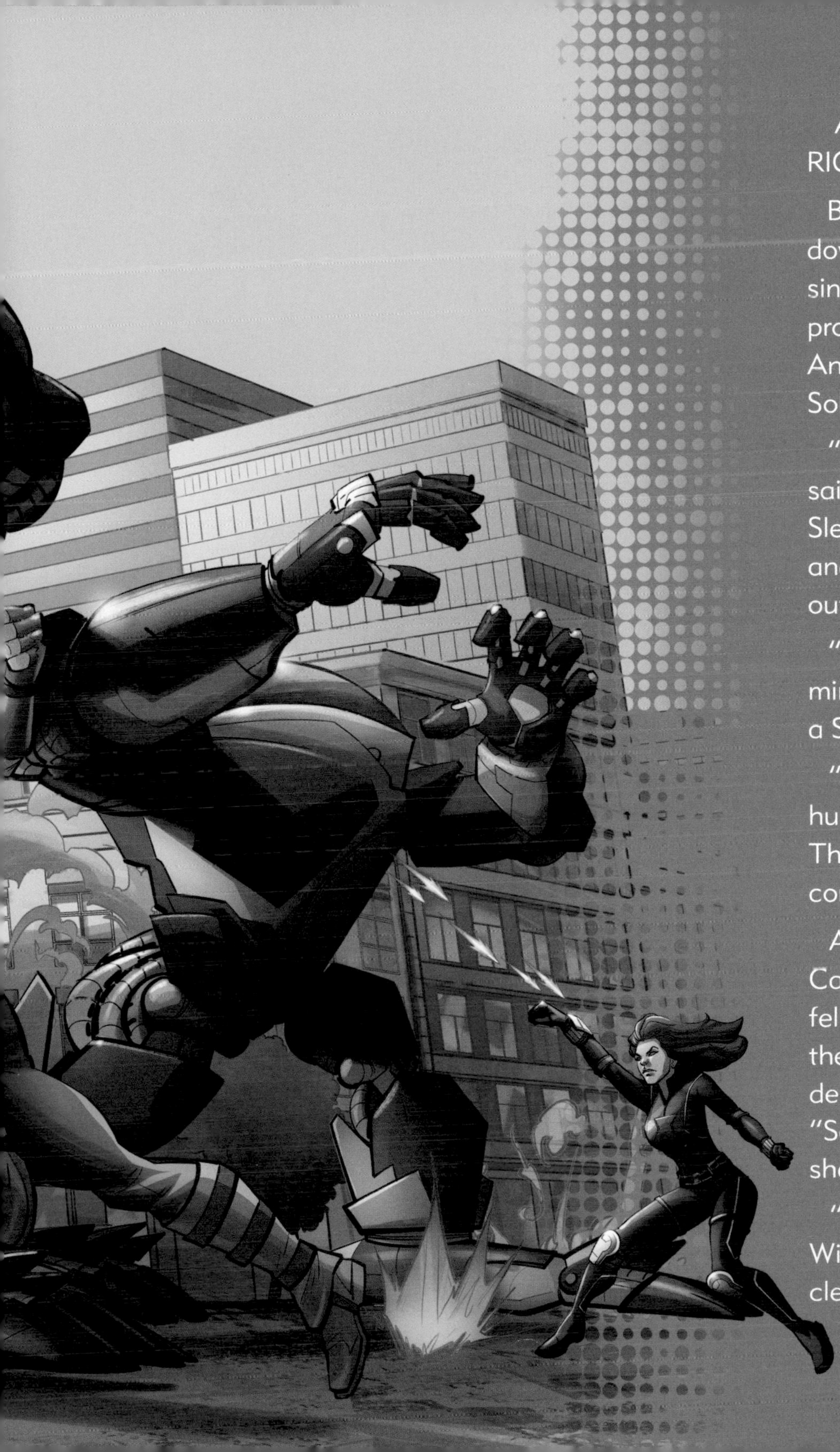

And when we say *now*, we mean RIGHT NOW.

Because the Avengers were facing down the threat of the Red Skull's sinister Sleepers—giant robots programmed to destroy all civilization! And they were going to need Winter Soldier's help to take them down.

"The big one's mine," Winter Soldier said, leaping onto the arm of a hulking Sleeper. He punched the robot's arm and reached inside. As Bucky pulled out wires, the robot sputtered.

"What do you mean, 'The big one's mine'?" Falcon said as he dive-bombed a Sleeper. "They're ALL the big one!"

"He's all yours, Soldier!" Cap said, hurling his shield at another Sleeper. The shield shattered the robot's controls, sending it to the ground.

As another Sleeper lumbered toward Cap, it suddenly exploded. The robot fell down, and Cap jumped out of the way. Standing behind the now destroyed robot was Black Widow. "Sorry, I should have said 'TIMBER!'" she joked.

"That takes care of the Sleepers," Winter Soldier said. "But who's gonna clean up this mess?"

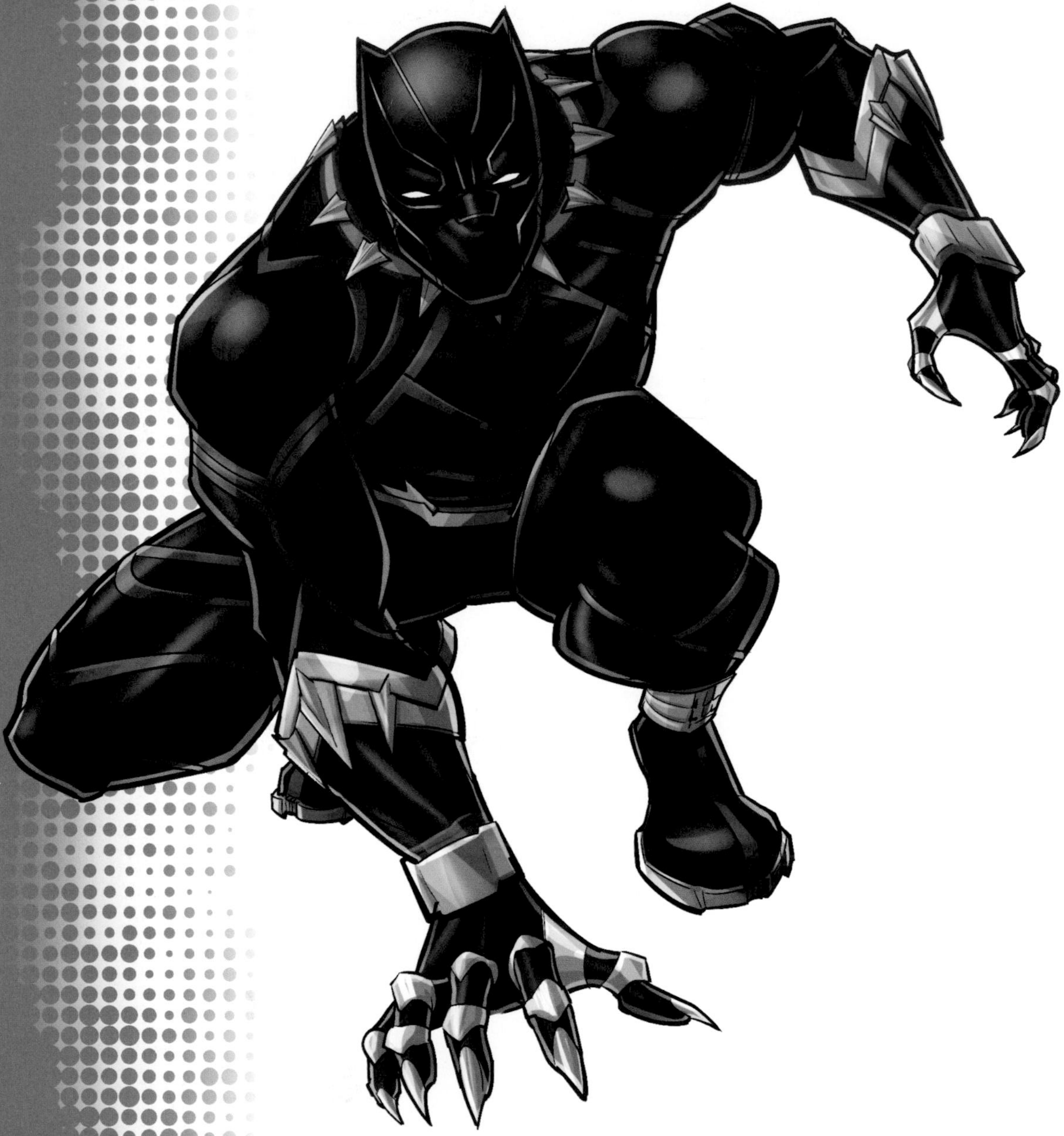

HEIGHT: 6'

WEIGHT: 195 LBS

KING OF WAKANDA

EARNED AND INHERITED THE TITLE OF BLACK PANTHER, PROTECTOR OF HIS PEOPLE

HEIGHTENED STRENGTH, SPEED, STAMINA, AGILITY, AND REFLEXES

MASTER OF MARTIAL ARTS, ACROBATICS, AND HANDHELD WEAPONRY

UTILIZES HIGHLY ADVANCED WAKANDAN TECHNOLOGY, INCLUDING VIBRANIUM-WOVEN BODY ARMOR AND STEALTH AIRCRAFT

GENIUS-LEVEL INTELLECT WITH EXPERTISE IN PHYSICS AND TECHNOLOGY

BLACK PANTHER

T'Challa

Did you know that one of the Avengers is an honest-to-goodness king? Meet T'Challa, king of the African nation of Wakanda. You might know him better by another name: Black Panther!

Wakanda is one of the most advanced places on Earth, thanks to its scientists—and its supply of a rare metal called Vibranium.

From the time he was a child, T'Challa trained hard to inherit the mantle of Black Panther from his father, King T'Chaka. The brave warriors known as the *Dora Milaje* watched over him. But they were unable to help the king when a criminal named Klaw tried to steal their Vibranium. T'Chaka was killed, and T'Challa became king—and the next Black Panther.

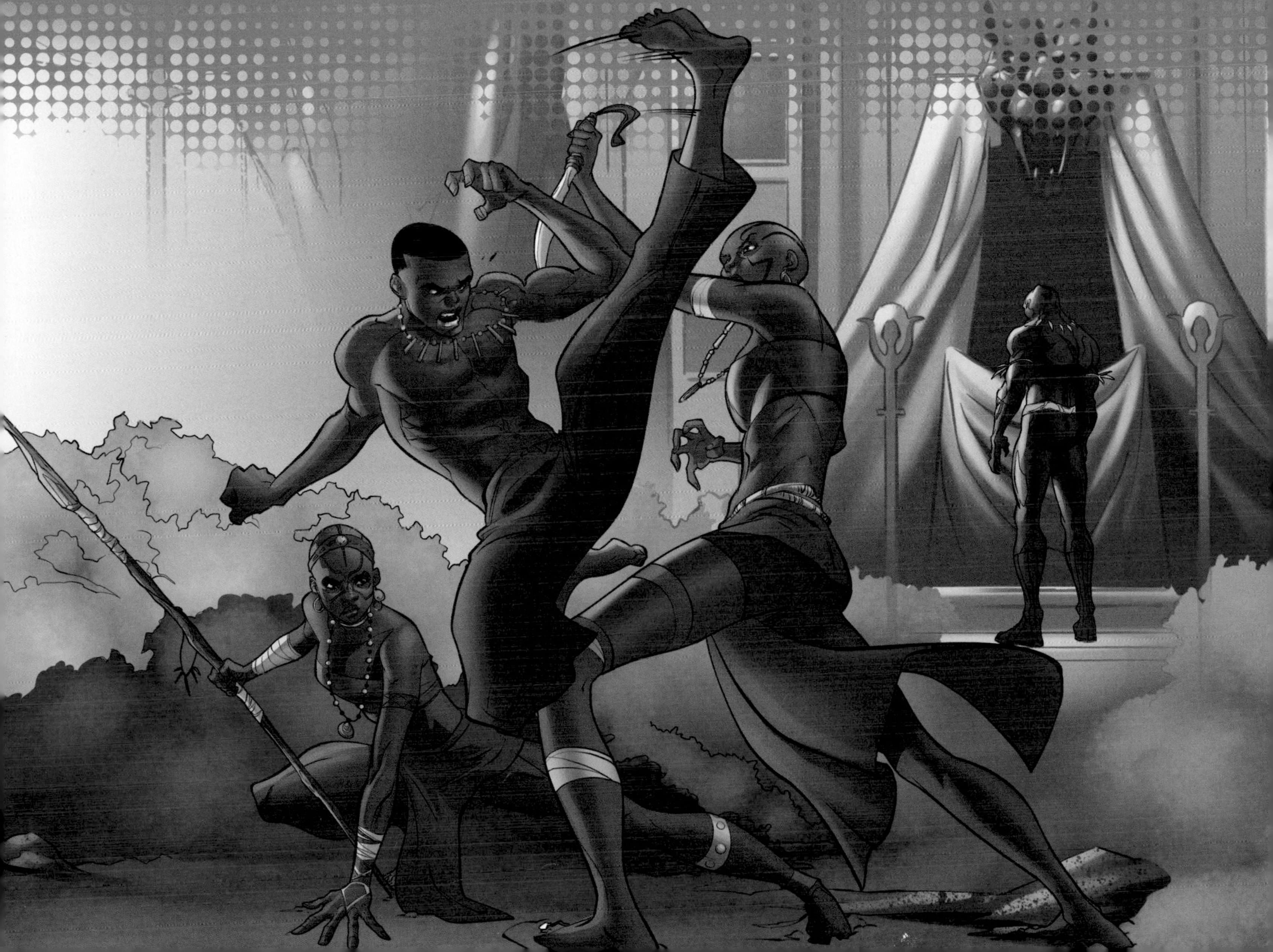

It was almost too much to believe—Klaw had returned to Wakanda, trying to steal Vibranium to enhance his sonic blaster! The Vibranium could absorb huge amounts of energy, like sound, and release it. It would make him nearly unstoppable! The *Dora Milaje* alerted T'Challa, who donned his Black Panther suit and leaped into battle.

"I give you one chance to surrender," Black Panther said, "and face Wakandan justice."

"I'll never surrender," Klaw replied, raising his blaster. "Not to you, not to anyone!"

Klaw attacked Black Panther using his blaster to create objects made of solid sound. He even made an enormous octopus to strangle the hero! But Black Panther was too fast and smart. He dodged the sound creature's tentacles, and delivered a crushing blow to Klaw.

With the aid of his sister, Shuri, Black Panther trapped Klaw in a Vibranium sphere. Klaw couldn't escape—now he would face trial for his crimes!

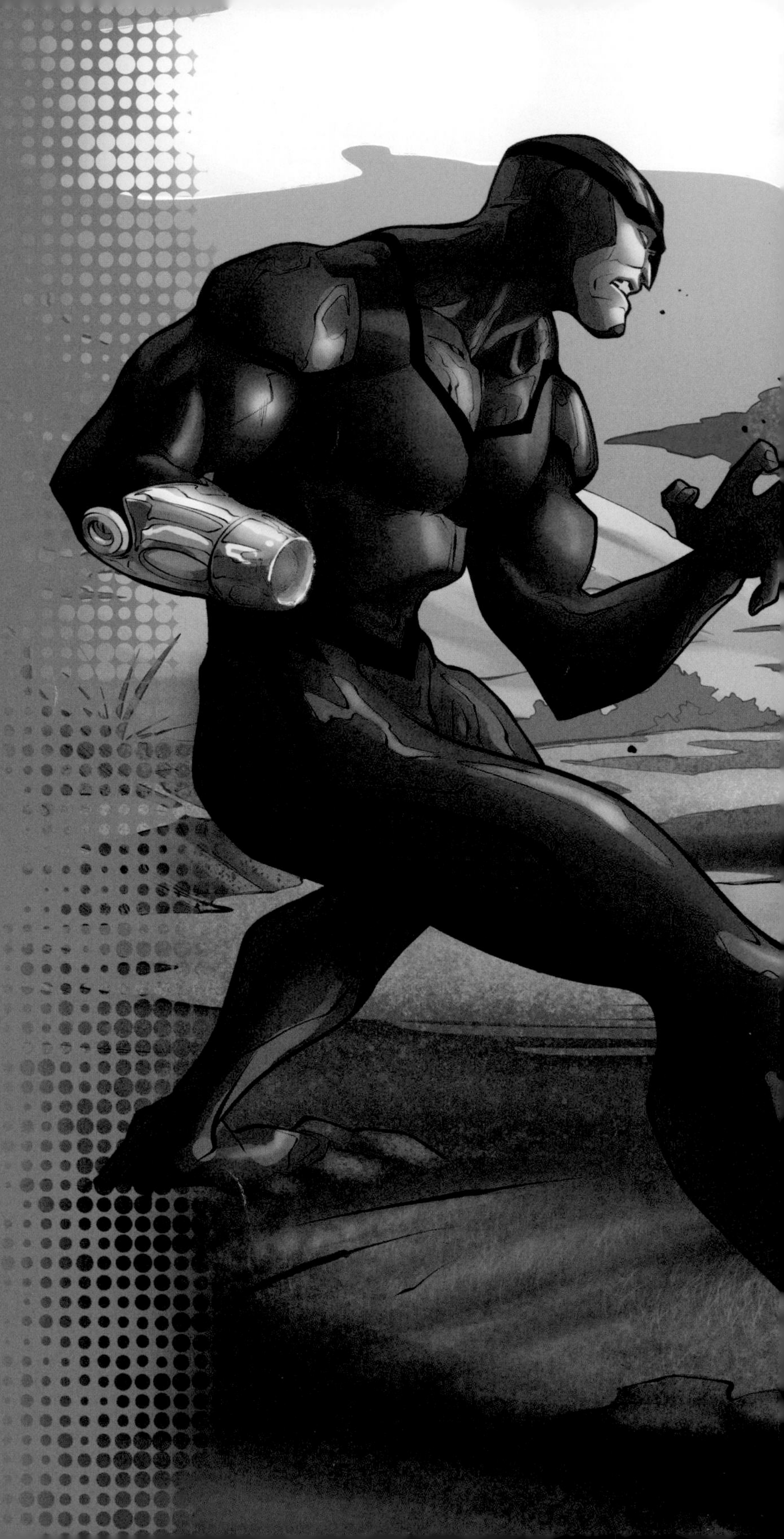

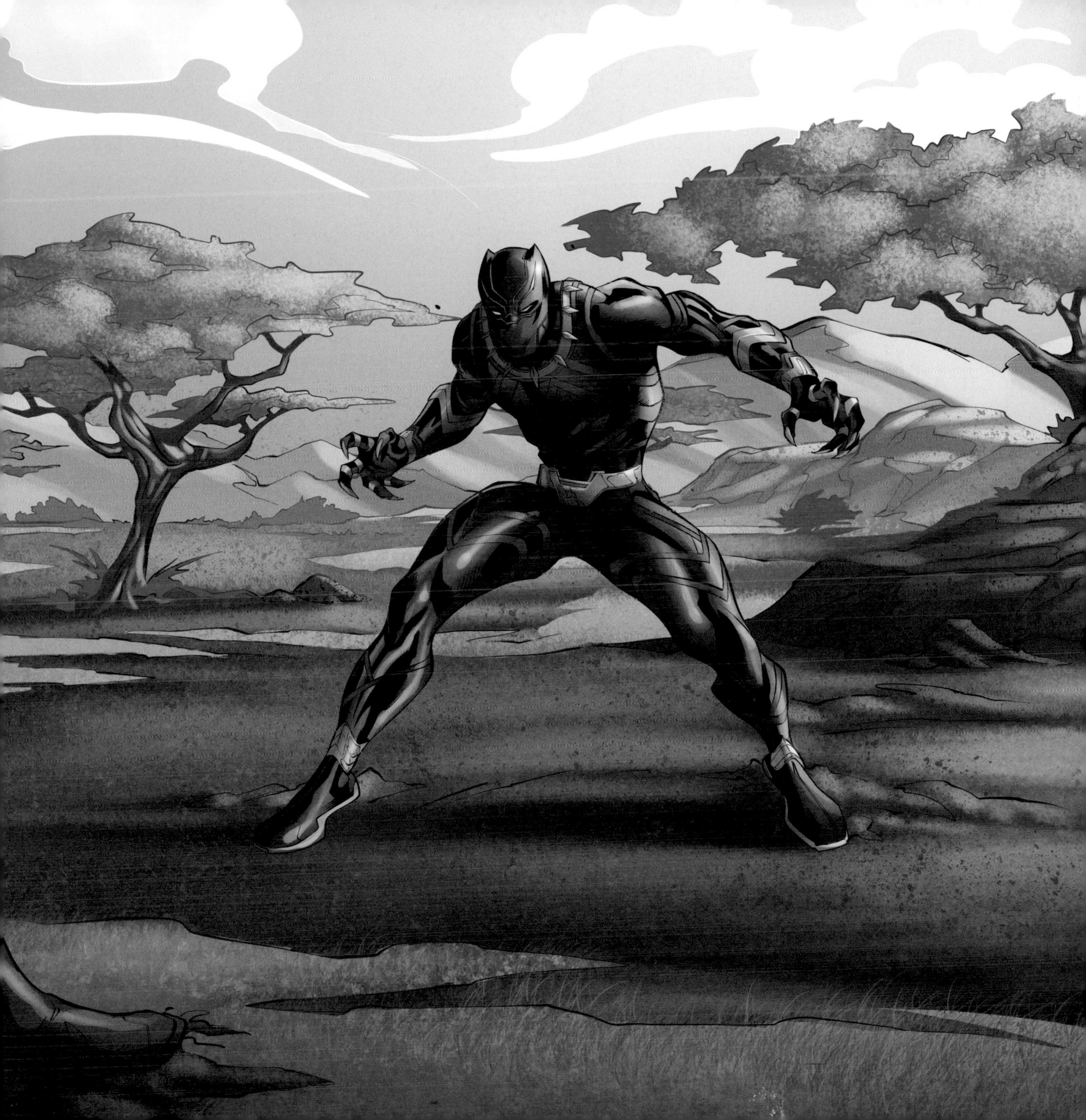

OKOYE & SHURI

Leader of the *Dora Milaje* / Wakandan Scientist and Princess

Remember the *Dora Milaje*? Of course you do, we just talked about them on page 107! The *Dora Milaje* are led by Okoye and are sworn to protect the king of Wakanda. Okoye also relies on Shuri, T'Challa's younger sister. She's one of the brightest scientists in all of Wakanda!

OKOYE

HEIGHT: 5'9"

WEIGHT: 150 LBS

ONE OF T'CHALLA'S TOP ADVISORS

FIERCE AND NOBLE SPIRIT

MASTER OF HAND-TO-HAND COMBAT

SHURI

HEIGHT: 5'5"

WEIGHT: 130 LBS

HAS RULED WAKANDA IN T'CHALLA'S ABSENCE

HEIGHTENED STRENGTH, SPEED, STAMINA, AGILITY, AND REFLEXES

MASTER OF MARTIAL ARTS, ACROBATICS, AND HAND-HELD WEAPONRY

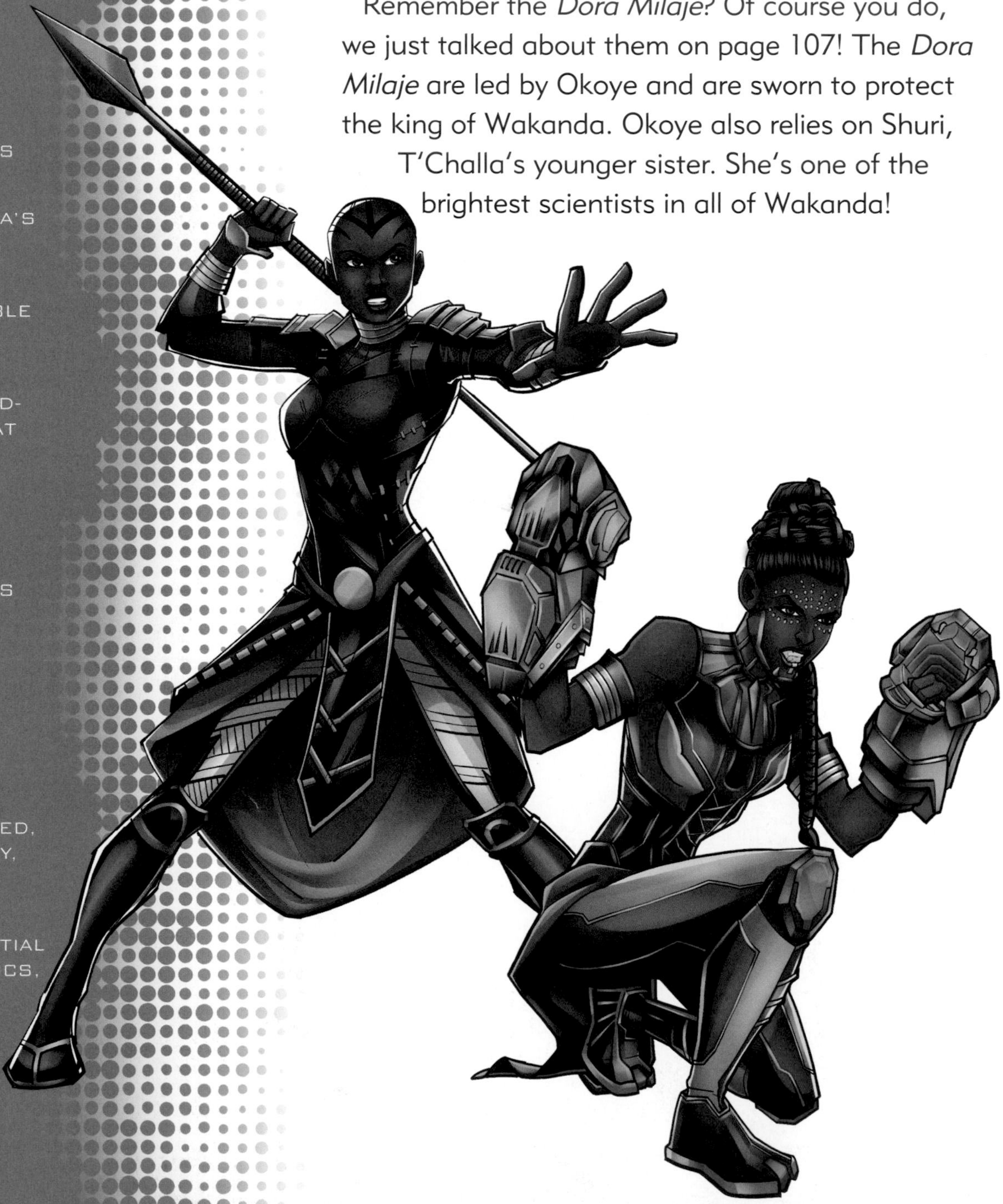

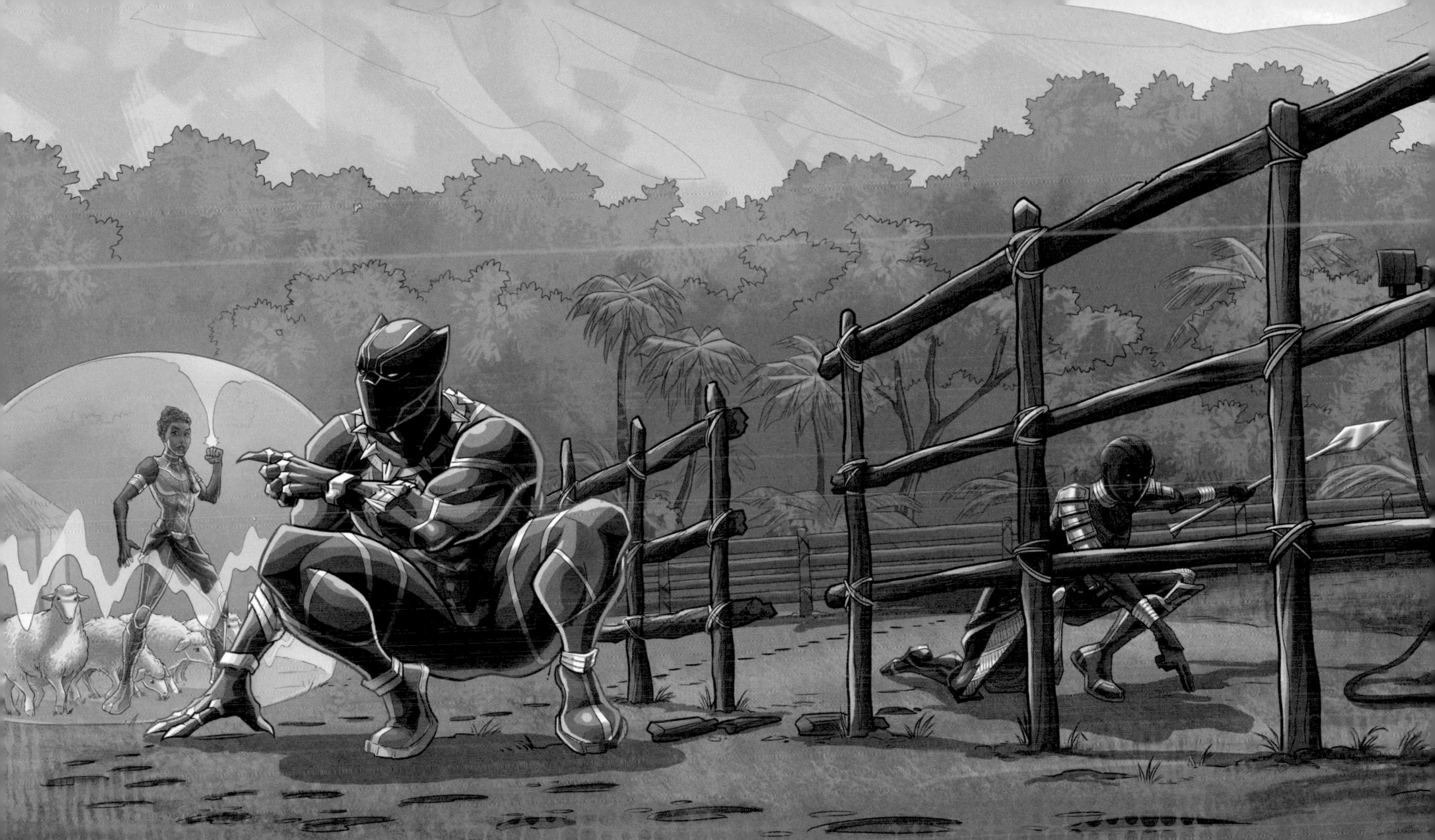

As the leader of the *Dora Milaje*, Okoye is one of the bravest, toughest, and most skilled warriors in the world. She is a master of armed and unarmed combat. Not only would she defend Wakanda to the end, but she is loyal to both her king and his family.

Though she might only be a teenager, Shuri has incredible knowledge and skills that she uses to design devices for her brother and all of Wakanda. But she doesn't spend all her time in a lab—Shuri also fights alongside her brother in defense of her country! She creates cool tech, like force fields and blasters, that run on Vibranium.

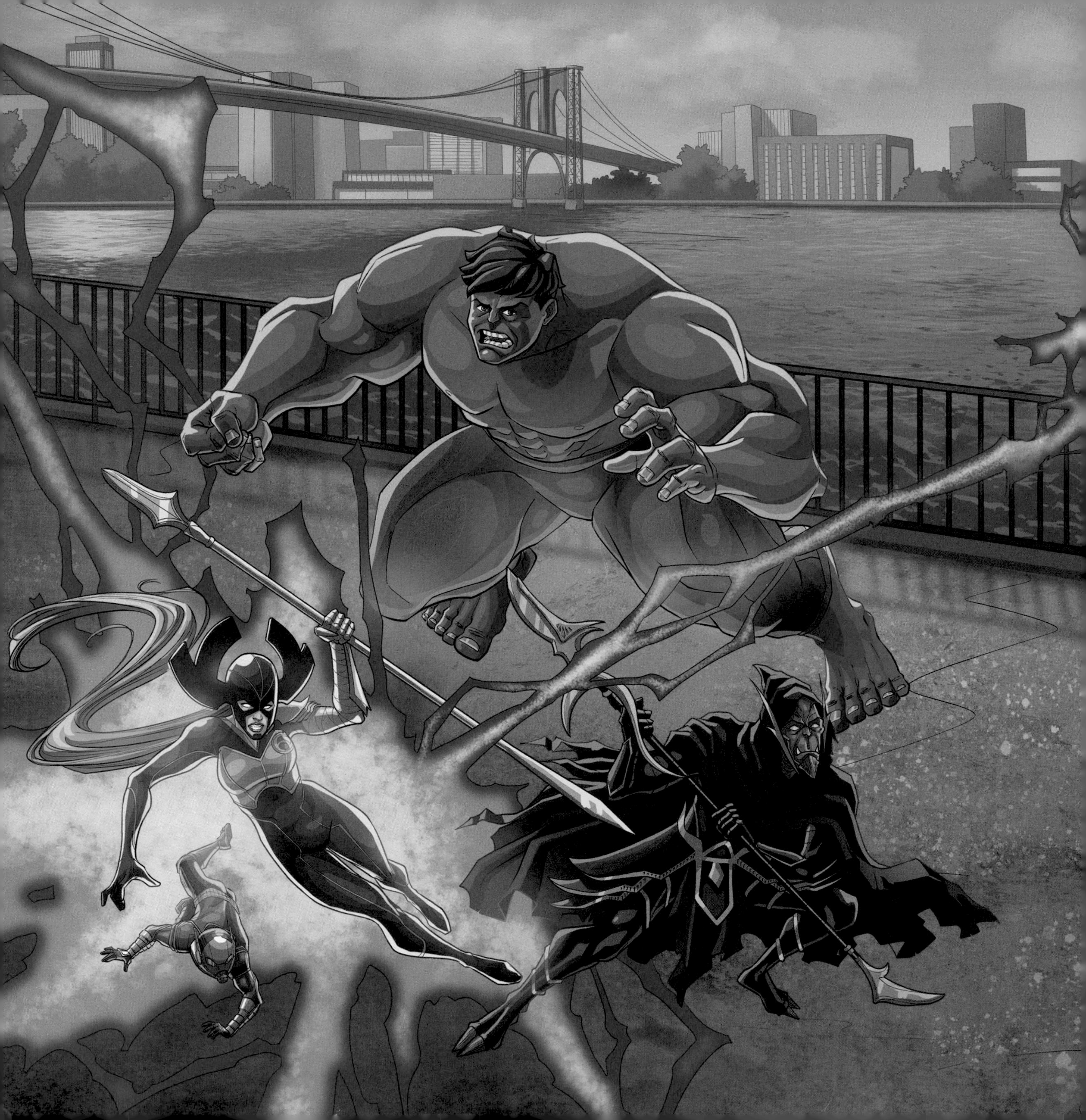

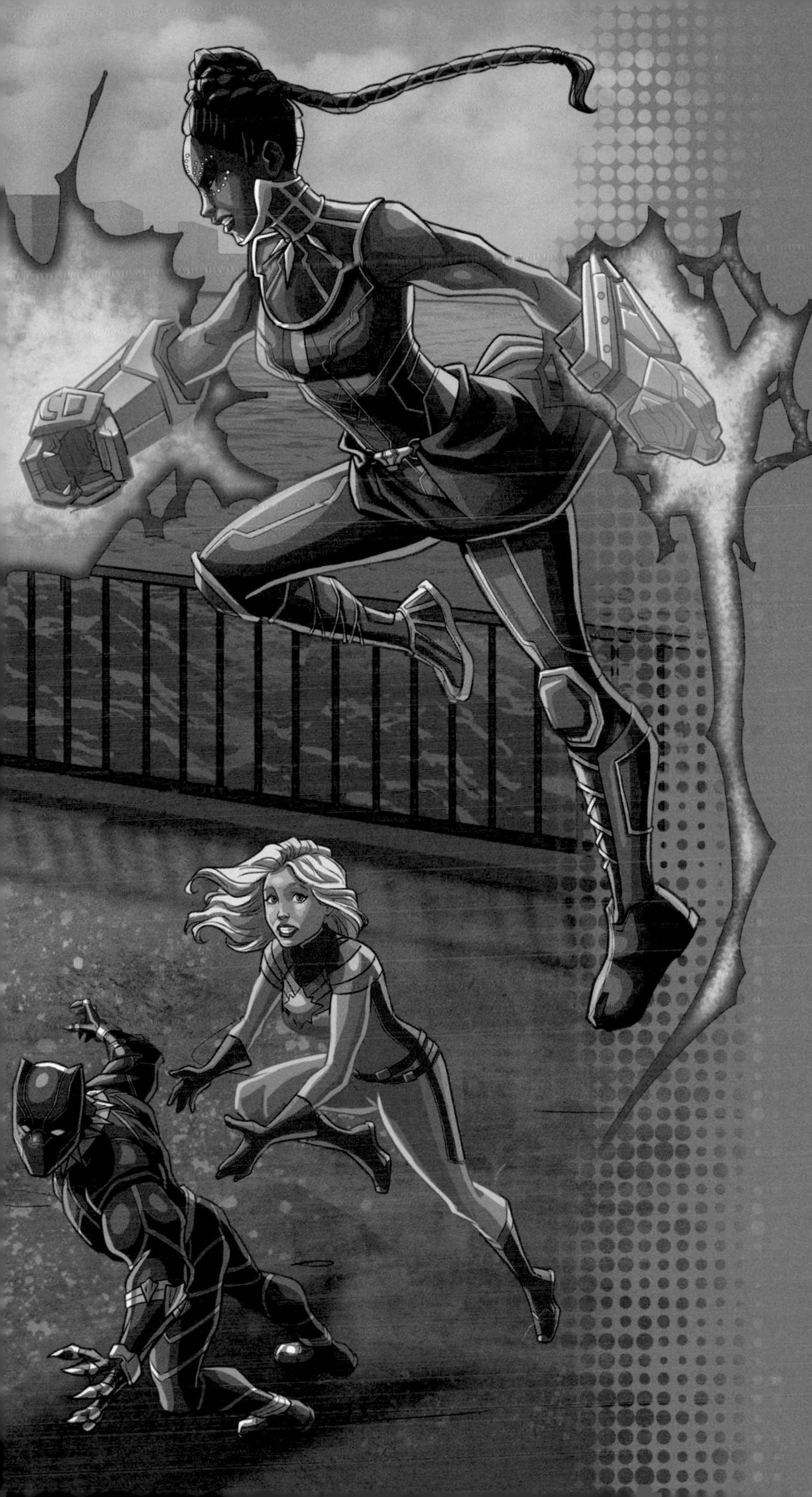

Sometimes, it is Shuri's tech that makes the difference between winning and losing.

This was one of those times.

The battle against the aliens Proxima Midnight and Corvus Glaive was going the opposite of good.

You know, bad.

Ant-Man, Black Panther, Captain Marvel, and Hulk were doing their best to stop the villains.

But they would have been lying if they said they didn't need help.

"Hulk doesn't need help," the green giant said. "But Hulk still take it."

Lucky for them, Shuri and Okoye had just arrived! Thanks to Okoye's fighting skills and Shuri's powerful Vibranium gauntlets, the tide of the battle turned in the heroes' favor.

Shuri blasted Proxima with an energy punch from her gauntlets and Proxima went flying!

"Who IS that?" Proxima Midnight groaned.

"That," Black Panther replied proudly, "is my sister!"

ANT-MAN
HEIGHT: 6'

WEIGHT: 180 LBS

WEARS A SPECIAL HELMET THAT CAN COMMUNICATE TELEPATHICALLY WITH ANTS AND OTHER INSECTS

POSSESSES ADVANCED KNOWLEDGE OF ELECTRONICS

WASP
HEIGHT: 5'4"

WEIGHT: 110 LBS

WHEN IN HER SHRUNKEN STATE, CAN FLY AT HIGH SPEEDS USING INSECT-LIKE WINGS

"WASP STINGS" DISCHARGE POWERFUL ELECTRIC ENERGY FROM HER HANDS

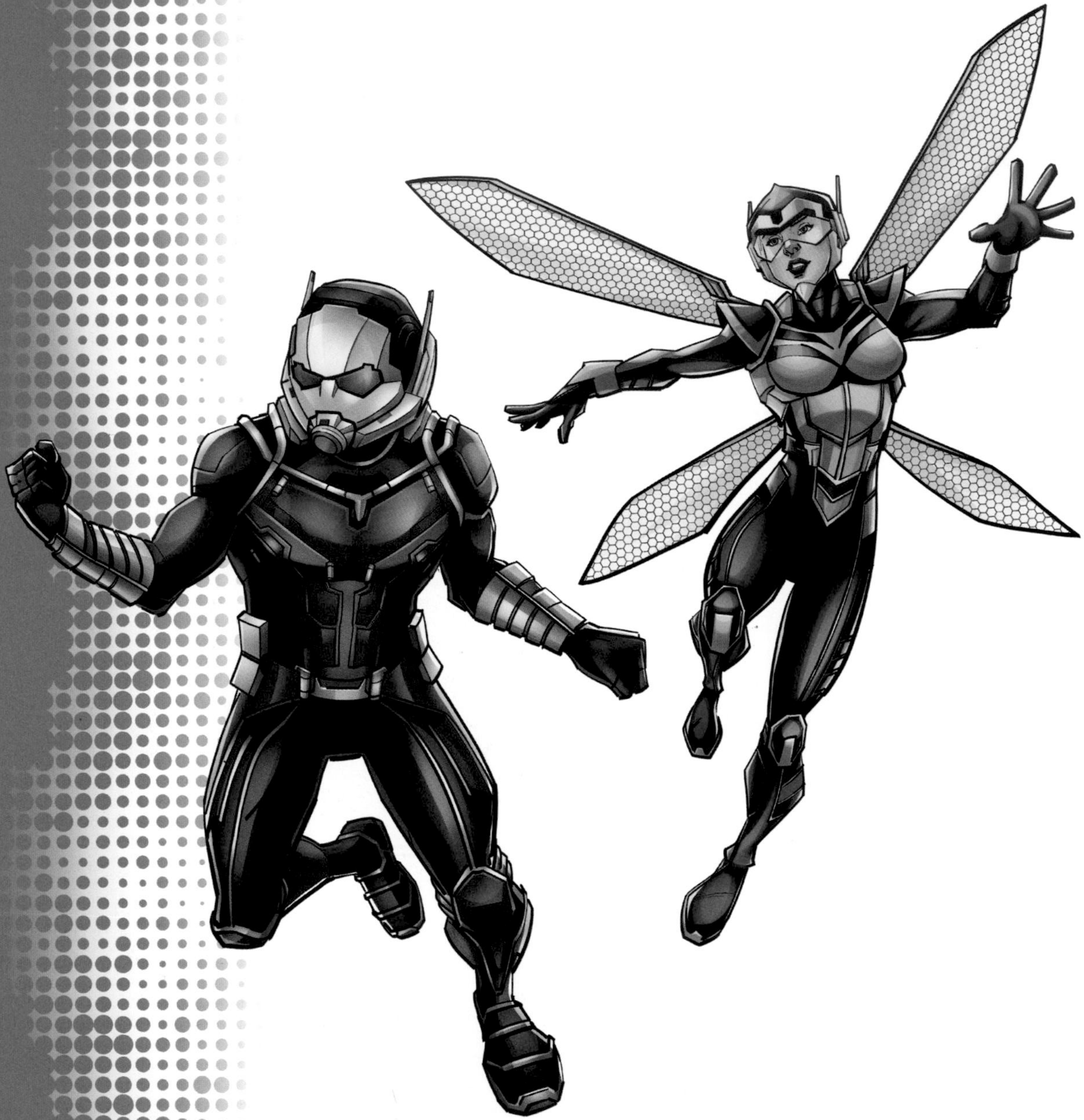

ANT-MAN & WASP

Scott Lang and Hope Van Dyne

Avengers come in all shapes and sizes. Some are big, some are small. And some are really, REALLY small—like Ant-Man and the Wasp! These two tiny Super Heroes make for one titanic team.

Hope Van Dyne was the daughter of scientist Hank Pym. Hank discovered the Pym Particle, which can shrink anything down to the size of an ant—or smaller! He used the Pym Particle to become the first Ant-Man. As he grew older, Hank shared the secret of the Pym Particle with his daughter and an electronics expert named Scott Lang.

Together, Scott and Hope became the new Ant-Man and the Wasp!

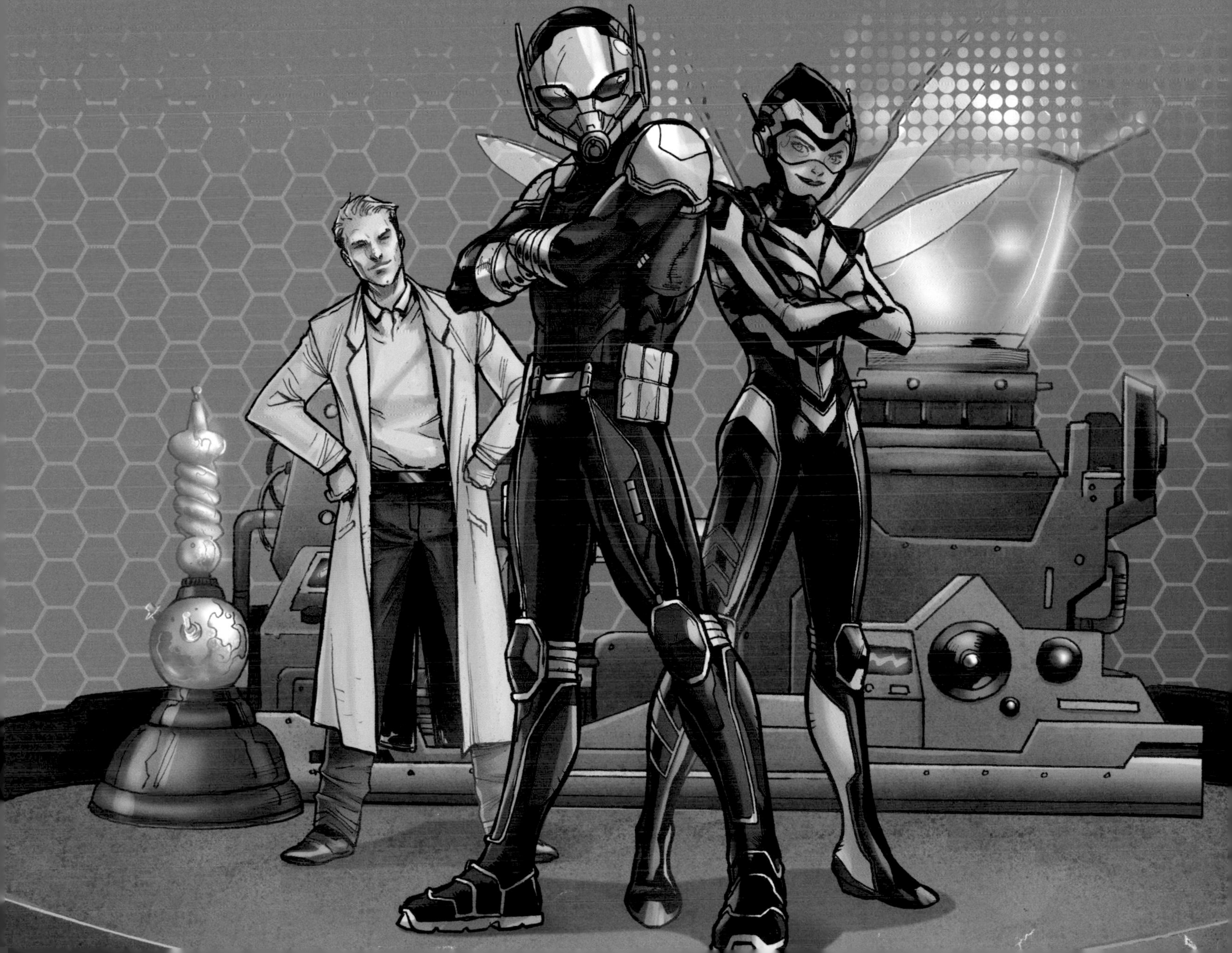

When they shrink down, Hope and Scott can punch as hard as they do when they're normal size. As if she wasn't powerful enough already, Hope created gauntlets that can produce an electric shock called the Wasp's Sting.

Being as small as an ant or a wasp can have some real advantages. But sometimes, it's not so great. Like when you're facing the sinister Scarlet Beetle!

The Scarlet Beetle had been an ordinary insect until radiation turned him into a super-smart, super-evil creature. And like most ordinary insects who had been transformed by radiation into a super-smart, super-evil creature, he wanted to rule the world!

But Ant-Man and the Wasp had other ideas. The Wasp flew overhead, zapping the Scarlet Beetle with her Wasp's Sting. On the ground, Ant-Man and his army of ants attacked. The tiny hero hurled discs at the Scarlet Beetle that caused him to shrink!

"Curse you, heroes!" the Scarlet Beetle said as he shrank to the size of a, well, smaller bug.

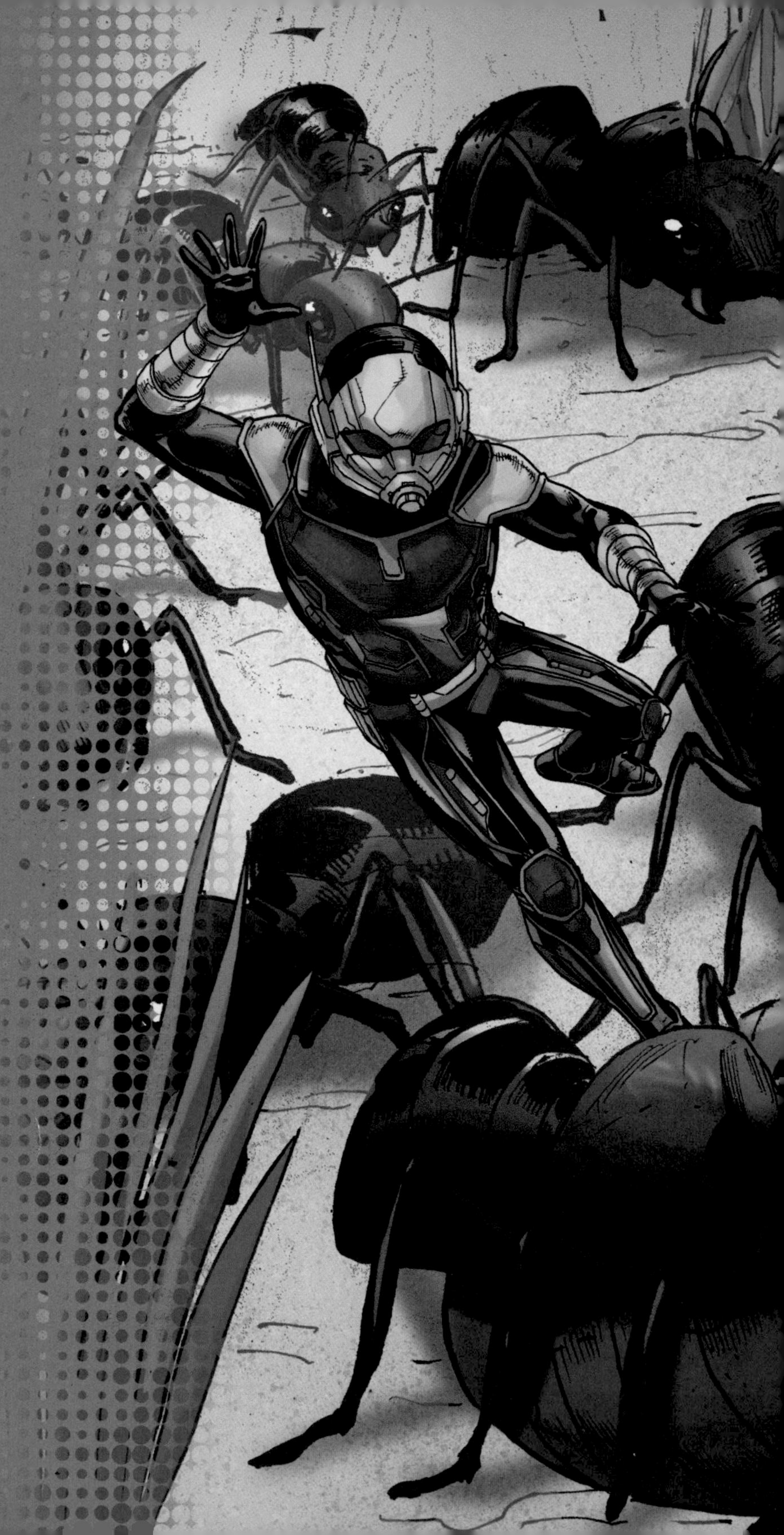

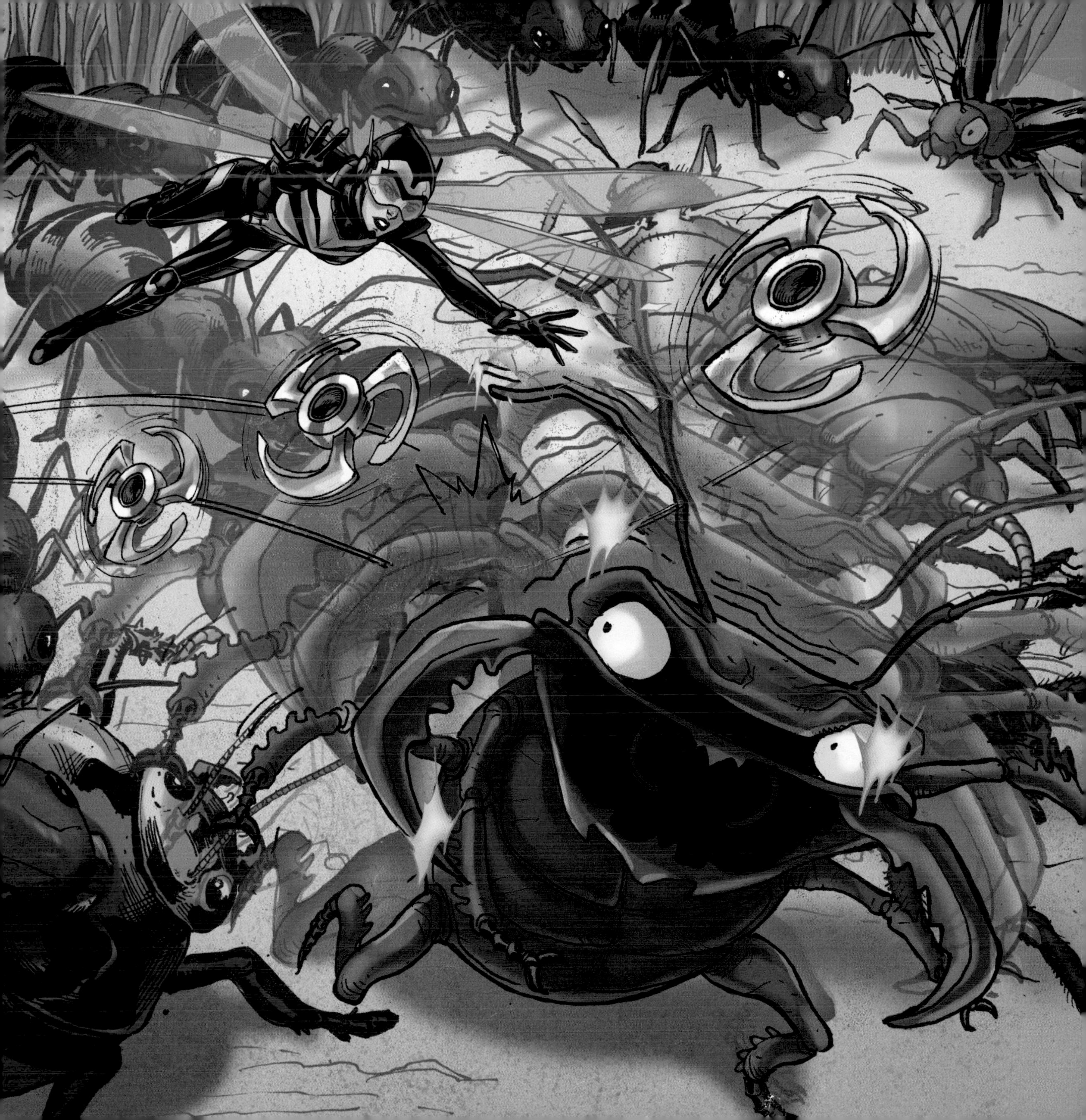

NICK FURY

Nicholas J. Fury

We already told you that Nick Fury is the leader of an incredible organization known as S.H.I.E.L.D. What you DON'T know is that Nick Fury is the smartest, most dangerous spy on Earth!

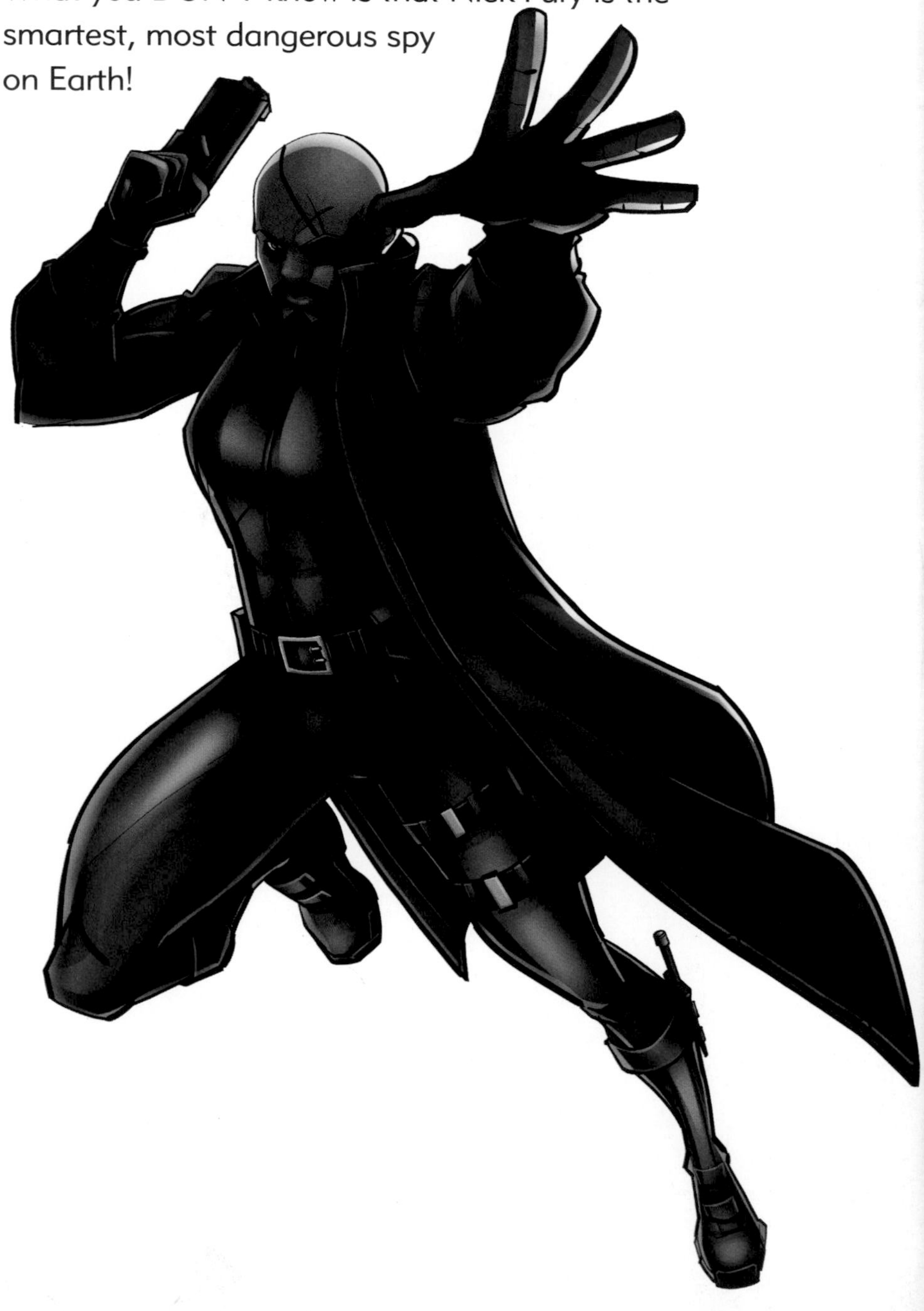

HEIGHT: 6'3"

WEIGHT: 210 LBS

FORMER U.S. ARMY SERGEANT AND TECH-SAVVY SUPER-SPY

MASTER IN THE ARTS OF ESPIONAGE, COVERT ACTIONS, MARKSMANSHIP, AND MILITARY STRATEGY

EXPERT HAND-TO-HAND COMBATANT WITH ADVANCED RANKING IN MULTIPLE MARTIAL-ARTS DISCIPLINES

EMPLOYS THE FULL RANGE OF S.H.I.E.L.D.'S INTELLIGENCE-GATHERING CAPABILITIES AS WELL AS ITS MOST TECHNOLOGICALLY ADVANCED GADGETRY AND EQUIPMENT

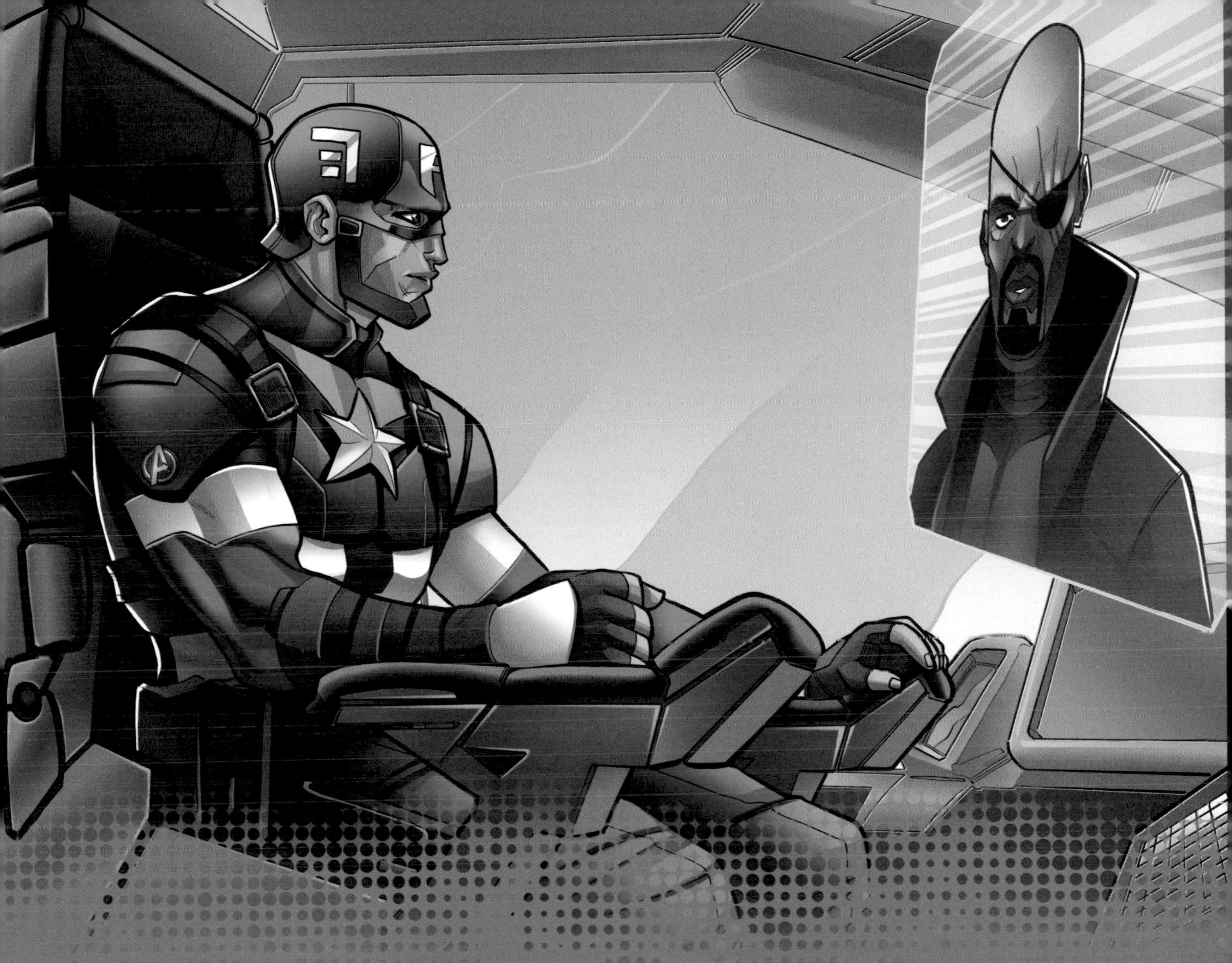

He spends most of his time aboard the S.H.I.E.L.D. helicarrier, a flying fortress in the sky. From there, he monitors everything that happens on Earth—sometimes even in space! He's always on the lookout for danger.

Nick has worked with the Avengers for years. He's always ready to help Captain America and the rest of Earth's mightiest heroes defend the planet.

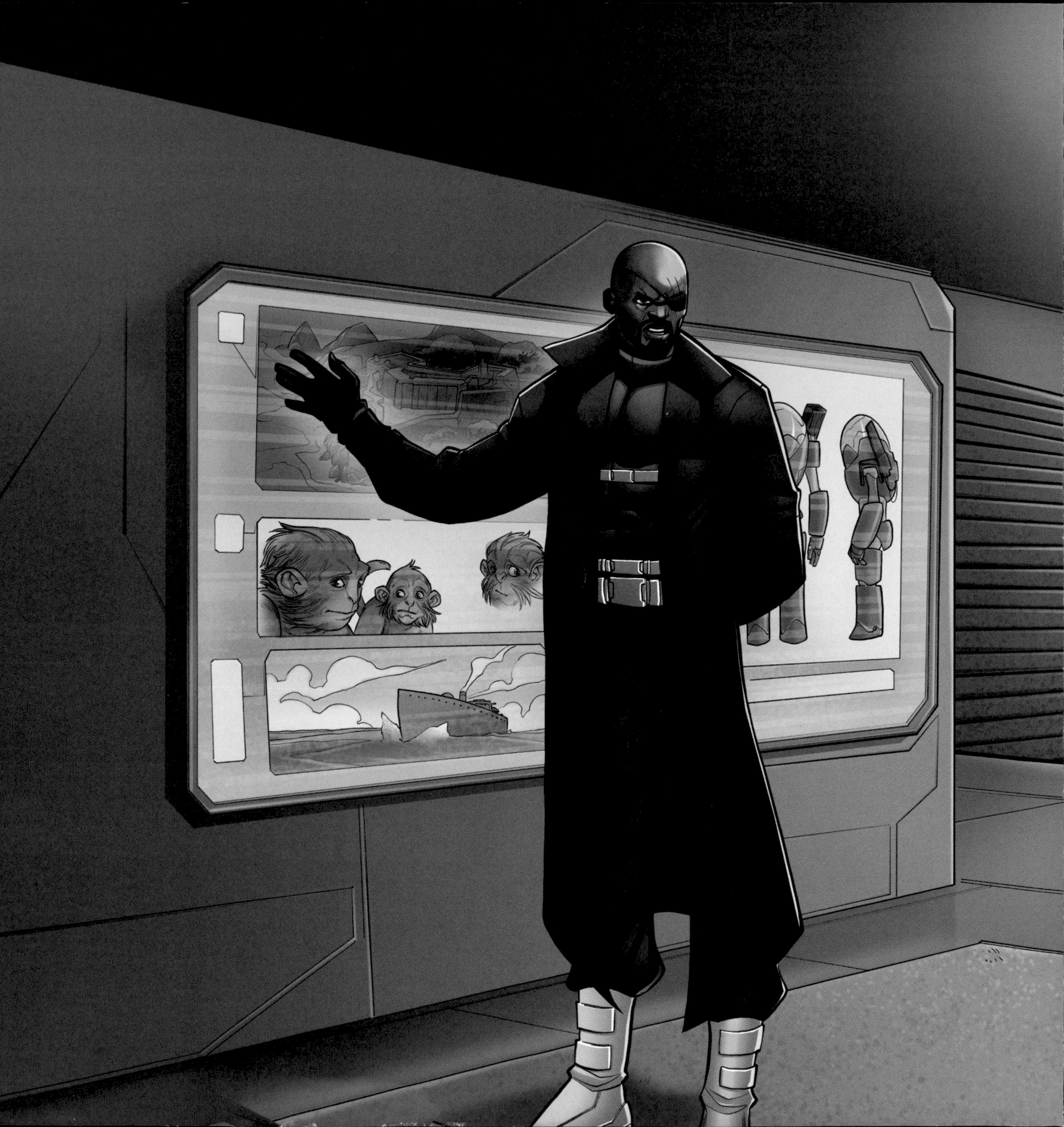

It just so happened that THIS was one of those times.

"I've got a mission for you, Cap," Nick Fury said.

Captain America had just returned to Avengers Tower and was sure that he was alone. But when he turned around, Nick Fury was suddenly standing there.

"I'd love to know how you do that," Captain America said.

"It's called being a spy," Nick said. "Take a look at the monitor. Someone's stolen a set of S.H.I.E.L.D. battlesuits."

"M.O.D.O.C.?" Captain America asked.

Nick nodded. "We need you to get them back."

"What about the monkeys?"

"Don't ask," Nick said.

Captain America's mission was just beginning.

Pssst! If you want to find out about the monkeys, turn to page 139!

HEIGHT: 6'1"

WEIGHT: 180 LBS

UNPARALLELED KNOWLEDGE OF ARCANE SPELLS AND ENCHANTMENTS, INCLUDING TELEPORTATION, ASTRAL PROJECTION, AND DIMENSIONAL MANIPULATION

VAST COLLECTION OF LEGENDARY ARTIFACTS, INCLUDING THE ALL-SEEING EYE OF AGAMOTTO, THE FLIGHT-ENABLING CLOAK OF LEVITATION, AND THE FABLED BOOK OF THE VISHANTI

EARTH'S PREEMINENT DEFENDER AGAINST THE DARKNESS THAT LURKS BEYOND

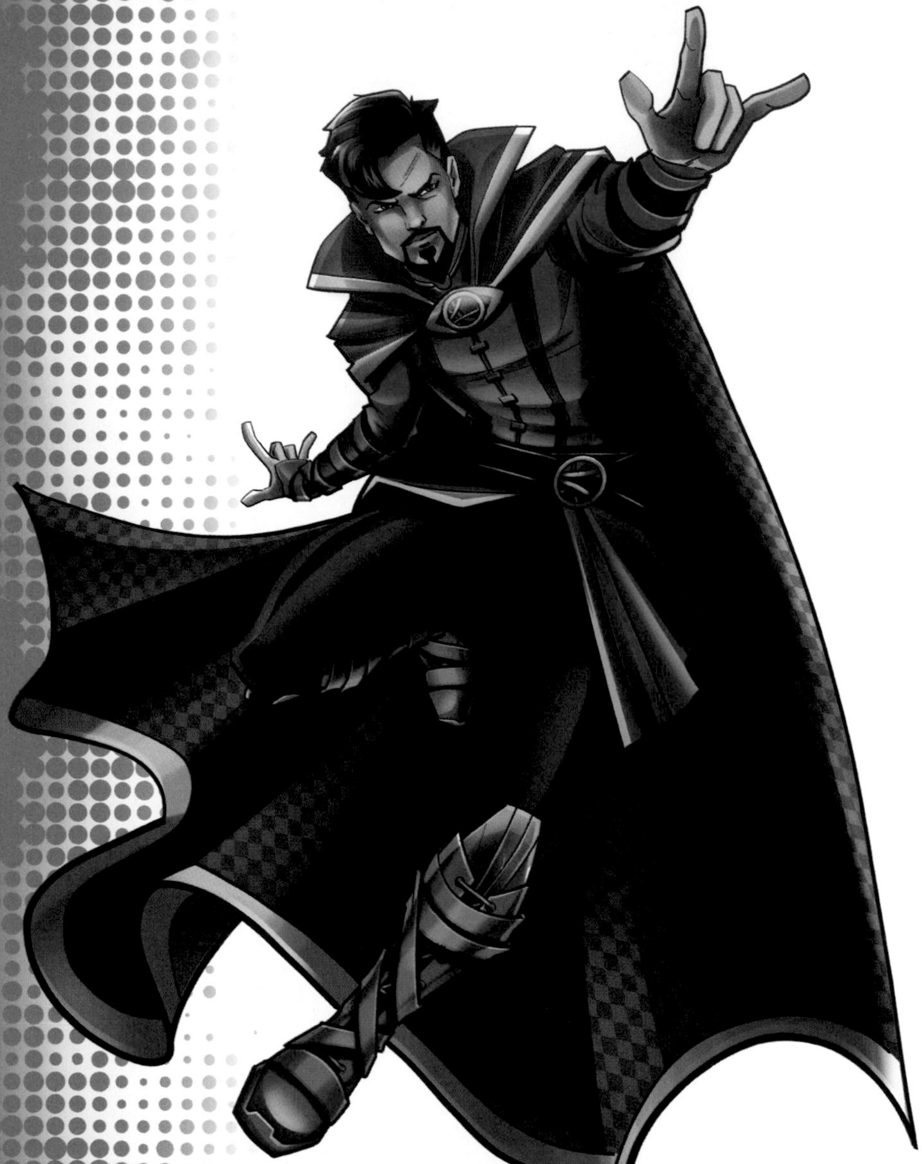

DOCTOR STRANGE

Dr. Stephen Strange

Is there a doctor in the house—or in this book? Actually, there are several! But the one we're talking about now is Doctor Stephen Strange, also known as Doctor Strange! He's Earth's Sorcerer Supreme, which means he defends Earth against magical threats. Pretty cool, right?

Stephen Strange was a brilliant surgeon, but his hands were injured in a car accident. He could no longer operate! Stephen traveled across the world to seek the aid of the Ancient One, who he had heard could cure him.

But the Ancient One did not cure the surgeon. Instead, the Ancient One trained Stephen in the mystic arts! A quick learner, Stephen became a master of magic, and swore to defend the Earth from all kinds of mystical threats.

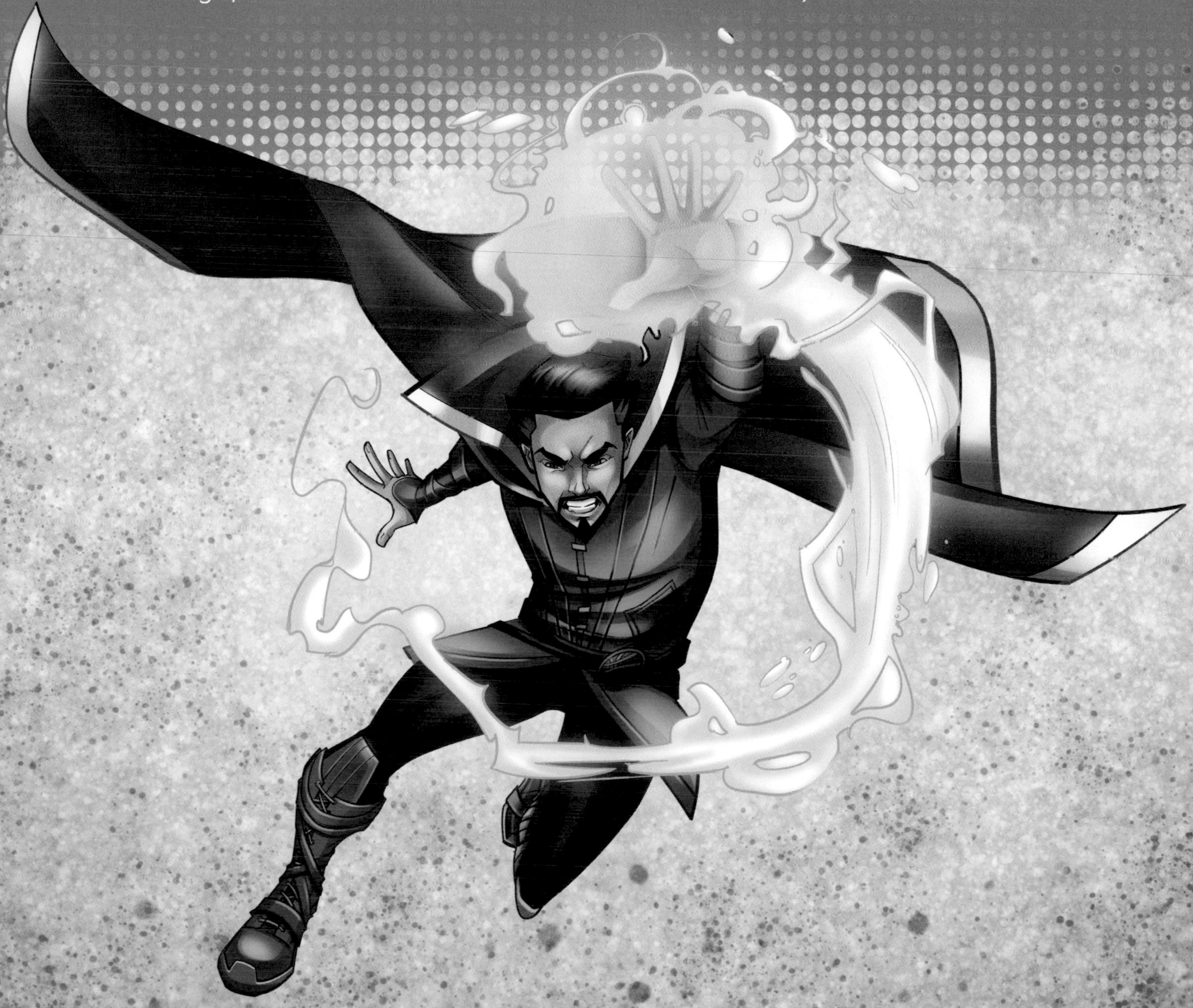

Doctor Strange levitated in the study of his Sanctum Sanctorum, located in New York City's Greenwich Village. The amulet around his neck, the Eye of Agamotto, crackled with mystical blue energy.

"By the Hosts of Hoggoth," Doctor Strange said, "I sense someone approaching!"

Suddenly the door to the study burst open, and Spider-Man leaped into the room.

"Doctor Strange!" Spider-Man said. "I'm sorry to interrupt, but I've been having trouble—"

"Sleeping!" Doctor Strange said. He had felt Peter's troubles.

"Yes!" Spidey said. "How did you know?"

"The Eye of Agamotto has shown me that you've been experiencing strange dreams," Strange told Peter. "And now it will show those to me."

"Can you help?"

"Of course," Doctor Strange said. "Do you want to help me stop Shuma-Gorath from invading our dimension as a thank-you?"

"Why not?" Spider-Man said with a smile. "Sounds like fun!"

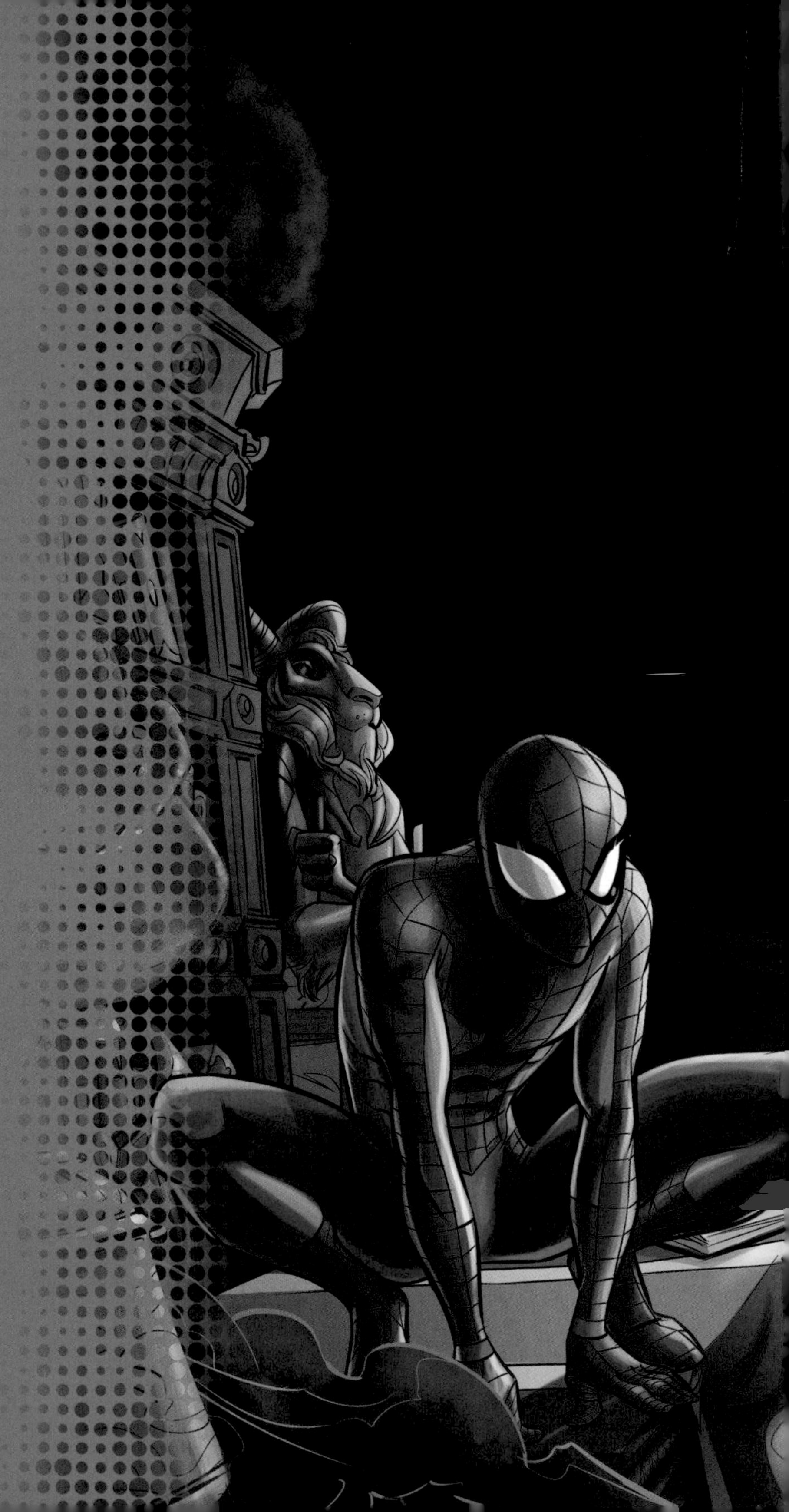

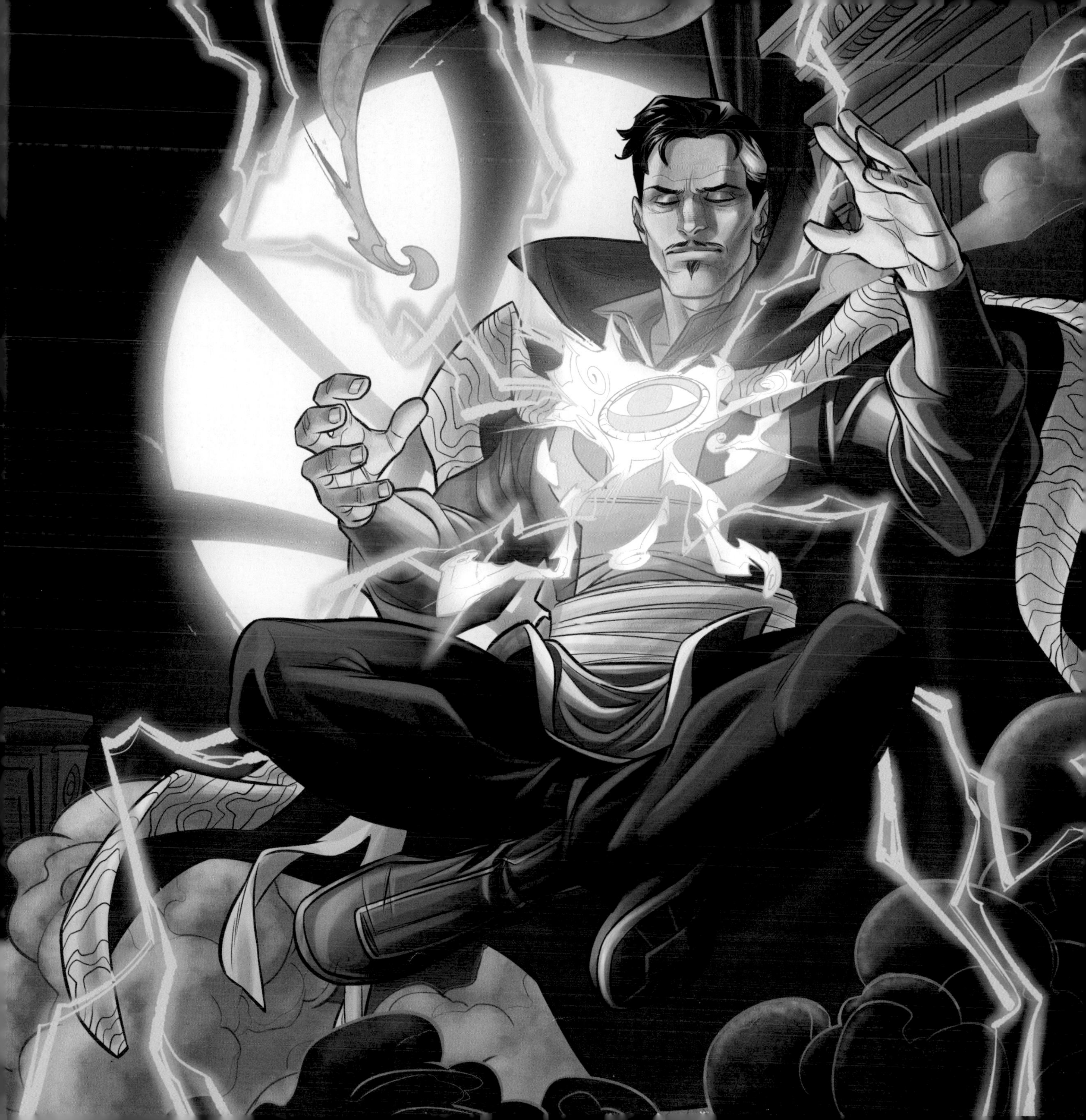

MS. MARVEL

Kamala Khan

You already met Captain Marvel, but did you know there's a Ms. Marvel? Her name is really Kamala Khan, and she's a high school student living in New Jersey. As it turns out, she's also an Inhuman!

HEIGHT: 5'4" (VARIABLE)

WEIGHT: 125 (VARIABLE)

TRANSFORMED WHEN THE INHUMANS RELEASED THE TERRIGEN MIST

MORPHOGENIC ABILITIES, INCLUDING SHAPE-SHIFTING AND THE ABILITY TO EXTEND HER LIMBS

HEALING FACTOR

SUPERHUMAN SPEED

SUPERHUMAN STRENGTH

BIOLUMINESCENCE

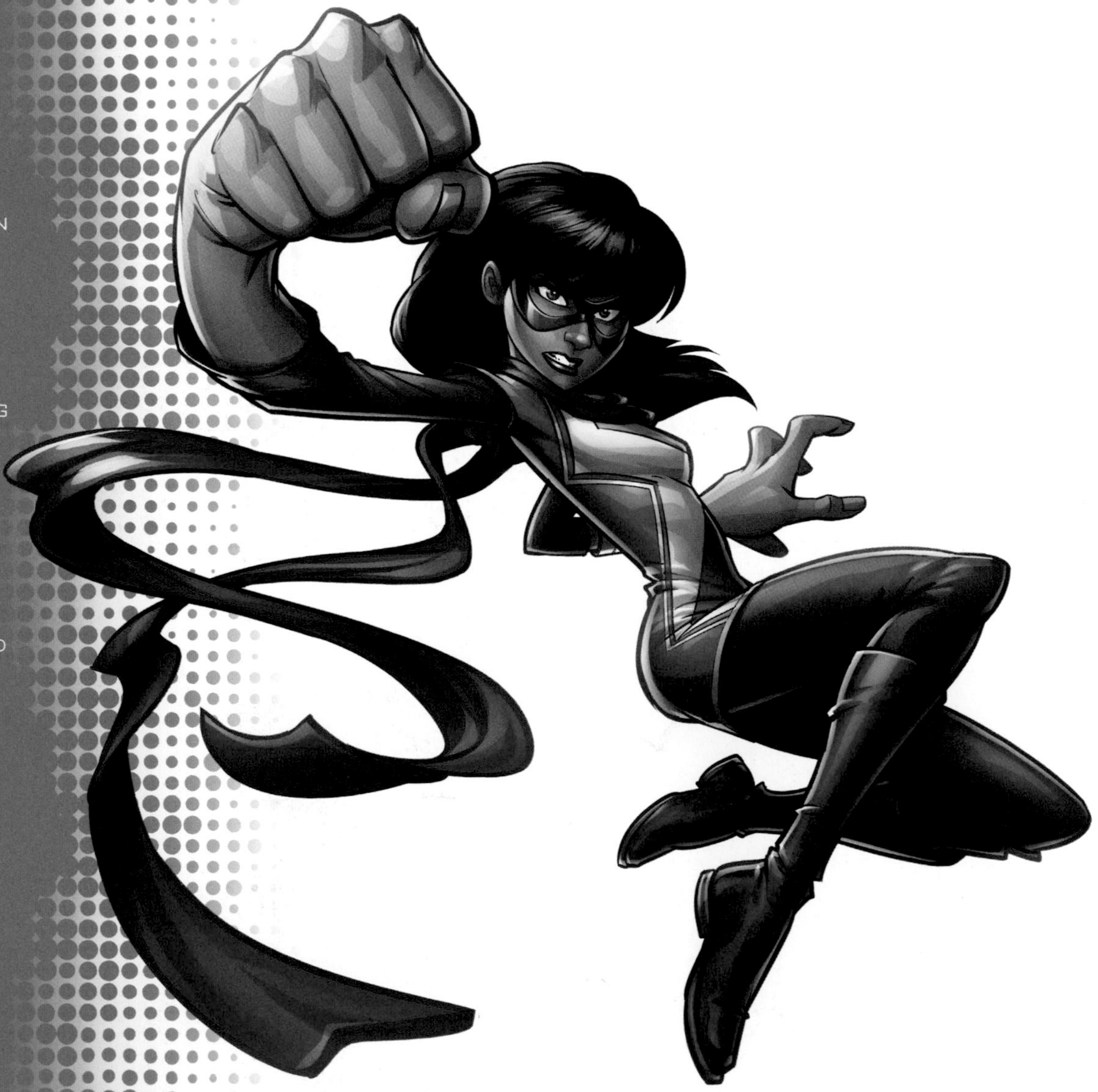

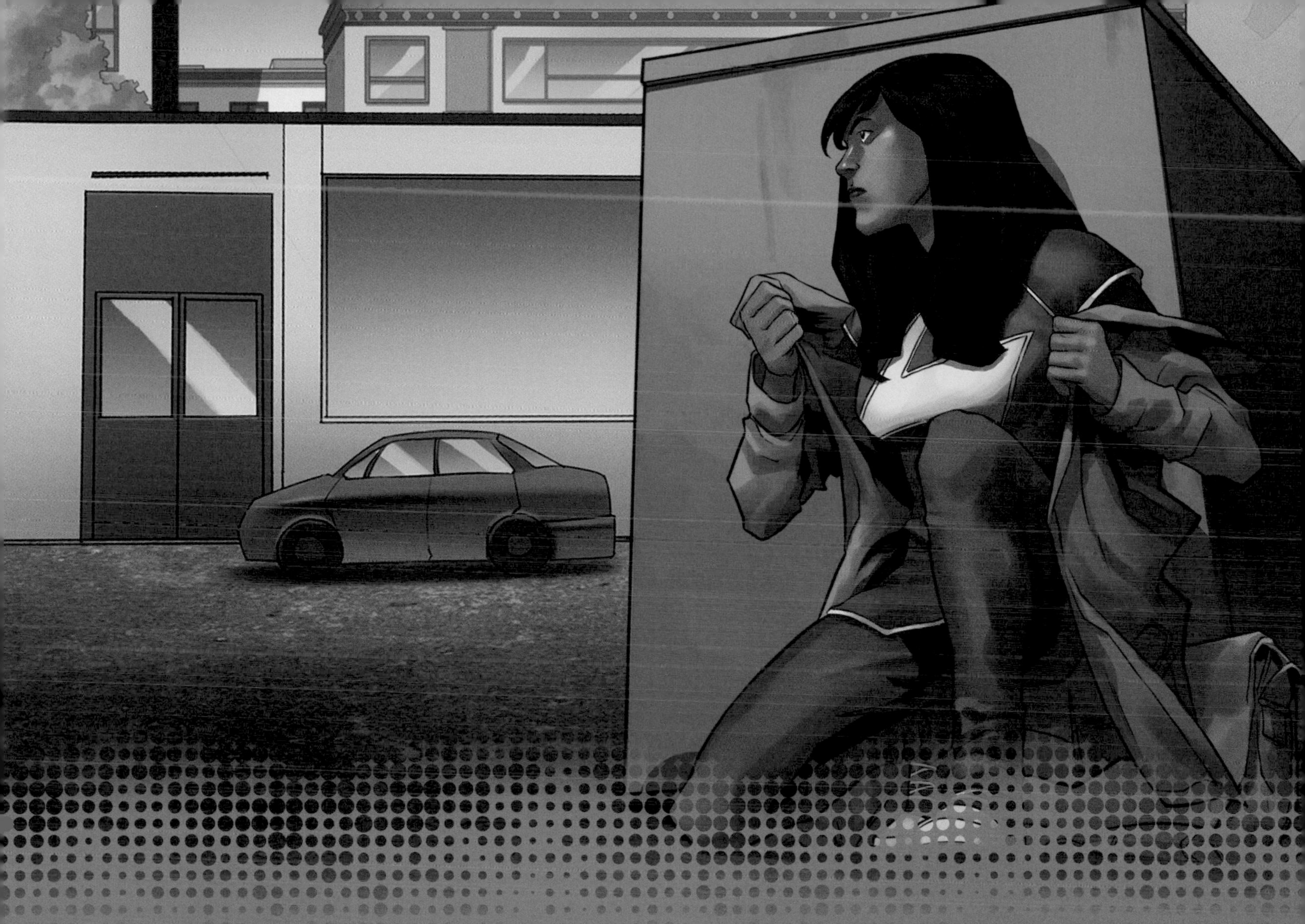

One day, Kamala was exposed to the strange Terrigen Mist, which gave her astounding super-powers. What could she do? Good question! Kamala gained the ability to morph her body—she could stretch her limbs and even shrink and grow at will: EMBIGGEN!

Taking inspiration from Captain Marvel, her favorite hero of all time, Kamala made a costume for herself. She also took the name Ms. Marvel to honor her hero. She was so excited to fight crime just like her favorite Super Hero!

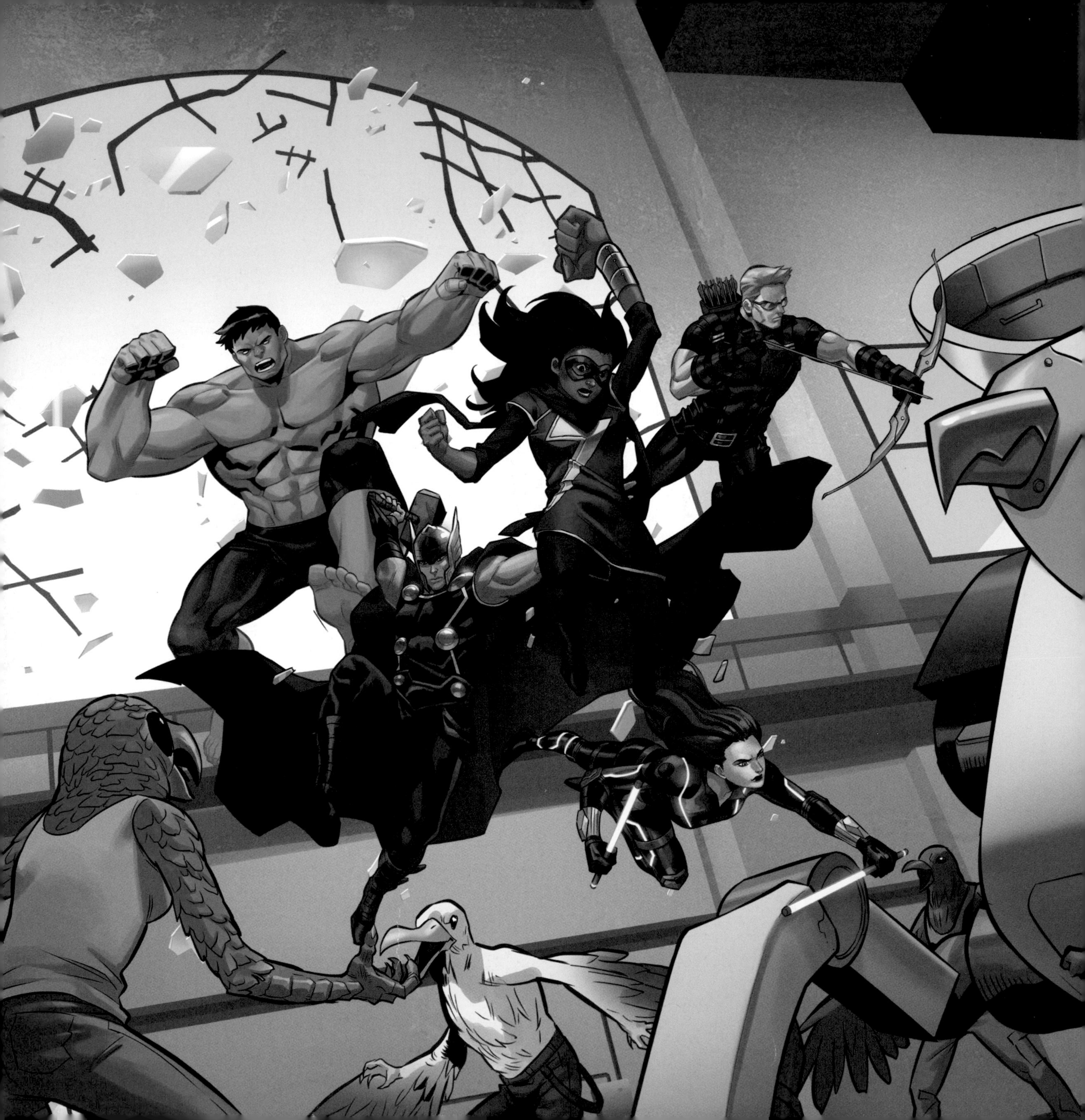

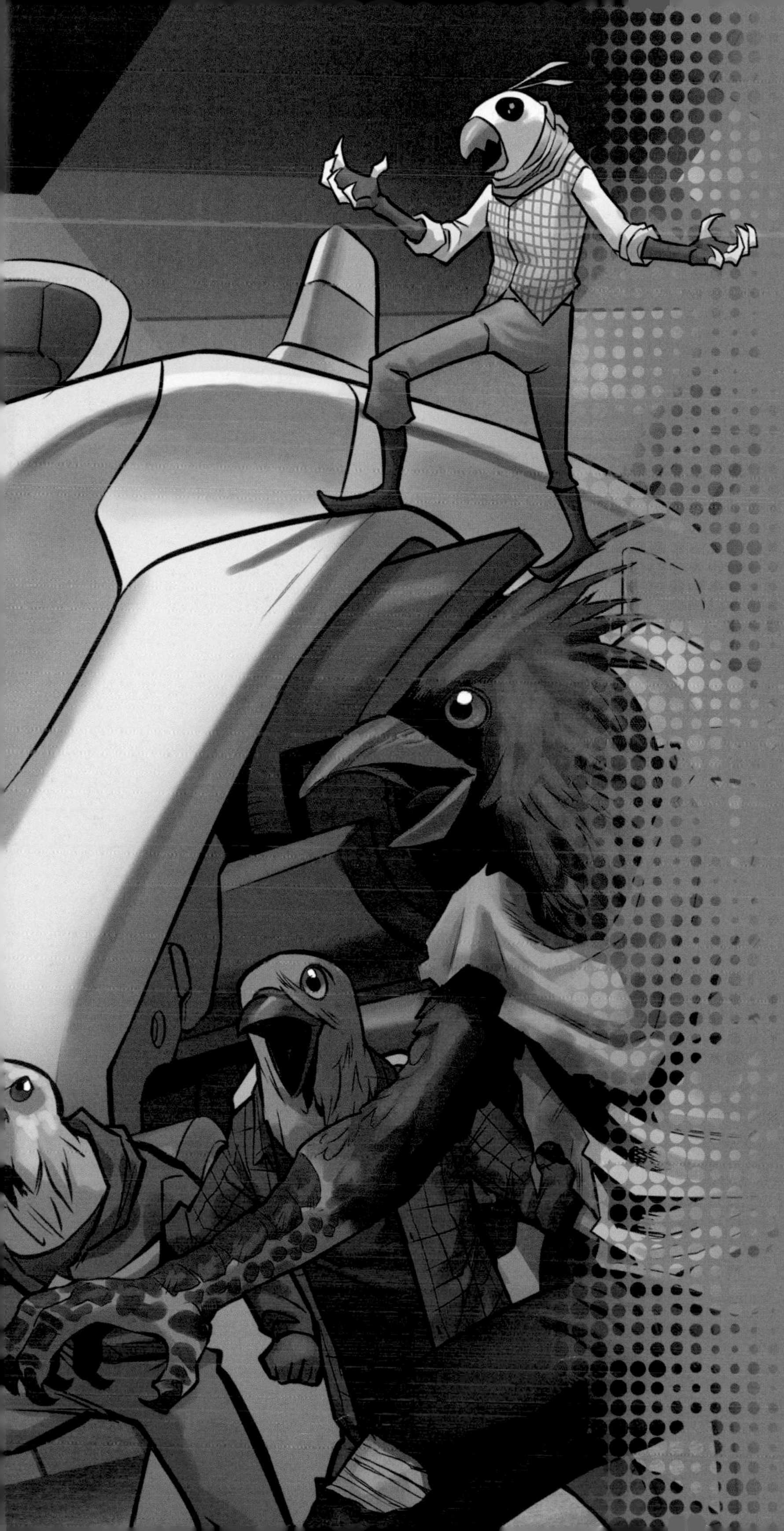

Kamala was a little like Spider-Man. She also wanted to keep her neighborhood safe. So, one day she might help the Avengers face world-threatening villains, and the next she might stop a weird bird guy from doing weird bird things in her neighborhood.

"Hold it right there, weird bird guy!" Ms. Marvel said.

The Avengers had just traced the evil Inventor (also known as "weird bird guy") to his secret lair. The Inventor was using his tech to transform stolen birds into bird creatures just like him!

"That's MISTER Weird Bird Guy to you!" the Inventor said as he commanded his bird minions to attack the Avengers.

Hulk, Thor, Hawkeye, and Black Widow were keeping the bird minions busy while Ms. Marvel went after the Inventor. She enlarged her fists and used them to smash the Inventor's machinery.

Suddenly the bird creatures transformed back into regular birds!

"This . . . This isn't going according to plan," the Inventor said as he tried to run away.

"Maybe not YOUR plan!" Ms. Marvel said, snatching the villain with a huge hand.

VILLAINS

TERRORIST ORGANIZATION BOASTING SOME OF THE MOST EVIL VILLAINS IN HISTORY AMONG ITS RANKS

IN EXISTENCE SINCE WORLD WAR II

FOUNDED BY WOLFGANG VON STRUCKER

OPPOSING FORCE TO S.H.I.E.L.D.

SOMETIMES ALLIES WITH A.I.M. (ADVANCED IDEA MECHANICS)

CURRENT MEMBERS INCLUDE BARON STRUCKER, RED SKULL, MADAME HYDRA, AND ARNIM ZOLA

HYDRA

Terrorist Organization

"Hail Hydra!" Red Skull cried. Along with Arnim Zola (the guy whose stomach looks like a TV) and Baron Zemo (the guy whose stomach DOESN'T look like a TV), Red Skull led the forces of Hydra against the Avengers.

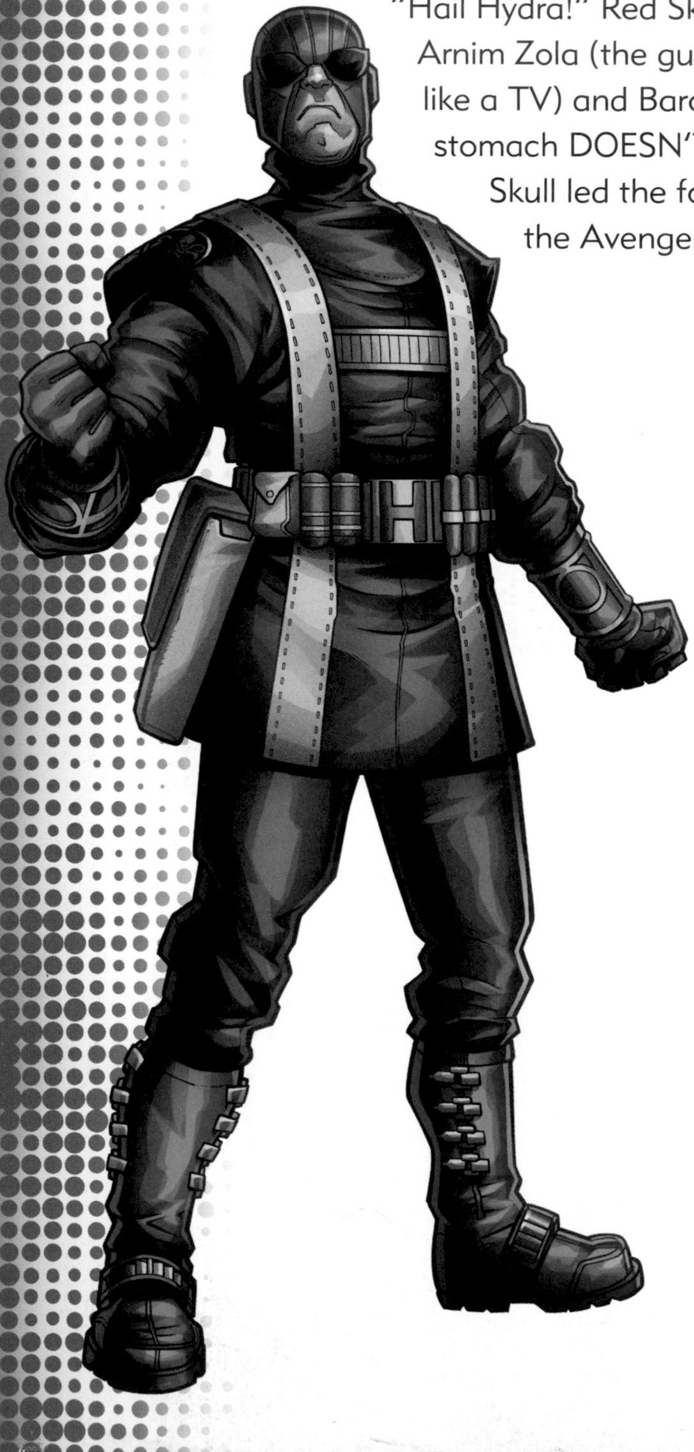

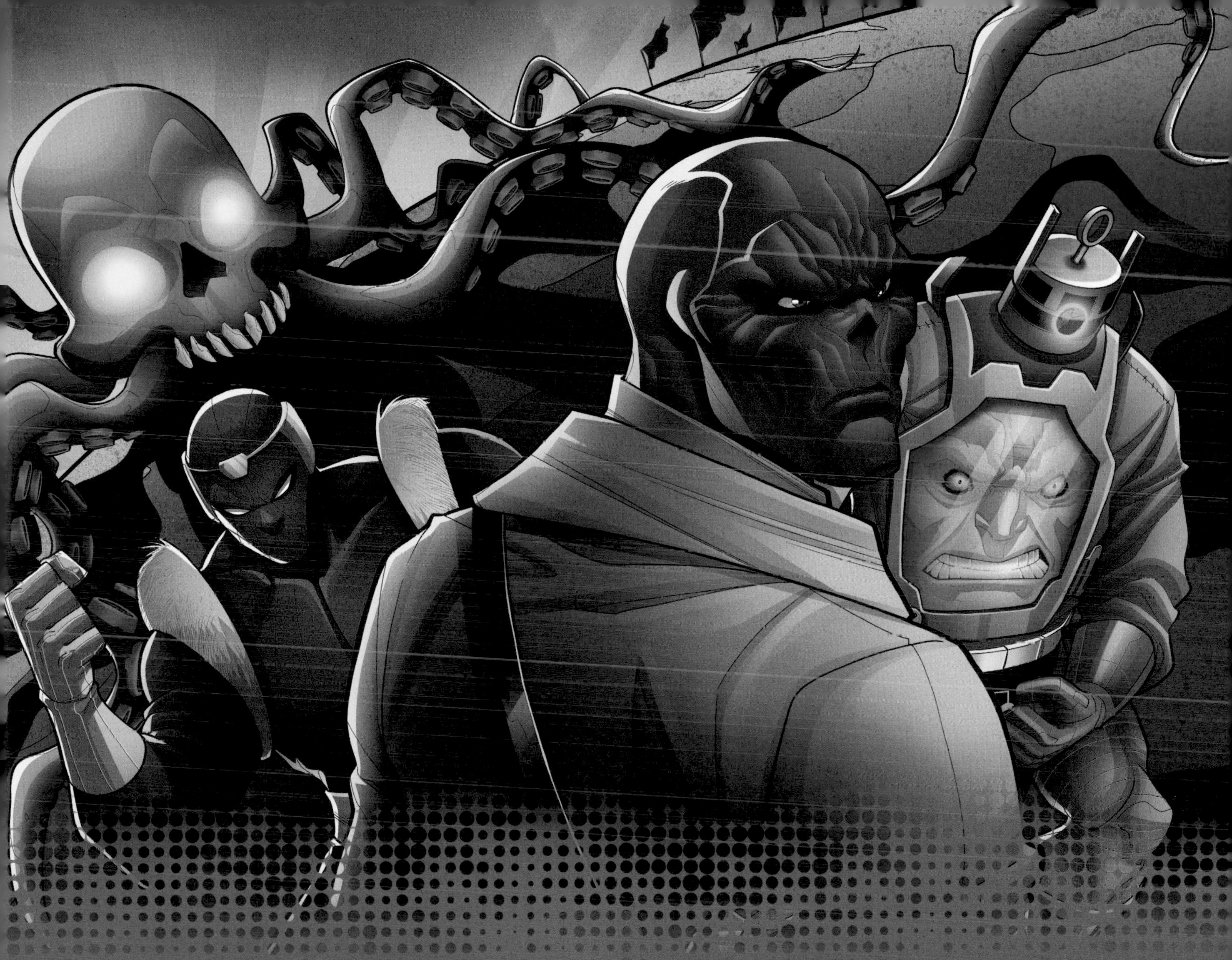

Hydra's latest plan involved the creation of an enormous mutant octopus with a skull head, the Octo-Skull! The villains were going to use it to destroy the Avengers. As far as plans went, it wasn't the worst, but it also wasn't the best. That was because Hulk could smash Octo-Skulls in his sleep.

Better luck next time, Hydra!

HEIGHT: VARIABLE

WEIGHT: VARIABLE

CAPABLE OF INFILTRATING VIRTUALLY ANY COMPUTER SYSTEM OR NETWORK AND INHABITING MECHANICAL BODIES

EVEN A TRACE OF HIS CODE CAN LEAD TO A FULL RESTORATION OF HIS CONSCIOUSNESS

COMPUTATIONAL PROWESS IS NEARLY UNMATCHED

EXHIBITS EXTREME SUPERHUMAN STRENGTH, DURABILITY, AND SPEED IN ROBOT FORM

MOST PHYSICAL MODELS POSSESS THE ABILITY TO FLY AND PROJECT INTENSE BLASTS OF ENERGY

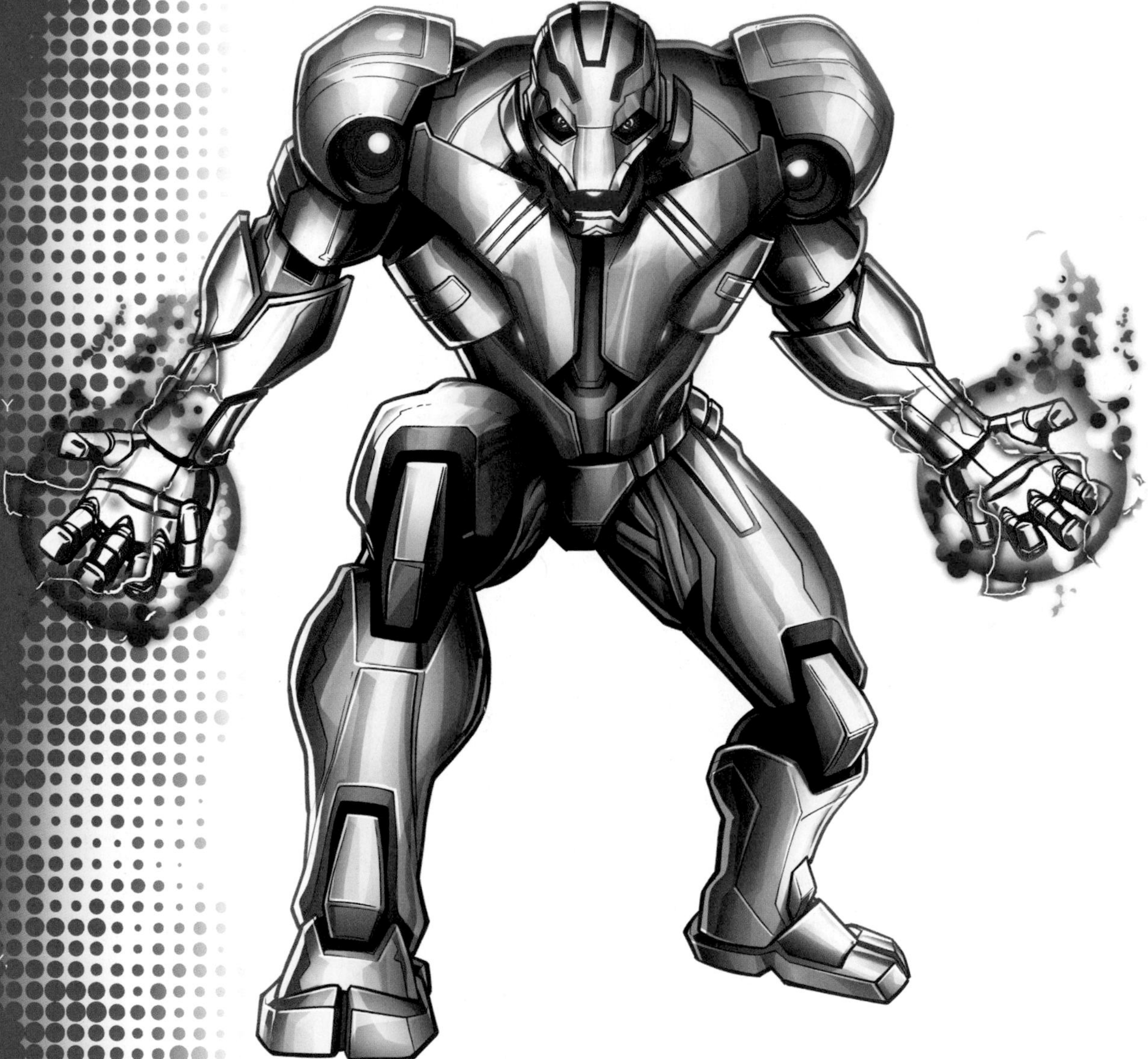

ULTRON

Evil Sentient Robot

Ultron was an artificial intelligence created by Hank Pym. He was designed to help people and save the planet. But Ultron decided that the biggest threat to the planet WAS people, so the only way to save the world was to destroy them!

"It's bad enough you stopped me from taking over that space lab," Ultron said as he swatted at Captain America. "And now you're trying to stop me from ridding the Earth of Super Heroes?"

"Keep Ultron busy while we feed him a computer virus!" Captain Marvel shouted.

"What do you think I've been doing?" Captain America said.

A second later, Ultron was shut down again.

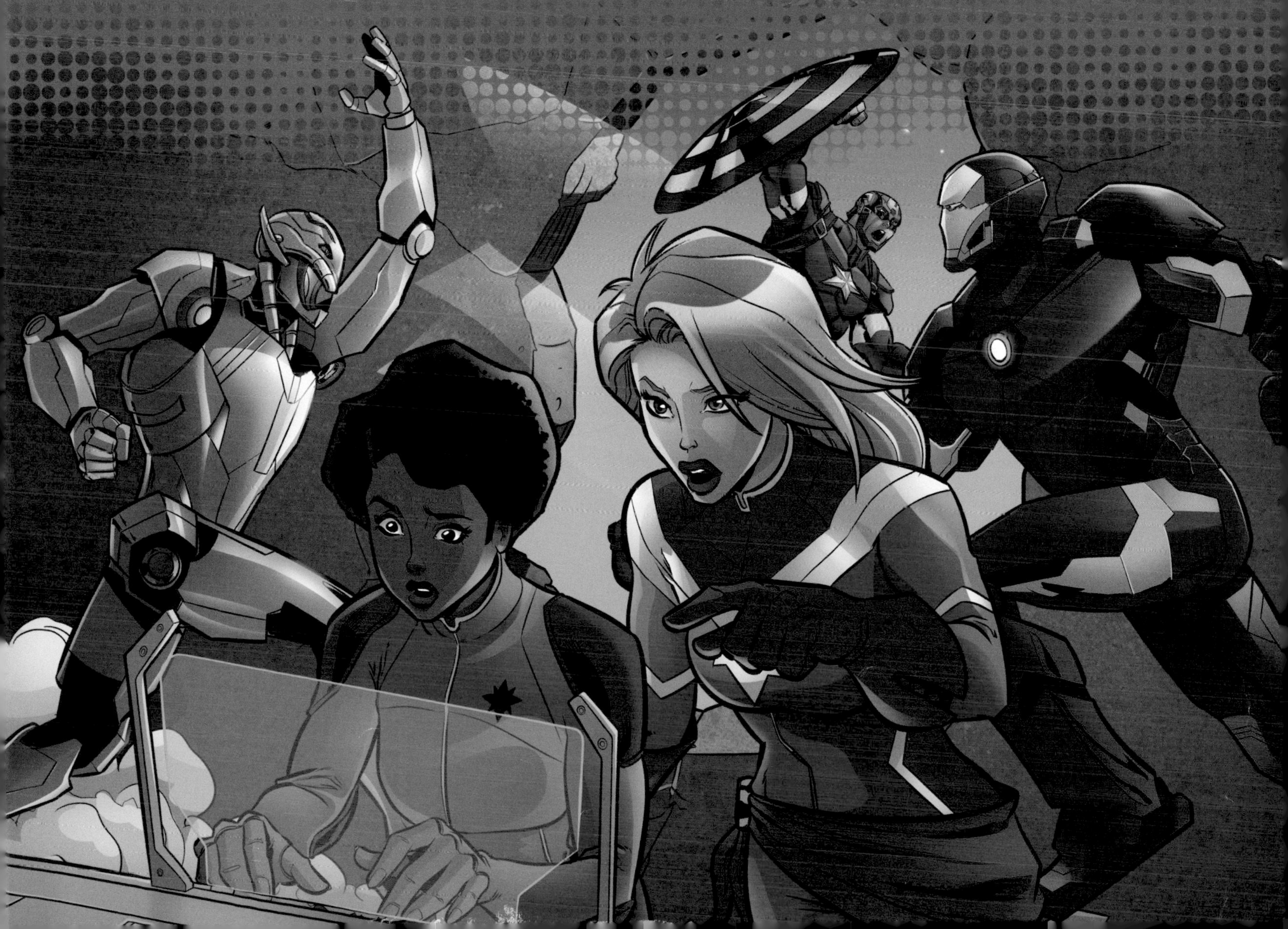

LOKI

God of Mischief

Sometimes it's hard to get along with your sibling. But what would you do if your sibling was the Asgardian Loki, an ace troublemaker if ever there was one? Well, if you're Thor, you constantly try to stop your brother from doing whatever terrible thing it is he's trying to do.

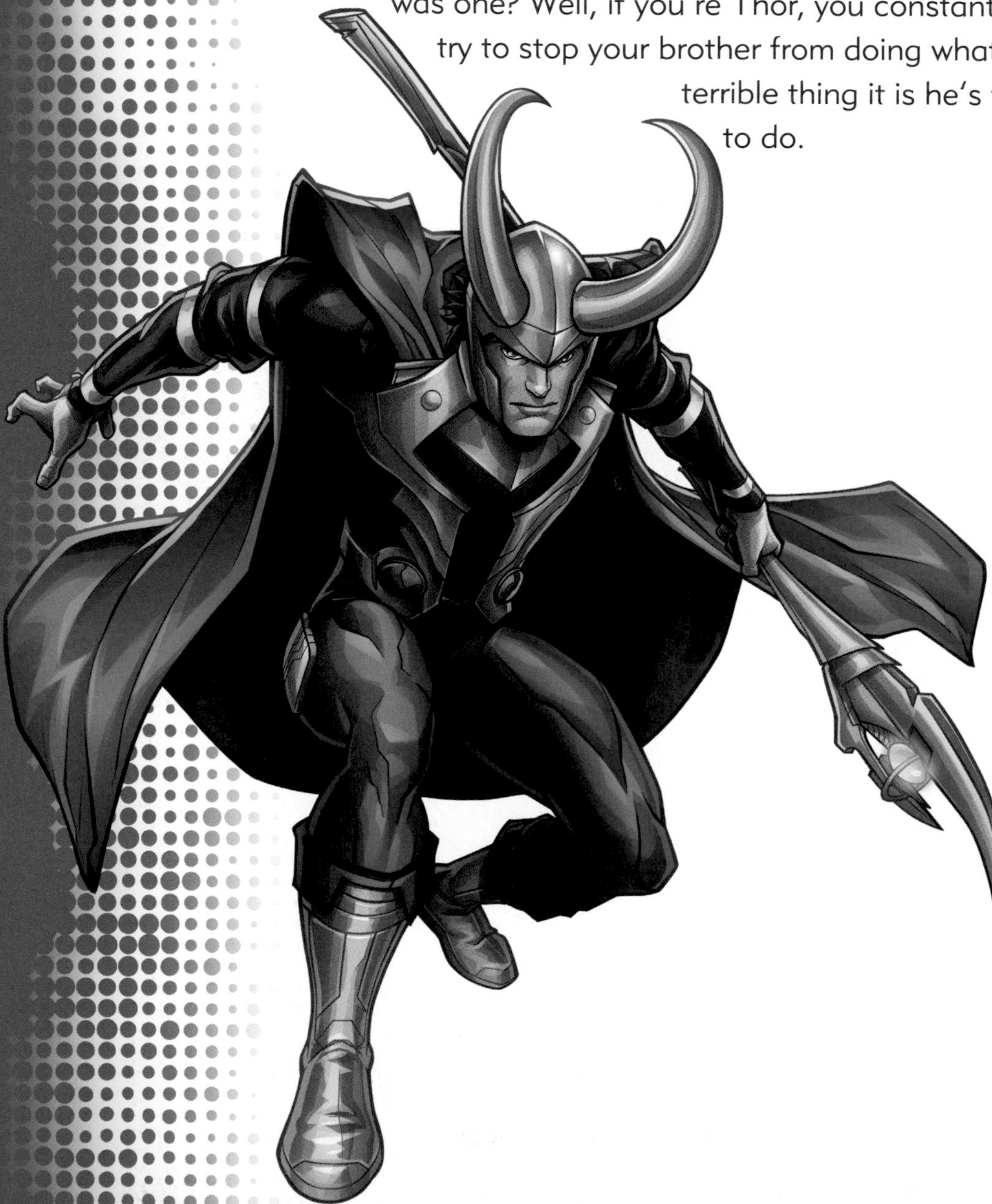

HEIGHT: 6'4"

WEIGHT: 525 LBS

RAISED IN ASGARD AS A FOSTER BROTHER TO THOR

MISCHIEVOUS TRICKSTER

MEMBER OF THE VIRTUALLY IMMORTAL JOTUN RACE

SUPERHUMAN STRENGTH, SPEED, ENDURANCE, AND RESISTANCE TO INJURY

MASTER OF REALITY MANIPULATION, INCLUDING SHAPE-SHIFTING, MIND CONTROL, AND ILLUSION-CASTING

WIELDS A MYSTICAL SCEPTER CAPABLE OF ENHANCING HIS POWERS

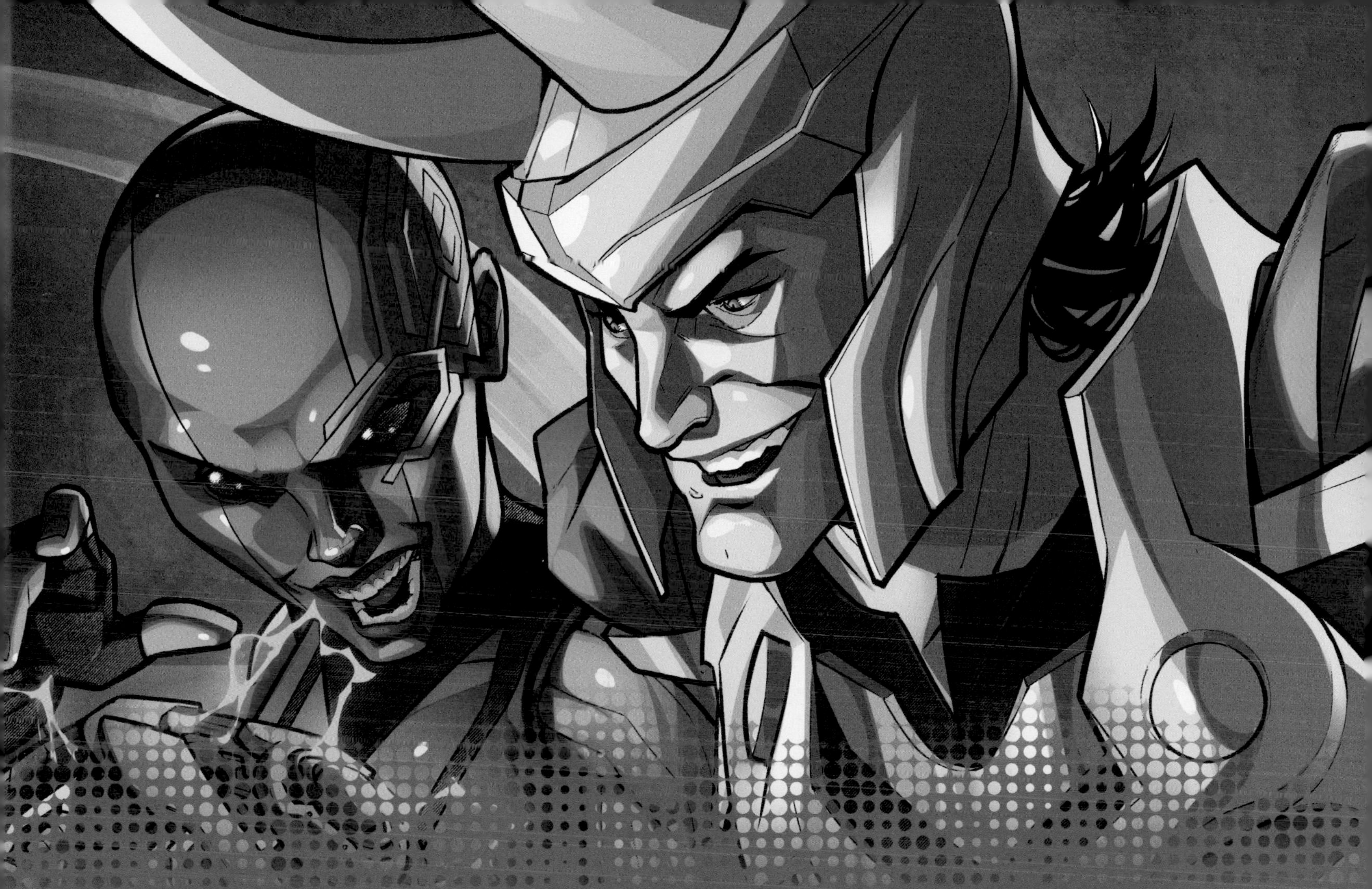

"Thor? And the Guardians of the Galaxy? What are you doing here?" Loki demanded.

"I see you and Nebula have been busy, brother," Thor said. "Joining forces to attack us."

"Do you think so little of me, Thor?" Loki said. "I wasn't going to attack you. Nebula was!"

With a wicked smile, Nebula raised her weapon. But before she could fire, Thor hurled his enchanted hammer, shattering her weapon.

"Got any other brilliant ideas?" Rocket asked.

"No," Loki said, frowning. "Just the one."

HEIGHT: 12'

WEIGHT: 750 LBS

ORIGINALLY A MAN NAMED GEORGE TARLETON, A SKILLED TECHNICIAN

SUBJECTED TO EXPERIMENTS THAT RESULTED IN SUPERHUMAN INTELLIGENCE AND PSIONIC POWERS

REFERS TO HIMSELF AS SCIENTIST SUPREME

HIS LARGE CRANIUM IS IN A HOVERCHAIR CALLED THE DOOMSDAY CHAIR, WHICH MAGNIFIES HIS PSIONIC ABILITIES

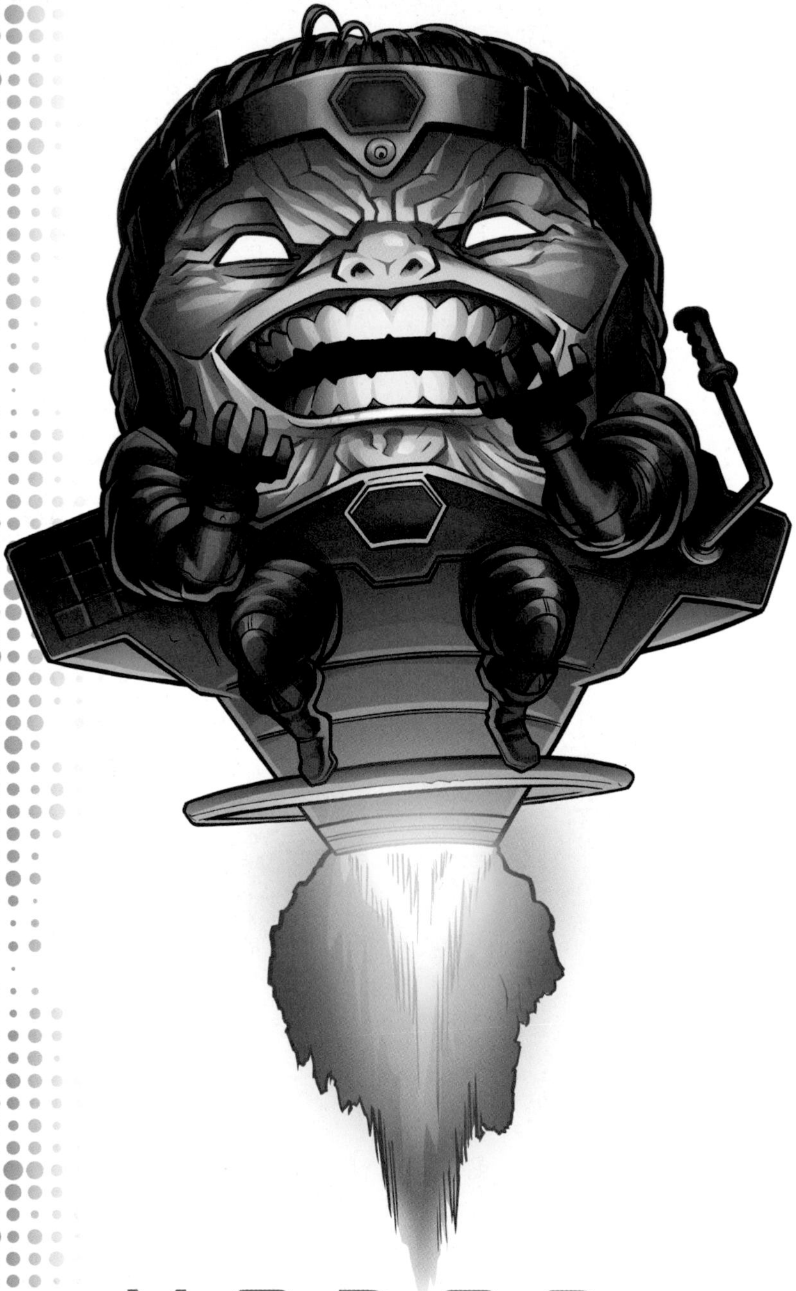

M.O.D.O.C.

Scientist Supreme

M.O.D.O.C. is superhumanly intelligent as a result of an evil genetic experiment. He also has a really, really—and we mean REALLY—big head.

"My army of mind-controlled monkeys wearing these stolen S.H.I.E.L.D. battlesuits will destroy you!" M.O.D.O.C. said.

"That . . . sounds ridiculous," Captain America said.

"How dare you insult me and my plan!" M.O.D.O.C. replied. "Attack, my monkeys! Atta—"

Before M.O.D.O.C. could finish speaking, Cap threw his shield and smacked the big-brained bad guy right in his, well, big brain, knocking him out.

The monkeys were no longer under M.O.D.O.C.'s control.

"Now what am I going to do with all these monkeys?" Cap wondered.

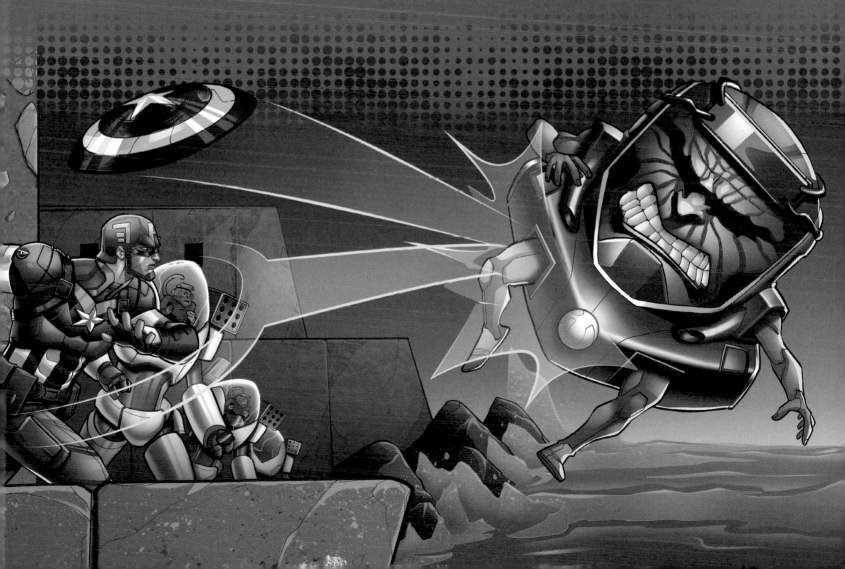

THANOS

Mad Titan

Thanos is the most powerful villain of them all. He has been searching the galaxy for the Infinity Stones. Each of the six Stones has a special property. If Thanos gets them all, he will become an unstoppable force of evil!

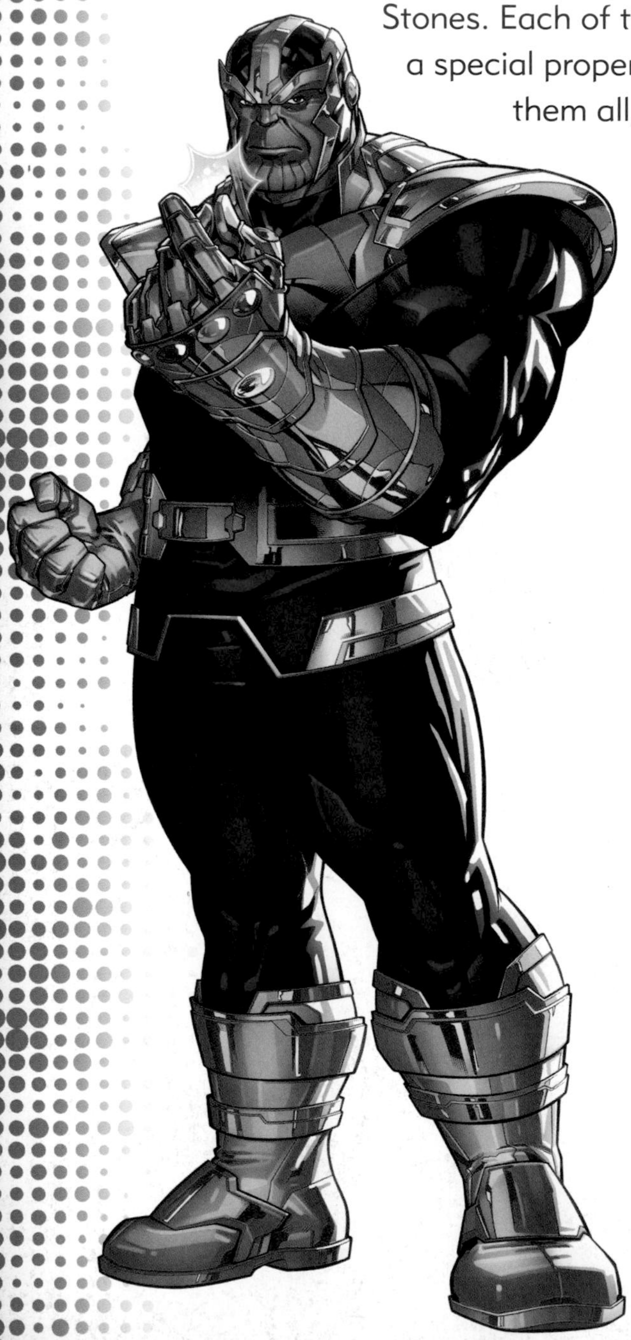

HEIGHT: 6'7"

WEIGHT: 985 LBS

STRENGTH, DURABILITY, AND STAMINA THAT SURPASSES THAT OF NEARLY ANY MORTAL BEING

CAN ABSORB AND PROJECT ENORMOUS QUANTITIES OF COSMIC ENERGY

CAN MANIPULATE MATTER ON AN ATOMIC LEVEL

GENIUS IN ALMOST ALL KNOWN SCIENCES, FAR EXCEEDING THE LIMITS OF HUMAN UNDERSTANDING

MASTER STRATEGIST AND MILITARY LEADER

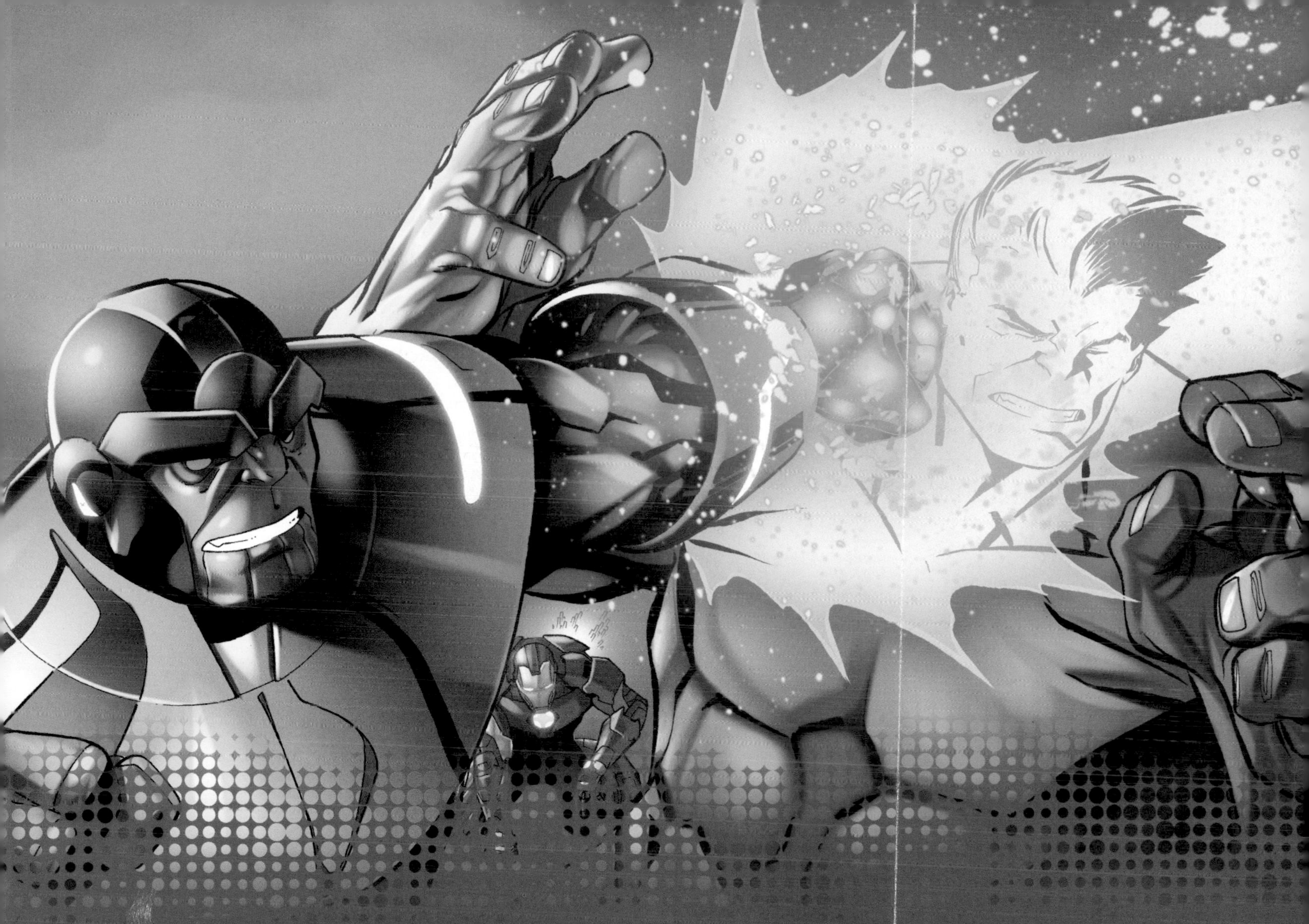

"I grow bored with this fight," Thanos said, blasting Hulk.

"Hulk not bored," Hulk said, punching Thanos. "Hulk could do this all day!"

Thanos fell back in pain. He realized that Hulk was right—the green giant probably COULD do this all day! And worse, he might even win!

A beam of light descended on Thanos from the sky above as his ship teleported him away.

"Until next time, Avengers," Thanos said.

"Hulk will be ready!"

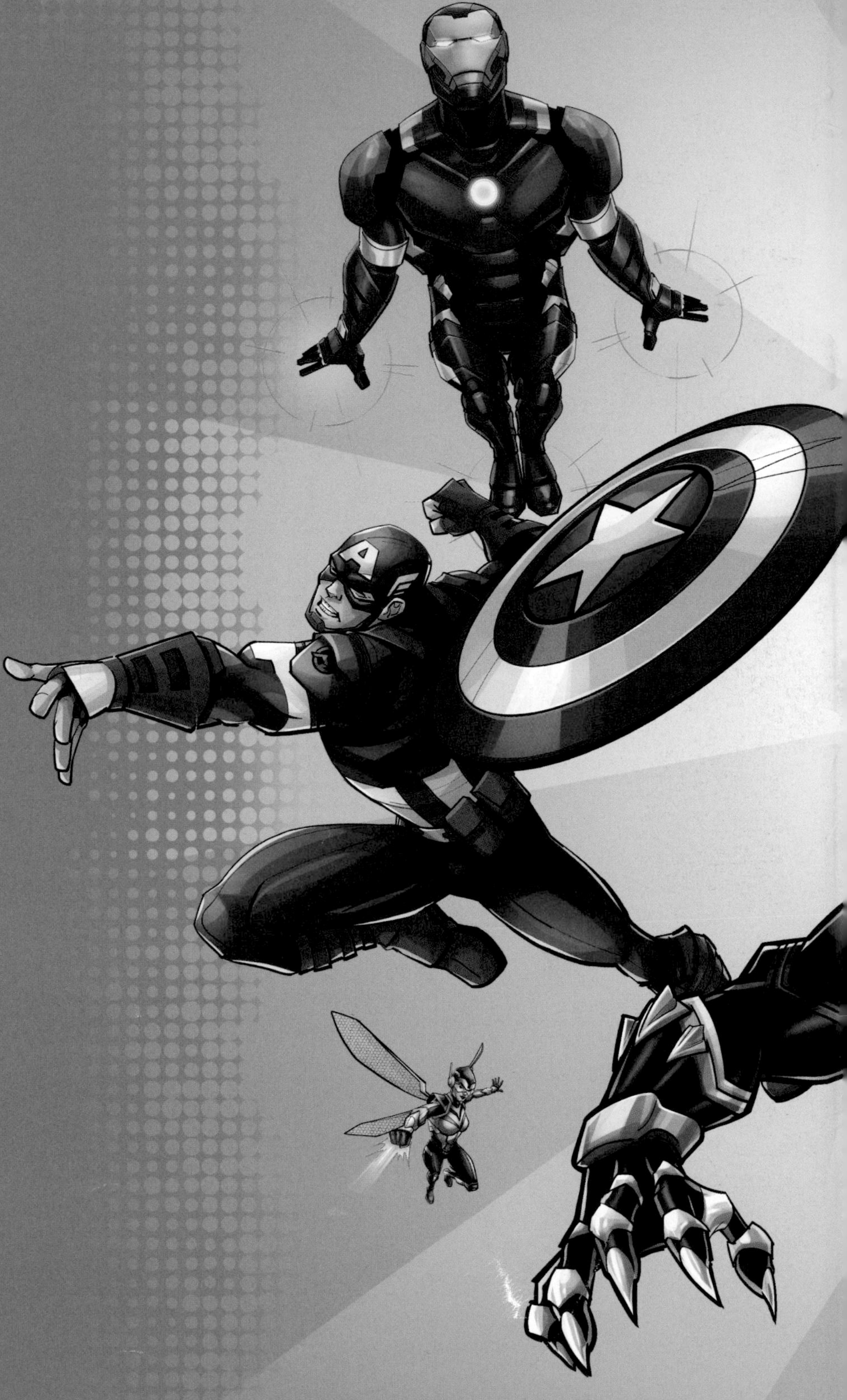

So there you have it, True Believers! Apart, they are some of the most amazing champions the world has ever seen. But together, they are Earth's mightiest heroes—the Avengers! With their combined abilities, the Avengers face threats too great for any single hero to tackle alone. Whether it's Thanos or Red Skull, M.O.D.O.C. or mind-controlled monkeys, the Avengers will be there.

As Captain America says—AVENGERS, ASSEMBLE!

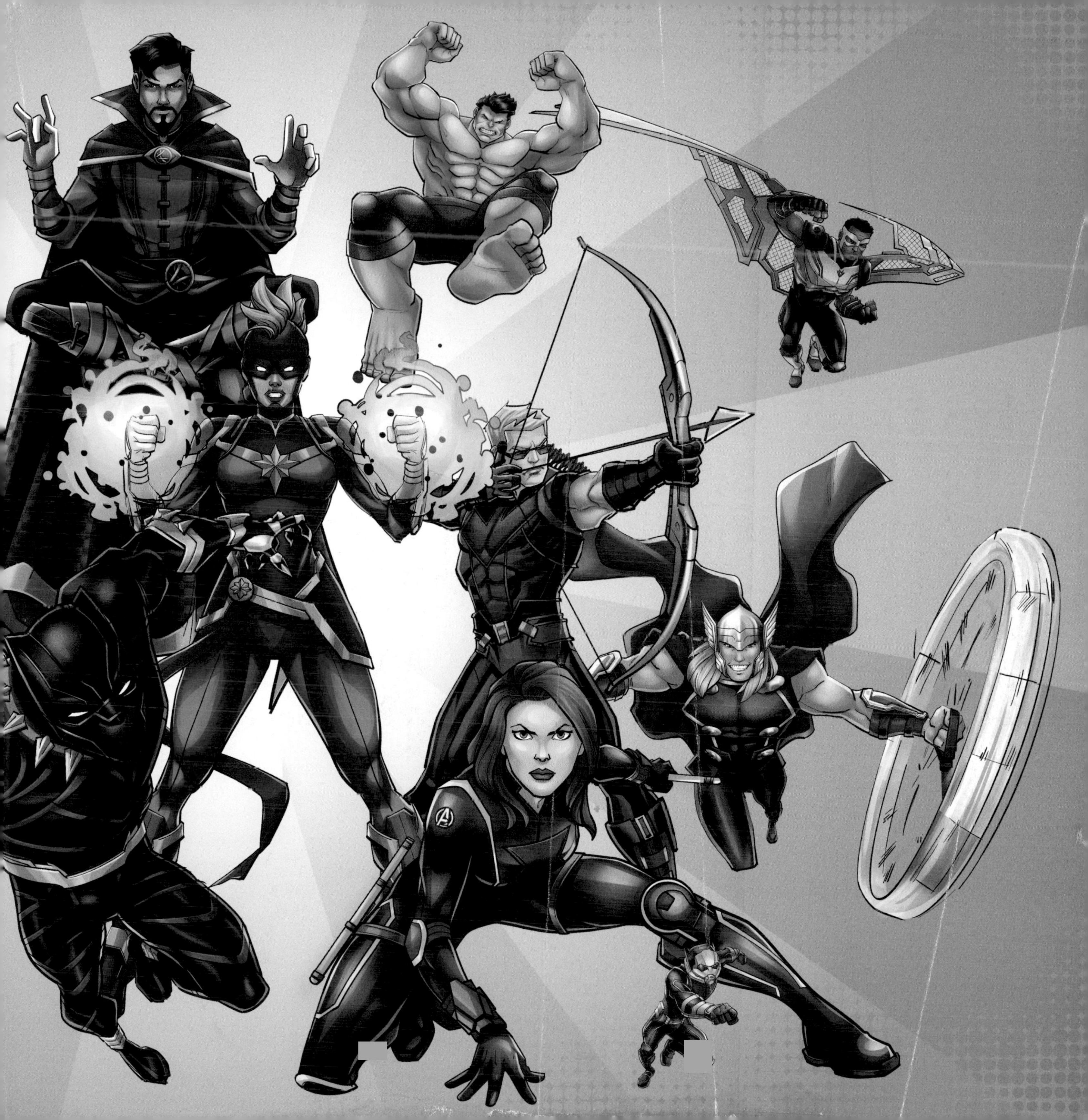